GIACOMO'S DAUGHTER

ROSANNA SAVONE & DIANA SAVONE

Liv Luhv Rahyt

Trigger Alert:
Giacomo's Daughter is a Mafia story and contains descriptions of sexual and physical violence that some readers may find upsetting or traumatic.

For additional information, contact us at
www.rosannasavone.com

Library of Congress Control Number:
ISBN 978-1-7344688-0-9 (paperback)

For Mom, who believes I can do anything
For Evan, who inspires me to do anything
For Diana and Elena, who support me through anything
-Rosanna

For every woman who tried to take flight but had her wings unjustly
clipped by societal constraints yet, still dared to fight the system that
kept her down so her future sisters could have the opportunity to soar.
-Diana

ONE

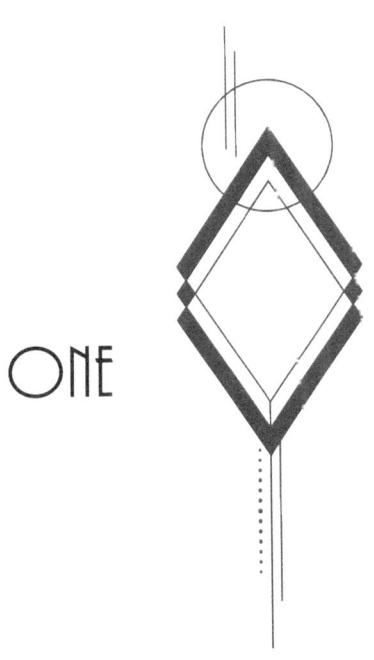

Mrs. Sofia Denaro was only eighteen years old. Still, she had already lived a lifetime, although you would never know it from the looks of her. Despite it all, she always somehow managed to have an air of innocence -- the most likely reason being she was once truly a sheltered girl.

She was a dark-eyed beauty reminiscent of a Roman goddess. Some would say she even looked like an angel in her white terry cloth robe as she glided effortlessly through her walk-in closet packed to the hilt with a luxurious wardrobe.

She had an outfit already carefully planned for this special evening. She combed through each hanging dress skimming them all with her fingertips on her way to the perfect ensemble. As she did so, Sofia caught a glimmer of the gigantic pear-shaped diamond solitaire on her left hand.

For a split second, it reminded her of the day that ring was first put on her finger.

The ring, being so conspicuous, made it hard not to be continuously reminded of that moment. It was easily five carats, although she couldn't remember exactly.

She had been in such shock when she first saw it nestled within its black velvet box. As she stared at it, wide-eyed with her hand covering her mouth to hide how her chin had dropped, her whole world had fallen silent. His instant bragging about its enormous size became nothing but muffled background noise.

Since then, Sofia never bothered to ask what he had said that day since things like diamond rings didn't seem to matter much anymore.

But for something that didn't even matter to her, this ring wasn't allowed to ever leave her hand. Max Denaro made sure of that. Since the day he nonchalantly slid it on her ring finger with the coolest confidence she had ever witnessed in a person in her entire life, the world had to know at all times that Sofia belonged to Max.

Because whatever Max wants, he gets.

And he wanted Sofia Spera since the moment he laid eyes on her on stage at the grand opening of the Book-Cadillac Hotel singing her heart out. She knew this to be true because Max could never resist reminding her, repeating the story often in the short time they'd been married.

Sofia was reared by her parents to be nothing more than a good Italian girl virtuously molded, thoroughly trained to excel in domestic chores, and patiently waiting to be chosen by an equally good man and provider.

There wasn't a day that went by; however, that she wasn't sing-ing along with her Victrola, although becoming an actual singer was out of the question for her. According to her strict Catholic parents, well-behaved women didn't run around on stage making spectacles of themselves. Good women weren't created for enter-tainment. At least, not for wide audiences. They were created for a higher purpose, a more noble cause, only to be enjoyed by one special man. Her future husband.

But her Sicilian father always had to add that women had it easy. Because they only had three choices to make in their entire lives.

Sofia could hear him now. In her mind's eye, she could see Giacomo sitting at the scuffed table tucked in her family's kitchen corner. Wearing his blue jean overalls with the oval Ford emblem stitched across his chest, he'd be twirling his spaghetti with his fork, stopping every so often to puff on one of his short, hand-rolled cigarettes. Papa would always count on his first three thick fingers, rough and blackened by the manual labor required of him on the automobile assembly line. He'd say in his thick Sicilian dialect with his husky voice that women had only to choose to be a *mugghieri, soru,* or *una puttann'*.

Every time he would say it, her father would pull on his long, scruffy, salt-and-pepper beard with a cheerful slap on the table. With a chuckle, he would be so amused with himself for coming up with such an apt observation on his own.

But then he would add with a cheerful snicker and sometimes a playful pinch on Sofia's cheek, that she had it even easier than the rest because she had only one choice. To be a wife, of course.

Evidently, Papa didn't see her being either of the other two extremes, a nun or a whore. So Sofia, being limited in options, resigned herself to societal fate quite early on in her teens.

What else was a girl to do in 1924?

Sofia finally made her way to the full-length mink in the corner of her closet. It was a wedding present from Max, and whenever she wore the soft, beautiful, brown fur, he couldn't seem to resist her. Her warm eyes almost matched the coat precisely, except for the flecks of gold that seemed to sparkle like glitter when she smiled.

Sofia dropped the robe from her shoulders to the floor, as she caught a glimpse of her naked body in the mirror, revealing her voluptuous curves before replacing the robe with the mink. Sofia wasn't rail thin, which was all the rage to be in the 1920s.

As much as she would love for a flapper dress to hang on her as if she were a human hanger, she had no choice in the matter. Sofia had a full bosom and equally round behind since she was thirteen years old. It wasn't like she could take her breasts off and hide them away in her purse like a soiled handkerchief.

But what Sofia had also learned early in life is that men didn't seem to mind big bosoms one bit. Since the day she had fully matured into a young woman, she noticed a shift in how she was treated by the so-called stronger sex.

Schoolboys her age, boys that Sofia had known since she was a child and would often play with at the park, could no longer help themselves and would always ask to touch them. Old men in church, even fathers with children her own age, would stare as if they were about to lick their chops when she walked by.

And Sofia wasn't the only one that noticed the difference.

Sofia's mother, Silvia, suddenly began lessons about how to ward off men's advances. They ended up not being much help to Sofia because Silvia was incredibly uncomfortable by the mere mention of sex.

The bulk of her mother's training consisted only of advising Sofia to politely say no with a friendly smile to be sure not to offend him if ever propositioned. She would emphasize that it was dire to make sure not to make a man ever, ever feel bad. A rejected man, evidently, was capable of anything. At the time, she thought Mamma was being dramatic. Now, as Sofia thought back to that particular lesson, she couldn't help but agree on that last point.

Giacomo, on the other hand, had a personal mission to make sure the chance to proposition her never happened in the first place. Sofia suddenly was never allowed to go anywhere alone with just her girlfriends. She couldn't go to birthday parties at all. Forget about school dances! Giacomo would never allow a man to lay a finger on her, let alone place his entire arm around her waist. Her father even walked her to school like he did when she was a child, which was embarrassing beyond belief.

But what was even worse, she wasn't allowed to sing anywhere in public except at their church, the heart of the Italian community in Detroit, *La Chiesa Della Sacra Famiglia*, or as it was called in English, Holy Family Parish. Her parents reasoned that she shouldn't draw any attention to herself and told her to be grateful and satisfied with singing in the choir. To her dismay, Sofia also couldn't help but note that they were, once again, right.

True to Sofia's past experience, Max also loved her *bubs*, as everyday 1920s slang called them, reassuring her they were never out of style. He told her the problem wasn't her body. It was that fashion was dictated by a bunch of fairies who had no interest in women. If anything, they were going out of their way, nowadays, to try to get women to resemble boys for their own sick satisfaction.

Not that Sofia ever asked to be reassured about her body. Max just volunteered that bit of information, as he did everything he felt he needed to explain to her.

So, knowing how effective her bubs could be, today Sofia practiced in the mirror. She nestled her coat innocently against her chin, with her big doe-eyes seductively gazing up under heavy lids through her thick, bristly, black lashes. Then to raise Max's temperature just enough, she offered a quick flash of her naked breasts.

Satisfied with her performance, she thought to herself that it was finally her turn to surprise Max for a change.

She then walked over to the jewelry box proudly on display in the middle of her massive closet. It was a large, ornately carved wooden box, which was another wedding gift from Max. Sofia had received many gifts from him that night. Too many, in her opinion, although he never really cared what she thought. That man did whatever he wanted, whenever he wanted.

She pulled open a few drawers, clearly on the hunt for something specific she had in mind. Each drawer was filled to the brim with gold and diamonds as she casually rummaged through it like it was nothing more than a kitchen junk drawer. Finally, her search came to an end, and a smile spread across Sofia's face.

Each wave of Sofia's perfectly styled bob shined brightly in her mirror's reflection as she carefully placed a diamond-crusted hairpin in it. She stepped back to take a look at her completed outfit and gave herself a reassuring nod.

Sofia looked perfect for tonight.

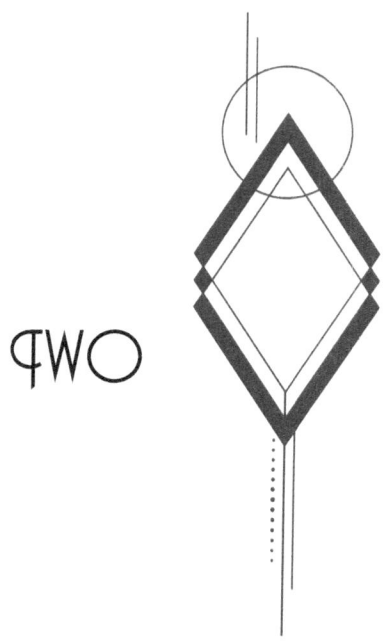

TWO

Meanwhile, in the Denaro's grand stone kitchen below, the housemaid, a mousy Polish gal named Marta, was adding utensils to a picnic basket as Catalda, the Sicilian cook, a portly, old woman, hobbled over to the oven and removed a golden baked chicken.

As she set the roasting pan down to cool on the massive butcher block, Catalda curiously asked Marta in her thick, broken accent, "The missus has-a been primpin' all day. Whatta you think why?"

"Oh, I do not know... They are newlyweds, dat is all."

Not curious in the least, Marta kept her attention on the task at hand. She continued to pack a feast of Italian food within the picnic basket. Marta knew that if she wanted to keep her generously paid job, she should not ask questions in the Denaro home. Mr. Denaro definitely made that clear to her with the intense glare he gave when he explained the rules of his household. She never dared to cross the line.

But today, even though she knew better as well, Catalda couldn't help herself. "Hog-a-wash!" She replied. "All the food, the love boat outta back. The missus is going to tell Mr. Denaro she's with-a child. *Certo!*"

The love boat that Catalda was referring to was a large houseboat that suddenly appeared that afternoon. It was currently docked at the end of the usually empty pier on the dark, brooding Lake Saint Clair.

Outdoors in the evening dusk, the peaceful lake reflected the dark hues and mood of the sky above. A thick blanket of dark pillowy clouds hung low and endless across the horizon. The dense forest trees hugged the 26-mile shoreline so serenely that all one could hear was the soft lapping of the gray water as it bumped against the pier. Red rose petals provided a splash of color as they were sprinkled down a path along the long, narrow pier to the boat.

Looking back to shore from the docked boat, one could see an elegant English manor with a gray fieldstone exterior that stared coldly back in silence. Similar to all the other majestic estates of upscale Grosse Pointe that surrounded the lake, the Denaro mansion's tall roofline jutted out here and there amongst the thick forest trees camouflaging its existence.

In the kitchen, the cook took over, packing the picnic basket with her baked chicken as the housemaid tidied up. As she swept the floor, Marta said, "What do you mean? It is much too soon after wedding."

"Thatsa if they were not already giving it a go before. Don't forget we're talking about the rich people," Catalda replied with a couple jabs of her fist in the air, a standard Italian gesture clarifying she means sex.

She then hobbled over to the tall, wooden wine rack spanning the entire wall of the large kitchen pantry. As the old cook grabbed a bottle of wine, she called out to Marta, "There's no problem trying each other out before-a the nuptials. If it doesn't work out, eh, someone else will always marry them because they filthy rich." Catalda hobbled back to the massive butcher block island and placed a bottle of wine inside the basket.

"I do not think dat is case. Mrs. Denaro come from humble place herself, I know," Marta argued.

A smile spread across Catalda's face, amused by how naive her much younger coworker was, and added with glee, "Butta the missus is-a beautiful. It's only the ugly girls that have-a to be fresh as a spring daisy on our wedding night."

Annoyed by both the condescending tone in the cook's voice and by her implication that she must be one of the ugly girls Catalda just referred to since she fit the profile, Marta retorted in the defense of the lady of the house. "Here, I wash bed sheets, and I tell you, it is too early for a baby. They are newlyweds, dat is all."

Wearing her mink, Sofia entered, catching the cook and housemaid off guard. Shocked to see her in the kitchen of all places, they both immediately stood up at attention at the sight of her.

Catalda tried to disguise her worry that her employer may have heard them gossiping about her. She did the best she could to muster her usual deferential tone when she asked, "Mrs. Denaro, you should have ring-a bell. Whatta you need, dear?"

Sofia, casual and seemingly unaware of anything being said before her surprise arrival, double-checked the contents of the picnic basket and replied, "Nothing at all."

She pulled a couple of crisp bills out of her mink coat pocket and handed one to each of them and told them with authority, "Here's a couple fins. Take the rest of the day and spend some time with your families. Tony is waiting out front to take you." As indeed the butler was.

With big smiles of gratitude, both Catalda and Marta looked down at the five-dollar bill, far more than a day's pay for them, sweetly placed within their palm.

Overwhelmed by her generosity, the cook was speechless for a moment before she finally could reply, "Thank-a you very much, Mrs. Denaro."

However, Marta, although happy as well, was also a bit worried. At first, all she could say was, "Yes, missus. It is very kind of you, very kind, indeed."

The shy housemaid then hesitated but thought it best to drum up the courage to add, "Excuse me, but does Mr. Denaro know of dis? He usually like us do work until he bids us good evening." Marta's nervousness made her strong Polish accent come out even more, making her harder to understand.

But Sofia expected her apprehension. She calmly responded, "Don't you worry about Mr. Denaro. I'll take care of him."

Not needing any more convincing, the cook and the housemaid dutifully grabbed their things and headed out the back door. As they left the gray stone manor, the cook whispered to the housemaid, "I no care whatta you say. She's having a baby."

Marta couldn't help but reply, "Whatever it is, she is a godsend to us all. We must go before Mr. Denaro returns home, and we are both cooked for leaving early."

They both scurried around to the front of the house to return to their homes before their chance to escape somehow failed. Extra time with family was a real treat for them because their hours were normally so long they usually just slept at the Denaro home during the week.

As their footsteps faded in the distance, Sofia looked out the kitchen's back window. Standing next to the houseboat, she could see its new captain, dark and weathered, waiting at the far end of the pier. His jacket collar was up, blocking his clean-shaven face from the cool spring wind that whipped him as it swirled around the flat lake. He acknowledged he was ready for duty with a curt wave to her. He had a face different from his, but the same familiar rough and blackened hands of the father she loved dearly. It made Sofia wonder if only crooks and criminals had soft, clean hands.

Sofia returned her attention to the picnic basket. She pulled out the wine bottle and returned it to the rack. She then reached high above, on her tiptoes, and grabbed an alternative selection from the very top shelf. She checked the label, confirming with a nod that this was, indeed, the right one, and replaced the old with the new.

Sofia emerged with the wooden picnic basket in hand from the back door. She looked up, checking the weather for the possibility of rain. The sky was as gray as any other typical day, with rolling clouds so low it felt as if you could reach out and touch them. Because of the constant cloud coverage that often went on for weeks on end, it was difficult to predict with any certainty whether it would rain in Michigan.

Sofia was especially nervous about it raining today. It had taken her a considerable amount of time to plan this evening's events. Spring showers would spoil everything. But luckily, the clouds didn't look sufficiently dark enough for anything more than perhaps a foggy night. And fog would only help her by providing more privacy.

As she stepped toward the boat, she heard a loud crunch from a twig her foot landed on. The sound instantly brought up an old childhood memory, one that she had been thinking about a lot lately, and she wasn't surprised it came up for her now.

She remembered that same crunch when her small leather boot had stepped on a twig when she was out hunting with her father as a girl. As soon as she had done it, she immediately hid behind a tree.

A mighty buck's head had popped up, alert, with nostrils flaring back and forth as if to smell out whether the sound meant there was truly danger nearby. When he neither heard nor saw anything else, he returned to his supper of leaves.

Behind another tree, Giacomo, then with a darker but equally scruffy beard, waved for the young Sofia to proceed on. When she hesitated to move, he impatiently motioned for her to pull back her arrow.

Giacomo was an avid hunter who had hunted often with Sofia's two older brothers, Enrico and Alessandro. But once they both perished in the Great War, Giacomo decided that his 12-year-old daughter would now have to do as a hunting partner. It was the best he could come up with, since he didn't know how else to spend time with her as she grew up into a young woman.

But he found her hesitant and unwilling to kill, which he reasoned was simply because she was a girl and didn't have it in her. He didn't expect her to be anything like his sons were, but seeing her timid nature made him miss them all the more.

Sofia could tell that her father wasn't thrilled to be left with only her to hunt with, but she at least was able to spend time with him alone. It was a luxury she had never experienced before. Back then, Giacomo was either always working the line or hunting with her brothers.

Careful not to make another sound, she pulled back her arrow. Slowly, she allowed her bow to emerge from behind the tree ever so slightly. She certainly didn't want the buck to see her weapon aimed at his neck as he feasted on his last meal.

Her chocolate brown eyes focused as she aimed at the deer. She remembered glancing over at Giacomo, who was still hiding behind a nearby tree, encouraging her to release the bow with his usual hand signal.

But when she did let go of the arrow, hoping her father wouldn't notice, she bumped up her bow ever so slightly. As the arrow flew swiftly in the air, it skidded right above the mighty buck's head. It narrowly missed causing him to bolt away in the opposite direction.

Sofia thought about how disappointed her father had been in her for missing that shot. Nothing ever got by Giacomo, so, of course, he had caught on that she purposely missed. He berated her for costing their family some much needed free venison.

She winced as she remembered he had called her weak that day. He then dismissed her actions as something a typical woman would do, grumbling to himself all the way back to their Model T that he really shouldn't expect much from her.

Sofia wondered if her father still felt that way about her -- after everything she had gone through this past winter.

Perhaps he still doesn't think I have it in me?

She snapped out of her reverie when she suddenly heard the sound of her husband's deep voice.

"What's this all about?" Max demanded.

Sofia met his question with an instant smile sweetly on her face, completely over the moon to see him.

ꞯHREE

"It's your invitation to a proper honeymoon, Mr. Denaro. It's about time, don't you think?" Sofia said playfully with a flirtatious smile.

Massimo Denaro had just turned 25 years old, but he already had the commanding presence about him of a man twice his age. Although, for the most part, it was his flippant charm that would render just about anybody defenseless.

Besides his dark, handsome looks and smooth ways, he was always dressed to the nines just as he was at this very moment. His black pinstripe suit was made of the finest Italian wool. It was cut to the exact measurements for solely his own broad shoulders and trim waist. His polished, black leather wingtip shoes with white spats with pearl buttons along the side looked out of place on the cold, dewy grass of his sprawling backyard.

Despite his elegant clothes and slick talk, Max, as he was called since he was orphaned at the age of four, was actually as tough as nails. He had no choice but to be. He was well-aware that he was second-in-command of the Scalici Squad, the toughest faction of the Detroit Italian Mafia, *La Cosa Nostra*.

Max's brother-in-law, Salvatore 'Sally Bottoms' Scalici, was his boss and was made by none other than the head of the entire Detroit Mafia, Salvatore 'Singing Sam' Cattalanotte, the last Gianolla family leader left standing after the bloody four-year Gianolla/Vitale Mob War that killed more than a hundred of their guys combined.

To restore the peace and maximize their profits amongst all the competing Mafia families within the city, Singing Sam took it upon himself to call a conference of mob bosses on Thanksgiving Day in 1920, dividing up the territory with clear boundaries to avoid future conflict. The Scalici Squad was granted a large segment of the eastside of Detroit, answering only to the former Gianolla lieutenant, William 'Black Bill' Tocca, in the chain of command.

Since Max was an orphan, Sally Bottoms was the one who reared him alongside Max's older sister, Teresa. When Teresa was apparently unable to give her husband any sons of his own (having given birth to five daughters instead), Max was groomed to take over the booming family business one day, which first engaged in blackmail and extortion and then, due to Prohibition, morphed into the most insanely profitable booze-smuggling operation in the country. So Max was destined to be the next boss.

And he was very much looking forward to it.

In 1924, Detroit, Michigan was the crown jewel of the country, where imagination and hard work spun innovation unlike anything ever experienced on earth.

Birthed by the hard-nosed Henry Ford, the auto industry literally drove the world forward in both miles traveled and bank balances achieved. Ford's unprecedented high pay, a whole five dollars a day, gave men incomes never experienced in history before. More money meant houses, cars, clothes, and, most importantly to Max, lots of parties with lots of booze.

Detroit was also responsible for a whopping 75% of all the alcohol supplied to the entire United States during Prohibition. Because of, yet again, Ford and his desire for a sober workforce, it was the first city to go dry in 1918, a whole year before the rest of the country. This gave mobsters living there a head start on building a network. By 1924, the smoothly run operation to bootleg hooch from Canada was dubbed *The Funnel*. About 500,000 cases of Canadian whiskey alone was making its way through the funnel every month.

When there were once only 1,800 licensed saloons, Detroiters, fighting for their right to party, now often frequented the 25,000 illegal *blind pigs*, also known as *speakeasies,* in the 1920s. The area of Detroit called Black Bottom, a hotbed for pure jazz music (and the breeding ground for the future Motown), supplied the legendary entertainment at these equally legendary parties, while several major gangs made sure the booze never stopped flowing.

But two gangs in particular made sure the fun times never ended for the city's most upstanding citizens. There was the Purple Gang, a group of Russian Jews so bad they were dubbed after the color of rotten meat. And then there was the Scalici Squad, equally as cutthroat in its attempts to gain a larger share of the second-most-profitable business in town.

Their greed flowed as freely as the whiskey they smuggled, and a fierce rivalry between the two gangs had developed because of it. That meant Max had to work double-time to make sure his boss was the biggest Big Cheese in Detroit. So it was extremely rare for him to take an entire night off for personal pleasure and relaxation. Especially on a Tuesday, when the largest shipments of the week would arrive and he would then have to provide the supply for all the big party nights that occurred nonstop continuously from Wednesday through Saturday.

Max held up a formal invitation to meet in the back by the lake that was addressed to him in Sofia's elegant cursive handwriting, and he wasn't amused at all by it.

"Whattaya up to, Sofia?" He huffed.

But she ignored his condescending tone laced with impatient impertinence. Instead, she responded with the same robust flirtatiousness as before, "I've been eagerly awaiting your arrival."

Sofia then blinked seductively as she gazed up at Max through her bristly eyelashes while she held her cozy fur close, nestling it under her chin. And just as she had practiced earlier in the mirror, she let her coat fall slightly open. When his eyes widened at the tempting flash of her bubs, Sofia knew she had gotten Max's attention.

With a graceful extension of her arm, she motioned for her husband to follow the trail of rose petals down the long, wooden pier. This, of course, caused her mink coat to open even further, allowing Max to see just enough to know she was completely nude underneath.

But, surprisingly, Max didn't budge.

"Somethin' came up at work. I can't make whatever this is ya got planned. I thought we were just havin' a quick dinner before I drift."

"Aw, things always come up at work. Don't be such a flat tire, Max. Enough with work. It's time to play..." Sofia showed him a glimpse of her bare shoulder from underneath her soft and luxurious mink before adding, "...with me."

"You do know how hard I gotta work for ya to own that fur?" Max asked.

"*Amore*, if it means more time with you, I could easily lose it."

Sofia then dropped the fur from her body, but before it could even go past her shoulders, Max stopped it from falling to the ground.

"Have ya lost your mind? What if someone sees you?"

"Who's going to see me out here?"

Sofia seemed to have a valid point since the entire property appeared isolated between the surrounding tall, thick forest that shielded the whole property and the immense lake. The only thing one could hear were the chirping of crickets in the dusk.

She continued, "Besides, you promised we were going to spend tonight alone together. Come on, Max, give me just one evening. Please, Max. It would mean the world to me."

Adding to her persuasive argument, Sofia raised the picnic basket and said, "You have to eat anyway."

He was now regretting appeasing her earlier that day when she asked with a sweet smile and gentle touch of his arm if they could get together tonight. He didn't recall whether she had referred to the evening in its entirety, having popped back home solely for dinner and a quick fuck before returning back to work. But not having the time to deal with this nonsense, he simply replied, "Let's just go inside."

Sofia instantly responded with her best sexy pout. Within their short relationship, she had quickly learned that Max liked it when she behaved like a spoiled child. If she wanted to get her way, as Sofia desperately wanted now, she was going to have to use every trick she could muster at that moment.

With her plump, red lips still protruding, she whined, "But I went through all this trouble, making it a surprise for you."

"I ain't gettin' on that boat, Sofia," Max snapped back.

"But I don't understand why not? Do you know how long it took me just to convince Bambino to help me? I practically had to beg him to get me this boat and driver."

Max's extremely loyal bodyguard, Bambino Cercone, or rather, Bambi as he was called for short by his fellow thugs in the Scalici Squad, was the most gigantic goon one could imagine, standing thick and tall at six feet four inches. By just the look of him, one could easily conclude that getting this intimidating man to do anything he didn't want to do would be impossible.

"That doesn't surprise me one bit. Bambi knows I hate boats. I'm surprised he got it for you at all."

Sofia knew it would be tough to get Max to agree to her plan. Still, she never in a million years thought it would take this much convincing to get her own husband interested in spending some uninterrupted time with her for a romantic evening. Sofia did her best to hide how absolutely irritated she was at the irony of the situation, considering their history together. Then again, she reasoned everything about Max was difficult.

Sofia mentally went through a list of her tricks. She had to be careful because one wrong move could make this entire evening end quickly and even terribly. Not sure what else she could do to get him to agree, she decided to change tactics, so her tone with him went from playful and flirtatious to cold and filled with disappointment.

"And Bambino said you'd never agree to this, but I assured him this was the only way I could get you all to myself with nobody dropping by unannounced. Or worse yet, your sister just hanging around for as long as she pleases. But you know what? It's okay. You go to work. I'll find someone else to play with."

Sofia spun toward the pier to depart without him, but Max grabbed her by the arm, stopping her. He was angered by her insinuation. He wanted to smack her right across the kisser for even daring to suggest such a disrespectful thing to him. But he didn't want to have a bad night between them, especially since she seemed so eager to please him.

Besides, Max knew she didn't mean it. Sofia may be a woman, but she wasn't dumb enough to do anything like two-time him. Just over a month ago on their wedding night, Max made sure Sofia was well aware of what the consequences would be if she ever dared to make such a decision.

Since then, Sofia had proven herself to be a dutiful wife by doing whatever Max wanted, whenever he wanted it. She never even complained, until now, about his long hours away in the city. It was also true that between his workload and her morning sickness, they were prevented from ever having a real honeymoon together.

It then occurred to him that this may be his last chance to really enjoy her hourglass figure. It shouldn't be much longer before the baby showed and she started to get fat. So Max decided it would be best for him to at least smooth things over.

"We have a perfectly good table in the house. Why don't we just eat inside? Then we can fuck in our own bed and not in some stranger's boat."

Surprised, Sofia raised an eyebrow. It had nothing to do with his vulgar language. She was used to that by now but instead, it was about his response as a whole. She asked, "I thought you said something came up at work? I don't understand why you can eat at home, but you refuse to…"

Suddenly, her eyes widened with a realization. She finally understood the problem at hand, and knowing full well he wouldn't like it, she blurted out, "You're afraid of the water!"

Max quickly retorted in his defense, "Me, afraid? No, Mrs. Denaro, you are mistaken."

She put her hands in his and tried to pull him onto the pier, but Max pulled his hands away, clearly anxious.

As an excuse, Max muttered, "To avoid a watery grave, I stay on the ground. God knows in my line of work how many have given me the *malocchio*."

The *malocchio*, as it was said in Italian, is an age-old superstition called *the evil eye*. And Sofia was in agreement with her husband that many people in town would have eagerly given it to Max, considering his brute power and immense wealth. With all the booze he bootlegged, he was one of the wealthiest men rivaling the likes of the auto titans in town. But she wasn't going to let any superstition, even one likely to be true, to get in her way tonight.

Sofia let her mink fall open again, giving Max another teasing glimpse of her naked breasts. Stroking his ego, she added with a seductive purr, "Since when are you afraid of the *malocchio*? The Max Denaro I know isn't afraid of anything."

Sofia knew she was pinning Max in a corner. Making him prove his manliness to her by showing he was not afraid of getting on the houseboat, as she desired.

But it never occurred to her that a man like Max would be frightened of anything, especially a fear of water considering all the many massive lakes that outlined around and throughout Michigan. Had she known he hated boats because of it, she would have come up with a different romantic getaway. But now, she had to make the situation work.

"I said I'm not afraid."

She pulled him closer and pressed him against her naked body, enclosing him within her soft, warm coat. "Then, this is one boat ride you're going to love," she said with a sly smile.

Max couldn't hide how clearly enticed he was by his beautiful wife's tempting body as her hand began to grope his throbbing shaft, giving him a small sample of the night to come if he finally acquiesced.

24

"I guess I gotta eat anyway." Making sure he kept his position as the one who called the shots in their relationship, Max quickly set a clear boundary, "But just this once."

He then playfully squeezed her ass hard as Sofia squealed with delight that she was finally able to convince him. She rewarded him with a long, passionate kiss.

With both arms wrapped around his neck, she looked him in the eye and promised, "You're never going to forget this night, Mr. Denaro."

To ease his anxiety so he would surely get on the boat, Sofia did her best to keep the moment light with her smiling radiant face locked onto his own. She gently took Max by the hand and led him carefully down the pier with her.

She could feel his apprehension with each wooden step he took, but she pretended nothing was amiss with him. She couldn't risk upsetting him right now by highlighting how afraid he actually was about walking above such shallow water.

One thing she had already learned for sure at her young age is that men had the tendency to act like big, fat babies if anything didn't go their way, so the last thing she should do was make Max feel weak. She knew that would cause his temper to blow, and he'd stomp back to the house in a huff.

However, that didn't stop her from marveling to herself about how scary Max could be; yet, he seemed now like nothing more than a scared, little boy. She would never have thought that was possible if she hadn't seen it with her own eyes.

When they finally made it to the end of the narrow pier, to get it over with quickly, Max hopped onto the houseboat without hesitation while Sofia easily entered the vessel without getting or needing his help. Once he was on board, it didn't seem as bad as he had imagined, but he was still relieved when she immediately led him inside.

Within the houseboat, a romantic setting had been carefully arranged with brightly lit candles scattered throughout the room, and in the middle was a small table set for two on a luxurious fur rug. However, Max opted to continue following the path that led straight to the soft, pillowy bed waiting with a large heart made of the same red rose petals.

"Going straight for dessert, are you? But I don't want to spoil your dinner."

Sofia placed the heavy picnic basket on the table as Max sat down on the bed, causing the flower petals to lose their shape and disperse everywhere. She immediately pulled out the bottle of wine she had carefully picked out for this particular romantic evening.

"Don't worry about me. I gotta big appetite."

Max gestured toward his full erection that he wasted no time with freeing from his constraining pants.

"But, the chicken will get cold."

"Somethin' you need to know about me if we're gonna have a happy marriage. I love cold chicken."

Even at this early point in matrimony, Sofia knew Max well enough to know that he wouldn't take no for an answer. So she stopped unpacking the carefully prepared meal and reluctantly put the wine down without opening it.

As much as she wanted to be pouring a glass, she didn't want to risk his mood changing for the worse with him stomping off in anger. Everything wasn't going exactly as she wanted, but at least she managed to get him on the boat.

She reassured herself that all she would have to do is screw him good and then they could have a drink followed by her carefully orchestrated conversation, as she had initially planned.

As Sofia approached, Max roughly grabbed her by the coat and pulled her close to him so aggressively that it made her stumble into him. Within seconds, Max threw Sofia's mink on the floor.

"Wait. The windows. The captain."

Max replied, teasing her, "So now you're worried about someone seein' you."

He reached over, pulled the window shut, and the curtain closed. Without another word, he then proceeded to push his naked wife down to her knees before him, giving Sofia her next cue.

¢OUR

Max abruptly popped open his eyes at the deafening sound of the bullet that woke him. Knowing that distinct sound intimately even in his sleep, he quickly sat up with a sense of urgency. Like the pro that he was, he instantly went to grab his gun, but after vigorously patting his surroundings down, Max realized that the gun was, indeed, missing.

Instead, he discovered that he was lying on the houseboat bed without his pants. Max quickly recalled how Sofia had asked him to take it out of his holster earlier, because it was jabbing her ribs when he was on top of her in bed.

"You work much too hard," had said Sofia nonchalantly.

With his prized Smith & Wesson in her hand, Sofia was back in her mink coat, standing in front of the prepared meal now laid out on the table, beautifully set for a candlelight dinner for two.

She continued, "And you clearly don't get enough sleep. You fell asleep within seconds afterward."

"Gimme that."

Sofia waved him over with the pistol and then pulled his chair back from the table. "No, come and get it, *amore mio.*" As if it were nothing more than a salad fork, she placed the gun on the table next to his plate.

Max couldn't remember the last time he heard Sofia utter the word *no* to him, and he quite frankly had no idea what gave her the confidence to do it now. But at least there was no one around to hear. And her insolence appeared playful, so he obliged Sofia as he was hungry anyway.

He gathered his nearby pants and pulled them on one leg, one step at a time, as he walked over and took the offered seat. Max warned, "Don't ever touch that again. Ya follow me?" He pointed at the smoking piece on the table with his index finger to make sure there was absolutely no chance Sofia could misunderstand what he meant. "You could have killed someone," he warned.

"Whatever you say, Max," Sofia replied brightly with a sweet smile. She said it in such a lively way, he couldn't help but note that she was glowing and much happier than usual. Her cheeks even seemed a rosier red to him, and her eyes had a glint of joy to them.

He wondered whether it was the baby that was causing her cheerful mood or whether it was spending time with him. For a brief second, he wondered if Sofia finally loved him as much as he wanted her to love him. Her initial lack of enthusiasm for their relationship was a reality he had known about from the start but one he would never ever acknowledge out loud. Sofia was the toughest dame to crack, that's for sure, Max thought. He always loved a challenge, though. It made the reward even sweeter.

Since their wedding, however, Sofia had exhibited a consistently pleasant mood even until this very moment. It made Max ponder whether she could have possibly changed as quickly as it appeared. Whenever he tried to push her buttons, to keep her on her toes, Sofia would easily submit. It didn't matter what he did.

Instead of a bitter tongue in response, she would only remind him that she was reared to be dutiful, and she now was his obedient wife. He was the man, and whatever he wanted was always best for them both. She assured him that her satisfaction was derived entirely by giving him satisfaction.

Regardless, Max was at least satisfied with her usual compliant reply for now. He then allowed Sofia to take a large napkin to make a bib for him, placing it around his neck.

As she did so, Sofia explained, "That's a good white shirt. We wouldn't want to stain it now, would we?"

As soon as the knot was tied, Max didn't wait for Sofia to take her own seat, but instead, he dove right into his meal, grabbing the roasted chicken leg on his plate, and taking a monstrous bite. He muttered with his mouth full, "This is exactly what I need."

He did enjoy finally having a woman to take good care of him, and Sofia had proven herself to be an attentive wife, so far.

Pleased by his statement, Sofia smiled warmly as she poured him a generous glass of red wine. As she did so, she gazed into his eyes, smitten in love.

Max barely let her put the bottle down before picking up his glass and taking a large gulp to wash down the chicken.

"Looks like that old cook of yours really outdid herself this time," Sofia said with a giggle to herself.

Barely looking up from his plate, Max asked, "What's so funny about that?"

As Sofia finally took her own seat across from him, she responded casually, "Nothing really. I was just thinking about how hard my mother worked all these years to teach me to cook. Because what Italian man would marry me if I didn't know how to cook? Now, here I am. I've been married for over a month, and the first time I stepped into the kitchen was today."

With a playful smile filled with chicken, Max teased her, "Give 'em a break, Mrs. Denaro. They had no idea you were gonna meet such a catch."

Sofia smiled, amused by his childish antics, and watched as Max quickly consumed his meal. She needed the perfect response that would somehow still be true yet simultaneously flatter him. She knew that if Max was going to be at ease this evening, she had to stroke his manhood excessively in every way possible.

"That's true. My parents definitely didn't prepare me for you."

"For I am one-of-a-kind. But you are, too. That's why I had to have ya."

Max never looked up from his plate, so he didn't notice the sly smirk that crept onto Sofia's face rivaling that of the famous Mona Lisa. He had literally given her the perfect response she needed to take this conversation exactly where she had planned.

"Really?" She feigned surprise and added, "When did you know I was to be yours?"

Max responded without hesitation, "Ya know. The first night

I met ya."

"Do tell, Mr. Denaro."

At the sound of her suggestion, Max abruptly stopped chewing and washed down another mouthful of chicken with wine. He eyed Sofia carefully, wondering why she was bringing this up now. He didn't know what it could possibly be, but he sensed something seemed off about her response.

He was often asked how he had met Sofia, and he did tell the story equally as often. Max wasn't stupid. Although nobody had the guts to say it to his face, he could tell no one could believe he had managed to get a nice doll like Sofia to actually marry him. Good girls like her don't marry bad guys like him. So he made sure everyone knew that Sofia was into him and nobody else through his constant recounting of the first time he laid eyes on her and fell in love. Max Denaro, of course, was no *cornuto*.

But he was curious about her response tonight because Sofia had never been one of the people who had ever asked him to tell it before. And she didn't always react well when he told the story when others asked for it. Sometimes she would just sit there with a forced, straight smile without adding much in details of that fateful night.

One time, Sofia suddenly excused herself midway through the story because she was either tired or had a headache or didn't feel well. Something like that. She then went straight to their bedroom for the rest of the night.

Another time, Sofia even got argumentative, which now prompted him to warn her. "Don't start with me, Sofia. It won't end well for you. Ya know I always win."

Sofia leaned over the table, allowing him a view of her round, full cleavage as she pouted seductively. "Do I look like I want to start a fight? Come on, Max, humor me. I'll be a good little girl. I promise."

Knowing she would be a damn fool otherwise, Max figured he'd once again oblige his wife. He thought, what else are we gonna do on this damn forsaken boat anyway?

Sofia sat at the edge of her seat, listening attentively with a sweet smile, as Max began, "It was at the grand opening of the Book-Cadillac Hotel. I had to work late that night. Later than planned anyway..."

₣IVE

Max sat in a high-back leather chair at a desk smoking a cigar while reading the *Detroit Free Press*. A desk lamp provided just enough dim lighting for him while the outskirts of the room remained camouflaged by darkness with the drapes drawn tightly shut. This created an eerie feeling which Max always did purposely to give his visitors the heebie-jeebies. He had learned quite early on in his work that the best way to keep people in line was to keep them scared of him at all times.

There had been a knock on his hotel room door. Bambi's key jiggled in the lock, then he opened it, and shoved in an Irishman, Fred Moore, who wore dirty Ford overalls. Despite his tough, weathered exterior made possible through years of manual labor, Fred hesitated timidly by the door until Bambi gave him another firm shove inside, causing him to stumble toward Max.

"Where's my shipment, Freddy?"

Fred, nervous, stood as far from Max as he could get away with. His anxious eyes surveyed the large lavish hotel room, searching for a possible exit route.

Impatient as always, Max lowered his newspaper, revealing his gun in his hand, causing Fred's eyes to widen in fear.

By the time Max was done with work and had entered the grand ballroom that night, the party was in full swing. He remembered straightening his bow tie and pulling on the end of each of his coat sleeves, smoothing them back to his usual impeccable self. He had made his way through the crowded room, which parted for him like Moses and the Red Sea.

The only thing Max loved more than watching all the veiled glances and hearing the muffled whispers that always occurred between guests when they noticed him entering the room was bragging about it to others later. So he went into gleeful detail about all the quick glances and quiet comments that occurred that night. Max was particularly proud that even Henry Ford, himself, wouldn't dare look him in the eye as he confidently strode by the auto titan toward the bar.

On stage, a bright light illuminated a sensational lead singer named Princess O'Sullivan, whose voice was as luscious as her milk chocolate skin. Flanked on either side of Princess were two young, white women. One he knew, the sweetest blonde you've ever seen, Irene Kolasinski. But the other was new to him. It was the stunning Sofia, who at that time had long, wavy, dark curls instead of her present-day, stylish bob.

The three beauties had all sung their hearts out on stage in what was later deemed by the *Who's Who* of Detroit as one of the most magical performances ever seen in town. Considering all the extraordinary talent that emerged from Black Bottom, Detroit's only Negro neighborhood, that was quite an accomplishment.

Max was proud of Sofia's performance. He could tell Sofia was proud of it too, although she was smart enough now not to admit it. Max had made it abundantly clear that her whole existence was solely to be his wife and the mother of his children, just as God intended. And it didn't help that he hated the idea that his wife would be singing backup behind a Negro, even if that black woman was as beautiful and beyond talented as Princess.

But the moment Sofia first caught his eye, Max remembered stopping in his tracks. It was as if he had been struck by lightning, and then the world had gone absolutely quiet around him. For a split second, his guard had fallen, his chin had even dropped, and he could do nothing more than stare at her. She looked breathtaking in her shimmering flapper dress and as she sang, her exuberance electrified the room. Especially Max.

He couldn't help but notice that Sofia had gathered quite a large fan base of men near the stage. As Max leaned against the bar, amused by the flirtatious men hooting and whistling, he couldn't blame them for their enthusiasm because he, himself, couldn't take his eyes off Sofia. From then on, all he could think about was having her.

At a table near the stage, four squad members stood guard around the boss, Sally Bottoms. He also eyed the stage with the same persistence but with his attention focused squarely on Princess instead. As long as Sally wasn't interested, this gave Max the go-ahead to pursue Sofia, if he wanted.

With a drink in his hand, Max had made his way from the bar toward the boss' table.

Along the way, with an eye still on Sofia, he casually eavesdropped on Henry Ford, Ford's son, Edsel, and Thomas Edison, all standing like kings in the middle of the grand ballroom.

Max overheard the elder Ford say in mid-conversation, "Detroit has the best schools in the country, and with our auto industry dominating the economy, we're sure to surpass Chicago, even New York, as the place to be."

Then Edsel chimed in response, "Father, you know Mr. Edison isn't from here. We don't want to offend our friend."

Edison teased, "Edsel, let him brag. Any man that put as many wheels into operation as your old dad… He's earned it."

Since nothing of importance was being discussed, Max merely continued on his way to join his brother-in-law while Princess, Irene, and Sofia shifted gears on stage with a romantic ballad. He vividly remembered sliding into the empty chair reserved for him next to his powerful brother-in-law as he asked, "Who's the new doll?

A satisfied smirk appeared on Salvatore's thin, wrinkled face as his gravelly voice replied, "I thought you'd ask. Her name is Sofia Spera. Her pop is a *paesano*. Works the line over at Ford's Highland Plant."

Max confirmed, "So she's Italian? She's perfect."

Salvatore responded, speaking now in his own Sicilian dialect, "Sicilian. But don't bother getting too excited. She's only here for one night because Ruth up and quit."

Max shifted in his chair at the ridiculousness of Salvatore's suggestion and exclaimed back in English as if he had lost his mind, "Don't bother? She's the best lookin' dame in Detroit!"

Salvatore, not getting his feathers ruffled at all, retorted dry with complete seriousness, "And she's the kind of dame you marry."

Never one to give up easily, Max pointed out, "My mamma, God rest her soul, was the marrying kind."

Not feeling well, Salvatore hacked a cough causing the conversation to stall before he could respond with the obvious. "And your mamma didn't marry no gangster like you."

It was right then Max noticed that the romantic song had ended. All three dolls on the stage gave the audience a simultaneous wink, causing the men to go wild with a roaring standing ovation.

The synergy between the singers transcended any performance Max had ever seen, and considering all the parties he had attended in his line of work, that meant something significant. It was hard to believe this was the first time these three dames had performed together.

Seductively, Princess called out to her adoring fans, "Ladies and gentlemen, we'll be on back after a short break."

Max, knowing an opportunity when he saw one, knew this was his chance to meet this dynamic beauty. Without any hesitation, Max retorted back to his brother-in-law, "Says you. Mamma always said nothin' but the best for her boy."

And then he cut right past the surrounding crowd of competition to approach Sofia directly, offering his hand to help her off the stage. He remembered not letting go of her hand but, instead, leading Sofia straight up to the bar. As always, a couple of seats seemed to magically appear available for him as the previous occupants recognized him and smartly decided to vacate quickly to avoid any contact with the known mobster.

As they sat beside each other, Max didn't even say hello but only asked, "What can I get ya?"

"A glass of water would be great," Sofia politely replied with a sweet smile on her face.

"Water? Ah, come on! We're celebrating."

Max had impatiently waved his hand at the bartender. He noticed Sofia's eyes were drawn to his gold ring on his left pinky finger and its gleaming white diamond encircled by several smaller diamonds. The ring was hard to miss, which was the point. Max especially liked that the sight of it made Sofia flush a soft pink hue in her cheeks, and he couldn't help thinking of her as his own blushing bride.

He was also proud that Sofia was able to witness the bartender halt in the middle of another's order to accept Max's order instead.

"One for me and one for this lovely lady," Max commanded and then immediately returned his full attention directly to Sofia.

The bartender's brow beaded with sweat below his carefully slicked-back hair as he nervously replied, "Sure thing, boss. Two punches coming right up." Noticing that his statement could be misconstrued as two actual punches instead of the sugary red drink special of the night, the bartender quickly corrected himself, "I mean two glasses of punch coming right up."

Sofia softly added, "And water, please."

Just as the bartender rushed away to get their drinks, Sofia seemed to care about appearing rude, so she explained to Max, "It helps with my voice."

"You're quite the canary," said Max, as he turned her seat to face only him. He couldn't help it. He wanted her all for himself.

He used the same finger that donned his pinky ring to push back a stray hair that had fallen in front of her face and noticed how her gold speckled, chocolate brown eyes seemed to sparkle just as brightly as his diamond.

Sofia, again blushing and flattered, responded demurely with nothing more than, "Thank you."

Max also noticed that Sofia's eyes quickly darted away from his own. Instead of looking at him, she looked all around, wide-eyed like an innocent young girl, observing the magnitude of this extravagant party. He noticed that she caught a glimpse of Sally's table where both Princess and Irene were seated.

To regain her attention, Max scooted in closer to her and asked, "So what's your name, doll?"

Shifting her gaze away from the table, her soft-natured voice responded, "Sofia Spera."

The bartender finally returned and shakily set down two freshly poured glasses of punch and a glass of water in front of Max and Sofia. "Here you are, sir."

Max gave him a quick nod and reached into his breast pocket. He pulled out a stack of lettuce that was neatly folded in half and held together by an ornate gold money clip. He fingered through the crisp bills until he pulled out a fin and threw it onto the white marble bar as if it were a mere penny.

The bartender's eyes widened happily at the sight of it. As he carefully picked up the crisp five-dollar bill, he said gratefully with a bow of his head, "Thank you, sir. Much obliged."

With another nod, Max sent the bartender on his way. He returned his money back into its designated place and then pulled out a small silver flask from the same inner coat pocket. Unscrewing the top and spiking both drinks, he gave Sofia a wide grin as he said, "It's nice to meet ya, Sofia."

Max offered her a spiked punch, but surprisingly the bashful Sofia politely declined, "I'm sorry... I don't drink alcohol."

"Don't be a Dumb Dora. We're at the grand opening of the tallest, the grandest, the one and only Book-Cadillac Hotel. And it's in our very own Whiskeytown. How can ya not at least toast to that?"

He got Sofia to change her mind as she decided to take the glass from him after all. Holding up his own to clink against hers, he announced proudly, "Take that, Chi-town." He clinked her glass and observed as Sofia took a small sip. He watched how pleasantly surprised she was by how delicious the liquor ended up being and how she continued to drink it despite her initial refusal.

Max confidently noted to himself that he could do good by a dame like her. After all, he knew what was right for her more than she did for herself.

"Do you know there's over a thousand rooms in this baby? Each one got its own private water closet. First one in the world."

Sofia flirtatiously responded, "You don't say?"

"And they're huge. I know because I got one. A penthouse, I

picked out myself. I'm makin' it my office in the city."

He watched as Sofia's big eyes had widened with excitement. He wanted to impress her and was pleased that his plan was, in fact, working.

"What kind of business are you in? Having an office like that, you're not that music producer, are you?"

This time, she allowed those seductive eyes of hers brimmed with thick lashes to meet his own piercing gaze as she took another sip, coy as ever.

Although Max found it hard to believe she had no idea who she was talking to, he played along with her little game. He answered, "No, I ain't no music producer." And then added, teasing her, "Are you disappointed?"

"No, I don't care about no music producer. I'm just doing a favor for my friend, Renie. They needed a singer at the last minute."

Sofia had turned back toward the bar, allowing Max to lean in and whisper in her ear, thick with his likeable charm, "That's too bad. Because I think a music producer would be very interested in a gal like you. You're very talented, ya know. And beautiful. The most beautiful doll I have ever laid eyes on."

Clearly embarrassed by compliments delivered in such a direct manner, Sofia reacted this time only by lowering her face modestly to finish her drink. She seemed to not know how to respond to him so she then cleared her throat and curiously asked, "So what's your name then?"

"Massimo Denaro. But everyone calls me Max."

He watched as Sofia stopped drinking mid-drink at the mere mention of his name. It occurred to him that she did know him by reputation. However, she had somehow managed to live in Detroit her entire life without putting his name to his face. She gave a little cough to cover her surprise and explained, "Just went down the wrong pipe."

But Max wasn't buying her little act for a second. He knew what she was trying to pull by faking a cough, so he replied amused, "Looks like ya heard of me?"

Suddenly, Irene appeared beside them, tapped on Sofia's shoulder, and said, "Break's over, Sofia. We gotta go."

"What? So soon?"

"We're paid to sing, not chat with you, Max," Irene retorted coldly.

Max paid no attention to Irene or her insolent tone, as all he cared about was Sofia. He wasn't going to let anyone distract him from his mission. He was also hoping Sofia wouldn't want to go back on stage now that she knew who he was and how clearly interested he was in getting to know her.

However, Sofia obediently listened to her friend and instead offered her remaining punch back to Max, only adding, "Thank you for the drink. It was delicious." He noted the girlish yet sexy smile that she flashed him before departing from her bar stool and following Irene back toward the stage.

As Max held Sofia's delicate punch glass in his large, well-manicured hand, he couldn't help but stare at her curves as she made her way toward the stage. Like a pocket watch used by a hypnotist, he felt entranced by the glittering sequins and beads on her dress that swayed side to side along with her hips. It didn't help that she had the best ass he had seen on a dame in ages.

Max, unable to have her as he desired, took down the remainder of Sofia's punch in one effortless gulp. Setting the empty glass onto the bar, he opted to return to his reserved seat at the Scalici Squad's table.

Max recalled that as the night continued he didn't move from that seat for the rest of the party. He didn't care to talk or interact with anybody else besides an occasional comment to his brother-in-law. Max only wanted to sit there watching Sofia sing, while smoking one ciggy after another. He didn't know how many he smoked that night. Maybe twenty or so. But the whole time, he was well aware of the effect this dame was having on him when he couldn't keep his eyes off her for even one minute.

It also amused him that the men who had once surrounded the stage earlier had now disappeared for the rest of her performance. Max smirked to himself, reveling in the fear he must have put into them. Smoke escaped Max's satisfied grin as he ashed his ciggy into the full ashtray at his table. He felt that his gaze on Sofia was becoming weighed down by the bootleg gin that once filled the now-empty flask in his breast pocket.

Princess, Irene, and Sofia swung their arms and legs about in perfect unison as they effortlessly alternated between the Charleston and the Jitterbug. Princess landed her feet at center stage as she raised her arms above her head and belted out the final note of their last number. The song ended with a bang, and the girls held their pose as the crowd went wild. The sounds of clapping, cheering, and whistling echoed inside the ballroom for the trio as they collected their breath and bowed to a standing ovation.

Max had sprung to his feet, shooting sharp whistles with his pinky ring hand over his mouth. His whistling cut through the air like a freight train, all for Sofia. He made damn sure that he clapped and whistled louder than every egg in that ballroom.

He remembered that Sofia's smile stretched from ear to ear across her face as she took in the adulation from the cheering room. He had waited patiently for her gaze to finally land on him, and when it finally did, Max shot a wink back at her.

Sofia, playing hard to get, immediately turned her glowing cheek away from him.

After blowing kisses to the audience, Princess wrapped her white satin gloves around the ribbon microphone stand. Into it, she said, "Thank you, ladies and gentlemen, for celebrating the grand opening of the Book-Cadillac Hotel with Princess and the Princess O'Sullivan Band!"

The tipsy audience (supplied booze on the sly by the Scalici Squad, of course) roared with wild applause. Max expected Sofia to continue to soak in all the hoots and hollers geared toward her and her spectacular performance. But, to his surprise, she didn't.

Instead, with a sudden sense of urgency, almost as if she would turn into a pumpkin at midnight, Sofia, quickly and unexpectedly, descended from the stage. Max observed her every step while she walked straight across the crowded ballroom toward the dressing room, doing her best not to be stopped for more than a moment by all her new adoring fans.

Max debated whether he should head toward the dressing room, but reasoned the place would be crawling with people. He wanted to get Sofia alone. So, without a word to anybody, not even Sally, he nonchalantly headed to the lobby of the Book-Cadillac

Hotel.

As he waited, he couldn't help but look up at the ornate ceiling above. It was hard not to, even though he knew he should be keeping a sharp eye out for Sofia. But the gold leaf paint coated the raised edges of the carefully handcrafted plaster ceiling precisely matching the massive gold and crystal chandelier that dangled above the guests' heads. He remembered concluding that this hotel certainly earned the accolades it was receiving that evening as an architectural masterpiece.

But luckily, despite the distraction, he did spot Sofia from across the room. It was hard not to, she was so beautiful. She had appeared wearing a modest brown wool coat with her gloves in hand and her head down as she briskly made her way toward the gold-gilded front entrance door.

He quickly made his move and barricaded her exit with his body.

"You weren't gonna leave without sayin' goodbye?

"Of course not."

Max could tell Sofia was lying, but he didn't care. He reasoned she was obviously being polite, which meant she cared about his feelings.

"Let me take ya home."

Sofia slipped one of her delicate hands inside one of her short gloves as she responded, "Thank you, but it's not necessary. I have cab fare."

Alluding to the large crowd of guests departing at the same time as she was, Max replied, "You'll never catch one now."

And then, Max, once again, couldn't help himself. He gave Sofia a bold, daring kiss as though he'd been waiting years instead of hours to do that.

SIX

"Are ya happy now?" Max asked his wife, hoping his detailed and rather romantic rendition of the night they met and he fell in love would satisfy her.

Sofia was seated directly across the tiny table listening closely to his every word. It allowed him to study her face intently and monitor her reaction as he told his side of the story. The last thing he wanted was to be stuck on this damn boat with Sofia sulking like a spoiled brat.

Fortunately, her mood didn't seem to sour at all. Instead, Sofia seemed amused as she rose from her seat to pour him another glass of wine.

Max was also glad because he needed a refill. After his first glass, that familiar tingling feeling was just beginning to course through his veins. It helped keep his mind off this houseboat, slowly and steadily going farther and farther away from shore. He wanted to ensure Sofia was unaware of exactly how uncomfortable he was, being God-only-knows where on this massive lake.

Once she finished pouring the wine, she handed it to him as if to say drink up. As she did so, Sofia added with a sly smile, "Our first kiss. Very romantic. Especially for you."

"What can I say?" Max retorted smugly, believing he had done a bang-up job. As usual, he was delighted with himself.

But then, unexpectedly, Sofia started to laugh. And not just any laugh. But a good, hearty one.

"What's so funny?" Max inquired, honestly wondering what she thought was so hilarious.

Sofia only managed to laugh even harder in response.

At first, he thought she was being playful. But when she didn't stop, Max wondered if she was the one getting zozzled tonight. He noted that she hadn't taken even a sip of wine. Sofia had already told him that drinking wine was making her feel ill lately due to the baby. Max had no choice but to conclude her brash behavior had nothing to do with booze.

Max sensed Sofia was now mocking him instead of snickering at some random thought about learning how to cook and being in the kitchen for the first time.

And it annoyed him. Down to his core.

Max demanded to know, "Tell me, what's so funny?"

Sofia responded, bent over as she tried to reign in her giggling, "You want to know what's so funny? You. A romantic!"

She then practically fell out of her chair with how ridiculous a thought that was to her.

There was no mistake about it, Sofia was clearly taunting him. Max took a gulp of wine, wondering how he misjudged her. She was clearly sour about something, and he was in no mood to deal with it.

Then again, he never was.

Sofia finally stopped laughing, sensing she may be pushing Max too far, too quickly.

But she was also a woman on her own mission that night. So she continued with the very conversation she had planned for more than a month to have at this exact moment.

"Nothing about it was romantic. You asked me once to tell my version of what happened that night. Do you remember the night you asked me that?" Not waiting for Max's response or approval, Sofia added, "Well, now, you're going to get it."

SEVEN

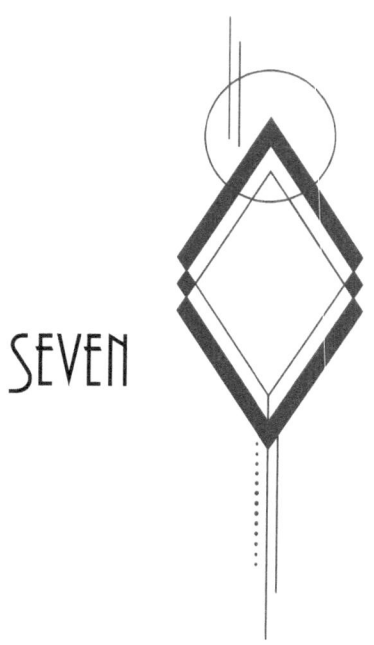

Sofia remembered she had been reading Jane Austen's *Pride and Prejudice* when a snowball landed on her bedroom window, causing her to jump at the sound. She scurried over to the glass. Sofia saw Irene shivering in the gray Michigan weather, as her best friend stood there in the cold forming her next snowball.

Sofia quickly opened the window before Irene had a chance to throw another. Something was clearly going on. Sofia didn't want her nosy mother also to be alerted to Irene's presence outside her home until she was able to get the scoop from her first.

"What's the big idea?" Sofia asked in a loud whisper. Her long, wavy locks fell delicately to her waist as she leaned out her window.

Irene immediately dropped her freshly made snowball and responded in her own loud whisper, "Am I glad to see you, Sofia!"

"Yeah? You could have just knocked at the front door like a normal person." It was an honest answer considering her friend had never done something like this before.

With a sense of urgency, Irene responded, "Hush… We don't need your daddy hearin' this…"

Irene then took a cautious look around, making sure Giacomo, or even Silvia for that matter, wasn't peering out another window eavesdropping. When she was satisfied that neither of them was around to hear her, she proceeded with her explanation. "Ya know, Ruth, the other girl that sings backup with me? She got cold feet and just up and quit."

Meanwhile, in a panic over the dire situation at hand, Irene pulled out her cigarette case and lit one to calm herself.

"Before the opening gala? At the Book-Cadillac? Tonight? What are you going to do?" Sofia was genuinely concerned for her best friend as she knew how important singing was to Irene. They both had that in common.

Sofia also knew how hard Irene had worked preparing for this big event since she had helped her friend rehearse for several weeks. Wherever the two young women were together, whether it was at home, school, or church, they were singing in harmony.

"Why do ya think I'm here?" Irene couldn't believe that Sofia didn't know what her point was in being there, but then again, at the same time, she could totally believe it. They had known each other since they were six years old. And Irene knew Sofia to be the most sheltered, and consequently the most innocent, girl primarily due to her overprotective Sicilian father by whom Irene was currently trying to avoid detection.

"Renie, really? Papa's never going to let me out till all hours of the night singing at some gala at some swanky hotel."

Sofia meant it. She knew her father well enough to know that he would not approve of her singing on stage in front of all those strange men. After all, he had made it abundantly clear on several occasions that she could only sing in the church choir.

"Come on, Sofia! Don't say no yet."

Dramatic as always, Irene took a long, suspenseful drag of her ciggy before continuing on. "Tell them we're goin' to bible study at Holy Family. Then midnight mass. Even *your* daddy can't say no to that."

There was a strong emphasis on the word *your* that Sofia picked up on. But she didn't mind Irene's criticism of her father. In fact, it happened all the time, and it never caused any friction between them.

For Sofia, her papa completely earned and conclusively deserved his reputation as the strictest father in town. She was chaperoned at all times except at night when she lay in her twin bed dreaming of singing on stage. The way her parents were with her, Sofia was surprised Giacomo didn't make her sleep at the foot of their bed.

Still, Sofia didn't like the idea of lying to them, especially since she prided herself on being a good Catholic girl. Although her parents' small-town Sicilian ways were suffocating, Sofia understood that they were only trying to protect her from what was to them a foreign land filled with rapists and other dangerous risks.

But then Sofia couldn't help but imagine herself singing on an actual stage in front of a real audience at the Book-Cadillac

Hotel. The thought had brought a pitter-patter to her heart. It was a pitter-patter that until now, she had felt only when singing at church.

How could I pass up an opportunity like this?

Even the Lord would be able to understand my desire, right? After all, He put it there.

Irene impatiently took another drag from her ciggy before letting the smoke billow out of her mouth as she said, 'When else are you gonna get a chance like this again? Princess O'Sullivan is the rage in Black Bottom. Besides, you're the only one that can help us."

Sofia remembered the mix of nerves and excitement that felt as if they were dancing the Lindy Hop inside her stomach as she responded in surprise, "Why only me?"

Irene threw her toasted ciggy into the pure white snow that covered Sofia's lawn like a soft blanket as she replied matter-of-factly, "Anybody who is remotely up to Princess' standards, that's available at the last minute, fucking hates her."

Sofia was shocked by her friend's crass explanation, causing her to cross her arms obstinately. She sternly reprimanded her with a harsh whisper, "You don't have to use that sort of language, Renie."

Irene knew that convincing her goody-two-shoes friend wasn't going to be easy. So she clasped her hands and shook them in the air as she begged, "Princess says that her daddy, Sally, knows this big time music producer who's gonna be there tonight. She'll be in Hollywood before ya know it, and I could go with her."

Sofia's eyes widened as soon as she heard her best friend say

Hollywood.

Irene continued, "Just think of it. You could come with us to *Hollywood.*" This time, having seen the effect it had, Irene purposely placed extra emphasis on the last word.

Sofia remembered how her body froze at the thought of one day being a professional singer in show business.

"Hollywood?" Sofia allowed herself to say the word out loud. Then she imagined herself starring in a movie with none other than the Sheik himself, Rudy Valentino.

How amazing would that be?

These days, she rarely let herself dream anymore, let alone say it out loud. It hurt too much. But somehow, Irene had managed to get her to do it. And like Sofia knew it would, it caused the happy pitter-patter that had just filled her chest to turn into longing and sadness.

But Sofia's sudden somber expression wasn't going to stop Irene as she persuasively added, "And, the richest men in Detroit will be there. Who knows? You could snag yourself a new daddy. One that won't keep you prisoner like your pops."

Ah, yes, the promise of a husband.

Sofia thought that was a much more likely benefit of her performance at the grand opening that night.

Just then, Sofia heard the rustling sound of Silvia's skirt in the hallway outside her bedroom. So she shushed Irene, knowing her mamma would find it strange that her friend didn't just come to the front door of the house. One thing Sofia knew for certain about Silvia, her mother was always suspicious about everyone, anyway. Sofia couldn't begin to imagine how suspicious she would be under these strange circumstances.

"I'll try. Give me thirty minutes."

"You're the bee's knees, Sofia!" Irene exclaimed as quietly as she could in her excitement.

"No guarantees."

But Irene knew that her friend would come through for her in the end. She had always been able to count on Sofia throughout her entire life. With justified confidence, she let out a little squeal of enthusiasm.

Sofia, once again, shushed her as she abruptly shut the window. She could hear Irene's next response muffled through the glass pane, "But it's cold out here…"

Not wanting her friend to freeze outside, Sofia knew she couldn't waste any time.

Besides, Sofia knew herself as well.

The more time she had to think about it, the less likely she'd be able to pull it off. Sofia was a terrible liar. She had been vigorously reared to tell the truth, so immense guilt always bubbled up across her flushed face whenever she attempted a guise. Her pink cheeks were always a dead giveaway and caused her to fail miserably in her lie every time. The consequences usually resulted in her parents making her already constrained life become fully constrained. This made her avoid lying at all costs.

But this time, it was worth it.

Sofia knew she would never be able to go to Hollywood. Papa would never allow it. But she reasoned that Irene could actually go. This really was a once-in-a-lifetime opportunity for Renie. Sofia had to be there for her friend.

Plus, Sofia couldn't think of a more delightful way to help her best friend out. It truly was a once-in-a-lifetime opportunity for her, as well.

Oh, the fun I would have!

As straight-faced as she could muster, Sofia asked her mother for permission to attend an impromptu bible study class at Holy Family. One filled with such devoted young worshippers that they planned on attending a special midnight mass afterward. Sofia did her best to pretend that the words she was saying were actually true. She even imagined walking with Irene up the church steps together to help it feel real to her.

Silvia had been kneading pasta in the kitchen as she listened to her daughter's unexpected request. She was inclined to say no because it was pasta night, and she needed help turning the machine's handle that transformed her ball of dough into long, straight pieces of spaghetti. As she powdered her sticky dough with a couple of generous pinches of flour, Sofia's mamma asked, "How will you get there? Papa is at work."

"Renie is outside waiting. I won't be alone. She will be with me the entire time."

"Why is she no here?"

Sofia immediately regretted not telling Irene to just come in. She had been fearful that Renie could have said something stupid and give the whole thing away. But as Sofia suspected she would, Silvia did, in fact, find it odd that Irene wasn't waiting for her daughter in the foyer inside the house.

So Sofia had to come up with the perfect answer for her mamma's excellent question to make up for it. Otherwise, there was no way Sofia would be able to convince her, especially when it meant Silvia had to make a week's worth of pasta by herself.

Whatever the answer was, it had to be close to the truth, or she would never be able to pull this off.

Sofia could feel the temperature rise in her cheeks. She fanned herself, hoping it would help cool her down as her mind raced for the perfect answer.

What can I say?
What can I say?
What should I say?

The only thing Sofia could think of that both made sense and had any chance of working was one she knew her mamma also wouldn't like hearing. Sofia considered the pros and cons of it and decided it was the best she could come up with and worth a try, so she blurted out, "Renie's smoking a ciggy."

"Sofia! It is so ugly for a woman to smoke! What is-a happening to Renie?"

Renie was the endearing nickname that Sofia's entire family had referred to Irene by since they were little girls. The whole family had accepted her as part of the family, despite the fact that Renie was Polish and lived in the nearby neighborhood of Poletown. The Speras, like many Americans, bought into the idea that the Poles were a bit dumb. Although Renie didn't seem to fall into an exception, she was such a sweet girl, one couldn't help but love her. So the Spera family brought her along everywhere as part of the family, even to their church.

"I agree, Mamma. That's why we need to go to bible study. She wants guidance to help her quit. I want to be there for my friend. We'll be together the entire time. I promise."

Noting her daughter's rosy cheeks, Silvia knew this was nothing more than an excuse for Sofia to get out of her chores to spend time having fun with her best friend. Sofia's mother had been young once, too. Before Silvia was a weary and sagging middle-aged woman in a plain, conservative house dress with a perpetual frown, she was a vibrant, bright-eyed girl who wanted to see the world. It's the reason she was attracted to Giacomo as her suitor. He wanted to leave their small boring town in Sicily to make a better life in America, too.

Silvia saw that same spark within her own daughter. She also knew that Sofia really was a good girl who could be trusted. After all, she had just admitted that Renie was smoking even though her daughter knew she disapproved. Sofia had never rebelled growing up despite their strict rules. She never gave Silvia a reason to warrant distrust, and Sofia rarely asked for anything, especially since the boys...

Silvia couldn't even finish her thought, it was so painful. She missed her sons terribly since...

...they went away.

Trying to push the excruciating memory away, she quickly changed the subject. She offered an excuse to cover up for the melancholy that hit her out of nowhere. "It's so hot in here," Silvia said with an exasperated huff.

Sofia immediately cracked the kitchen window open to let a little cold air in. She was grateful Mamma was also hot. It offered another viable explanation for her own flushed cheeks as well.

Silvia abruptly blurted out, "Okay, you can go."

"Really?" Sofia's face lit up with such surprise. She never thought Mamma would actually say yes. Usually, her mamma was a strict enforcer of Papa's rules, especially when he wasn't home to do it in person. Silvia often told Sofia that she also had no choice in the matter. If she went against Giacomo's wishes, her father would never let her mother hear the end of it whenever they were alone.

But something, unknown to Sofia, caused Mamma to say yes anyway.

Sofia was beyond grateful that Papa had picked up an extra shift on the line that night. If he were home, he would have never said yes, and if, by some miracle he did, he would have personally walked her up to the church. Her father would have made sure to speak to whomever was in charge. He didn't assume anybody, not even the priest, was fit to be around his only daughter and now, his only child, without his prior inspection and careful approval. If they didn't pass, without a moment's hesitation, Giacomo would have immediately walked Sofia back home.

As Silvia pushed aside some stray hairs from her face with her shoulder while her hands continued to knead the dough, she added some boundaries, "Butta you better be back before midnight. No mass. I no wanna worry Papa. Take-a little money from the cookie jar. Call for-a cab home. At least, thatta way, you no out on the street at night."

As Sofia scurried joyfully after her coat, Silvia added her final condition, "And no tell Papa about going with Renie by yourself there. I walked you. *Capisci?*"

EIGHT

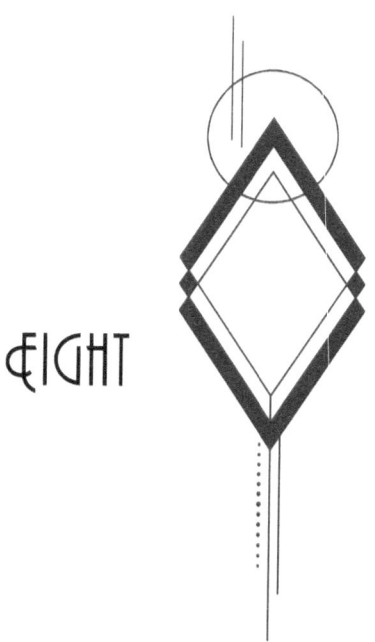

From across the street, Irene smoked one ciggy after another as she anxiously stared at the front door of the Spera's quaint bungalow home. As she waited for Sofia, a gentle snowfall was now adding to the already snowbanked lawn as well as to Irene's shivering chill, which continued to intensify.

Irene later told Sofia that after some time had passed, she started to second guess whether her friend could actually pull this off. She knew how dependable and loyal Sofia could be, but she also knew Sofia was a terrible liar. It's something, Irene had told her time and again, that takes dedication and practice to get good at, a lot like singing.

Irene was also well aware that this favor was a big ask. Especially for a girl like Sofia, who was restrained by her parents in every way. She then noted to herself that, in reality, whether Sofia could actually pull off this stunt was honestly a toss-up.

Dread started to fill the pit of her stomach.

Irene had no idea what she would say to Princess if she came back empty-handed. Having only two gals will make them appear as a duo. Equals on stage. The lead singer may very well decide to go on without her because of it.

Then, in what seemed like an eternity, Sofia stepped out of her family's front door wearing her best brown wool coat and matching short gloves. Irene couldn't contain yet another squeal of excitement that uncontrollably slipped out as she joyfully jumped up and down.

Sofia remembered how she, too, felt the same excitement as her dear friend but she, on the other hand, had to keep her cool. At least until she was out of her mamma's potential sightline. Silvia was known for spying on her daughter through the sheer white drapes that hung in the living room picture window. But as soon as they were safely off her street and onto Gratiot Avenue, Sofia actually skipped about like an excited little girl.

Upon entering downtown, they rounded a corner, arm-in-arm. Sofia and Irene were faced with an enormous advertisement for the Ford Motor Company. Although it was one of many throughout Detroit, they couldn't help but gawk at the towering billboard overhead that enticed them to buy the latest Model T.

Oh, how wonderful would that be!

Sofia gave herself a free pass for the rest of the night, allowing her to dream away without reservation. She decided that this was one of those rare moments in life where she wasn't going to let reality or probability squash exciting ideas. Just for one glorious night.

And owning my own Model T, that would be a dream!

So she let her mind linger on how beautiful it would be with the freedom that would come with owning your very own Ford. She would be such an anomaly since young women rarely drove, let alone had a vehicle. She wished she could be such a daring woman.

The girls then walked down to Michigan Avenue, where holiday decorations adorned the downtown shops in Detroit as the sky snowed on the bundled-up shoppers that were briskly passing by.

Sofia remembered how alive and exciting it felt that night in December as she gazed in awe at the many bustling shops. After all, she had never seen the city this late at night before because of her own personal fire extinguisher known as Giacomo.

While the many Fords, Cadillacs, Buicks, trolley cars, and a parade of pedestrians zipped by, she thought to herself that she was a city girl at heart. How badly Sofia wished she could wander the city streets whenever she wanted!

A police officer with a navy cap on his head, a club at his side, and a stop sign in his hand waved to stop the oncoming traffic, allowing the girls to cross the crowded downtown street.

"If Papa finds out, he's going to kill me, Irene." Sofia worried as she began to fear that any of these crossing pedestrians could end up recognizing her and telling her father.

Irene puffed a cigarette with her head held up pretentiously high as if she was a big starlet in town walking amongst the commoners. Sofia found this attitude was one of many changes that

Renie had undergone this past year.

"How's he gonna find out? Anybody Giacomo knows isn't gonna be there. I can promise ya that."

Irene had an idea and suddenly stopped in her tracks. She took out her cigarette case from her winter coat pocket. She offered a ciggy to Sofia, explaining, "It'll calm your nerves."

"A woman smoking is vulgar." Insulted by the mere suggestion that she would do such an unladylike thing, Sofia proceeded on her way, returning her attention back toward the delightful sights and signs around her.

"Of course, Silvia," replied Irene flatly, knowing damn well where Sofia got that idea from as she returned the cigarette case to her pocket.

Just then, another particular billboard caught both girls' attention. It read *The World Famous Detroit Auto Show*.

"Sofia, look! With everything goin' on, I almost forgot to tell you. We just found out that we're performing at the auto show, this year! We entertain the *Who's Who* of Detroit. Even Henry Ford."

Irene's dreamy eyes couldn't move from the advertisement. She was beyond excited about performing at the biggest auto show in the world. After all, everyone was going to be there. Everyone went every year. For her, this was yet another of what seemed like a string of lucky breaks lately.

With equally dreamy eyes, Sofia also gazed up at the billboard, and that pitter-patter in her heart suddenly returned. She replied to her friend as if in a daze, "You don't say? I wish I could do something like that."

"What are you talkin' about? Now's your chance. Ford is gonna be at the Book-Cadillac. Tonight!"

They celebrated the thought giggling like schoolgirls until their glee was suddenly silenced upon making eye contact with Bambino. His immense size, brooding demeanor, and severe grimace sent a shiver up both their spines. As they crossed paths, the giant goon acknowledged Irene with a nod, and she returned his gesture with a smile.

Surprised, Sofia whispered in Renie's ear, "You know him?"

Irene waited for Bambino to gain some distance ahead of them. He was escorting Fred Moore, who walked beside him like a prisoner heading to the lethal gas chamber. Once they were out of earshot, she replied with as serious a tone as an exuberant girl like Irene could muster, "Yeah, and my advice is to stay away. Bambino Cercone is a thug for some of the most ruthless gangsters in Detroit, the Scalici Squad. They're Sicilian, like you."

Sofia's eyes widened in surprise. To her, these people were nothing like her. Gangsters (or mobsters, as some called them) like this only existed in the fiction she read at home alone in her bedroom, not out in real life. "But how do *you* know him?"

"Princess shacks up with the Big Cheese, Salvatore Scalici. He goes by Sally Bottoms because you end up at the bottom of the Detroit River if you mess with him." As she explained, Irene straightened her shoulders and, rather confidently, picked up the pace.

It made Sofia wonder if Renie was proud of her new association with the Mafia, an idea she personally found gross at best. "Aren't you frightened being around...these types of people?"

Nonchalantly, Irene responded without a concern in the

world, "Frightened of Sally? Naw. Princess has him wrapped around her little finger."

But then, her mood grew more serious at a new thought, and Irene cautiously warned, "The one that scares me is Sally's brother-in-law. Whatever you do, steer clear of Max Denaro. And he can be a charmer when he wants somethin'. So beware!"

Sofia responded, "Max Denaro. I won't forget," at the precise moment when a dark, handsome, and rugged man wearing Ford overalls briskly passed them by. He had been heading in the same direction as the two women but at a faster pace and with a real sense of urgency. Making eye-contact with Sofia, the man clearly overheard her. It was as if he wanted to witness who dared to say such a name, out loud, on the streets of Detroit.

When her eyes met his gaze, however, she looked away immediately to the ground. His good looks and intensity felt like electricity that shot right through her. It made her heart pitter-patter wildly, and she felt an instant tingle down below. She could feel her temperature rise and her cheeks redden. Sofia just knew she was blushing a deep shade of red.

Her mind instantly wondered what it would be like to kiss him, but instead, Sofia kept her bashful eyes down as he hurriedly continued on his way ahead of them.

"Did you see how he looked at you? He's gorgeous. Do you know him?" Irene couldn't help but stare as he swiftly walked away.

"I wish." By now, Sofia felt it was safe to look up, and she, too, watched as her mystery man disappeared into the crowd ahead.

Playfully referring to his occupation as one of the many assembly line workers in town, Irene added with an elbow to Sofia's side, "I'd let him tend to my parts, that's for certain."

They, again, giggled like schoolgirls at what to them, at the time, was a very provocative joke. Just as their laughter subsided, Irene gave Sofia another little jab as they neared Washington Boulevard. She pointed ahead of them, "There she is."

Beyond the tip of Irene's finger was a towering Neo-Renaissance style hotel, complete with Corinthian pilasters and columns separating large arched windows, displaying a regal awning above the grand entrance that read, *The Book-Cadillac Hotel*. The 31-story, beige brick and limestone masterpiece made every building around it seem like a plain dwarf.

Sofia's doe-eyes widened as her jaw dropped in awe at the sheer mass and beauty of the elegant hotel. She gasped, "Wow, Renie, that is the tallest building I've ever seen."

Irene retorted with a giggle, "Well, it better be, it's only the tallest hotel in the entire world."

"The entire *world?*" Sofia exclaimed as her eyes widened to their maximum capacity. She noted that she really wished she could come downtown more often. She missed so much in life always staying close to home.

At that very moment, Sofia felt a surge of pride. She was going to be performing at the grand opening of the tallest hotel in the world! And, she didn't even have to travel to New York or Chicago to do it, either. This night was all happening right in her hometown of Detroit.

Under her breath, Sofia asked herself, "Could tonight get any better than this?"

As the two young women approached the front entrance,

Irene and Sofia were greeted by a doorman wearing a long double-breasted ruby red coat and a matching hat with a shiny black brim. His coat had polished gold buttons that matched the bright gold trim that traced both the edges of his notch collar lapel and circled around the cuffs of his sleeves. His uniform was completed by a pair of pristine gloves, white as virgin snow. Sofia wondered whether the ornate handle of that massive gold door had been the first thing his immaculate gloves had ever touched.

The doorman gave a nod of recognition to Irene, who casually nodded right back at him as he opened the door and said, "Good evenin', ladies. Welcome to the Book-Cadillac Hotel."

Sofia also noticed how the doorman's spine was perfectly erect. It made her wonder whether he was once a military man. Being about the same age as her two brothers, she questioned whether he could have fought in the war beside them.

The thought of Enrico and Alessandro made her instantly miss them. Sofia immediately shook the sad thought from her mind as she entered the glitzy hotel.

Tonight was not the night for sad thoughts.

Sofia and Irene's gently worn t-strap pumps tapped across the shiny cream marble floors of the magnificent hotel lobby. Crowded within were regal men who all wore sharp dark suits or coattails with starched white shirts. Many escorted elegant ladies in silk dresses covered in glass beads and fringe, shimmering and swaying under the grand chandelier overhead. The crystal masterpiece above was framed by ornate plaster, trimmed with touches of gold paint that swirled about on the ceiling.

Sofia remembered feeling like a dull brown mouse as she

walked past the ostentatious women donning sparkly jewelry and headbands with beautiful feathers. She had never seen such sophistication and splendor in her whole life.

The sound of jazz instruments improvising with each other from another room echoed through the gilded walls as Sofia and Irene approached the bronze doors of the elevator. Upon entering, the operator closed the door behind them, removing them from the hustle and bustle of the hotel lobby.

Irene proudly ordered, "The Grand Ballroom, please," and the elevator operator returned her request with an affirming nod, "Going up."

Sofia remembered how the rush of the elevator matched the nerves that danced in her belly. To take her mind off of her anxiousness, she focused her attention on the elaborate geometric shapes etched onto the doors in front of her. She noted to herself that not one detail was spared in the design of this extravagant hotel.

One floor later, the operator sharply announced, "The Grand Ballroom," right after a loud ding that preceded the opening of the elevator door.

Irene guided her into the Grand Ballroom, and as soon as they entered, Sofia stopped dead in her tracks. It was even grander than she could have ever imagined!

Sofia remembered how the oak floor was cut into precise chevrons that stretched as far as the eye could see, and how it looked so shiny, the shiniest she'd ever seen, since it had never been danced on before.

All around the room, waitstaff dressed in stiff white jackets with black lapels scurried about placing untouched crystal and flatware onto equally stiff white table cloths atop rows upon rows of round tables.

She also remembered how the ballroom ceiling was even taller than the one at the Catholic Church where she and Irene were supposed to be that night. She gazed up at one crystal chandelier after another crystal chandelier after another, all centered in an ornate plaster ceiling even more opulent than the hotel lobby.

Sofia remembered thinking that this ballroom felt holier than her church. She was surprised that something like that would occur to her so easily and she instantly did the sign of the cross across her chest while silently praying for forgiveness for having such a sacrilegious thought.

A spotlight on the stage illuminated Princess O'Sullivan, royalty of jazz music, as she sang like a superstar on stage.

This was the first time Sofia had ever seen Princess with her own eyes. Up to this point, she had only heard stories about the singer through Renie, and mostly felt like Princess was some sort of demanding mythical goddess. At the time, Sofia had thought her friend was being dramatic and exaggerating, as usual. But, after hearing her voice in person belting out the lyrics with such depth, range, and soul, Sofia concluded that the stories were, in fact, true. Princess certainly earned her reputation of being the best singer in town.

Sofia felt the nerves in the pit of her stomach multiply. She could only hope she wouldn't embarrass herself singing next to this immensely talented professional.

She then noticed that she wasn't the only one mesmerized.

The table nearest the stage had the only guests currently present in the room. She saw an old, fragile man, who she suspected was the infamous Sally Bottoms. He was surrounded by a standing crew of rough and tough gangsters as he sat and watched in awe at Princess singing her heart out. Sofia was surprised to see how frail and feeble this powerful man was in reality.

She was also surprised because it was clear to her from his beaming eyes that Salvatore Scalici was madly in love with Princess, which felt strange to Sofia. Although black women were never recognized for their beauty, Sofia knew no matter what anybody said, Princess was, indeed, showstopping.

But she also had never witnessed a white man openly showing real emotion for a black woman. That was stuff she hadn't even read about in fiction.

Next to Sally Bottoms was Bambino with the same man she had seen walking beside him earlier. She noted how the man anxiously stood there behind Bambi, skittish and uneasy. He looked utterly miserable as he waited for his escort to finish whatever business he had with the sickly mob boss. Bambi whispered into Sally's ear, interrupting his concentration on Princess' performance.

Sofia tried not to be obvious as she observed from the back of the room. She was still standing next to one of the many ballroom doors she had entered, as the two men briefly whispered what seemed to be top-secret business into each other's ears. Then Bambino abruptly rose from his seat and quickly exited with Fred, scurrying to keep up with his wide stride.

Curious, Sofia couldn't help herself, so she cracked open the nearby door and tried to catch a peek of them. However, Sofia didn't see Bambi's head towering above the other hotel guests loitering in the hallway. She concluded that he must have already made it into the elevator. Boy, that was fast, she thought to herself.

As she was about to close the door, she saw a man's legs wearing blue jean overalls with his upper torso and face hidden behind an open newspaper. She couldn't help but notice him because his casual clothes were conspicuously out of place in the glamorous, upscale hotel.

He then lowered the newspaper slightly as if to spy on someone around the corner, and that's when she realized that this was her mystery man!

It was at that precise realization when he caught Sofia's curious stare, and once again, their eyes locked. But this time, a smile spread across his face.

Embarrassed by having been caught staring at this attractive man, Sofia briskly closed the door. Her breasts heaved with each breath she took from the pitter-patter that began to drum a beat in her chest. Something about this mystery man had an air of fate to her.

What were the chances I would bump into him, again, so soon?

But Sofia gave her head a little shake as if that would help get the mystery man out of her mind. She did her best to conscientiously return her attention to Princess on stage as she reminded herself that at this important moment she needed to focus. This opportunity was a dream come true for her, and she couldn't sabotage it with lustful thoughts. No matter how gorgeous that man may be.

Instead, Sofia returned her gaze to Salvatore Scalici, who

continued to be overwhelmed by Princess' fantastic talent as she belted out her final note of the song. Princess raised both arms triumphantly in the air and then took a graceful bow.

Already standing, Sofia and Irene vigorously applauded Princess' performance as Salvatore gave her a standing ovation. From the stage, Princess blew him a kiss in return. But frail from illness, his only reply was coughing severely, which caused him to pull out his handkerchief to cover his mouth. He had to sit back down in his seat as well.

"Sally? Daddy, you alright?" Princess asked with genuine concern for him.

Despite the worry in the singer's voice, Sofia received the impression that this wasn't the first time Princess had asked this of her sugar daddy's well-being. Notwithstanding its authenticity, something about how she had asked the question felt uniform and familiar.

While he coughed, Salvatore had responded with a wave for her to not mind him, but instead to proceed on with rehearsal. "You don't have to worry about me, my princess," he managed to say between dry, hacking coughs.

Sofia saw Mr. Scalici checking the handkerchief he just finished coughing in. There was definitely a red smatter of blood on it.

Meanwhile, Princess didn't need to be told twice, and she quickly swung around toward the band. To show she meant business, Princess began to shout loudly at her band members, "This needs to hit on all sixes! And Horace, you're a snore. Perk it up from here on in."

Sofia noted that Horace dutifully positioned his trumpet up to his mouth with his middle finger up higher than the rest. She wondered whether that was the standard way to play or his way of letting Princess know how he felt about her cutting criticism in front of his fellow band members. Sofia already knew by this time that men rarely took direction or criticism well from women.

Then Princess waved to both Irene and Sofia, who still stood idly at the back of the ballroom, to come over to the stage. "You two. Nobody home?" She spoke to them like they were a couple of idiots for having to be asked to take their places behind her.

Irene and Sofia obediently scurried over. Their pumps echoed loudly with every step they took toward the raised stage at the end of the ballroom.

Princess shouted out, "Take it from the top!"

And then the jazz band instantly burst out, once again, playing the last song.

NINE

After rehearsal, Sofia and Irene had followed Princess in tow into the brand new ladies' dressing room. Sofia remembered how she once again felt like a plain mouse next to the most glamorous and talented singer she had ever witnessed.

The dressing room smelled distinctly of fresh paint. There were long built-in wood counters with rows of small drawers that created personalized stations for a potential group of performers such as themselves. Sofia concluded they looked freshly painted to her; hence, the bad smell's culprit.

There were also a series of six large rectangular mirrors framed by small round lights on each side of the room. Chairs were neatly tucked in front of each mirrored station, except for Princess', whose chair was ajar from having previously been there before rehearsal.

Princess grabbed an ornate red and gold perfume bottle that had a long black tassel dangling from its small black bulb. She gently squeezed the bulb to dispense a mist of roses into the freshly painted room.

"It still smells like chemicals in here. Damn paint," Princess exclaimed as she pumped a few more sprays of the floral scent into the air. "Sally gave me this perfume. All the way from France." Princess proudly took a whiff and added, "He knows I love roses. It's my signature flower."

As Princess set the perfume bottle back onto the counter, she leaned in gracefully to smell one red rose out of the two dozen arranged within two separate crystal vases, chisel-cut with geometric diamond designs, one on each side of her mirror.

Sofia had never seen so many roses together in her life. She had also never met anybody who had a signature flower. But it didn't surprise her that her first was a woman named Princess.

Giacomo would never buy flowers during his weekly shopping trips at the Eastern Market. They were insanely expensive, and as he phrased it, an utter waste of money. But standing near them, admiring them now, Sofia thought that they felt good to the senses. She began to wonder what her signature flower would be if she had one.

Princess then strode over to the end of the dressing room, where there was a rack filled with glamorous dresses that were distinctly color-coordinated like a rainbow. She leisurely swiped through each dress. Her focus was on selecting the winning one of the evening as she simultaneously asked Sofia, "Irene's been singing for me for months now. If you're such great friends, how come

I've never met you before?"

Before Sofia could even open her mouth to answer, Irene quickly chimed in, "Because she's practically a nun. *Papa* never lets her out of his sight."

Renie seemed peeved by Giacomo's behavior -- as if it was outlandish. She had always been critical of Sofia's parents but her tone was different this time. Her friend made it feel like there was more going on than a father solely protecting his daughter. It made Sofia question the nature of her relationship with him for the first time.

Was there anything wrong with the way Papa treats me?

Princess' eyes landed on a creamy white silk flapper dress. It had a drop waist made entirely of red beads that accented the red embroidered roses on its bodice. The skirt was made of long layers of shiny dip-dyed fringe that started as the same creamy white at the top and gradually changed to a deep red by the bottom.

Princess looked back over her shoulder at Sofia and said, "Would you mind making yourself useful?" Ending her request with a charming yet snippy smile.

Sofia hesitated slightly before responding as one would anticipate, "Oh, um, of course."

She then gently set her purse down along with her plain brown gloves, carefully placed directly on top. It was as if to not take too much room on the long, empty counter. She did this as fast as she could, which still seemed to take a bit too long for Princess.

To make up for lost time, Sofia scurried over to Princess' aid, who seemed to enjoy the apprehension she was causing within the girl.

Sofia tried to steady her shaking hands as best as she could, while she unfastened the row of tiny muted rose silk buttons. She was aware that it was also the first time she had ever touched a dress so fine. That only added to her anxiety.

When Princess was finally set free from her dress, Sofia quickly returned to where she had initially been standing near the entrance. She acted like she wanted to give Princess some privacy. But she also was hoping some space from the singer would alleviate the mounting nerves in Sofia's gut.

She watched as Princess carefully stepped out of her rehearsal dress and placed it neatly back in its color-coordinated spot. Sofia recalled how Princess' creamy white silk slip had the most delicate embroidered detail that swirled around the neck and hemline. And how the shiny silk looked as if it was floating over Princess' curvaceous body.

Sofia had never seen such an expensive slip before. Her parents could only afford the modestly cut, cotton slip that she was wearing at that very moment.

The fringe of Princess' floral dress swayed and shimmied as she slid the creamy white silk straps over her robust muscular shoulders. She then looked at herself in the mirror, and a smooth smile spread across her face.

Sofia could tell Princess was pleased with how she looked in that fabulous dress, and she didn't blame her one bit.

Princess did look breathtaking.

Sofia waited patiently as Irene then searched through the rack of flapper dresses. She had already been through the entire selection once. She was now going through it a second time to hopefully pick one out for herself during this next round.

Alluding to her own beautiful choice, Princess said, "Pick anything. You're not going to look better than me anyway."

Sofia was surprised to hear how direct and, frankly, mean Princess was to Renie. She wanted to stick up for her friend but knew better than to speak up. Sofia knew that Renie would be furious with her if she did so. She couldn't risk losing this opportunity for them both by starting an argument. So, she kept quiet and allowed Renie to ignore the local celebrity's unkind comment.

That's when Princess then turned her attention to Sofia, whose head was modestly tilted down toward the floor with only her eyes looking up quietly, observing the dressing room. She walked around Sofia and examined her looks like she was a thoroughbred horse and Princess, a prospective buyer. When she seemed satisfied by her inspection, she questioned her, "Where did you learn to sing?"

Sofia met Princess' gaze and remembered how her heart was racing as she proudly responded, "I'm in choir at church."

Princess' eyes were deadlocked onto Sofia as she delivered the following question to the back of the dressing room, "Irene, I thought you said she was a trained singer?"

At first, Sofia felt deflated.

Here she thought singing in the choir would impress Princess, especially since many black singers did the same. At least that's what Sofia had heard through the grapevine. After all, Princess was the first black person she had ever conversed with this much up until now. The neighborhoods in Detroit were segregated, so she didn't even have a chance to get to know any black women. She really only knew what she had been told or read about them.

But Sofia always admired their music. She was such a fan, it didn't even occur to her to care about Princess' race. Instead, Sofia had risked a great deal for this opportunity. Too much to give up now. She knew that she needed to prove to Princess that she deserved to be there. After all, she didn't want to end up lying to her mother and walking unchaperoned through the streets of Detroit just to have a stroll over to the Book-Cadillac.

So with a quick inhale, Sofia began to sing a bible hymn. Her warm mezzo-soprano voice gently filled the dressing room before she effortlessly transitioned into one of the hopping numbers they would be performing that night.

Princess was impressed but not quite finished sizing up Sofia. With a raise of her brow, she asked, "You know our songs?"

Again, trying her best to impress, Sofia responded with her chest up and chin raised, "All of them. Renie taught me."

And again, unexpectedly, Princess slowly turned her head back as she glared at Irene for doing such a thing.

Sofia didn't understand why that was a problem. But in an attempt to save her friend from getting heat, she interjected, "Renie and I are like sisters. Known each other our whole lives."

With Princess' eyes still fixed on Irene, she asked Sofia, "Then why didn't *Renie* introduce me to you earlier?" Then chastising Irene, Princess added, "She's ten times better than Ruth ever was."

As Irene slipped on her finally-chosen red satin flapper dress, she responded in her defense, "I told you. Her daddy is practically a watchdog. She never goes out anywhere. Wops would sew your legs shut if they could get away with it."

This wasn't the first time she had heard Renie describe Italians like this. Usually, she didn't mind because the observation was on point. But now, Sofia felt a flood of embarrassment rise up within her. Her parents' old-fashioned, old-world ways must seem so weird and foreign to a sophisticated flapper like Princess. Tears began to well in her eyes, causing her to look away in shame as she blushed a deep red.

Princess, however, softened when she noticed how sad Sofia had become by the mention of what she deemed was female indentured servitude. Except the term of service was for life and involved unlimited sex as part of the deal. Princess was almost twenty-eight years old, a whole decade older than the fresh faced, innocent Sofia, and working in show business since she was a young girl. She had seen more women being taken advantage of and abused than Sofia could ever imagine coming from such a sheltered childhood.

Princess understood the plight of women intimately, having grown up with a mother who passionately picketed for the suffrage movement. American women finally being granted the right to vote, and then to see it not given to black women equally in practice, made Princess particularly sensitive. Her life experience taught her that the constructs of Sofia's circumstances were ingrained within society for centuries and, undeniably, very complicated. None of which was Sofia's fault.

Princess realized that she couldn't have Sofia moping during their upcoming performance. So in an effort to make her feel better, she offered the young gal comforting wisdom, "Listen, doll, it ain't so bad having a watchdog in this miserable world."

As Sofia wiped the tears from her eyes, she nodded in agreement. She actually did agree with what Princess had said to her. Despite how stifling her papa could be, Sofia was also well aware that she was lucky to have a father looking out for her. It was a valid point she reminded herself of often, especially whenever she was stuck home alone because he couldn't chaperone her anywhere. She recalled sharing a smile with Princess, reassuring her she was feeling better.

Satisfied that her sentiment had helped, Princess returned her focus back to her own dressing room mirror. She picked up her lipstick to complete the final touch of her own look.

As the singer swiveled the lipstick from its tube, Sofia couldn't help but stare because she had never seen a tube of lipstick in real life before. In her Sears Roebuck and Co. Catalogue, yes, but in real life, no.

Sofia's mother would never get caught dead with *even* rouge on her face, let alone lipstick. Her mother cautioned Sofia against the practice, advising her that "painted women," as Silvia often called them, "were whores back in *Sicilia*. Good men don't marry whores."

But as Princess effortlessly glided the red pigment to the edge of her full lips with precision, Sofia thought it made her look even more attractive, if that was humanly possible.

She wanted to look as beautiful as Princess with her very own red painted lips.

Sofia felt a pang of guilt for wanting the very thing her mother despised. So she looked away and back to the floor, embarrassed because she was so weak and easily tempted. It then occurred to her that her mamma would be very disappointed if she knew where Sofia was at this precise moment. And it definitely wouldn't help if she knew how badly her daughter wanted to be here, on top of it.

Once Princess was satisfied with her own looks after patting down a stray hair here and there, she turned toward Irene and commanded, "Give her a dress. Something that works with what we got on."

Princess dramatically shook her head in pity at the conservative, plaid, cotton dress Sofia wore under her simple wool coat. She added an apt observation. "This ain't church, that's for certain." But then she gave Sofia a reassuring wink that it'll be alright after they're done with her.

It was true that Sofia had felt self-conscious about her appearance since she first entered the Book-Cadillac until that wink. Frankly, she wasn't confident about where to start with assembling her outfit and was relieved by the help. She had little chance to play with fashion before this, confined again only to what she had read in books or seen in store catalogues.

To Giacomo, following fashion trends was just another utter waste of money. He declared that overspending on clothes one didn't need, no matter the quality, was for vain, shallow suckers obsessed with little else in life than showing off. So Sofia never owned anything above her practical needs.

With sincere gratitude for everything, Sofia said, "Thank you so much for this opportunity, Princess. I won't let you down. I promise. And I'm a girl that values my word."

Princess leaned back in her chair, concluding her inspection of Sofia with a confident, "I think you'll round us out real nice tonight. And, who knows, with a little work, you could even snag yourself a new daddy."

Irene yelled out from behind the rack of dresses as she debated between two choices for Sofia, "That's what I said. Can you believe she's still a virgin?"

Luckily, there was a knock on the dressing room door. Sofia felt relieved that she didn't have to suffer through another lecture about how she shouldn't define her personal value with what's going on between her legs. To Renie, a girl liberated from the chains of abstinence by a schoolmate named Billy a year earlier, Sofia was needlessly saving herself for marriage.

If Silvia knew how much Renie had changed, Sofia was convinced she would no longer be able to spend time with her best friend. She could hear her mamma now, also lecturing her, but her lecture would be about how one must be very careful who you allow in your inner circle because they can make or break your life. Judging from what Sofia was about to do, in front of countless strangers no less, she would not be able to argue with any success that Renie had not become a bad influence.

"Who's there?" Princess responded through the door.

A man on the other side of it yelled loudly so as she could hear, "Delivery for Miss Princess O'Sullivan."

But he didn't wait for her go-ahead before popping his head in. It was a young man that Sofia recognized as one of Sally's goons from earlier in the ballroom. His black slicked-back hair almost matched the small velvet box in his hand precisely as he repeated to her, "Delivery for a Miss Princess O'Sullivan."

Princess only nodded, allowing him to enter.

"Where do ya want it?" he asked politely.

Princess patted the end of her vanity as she responded, "Right here will do."

He set down the box as instructed and explained, "Sally says it will give you luck."

"Thank you, Vito," was her only reply as she waited patiently for him to leave.

Vito stole a glance over at Irene and then Sofia. A little smirk appeared on his face at the sight of the new girl. But he felt Princess' glare and proceeded out the door with a, "Break a leg, Princess."

As soon as the door closed behind Sally's delivery man, Princess opened the box. Inside, there was a diamond solitaire, a huge rectangle, set in a white gold, art nouveau-style, filigree casing.

Sofia had noted at the moment that she was, once again, experiencing a first in her life. She had never seen a diamond before. Mamma, along with every other married woman in her eastside, working class, Italian neighborhood, wore only a simple gold band on her ring finger.

As Princess squealed with delight, she slid it on her right ring finger and then flashed it for the other two girls to see. "Take note, girls. Get all the perks without all the work."

She pulled her hand closer to her face so she, herself, could get a better view of the giant diamond as she added as an afterthought, "Poor Teresa."

Without thinking, Sofia's curiosity got the best of her, and she blurted out, "Who is Teresa?"

After hearing herself out loud, it didn't take but another second of time for her to get it. *Oh, Mr. Scalici is married!*

But Princess didn't seem at all offended. It was like she didn't care one bit about it. Instead, she patted her chair for Sofia to take a seat and said, "Doll, you've got a lot to learn. But let's start with those brows."

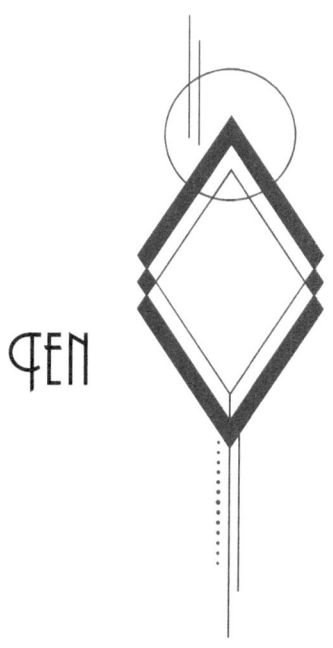

TEN

Sofia had finally come to her favorite part of the story. She gazed up wide-eyed and dreamy, trying to recall every vivid detail of her most favorable experience in life. She described it to Max with such yearning, as if she would do anything in the world to go back in time to that precise moment.

Max, however, didn't care to notice both the longing on Sofia's face or in her voice. Instead, he was focusing on doing his best to finish his meal as she yacked on and on. He didn't understand why he needed to know all the details about how she ended up there at the grand opening that night.

But he did notice that Sofia wisely made sure he was having a pleasurable time despite her long, drawn-out anecdote. When he finished the last drop of his wine, Sofia immediately paused and poured another for him. Max was glad for the bottomless glasses.

The constant lubrication made it all the more palatable to him.

After she finished filling his glass, yet again, Sofia continued with her story at the point when the trio first entered into the grand ballroom. Her entrance beside Princess and Irene was unlike anything she ever encountered in her entire lifetime.

ELEVEN

This night was a night filled with many, many firsts for Sofia.

The party guests, all dolled up in their finest garments with feathers and sparkles everywhere, had recognized Princess, by now a local favorite, instantly. Some tried to steal a glimpse of her. Others politely nodded in acknowledgment as they stepped aside to allow a pathway for the trio.

Sofia had never felt so many gawking eyes on her at once. She had already grown quite accustomed to being stared at by this point in her life. But this was at a new level, even for her.

This was also the night she wore makeup for the first time.

She recalled in striking detail how beautiful she felt with her *cupid's bow* lips that perfectly defined her full, red pout.

Sofia couldn't help but touch the apples of her cheeks as she described how they were delicately flushed like two powdery pink rose petals due to the rouge put on them.

How the soft matte black eyeliner made the gold flecks of her warm, brown eyes sparkle like glitter.

Or, how the weight of the cake mascara that Princess applied with a wet brush weighed down her eyelids just a touch. Giving her an effortlessly sexy gaze that Sofia had never before seen on her face.

Besides the makeup, it was the first time she wore the color black.

Traditionally, it was once a color reserved for mourners. Since her parents were traditional at best, old-fashioned at worst, Sofia was never allowed to wear the color. Mamma couldn't fathom why any young girl would go out of her way to look old before her time. Sofia could tell her mother was truly perplexed by what she thought as a strange new fashion trend.

But, despite her mother's opinion, black was now regarded as a color of class and sophistication. Renie had picked out the most stylish black dress Sofia had ever seen, let alone ever worn.

Sofia described the details of that dress on the houseboat to Max as if it were still literally clinging to her curvaceous body. She recalled the contrast between the shiny satin bodice and the angular, sheer lace straps that exposed the olive complexion of her shoulders beneath them.

Bare shoulders were definitely a first for Sofia as well.

The single strand of beaded fringe that extended past the shortest satin skirt she had ever worn, swung back and forth with every step toward the stage. Every strand was comprised of a stack of small black beads that had a creamy white pearl just above one large sparkly red glass bead at the very end.

To finish off Sofia's look, Princess had tucked a red rose behind her ear and placed one of her own super long string of white pearls around her neck. She clarified to Sofia that they were not a gift but on loan along with her spare black satin opera gloves. Sofia loved how they felt like heaven to her fingertips, and how the white necklace popped perfectly against the dark dress and swayed harmoniously right along with her skirt.

It was the first time Sofia purposely drew attention to herself.

They had practiced for almost an hour prior in the dressing room. Sofia did her best to follow Princess' precise instructions. As she walked, she swayed her hips with every step, so that long beaded fringe swooshed from side to side, drawing attention to *all the right places* on her body.

Sofia could tell it was working, too.

Many of the surrounding men had tipped their hats with blatant expressions of interest toward her. Some even attempted direct eye contact or daringly winked as she made her way to the main stage. Sofia noted that this must be how the royalty she read about in books felt when they walked amongst the common folk.

Sofia felt her heart pounding like a freight train as she stepped onto the dark stage for the first time.

Princess and Irene found their marks and turned their backs toward the audience, and Sofia quickly followed suit. She could hear sporadic hoots and hollers from behind as she waited for Princess to place her left hand onto Irene's shoulder and her right hand onto Sofia's shoulder. That was the signal to the band and lighting crew that they were ready to start the show.

Sofia recalled how her nerves continued to hop about in her gut as she waited for her cue. Meanwhile, she silently prayed to hit every note and land every step exactly as rehearsed. Sofia hoped with all her might she wouldn't end up embarrassing herself in front of such a large, prominent audience. If this was to be her only performance in her life, she wanted to at least be able to look back on it as a fond memory. Instead of becoming a laughing-stock.

As soon as she felt the smooth, warm touch of Princess' satin opera glove on her left shoulder, Sofia took a relaxing, deep inhale to calm herself. It was finally showtime.

As soon as the band burst into music, three round spotlights flashed onto the girls as they shook their hips and tapped their feet in unison to the roaring beat.

The crowd instantly began to cheer, but they went absolutely wild when the trio finally turned to face them. Sofia remembered how the bright light felt warm as if the sun was shining on her.

As the three beautiful women continued to sing one hopping jazz tune after another, the night became more and more magical for Sofia. On that stage, she was the happiest woman in the world. She almost felt like a deity being worshipped.

She recalled at one point that Princess practically purred to a stop and then smoothly transitioned into a soft love song. It was Sofia's favorite song of the night.

Always the apt pupil, Sofia was a quick study of Princess' sensual mannerisms. She had done her best to mimic the lead singer's graceful movements, trying to be as desirable as possible, as naturally as possible. And it all seemed to be working.

Despite Princess' fame and fabulous singing voice, Sofia had her own fan base forming, gathered alongside the right of the stage next to her. She noticed that with every note she sang and with every swoosh of her hips, the group just grew in size. All those men seemed enthralled as she now sang along with the romantic lyrics.

When the lovely song had finally come to an end, the trio gave a simultaneous wink, causing everyone, especially the men, to burst uncontrollably with applause.

"Ladies and gentlemen, don't go too far. We'll be right back," Princess had said as sweetly and seductively as she could without catching her breath first.

The stage lights then glared into Sofia's eyes, causing everyone in the audience to disappear from her field of vision and turn into one big, black blob. Sofia had lifted her hand to shade them. But, before she could regain her sight, a hand suddenly appeared from out of the blackness and helped her off the stage.

As her sight adjusted, Sofia realized to her satisfaction that the hand belonged to a rather handsome, well-dressed man, who was now easily cutting through the crowd. Everyone was clearly watching them as he did it, too.

The rather handsome man had taken complete control of the situation. He held her hand tight, and confidently led the way. She didn't know where he was taking her. She had asked, but he didn't seem to hear her.

Sofia didn't want to make a scene in front of all these people by pulling her hand away. She did wonder though who this take-charge guy could be...

They didn't have to go far before she finally realized he was leading her straight to Sally Bottoms' table in the front row.

As the handsome man pulled out a seat for Sofia, Princess was already beside Salvatore, flirting behind a colorful peacock feather fan. She first hid her entire face behind it. Then, she slowly and seductively moved it down until he could see only her lustful eyes. Sofia overheard Princess say, "Daddy, you'll never see this ring off my body. Now this dress... That's a different story."

As Sofia sat down, she couldn't help but notice the icy glare Renie was giving the handsome man from across the table. It sent chills up Sofia's spine. She wondered what her friend could be so upset about, but she had no idea. They had just had an amazing first set.

When Sofia looked around at the other men seated at the table, she recognized a few from when she had first entered the ballroom. She remembered that one even whistled at her. She couldn't help but notice that, unlike earlier that evening, they all avoided making eye contact with her now.

It was then when it occurred to Sofia that the handsome man could be the notorious brother-in-law Renie had warned her about earlier. But Sofia quickly rationalized that conclusion away. She figured with Salvatore Scalici being so much older, she assumed his brother-in-law would likely be closer to his age than this young man who kindly helped her off the stage.

After all, Sofia had never met an older man who could marry a much younger wife with an even younger brother. Because those unlikely circumstances only occurred to the rich. It hadn't occurred to Sofia how immensely rich Salvatore Scalici actually was despite the evidence in front of her eyes. Otherwise, young women like Princess had no time for old men.

Before the handsome man had a chance to say a word to Sofia, Princess accosted him for a compliment almost as if she were testing him, "How about my performance?"

He replied with a wide, white smile but turned his attention squarely on Sofia as he answered her, "You're quite the canary, Princess. But not like Sofia here. Ya did real good hirin' her."

Clearly flattered, Sofia had blushed and looked down to her hands folded demurely in her lap. She had been carefully reared to value modesty and humility above all other things. Yet, she had to secretly admit to herself, it felt great to be praised for the one thing she loved to do more than anything and from such a handsome man on top of it. Sofia noted he had a smooth, likeable way about him.

"You're telling me! Did you see that crowd around you?" Princess eagerly asked her.

Surprised, Sofia looked up at Princess. She had expected a cutting remark instead of compliments because she was taking some of the star's limelight. But Princess was taking it all with such grace. If anything, she seemed genuinely enthusiastic about it. It was as if she was so secure in her own abilities, she didn't have to be threatened by Sofia's success.

But Sofia didn't want to push her luck. So, also being thoroughly trained by her mamma in the art of treading lightly, she softly replied with a little white lie, "I couldn't see a thing. The lights were in my eyes."

"Good. She only needs to have eyes for me," the handsome man had interjected, confident as ever, as he proceeded to take out his flask from the inner pocket of his elegant tuxedo jacket.

He spiked his punch despite the Prohibition-abiding guests surrounding them at the party. He offered it to her and added politely, "It's nice to meet you, Sofia."

Sofia didn't know exactly how he knew her name. Still, he had clearly done his research, except for the fact she had never drunk anything but a small glass of dessert wine after Sunday dinners. As carefully as she could, so as not to appear rude, she replied with a friendly smile, "I'm sorry… I don't drink."

Expecting an equally heedful response back, Sofia was caught off guard when she received his abrasive retort instead. "Come on. You're singin' at the biggest fuckin' event of the year, and you're sharing a drink with the richest man in here. I say that's worth a sip." The handsome man shoved the cocktail in her hand.

Since he was insisting, Sofia didn't want to appear bad-mannered. She believed it was polite to appease him so Sofia graciously took a sip even though she didn't want it. To her delight, it did turn out to be delicious, which persuaded her that it wouldn't hurt her to try something new. So she quickly took another sip.

Sofia curiously asked, "Are you that music producer?"

She noticed his sly smile as he responded, "I'm no music producer." He flirted back, "Are you disappointed with me now?

Being a practical girl, Sofia shrugged off the desire to have her own music professionally produced, as she replied, "No, I don't care about no music producer. I'm just here doing a favor for Renie, that's all."

"That's too bad. Because I think a music producer would be very interested in a girl like you. You're very talented, ya know."

Judging from the reaction she was getting from men that

entire evening, Sofia had easily concluded that the handsome man was being sincere, which made her feel embarrassed by the compliment. He had such a direct way about him, she didn't know what to say in return. She decided to take yet another drink of the spiked punch to hide her blushing from him.

He acted like he had never met anybody like her before and just continued to admire her beauty as if she actually were the most majestic thing he'd ever laid eyes on.

Wanting to break his piercing stare, she then softly asked, "So who are you then?"

That's when the handsome man answered her, as matter-of-factly as anyone else answering this common question, "I'm Massimo Denaro. My friends call me Max."

Sofia remembered straightening up in recognition of the name. She instantly heard Renie's voice echo within her mind. Her best friend's warning came back to her clear as a bell.

"Why? Ya heard of me?"

Sofia could tell by Max's tone that he believed she had heard of him before, but she certainly didn't want to get into detail about what she had, in fact, heard. That would be inappropriate and offensive.

She felt it time to rely on a trick she had learned in one of her books. So Sofia played dumb and responded as innocently as she could muster, "Should I have, Mr. Denaro?"

Max had chuckled lightly at Sofia's response. He seemed to like her sweet little girl act, as he teased her back, "I did mention to ya I'm one of the richest men in Detroit, right?"

Suddenly, from across the table, Princess put down her feather fan and stood from her chair with an announcement. "Break's over, gals."

Sofia noted Max's disappointment as he questioned, "What? So soon? I barely had a chance to get to know Sofia here."

Irene aggressively pushed her chair back under the table as she responded sharply, "We're paid to sing, not chat."

Sofia offered her punch back to Max to finish it for her. "Thank you," she said as he took the glass from her hand. He made sure to touch her slender fingers as he did so, adding, "Join me later."

Sofia carefully pulled her hand away so as not to offend him by outrightly rejecting his advances. She didn't respond. She only smiled warmly back at him before heading back to the stage with Princess and Irene.

Irene had locked arms with Sofia as she guided her back toward the stage. She turned back at Max to give him one more disapproving glare before Sofia whispered to her, "I about died when I heard his name."

Irene was filled with ire as she shook her head and said, "I should have known he'd go straight for ya. A fresh flower waitin' to be picked."

Sofia responded, "Thank God our break ended."

Then the three ascended the stage and went their separate ways as they headed to their marks. It wasn't long into their next set that Sofia noticed all the men that once surrounded her side of the stage had disappeared for the remainder of the night.

It also didn't take long for Sofia to accidentally make eye contact with Max, who was staring at her like he wanted to devour her. Sofia didn't know what to do except quickly look away and pretend she didn't see Max look like a hungry lion licking his chops at a tender, young lamb. She recalled the conflicting feelings of flattery and simultaneous uneasiness she was experiencing within her.

At the end of the night, the fantastic trio performed their final number, ending with a bang. They held their final pose as they each caught their breath in front of the roaring crowd. Princess, Irene, and Sofia then walked downstage and bowed in front of a standing ovation.

Sofia remembered how the conflict within her continued to spread to the rest of the evening's events. She was on an absolute high from receiving a glowing reception from the crowd after an amazing performance with Princess and Irene.

It was a dream come true!

She also loved seeing the nightlife of Detroit in all of its glory, something Sofia had only heard about through the grapevine. She felt proud to be a Detroiter.

Sofia loved how she had never felt more beautiful in her life.

But, at the same time, Sofia felt low, knowing that her parents would be disappointed in her for the exact things she was enjoying at that moment.

It also didn't help that not a single soul stood near Max, who was standing near the stage right in front of Sofia, still eyeing her like fresh prey. He whistled and clapped louder than any other cat in the room as if to publicly declare his possession of her to everyone around with ears.

Sofia had received more praise and attention from Max than

anybody she had ever met before. But Renie's warning about him made her feel worried. Although Max had been nothing but kind and complimentary to her, she knew he would never make a suitable husband and decided to avoid the likes of him from here on in.

Princess wrapped her creamy white satin glove around the ribbon microphone at center stage as she said, "Thank you, ladies and gentlemen, for coming out and celebrating the Book-Cadillac Hotel tonight!"

The audience's applause swelled with excitement. It was clear that everyone, including Sofia, had an unforgettable night.

As much as Sofia wanted to stay to soak it all in, she needed to get home as soon as possible to make her midnight curfew. She quickly descended the stage and headed straight toward the dressing room, having to rebuff her new fans' attempts to get her to stop for a chat. The boisterous cheering of the audience was muffled as soon as she closed the heavy door behind her.

With no time to spare, Sofia undressed rapidly. She placed her borrowed dress back onto its empty hanger, but the smooth silk kept slipping off the wooden hanger until Sofia finally managed to steadily put it back onto the dress rack.

Sofia pulled her plaid, cotton dress over her head, slid her arms through her wool overcoat, and grabbed her purse and gloves before rushing toward the exit. She was halfway to the door when she caught a glimpse of her painted face in one of the dressing room mirrors, which caused her to stop dead in her tracks in front of Princess' makeup station.

As Sofia pulled fresh tissues from its cardboard box, she

thought how terrible it would have been if she had gone home with her face like this. There was no way she could have explained to her parents why her face was painted like a *puttann'*, especially when she was supposed to be at the Holy Family Catholic Church, of all places. Despite how marvelous this whole experience had been for her, the thought of being caught in a lie made Sofia vow to never do this type of crazy thing again.

Sofia unsuccessfully smeared the red lipstick from her lips before she noticed a jar of cold cream on the counter. She recalled reading in a Sears Roebuck catalogue that cold cream removed makeup.

Sofia sparingly lathered the thick mixture onto her smeared red lips until her lips and chin were a swirl of pink like a circus clown. The pink swirl alarmed her at first until she effortlessly wiped it away.

The oils from the cold cream then broke down her beautiful smoky eyes before she promptly wiped the glamour from her face, allowing her clean, innocent image to reflect back at her in the mirror once more.

Sofia then hastily pulled out the rose tucked behind her ear and decided to keep it as a memento, much like Cinderella with her one glass slipper. She placed it in her coat pocket, careful not to crush it.

Sofia then searched through her thick dark hair for the tiny bobby pins that kept her wavy locks in place. Once she removed every last hairpin, she tied her long hair back into a loose bun. She, once again, grabbed her purse and gloves and exited the dressing room as quickly as she had entered it.

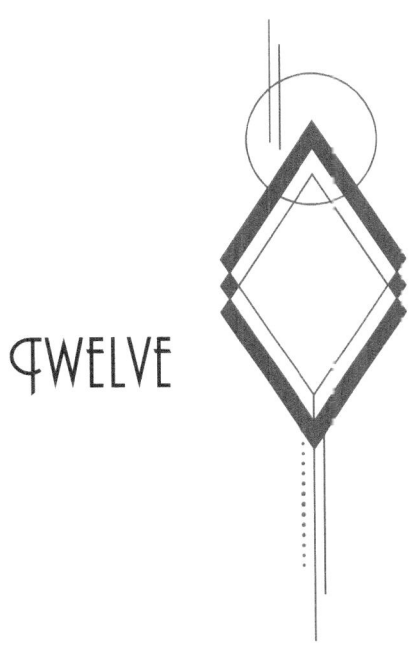

TWELVE

Sofia dashed out the gilded elevator across the hotel lobby toward the same grand golden door she had joyfully entered earlier that evening. She was focused on slipping her glove onto her hand when she suddenly heard Max's booming voice, "Ya weren't gonna leave without sayin' goodbye?"

Before Sofia had a chance to look up, Max gave her a hard, lustful kiss.

She remembered how the smell of cigarettes and whiskey on Max's breath stung the inside of her nose and how his coarse stubble scraped against her soft skin. She didn't know what to do as Max's tongue forcefully pushed about inside of her mouth. Her body had become frozen while she tried to process what was oddly happening to her.

Sofia pried herself away from Max, but he was the last kind of guy she wanted to anger. So she attempted to wipe his saliva from her face as discreetly as possible.

Max didn't seem to notice Sofia's discomfort; if anything, he seemed turned on by her surprised eyes and timid disposition. This big cat enjoyed having a little mouse to play with.

Wanting to simply move forward from the unexpected kiss to still make her midnight curfew on time, Sofia replied as respectfully as she could muster, "I'm sorry, Mr. Denaro, but I really must be getting home."

She then tried to step past Max, but he stepped in unison to block her with his broad body as he replied equally as politely, "Then let me do the honor of taking you home safely."

Sofia attempted to go around Max another time as she replied, "That's not necessary. I have cab fare."

Max seemed to enjoy how he easily intercepted her second attempt at exiting. While Sofia, on the other hand, wasn't enjoying their little dance since she desperately needed to get home.

Gesturing to the crowds of people now departing from the party, Max had replied confidently, "You'll never catch a cab now."

He had then patted down his coat, noting that his keys were missing. He pointed to the ceiling to indicate they were in his hotel room above. "Just let me get my keys," Max told her casually.

He then offered his arm to Sofia like a gentleman and added, "I insist."

Sofia felt in a bind.

She absolutely needed to get home before midnight, and she would if she could jump into a cab right at this exact moment. But she had missed her brief opportunity to skedaddle before the crowd formed and, as Max so aptly pointed out, there was now a long line snaking through the lobby waiting for one She could easily be late taking a cab at this point.

She certainly didn't want to go upstairs alone with Max to get his keys, either. Even if he is attractive. Her parents had taught her better than that.

Maybe it would be best if I just walked home?

Sofia debated if she could convince Renie to leave all the fanatics worshipping her at the marvelous afterparty to walk her home instead. But she quickly rejected that idea. There was no way Sofia could ask her friend to do that for her. This was Renie's big night.

She didn't know how to tell Max she wanted to leave on her own without risking rejecting him. She could only guess at how truly enormous the hot air balloon-sized ego would be on a guy like Max. But she couldn't just show up at her house being escorted by him on foot or by automobile. Sofia also felt better if he didn't know where she lived.

Still, she didn't want to seem demanding, so Sofia replied, "I really must go now. But I'm fine. You don't have to worry about me. I'm sure you're a very busy gentleman."

With Max's muscular arm still wrapped around Sofia's petite one, he responded with his devilish smile, "Don't be a silly dame. I'm not lettin' an ab-so-lutely gorgeous doll go home alone in the middle of the dark. I won't take no for an answer."

Feeling cornered, it occurred to Sofia that maybe Max was right. After all, she had never been in a cab alone before, and she would also be with an unknown man in that scenario as well.

Who knows where I could end up?

Max seemed so confident that she wasn't going to catch one anyway. "There's only so many hacks in town, honey," he already pointed out earlier.

Sofia also noted that Max had been nothing but attentive and eager to please her the entire evening. He clearly liked her and wanted to be in her good graces. Plus, he could get her home faster than a cab anyway. She concluded she could always have him drop her off down the street.

"Okay, I'll wait here while you get your key."

"You're a riot. It's faster if you come with me."

Sofia could feel the same firm grip he had on her arm as when he held her hand earlier. It was like Max would never let her go. It might have been romantic if she had felt the same way.

Who in their right mind would want to be with a notorious gangster?

No matter how handsome?

After a moment of apprehension, Sofia didn't know what else to do but nod. He wasn't going to just let go of her arm, and she couldn't think of a better option. She certainly didn't want to make a scene in the hotel lobby.

Max's been nothing but kind to me, Sofia reasoned.

ꟼHIRTEEN

Max gave her a playful wink as he guided her back toward the elevator. He beamed at her the entire way with his pearly white, crooked smile, chatting her up about her fantastic performance earlier that evening.

She could tell Max was smitten with her, and it was hard not to be flattered by it. He had a way, unlike any other boy she had ever known. They had walked arm-in-arm on the soft baroque carpet down the lavish hallway until he stopped in front of the last door on the right.

As Max turned his back toward her to forage through his pockets in search of his hotel room key, Sofia couldn't help but notice the placard placed beside his door that stated Penthouse #13. She hadn't seen such a large sign by any other. It was as if it was made especially for his door.

The unlucky number didn't feel like a good omen to her, but then she shrugged off the thought, concluding she was silly for being superstitious.

Sofia then caught a glimpse of Max finally pulling out a whole keyring, filled entirely with keys, from his coat pocket. The thought that Max had his keys on him the entire time flashed into Sofia's mind. She quickly dismissed it as her being neurotic.

Sofia reminded herself that Max knew she had to get home right away. She had told him several times. Surely, he wouldn't waste her time understanding how important it was to her.

Who would do that?

Nobody Sofia had ever known would do something like that.

Max used one of the many keys on the keyring to open the hotel door. He pushed it wide open for Sofia to enter as he said, "Welcome to my new home away from home."

Sofia remembered hesitating for a moment. She didn't understand why she needed to enter for him to merely grab the key to his automobile.

But then Sofia caught a glimpse of the moon like a giant saucer in the sky. The heavy silk drapes were drawn back, allowing the pale moonlight to pour in through the three large arched windows.

She could tell the surrounding decor was magnificent, even in so little light. But when Max flipped on one of the bedside lamps, Sofia's jaw dropped as she stood by the door and took in all the elaborate details of Max's opulent accommodations.

"Where do you normally live?" Sofia asked as she took a cautious step into the room. She had never been in a hotel room like this breathtaking one before. It was tempting her to explore it.

She could tell Max enjoyed watching her appreciate his impressive suite as he quickly responded with an equally remarkable answer, "Grosse Pointe Farms. Right on Lake Shore Drive."

Sofia recalled that Grosse Pointe Farms was an affluent town between Detroit and Lake Saint Clair. It's where a lot of auto executives had moved, but she had never been there before. She slowly inched further into the room as she asked Max, "Isn't that where Edsel Ford moved?"

Max casually responded, "We're neighbors, but it's usually all business with him."

Not understanding what he meant by that, Sofia remembered genuinely asking him, "Whatever do you mean?"

Then, she had turned her back away from Max for only a moment. She headed toward the nearest of the large arched windows to witness the spectacular view of the giant full moon hanging over the Detroit River and above the dark Canadian border in the distance. As soon as Sofia planted her feet in front of it to ogle at the landscape below, she heard the door shut behind her.

Max removed his black dinner jacket and tossed it onto a nearby chair as he casually replied, "I own Ford dealerships. Several of them."

He continued to remove his black leather shoulder holster where his most prized possession, his .38-caliber Smith & Wesson pistol, rested. Its mother of pearl handle shimmered under the soft light as he carefully placed it on the bedside chest.

Max untied his bow tie nonchalantly as he headed toward the wet bar and asked, "Can I make you a drink?"

Without waiting for Sofia's response, Max removed the crystal top from its geometric etched decanter and poured a glass of whiskey into a beautiful matching tumbler.

Sofia gazed out the window as she replied, "I've never been this high up before. It never occurred to me that it could be this stunning. What a beautiful view..."

Sofia could sense Max as he approached her from behind and handed her the glass. Sofia looked down at the whiskey tumbler then back at Max, who appeared to not have any intention of leaving anytime soon.

Sofia remembered the sinking feeling she had in her gut as soon as she looked back into Max's face.

There were those eyes again. Like a hunter locked onto his prey.

She immediately felt her breath leave her body. She was scared.

Trapped between Max and the large arched window, she asked with a thick gulp, "Your keys? I really do need to get home soon."

Sofia's body felt stiff, almost frozen, while she looked into Max's devouring eyes as he said, "Of course."

He patted his pant pocket and felt his keys in one of them. With a mischievous grin, Max added,"I guess I had 'em the whole time."

Suddenly, Max put his arms around Sofia's waist, pulling her close to him, as he said, "You're a knockout, ya know that?"

Before she could say a word in reply, he gave her a kiss in the same forceful manner as he did down in the hotel lobby.

Sofia managed to pull her face away, but Max's arms were still wrapped tightly around her body as she said, "Mr. Denaro, I really must be getting home now. If you…"

Before Sofia could finish her sentence, Max kissed her forcibly again. She could barely breathe between her fear…

And the stench of whiskey…

And the taste of cigarettes as he filled her mouth with his gyrating tongue.

Max effortlessly lifted her in his arms. She remembered how her small frame was no match against his brawny figure. Sofia felt like a puny mouse dangling from her tail in a lion's paws.

Not knowing what else to do to stop him, she threw the whiskey glass down to divert his attention to the mess she created on the expensive new Persian rug.

Max didn't even flinch in response. Instead, he seemed to interpret it as some sort of erotic display of impatience on her part. As if she were saying, "*Take me now!*"

So he continued on his mission undeterred.

Sofia's eyes had widened in shock as Max laid her down on the bed. She exclaimed as she attempted to spring back up from it, "Now, you have the wrong idea here!"

But that didn't stop him. Not even for a millisecond.

Instead, with one hand, he pushed her back down with ease. And, he climbed on top of her to keep her there.

He kissed her continuously, not allowing her to speak almost to the point where she couldn't breathe. He pinned her down easily with his body weight. As she gasped for air, she started to worry he may actually crush her to death.

Sofia knew, for a fact, that she didn't give Max a strong

enough sign that she wanted any part of this ordeal. Panicked, she desperately tried again. "Mr. Denaro, I barely know you!"

She again tried to block his hands as he tore open her cotton slip, revealing her bare breasts. Despite her attempts to swat his hands away, Max continued to maneuver her clothing up and off wherever necessary. Her efforts were as futile as a gnat against him.

Tired of her annoying resistance, Max merely pinned her right arm behind her and then held her left wrist above her head.

Sofia was no match against him.

She recalled feeling invisible as Max ignored every one of her physical and verbal oppositions. It was clear he wasn't concerned at all about what she wanted to happen between them.

That was when her best friend's warning popped into her mind. Sofia realized that it was too late to heed those wise words. She had been duped by this predator.

But Max was acting so polite a moment ago.

Sofia was about to learn a cruel lesson in life. People that do nice things aren't always nice people. On the contrary, for a predator, kind gestures are how they set their trap, like the cheese tempting the mouse. She had allowed Max's dark, handsome looks, persistent charm, and confident ways to prevail over her good judgment.

Sofia helplessly whimpered as Max entered her body.

Her next reaction was wailing out in pain while he forcefully penetrated her. His only response was to cover her mouth so his erection wouldn't be interrupted.

She immediately disappeared into herself like a ghost. It felt safer to disappear.

Sofia could feel the blank expression upon her face while Max aggressively pumped her stiff body.

Unable to move an inch, Sofia fixated on the small gold chandelier above to divert her attention from what was actually happening to her. She recalled its golden arms swirled about like vines with a single light bulb illuminating a floral bouquet that appeared at each end.

She didn't know what else to do because if she tried to look to one side, she saw his gun sitting there ominous beside the bed.

What if he shoots me, too?

If she looks to the other, she sees that damn full moon. And she doesn't want to end up hating the moon because of this.

So she just stared straight above until the details of the dangling fixture began to blur as tears brimmed her eyes.

I feel ab-so-lutely powerless.

She could feel Max's hot breath against her skin as he grunted into her right ear.

The odor of whiskey and cigarettes was so strong, it was his cologne. It continued to burn her nostrils.

Sofia could hear the squeaking of the bedsprings beneath her pinned body as she continued to stare blankly at the blurred chandelier hanging above.

She wondered how much longer she would have to deal with the sharp pain she felt every time he…

Although it felt like an eternity to her, it was only a few minutes more before Max buried his groin inside her with one final, painful thrust accompanied by a long groan. He then rolled off of her, allowing her to breathe deeply for the first time since this nightmare began.

Sofia watched as he took off his shirt. His white tank top underneath was drenched with sweat. Sofia couldn't help but think how ironic it was to see the crucifix hanging from the gold necklace that was nestled within his wet, hairy chest.

Sofia sniffled, trying to keep her tears away as she pushed the skirt of her plaid dress down. Earlier, it felt like such an everyday boring outfit. Now, it was the dress Mamma and Papa gave her for Christmas the year before. Sofia had thought about how her face lit up like their family's Christmas tree as she lifted the new dress from its paper box.

She found the straps of her cotton slip that Max had stripped down around her waist and covered her exposed breasts as she pulled them back onto her shoulders.

As Sofia searched for the sleeves, she noticed a tear at the neck and shoulder seam from Max's carelessness. Sofia would have to repair it before her mother noticed, and she knew she would always be reminded of this every time she saw the stitches.

Avoiding eye contact with Max, Sofia sat up from the bed and asked, "Is there a water closet?"

Max casually bragged with a lit cigarette now dangling from his mouth, "First hotel in the world to have one in every room. Whatever you need, doll."

Sofia stood onto her t-strap pumps that had never left her feet. Feeling light-headed, she wobbled for a second.

As Sofia teetered across the room, she could feel warm liquid dripping down her inner thighs.

Oh, God, what if I get pregnant?

She walked over to the nearest doorway that she assumed would most likely be the water closet and closed the door behind her.

Sofia stood in the darkness for a moment, taking a deep breath, preparing to see herself for the first time in the mirror. She had wondered if she would see the same person Sofia saw the last time she looked at one in the dressing room, not even an hour ago. But Sofia had a deep knowing she would never be the same person again, no matter what she looked like from the outside.

When she flipped the light switch, the warm, bright light filled the white tiled bathroom allowing Sofia to see the mirror ahead of her.

She looked into the glassy, forlorn eyes of the reflection staring back at her.

With her shaky hands, Sofia attempted to smooth her disheveled hair as best as she could. Still, despite her effort, her hair wouldn't entirely fall back into place. She didn't know where the ribbon had gone during this whole ordeal and desperately wished she could use it to sweep her hair back up in a bun.

She then inspected her pink nose and chin that had been made raw from Max's forceful kissing. Sofia remembered how she desperately wished there was a cold cream that could wipe Max's presence from her face like Princess' lipstick. She hated that she was helpless to do so.

Inspecting her torn neckline, Sofia was a little relieved that the tear was mendable.

Maybe it was best to just throw the whole dress out?

But then her mamma would wonder where it went because

Sofia didn't have but three dresses. Clothes were not cheap.

She then brushed her hands down her dress in an attempt to smooth out the unwanted wrinkles.

Grabbing a white towel hanging from the nearby rack, Sofia lifted the hem just enough to wipe the dampness from between her legs. She pulled it out from under her to find the once untouched towel now stained with blood.

Sofia whimpered softly to herself as she said, "Now what am I supposed to do?"

Tears welled in her eyes until one lone tear made its way down her face as she looked back upon her defiled reflection. She still was in frozen shock as to what had just occurred.

As she dropped the towel onto the floor, Sofia recalled how she desperately wanted to be home in her mother's arms at that moment.

Then Sofia felt a jolt of fear that struck through her.

She was scared about what Silvia might think of her now that she was no longer pure, just like the bloody towel that laid on the floor. The thought brought more tears to Sofia's eyes that she repeatedly wiped away.

Once her persistent tears subsided enough, she decided to exit.

As Sofia tiptoed out of the water closet, she heard Max snoring soundly in bed in the same, exact position she had left him. She was relieved to not have to get a ride from him after everything he had just done to her.

Giacomo might have been home by now from the night shift, and the last thing she needed was her father to witness her getting dropped off by this infamous man, alone and wearing a torn dress. As quiet as a mouse, she grabbed her crumpled coat and purse from the bed in the dim lighting and tiptoed out of Max's hotel room.

Sofia steadied her shaky hand as best as she could while she quietly closed the door behind her. She took a deep breath in a vain attempt to calm down, hoping to never see Max and this door to Penthouse #13 ever again.

Her teary, solemn eyes stared down the hall as she walked as fast as she could toward the gilded elevator. As she waited for it to arrive, Sofia placed her hands in her coat pockets. She felt her memento still in one of them.

As she pulled it out, Sofia discovered in her palm that the red rose had been crushed.

ҒOURTEEN

In the candlelit houseboat, Sofia wore those same teary, solemn eyes. Just like she did that night at the Book-Cadillac.

She bravely turned to face Max. She waited for his response, however bad it may be, to her accusation of rape on the so-called romantic evening they had first met.

Max remained seated behind his dinner plate, slowly chewing his food, buying another moment to decide how he was going to react to Sofia's story.

Sofia felt her temper rise with every second Max made her wait for his response until she finally blurted out, "Say something, damn it."

Max feigned a dumbfounded expression at Sofia and responded sarcastically, "What do ya want me to say to that?" As Max took in her heated disposition, he unexpectedly broke into laughter.

Sofia, on the other hand, was actually dumbfounded by Max's response. It was now her turn to ask, "What's so funny?"

Her question only made Max's maniacal laughter grow until it echoed within the walls of the houseboat.

A fuming rage was quickly building inside of Sofia as she commanded, "Come on, Max. Tell me. What's so funny? What did I say that's so fucking funny!"

Max's eyes widened in amusement by her unladylike demeanor as he retorted, "My, my, Mrs. Denaro, quite strong a word for such a proper woman as yourself. Or should I say such a proper woman like you pretend to be?"

With her petite feet planted squarely at Max, Sofia answered firmly with deeply held conviction, "I was a good girl until I met you."

Without missing a beat, Max retorted with a snort, "Bull! It's all bull. I didn't do nothin' to you that you didn't want comin'."

Standing her ground, Sofia stated with strength she didn't even know she possessed until that very moment, "That's not true."

Max rolled his eyes, smirked, and challenged Sofia's logic. "Then why did ya come up to my hotel room?"

Appalled and enraged, Sofia screamed in frustration, "To get your fucking keys!"

Having enough of her combative behavior, Max abruptly stood up from his seat. He pulled the napkin wrapped around his throat, and threw it down on the table with a bang of his fist, causing the whole table to shake, including the brightly-lit candlesticks.

Sofia feared he would end up burning the whole boat down.

But instead, Max pointed his index finger right at her as if he would drive it through her chest if he could, while he demanded, "Tell that guy to turn this boat around. I should be takin' care of my business. Not sittin' here wastin' my time with this bull."

Sofia realized that she had let things get out of hand. She had wanted to tell her story finally. She wanted to make sure Max absolutely, positively knew her point of view about the night she had to hear told through his own constantly. That was her plan.

But she didn't anticipate the raw rage that just boiled out from inside of her. That was unexpected.

She knew she needed to cool down and keep a level head if she was going to come out of this without a black eye.

Knowing that the night couldn't end here or her entire plan would have failed, Sofia instantly softened her disposition. She pleaded with as much regret as she could gather inside, "Please stay. I won't breathe another word about it. I didn't mean to ruin our night. Please."

Still heaving from his own anger, Max, once again, challenged her, "What did ya mean to do?"

Sofia sat down on the bed as if sorrowful for her behavior. She needed him to believe she was truly, truly sorry about it. Nothing less would do. She looked down at her feet, shifted them about anxiously, and then stomped them as if she was beyond frustrated with her own big mouth.

But then, she carefully turned her gaze with her soft doe-eyes from the floor to look him straight in his own eyes. She batted her lashes for added seductive effect and sensually offered, "Let me make it up to you?"

Having just consumed a large meal, Max rubbed his stomach. He answered her with his own utter conviction, "You bet you're gonna make it up to me, but first, get over here, now! And pour me some wine."

Phew! That was close.

She knew she would have to tread extremely lightly if she was going to make this night unfold perfectly. Relieved from having been forgiven quickly, Sofia smiled brightly as she obediently walked over to him.

Max stopped her before she could grab the wine bottle and pulled off her mink, revealing Sofia's nude body. He enjoyed the view as he aggressively touched and rubbed her as he pleased. Even pinching her hard to the point where she knew she would find bruises tomorrow.

It was clear to her that this was his way of letting her know that her body belonged to him for his pleasure, and there was nothing she could do about it.

With a hard slap on her ass, he ordered, "That's the last I ever wanna hear about that night. Ya hear me?"

Pretending the strike on her backside turned her on, Sofia answered smoothly, "I've been a bad girl, Max."

She could tell he didn't mean it erotically. This was one of his serious warnings to her. But she needed to buy some more time and disarm him before his mood turned even uglier. She noted that Max had almost finished the entire bottle of wine.

Being too full to fuck, Max didn't bite at her sexual bait as usual. Instead, he stayed focused on the point at hand. His pride had been punctured by her audacity to question his behavior. It was more important to get her under control than to have his physical needs attended to for a second time that evening. Nothing annoyed Max quite as much as a woman who didn't know her place, so he found a disrespectful woman intolerable. "I mean it, Sofia."

Knowing he meant business, Sofia answered, straight-faced and obedient, "Whatever you say, Max."

She then reached for her fallen coat, but Max stopped her as he said, "Don't even think about it."

Completely nude, Sofia didn't skip a beat. Max made her do this kind of thing all the time.

She continued to act as desirable as possible as she poured the last of the wine into Max's glass. She popped her curvy hip out, then bent over just a little to give him the best view of those useful bubs of hers and bit her lip, giving him a look of longing.

Finally appeased by her servitude and vastly improved attitude, Max lowered himself comfortably back into his seat as the red wine filled his glass. Happily content with how easily that problem was dealt with, he let out a deep exhale looking forward to enjoying the rest of the evening digesting and then, once again, fucking his beautiful, young wife.

After a brief moment of silence, Sofia finally broke in with seemingly small talk and remarked, "This is the last of my father's wine."

"It's good."

"I'm glad you like it... You know who else loved his wine?"

Max merely shrugged, having no clue what she was about to

say, nor did he care. He took a sip letting the subtle notes of the liquid sit and roll around on his tongue before swallowing it.

"Renie."

"Really..."

This time, Max let out an impatient sigh. Sofia's mention of her best friend, of course, caused the memory of the last night he was with Irene to appear in his head. He had flipped her over in bed to stop her from talking so much. He remembered how tired he was listening to her. Her tiny voice felt like little needles to his brain.

While Max was lost in the details of that particular evening in his mind's eye, Sofia casually remarked, "I can't believe she didn't make it to the wedding. It's unlike her. Renie just up and disappeared. Poof."

Max had a feeling where this conversation was headed. He took a big swig of wine as he withdrew even further into his thoughts. Max remembered that as he had screwed Irene from behind in his hotel bed, he had pulled her head back by her shiny, blonde hair as he told her off, "Ya know, Irene, you need to learn..."

Max then buried Irene's face into a pillow as he continued, "To mind your own business."

Max recalled how relieved he felt at that moment because he had finally solved the looming problem he had with Irene's very existence and proximity to Sofia.

He also felt a strange high at how powerful he felt compared to her. He enjoyed how Irene was no match at all against his strength, and how it wasn't long before he orgasmed into her motionless body. Her existence or rather, now her nonexistence, was, in fact, at his total will. She could do absolutely nothing to stop him.

He noted to himself that with all that church Irene went to, he ended up being her God in the end because he was the one that determined her ultimate fate. Max was immersed in what to him was a deep philosophical thought when Sofia asked, "Do you have any idea about Renie's whereabouts?"

Sofia's question snapped Max out of his inner trance and back into the romantically lit houseboat. He looked her straight in the eye without as much as a blink. Max flatly responded, "No idea what happened to Irene."

Unsatisfied with his blatant lie, Sofia pressed on, "So you have no idea about Renie's whereabouts, at all?"

The last time Sofia saw Renie alive was with Max. She knew her husband well enough to know that it was not a coincidence, and Sofia was done playing dumb for his benefit.

Max defensively retorted, "Why would I know where your lousy friend is?"

Sofia could feel the tension was again building back up between them, so she responded as pragmatically as possible, "Oh, I don't know… I have this idea that she went to you for help… Maybe to stop me from seeing Mrs. Stoner… And it angered you, and you did something to her?"

Despite being naked, Sofia squared her shoulders confidently at Max. She sincerely asked her husband, "Did you kill her for being the bearer of bad news? Because Renie told you what I was planning on doing. Please, Max, she was my best friend. I deserve to know what happened to her."

Max brushed off Sofia's question with his usual venomous laugh and an exasperated huff, "My dear Mrs. Denaro, your imagination is spectacular."

Not allowing Max to brush her question away easily, Sofia continued, "Again with the laughing. Do you blame me for thinking it? That's what you do, right? Besides being a bootlegger... You do kill people."

Growing wearisome of her antics, Max stared right into Sofia's eyes. Giving a severe warning to his mouthy wife with his deliberate glare, he replied, "Yes, I do kill people, but that's no laughin' matter."

This time, it was Max who picked up Sofia's mink off the ground and threw it into her arms.

Sofia knew he was sick of her line of questioning, so much so that not even sex would make up for it now. She knew once that was off the menu, she had little control of her husband.

But she also knew it was getting late, and she was getting closer to the truth, so Sofia courageously asked, "Then tell me, Max. What's so entertaining about my ideas regarding Renie's whereabouts?"

A sly smile stretched across Max as he responded like spit to her face, "That you think she cared about you. Irene hated you."

In total disbelief of Max's bold statement, Sofia instantly defended her childhood friend, "That's not true. Renie and I have been fast friends through school."

Max challenged Sofia's rosy perspective of her so-called friend, "Really? Is that why she thought it was hilarious that Giacomo guarded ya... What was the phrase she used? Ah, yes! That your papa guarded ya like Egyptian treasure. Yet I got the goods anyway. *Renie* even called ya a double-crosser."

Max said Renie with an emphasis that suggested Sofia was a complete fool for having an endearing nickname for someone who clearly hated her as much as Irene did.

But Sofia knew her friend, and she also knew Max.

She wasn't going to let him poison her reality. But, for some strange feeling, she had to acknowledge that she also sensed that what Max had just said was somehow not a total lie.

Renie's comments about Giacomo didn't surprise Sofia. Her friend had said the exact same thing to her about her father on several occasions. She also knew Renie meant it differently than how Max relayed it now.

Renie believed Sofia's situation showed that it was impossible to protect women if you don't allow them to be educated and independent of men. According to her best friend, it was Sofia's ignorance on the ways of the world and not her freedom that caused her to be in this mess. Renie knew this because her own father had done the same thing to her, although he was nowhere near as strict as Giacomo.

So Sofia knew it to be true that Renie did say those exact words. Their validity made her further believe that the double-crosser comment was also true, too. But Renie saying she's a double-crosser confused her.

Why would Renie have said that to Max?

Sofia needed to hear this story even if she knew not to believe a word of it. She knew Max well enough by now that he could say anything, true or not, without reservation, without even a flinch or a twitch.

But she had a feeling that this was the key to finding out what really happened to her friend and now was her only chance to get that information, so Sofia asked, "Why would she say that? I never did one thing to double-cross Renie."

Like the cat that got the cream, Max smiled wide as he said, "Yeah, ya did. You just didn't know ya did it."

Sofia instantly knew what he was referring to, but she feigned surprise, hoping she was half as good an actor as Max. As if her next thought had just popped in her mind from only God knows where, she said, "Irene was *in love* with you?"

All the practice she had done repeating that line over and over again paid off at that moment.

With his ego as full as his belly soaked with wine, Max said, "She begged *meee* to be with *herrr*."

Sofia heard Max slur, but she tried to maintain her focus and continued with her charade. Sofia quickly slipped back into her mink, and then she sat back down on the bed, supposedly stunned by his secret. As surprised as she could muster, she replied, "Renie never said a word. I thought she was my friend."

She looked down at her feet, forlorn and flabbergasted, hoping with all her might that Max was buying the whole bit.

Satisfied that he had burst Sofia's bubble, Max gloated, "Looks like your friend kept a lot of *secretsss* from ya…"

Max also had a tendency to keep Sofia in the dark about most matters, since most matters were, according to him, none of her business. But to get Sofia off his back about Irene, once and for all, Max needed to reveal some secrets of his own, starting with the same night he had just warned his wife to never speak about again.

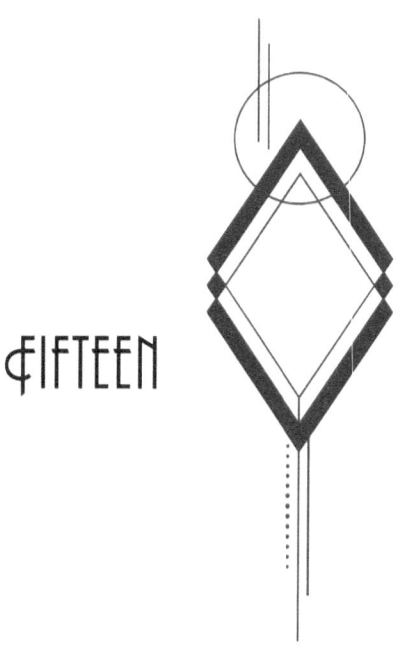

₣IFTEEN

Max confessed that he didn't actually go straight to the hotel lobby after he watched Sofia rush off stage immediately after the show ended. Instead, he sat back down at Salvatore's table to buy some time.

As soon as Sofia disappeared into the dressing room, her dear friend, Irene, slid into the seat next to him and said, "I see you're stuck on someone new."

Irene wasn't wrong, of course. It was a pretty safe bet considering his unbroken gaze upon Sofia the entire night. Everyone in the whole room could easily tell that Max was stuck on her.

But Max also liked to do as he pleased without any judgment or input from anybody else, so he replied flatly, "That's none of your business."

Attempting to soften his cold disposition, Irene seductively asked, "What about you and me?"

She then scooted closer to Max, nipped him on the earlobe with her teeth, and whispered, "I thought we were somethin' pretty great?"

Max described how he pushed Irene away because he didn't want Sofia to catch him with her slut friend and get the wrong idea.

Irene was miffed by Max's treatment, so she came back at him and said, "What's the big idea, tough guy? You can't just throw me away like a piece of garbage."

Max then grabbed Irene by the hair, something he often did to women that didn't know how to keep their mouths shut, and through his gritted teeth, he admonished, "Is nobody home in that dumb, blonde head of yours? I said what I do is none of your business. We're through."

Just before Max released his tight grasp, he pulled Irene's face away from him, causing her whiplash.

Jilted and holding her neck in pain, Irene scurried away from the table in tears just before a newly cleansed Sofia entered the grand ballroom with her coat on and her gloves in hand. As soon as he saw her return, Max had taken a short-cut out the kitchen entrance to beat her to the hotel lobby, not thinking twice about Irene ever since.

But Max needed Sofia to understand that he didn't have much choice in the matter, so he simply stated, "Irene didn't take no for an answer."

Max went on to describe how he became prey to Irene's persistent sexual advances. So, like any red-blooded Sicilian man would do, they began fucking again in secret like they had been doing for the entire previous year. He raised an eyebrow checking out Sofia's furrowed forehead in response to that doozy.

But one night, in bed with Irene in his hotel room, she had whispered into his ear, "Marry me, Max. I'd be the best wife to you. I'm no double-crosser like Sofia.'"

As soon as Max heard the words *double-crosser* come out of Irene's trap, it made him stop dead in his tracks. He felt like he'd been punched in the gut. He hated to think about what he would do to the man that put his hands on Sofia's beautiful body. A body that was meant for only him.

The mere thought made him so jealous with love, his jaw tightened as he interrogated Irene, "Why is Sofia a double-crosser?"

Max prided himself on his keen intuition and instantly became suspicious of Irene as she back-tracked, "She's not. I'm just jealous, is all. Don't stop."

When Irene came in for a kiss to change the subject, Max forcefully held her back and shook her by her shoulders. He was determined to find out if his *amore mio* was having an affair.

Max chose not to add the part of the story where he was ready to kill Sofia if his suspicions were found to be true. After all, he was no *cornuto*. Nobody, especially a woman, would make him a laughing-stock in his city by cheating on him.

Instead, Max re-enacted for Sofia to the air in front of him how he shook Irene as he demanded, "Has Sofia been messin' around with someone else? Spit it out, Irene."

He proudly described how Irene's eyes widened in fear as she exclaimed, "No!"

Max had thought to himself that Dumb Dora wasn't gonna weasel her way out of this, so he demanded from Irene, "Then, what is it?" He made it clear with his usual threatening glare that there would be painful consequences if she lied to him.

"Sofia's havin' your baby," popped out of Irene's mouth.

Words that had brought a surprised smile of joy across Max's face.

But after a mere moment of bliss, his smile disappeared as quickly as it came. He suddenly realized that there was only one way his pregnant fiancée could possibly be double-crossing him, and it was in an even unholier way than he initially imagined.

So Max persisted in interrogating Irene, "How does havin' my baby make Sofia a double-crosser?"

Irene tried again to get out of the situation by saying, "Max, you always tell me your relationship with Sofia is none of my business."

Frustrated, and determined to find the answer by any means necessary, Max couldn't help but strangle Irene as her eyes widened in shock.

Irene fought back, unsuccessfully, of course, grasping at Max's large hands tightly wrapped around her throat. Both of her entire hands couldn't even pry a finger loose.

Max chose to stop the very moment before he actually killed her and questioned, "Tell me why Sofia is a double-crosser?"

After Irene took several dry gasps for air, she croaked out, "She's gettin' rid of the baby. Next Sunday night." Knowing he would be angry, Irene pleaded for forgiveness for not confiding this valuable information to him earlier, "Sofia's the double-crosser. Not me. I'd have your baby, Max!"

He then nonchalantly added that the shocking news had upset him so much that he may have been guilty of overreacting. Implying that he did, indeed, murder Irene for being the bearer of bad news, just as Sofia accused initially at the beginning of the conversation about her.

He concluded his story by adding a little salt to her wound, "So ya see, my sweet Sofia, Irene didn't give a lick about you."

SIXTEEN

The confirmation of Irene's demise started to sink in as Sofia sat on the bed in silence, while Max remained unmoved in his dinner chair. She already knew in her heart that Max had killed Renie, but hearing his admission that her suspicions were very much correct made her sick to her stomach.

Avoiding his face to not give away her disgust, Sofia's unfocused gaze rested on the floor as she asked one more time just to be extra clear, "So you did kill her?"

Max shrugged like he, again, didn't have much choice in the matter and offered as a consolation, "She woulda always gotten between us."

Sofia took a moment to gather her thoughts. She knew she had to respond perfectly if she was going to succeed in getting the information she desperately wanted for Renie's family. Sofia needed to find out where her best friend's body was buried so they could put her to rest respectfully, like she deserved.

Sofia took a deep breath to gain some courage to proceed, and simply stated to her husband, as matter-of-factly as possible, "You're right. I'm glad you did it."

Surprised, Max couldn't help but smile at his wife's unexpected reaction. He thought for sure she would throw herself on the floor and dramatically cry like a typical slobbering woman over her dumb, slut friend.

But when Sofia didn't react as Max expected, he found himself turned on by her cold demeanor. He cocked his head to the side as he flirtatiously asked, "Mrs. Denaro, could you be jealous?"

Of course, you would think I'm jealous.

Knowing he was the most arrogant man she'd ever met, Sofia predicted with precision that Max would automatically conclude she was envious. But she checked her impulse to roll her eyes at his narcissism. Because Sofia needed Max to believe she was angry at Irene over her illicit affair with him.

Otherwise, if her husband thought she still cared at all about her best friend, Sofia would never get him to admit anything further. He never did anything for her, for anyone, out of pure kindness. If anything, Max, knowing she wanted it, would purposely keep the information from her so he could torture her in the future with ultimatums whenever needed. The only way Sofia could get it out of him was if Max was able to brag cruelly about what he had done with Renie's body.

So, instead of showing her true feelings about the situation, Sofia made herself appear to be happy over the devastating news.

Due to previous practice, she was becoming quite a good actress.

I guess those are the skills that sharpen when your life depends on it.

As if she couldn't care less about Renie's death, Sofia casually asked, "Where is she? What did you do with her? Is she fish food?"

With yet another shrug of his shoulders, Max acknowledged that Sofia was close to the truth, but just like Irene, the truth didn't really matter much to him.

Of course, unsatisfied with Max's vague response, Sofia pressed on, "Did you do it the night we all went to Black Bottom? Where did you go after you dropped me off?"

Her question made her think about the last night Sofia saw her best friend. She was seated with Renie in the back of Max's Lincoln Model L as they drove down Detroit's Gratiot Avenue. She remembered how Renie wouldn't even look at her, let alone speak to her because she was mad over Sofia's decision to get rid of the baby. Due to her regular attendance at Catholic Mass on Sundays, Renie compliantly believed that Sofia would be doomed to Hell for such a decision.

Despite Renie's earlier attempts to persuade her to change her mind, this was the first time Sofia went against her own similarly held religious beliefs. As much as she wanted children someday, her back was against the wall. Sofia needed to get out of this mess. She was convinced this pregnancy would doom her to a life of Hell on Earth if she didn't do it. This left the two friends at a stalemate and not talking over the matter.

Sofia also remembered her father, whose beard seemed to have become even more grizzled with gray since she departed alone with Max earlier that evening. When Max made his second to last stop at the Spera household, Papa had emerged from the front door before the wheels of the car even stopped spinning in the driveway. She recalled the relieved look on Giacomo's face upon her so-called safe return. By this time, Sofia was well aware as long as she was Max's girl, she would never be truly safe again.

While Sofia exited the car to return to her home, she recalled how Irene waved a friendly hello to Giacomo, as he waited for his daughter to approach the front porch steps. He didn't return the wave. Instead, Giacomo stood there, stern with a grimace, as if Irene were the Devil herself.

Sofia was also well aware by this time that her dear papa blamed Renie for her current predicament with Max. When Sofia tried to explain to Giacomo on more than one occasion that Renie was also a victim in this circumstance, he didn't want to hear any of it. To him, Irene chose to run around town singing and dancing like a *puttann'* and that was enough to make her guilty of being the cause of this mess.

Just as Sofia was about to close the front door behind her, she looked back at the Lincoln in the driveway catching a glimpse of Irene scooting closer to Max in his car. She remembered her stomach also felt sick at that time for her friend.

But, as Sofia recalled the unfortunate memory, she instead re-marked begrudgingly to Max as if he was dead-on right about her being jealous over his affair with Irene. "I thought she was a little too cozy for a gal that found you so frightening," Sofia spouted as catty as she could be.

Sofia continued to explain what she meant by her spiteful remark. She admitted to Max how she had seen Irene scoot awfully close to him after he dropped her off at home that night. Sofia even recalled Renie touching Max's hand earlier that evening.

Without having to be asked, she instantly went into detail about how it all occurred in front of her own eyes. As if admitting a new, inner observation for the first time, Sofia added, "I feel like such a fool for not having seen it until now."

SEVENTEEN

Jogging Max's memory, Sofia recalled how crowded the back alley of G. Washington's Funeral Home was when they had joined Salvatore, Princess, and Irene. It didn't take but two seconds before they were being escorted right past the long line of well-dressed people entering the unmarked back entrance.

They didn't leave things well the last time they spoke but Sofia didn't realize how upset Renie was with her until that moment. Sofia sensed something was wrong with Renie because she barely said a peep about her new dress and coat. She had merely turned hastily away from Sofia to follow Salvatore and Princess inside.

In his efforts to court her, Max had begun sending Sofia new silk dresses, fashionable hats, and expensive jewelry daily to her house. The gifts were beautifully packaged, wrapped to perfection, and hand-delivered by a member of the Scalici Squad with fresh flowers, much like Princess' gift from Sally Bottoms the night of the Book-Cadillac's Grand Opening Gala.

Sofia didn't, of course, mention to Max in the present moment on the houseboat that none of the objects softened the blow of what had occurred to her in his hotel room. So, most of the boxes were mounting in piles in her tiny, childhood bedroom completely unopened.

But that particular morning on the last day she would ever see her friend, her usual delivery guy gave her specific instructions. Sofia was to be ready for pick up at nine o'clock tonight, wearing whatever it was he had just handed to her. Max was taking her out for Valentine's Day.

Lucky for her, Sofia liked this one. It was a textured gold velvet dress with groupings of flowers that were scattered about in various shades of pink. The hem was trimmed in mink fur that brushed against her legs like a fluffy cat with every step she took. She loved how soft the velvet felt against her skin and how it tastefully clung to her body in just the right places.

The fact that it was not only sleeveless but had a scoop neckline was a bit controversial in the Spera household. But Sofia knew Mamma wouldn't complain since the dress was from Max. Sofia had already aptly observed that everyone around Max had to bend their own rules to accommodate him, and her mother was no different.

Silvia was bending backward when she bit her tongue about that dress. In the past, Sofia would never have been allowed to wear it, especially in winter. But it helped that she wore the long brown wool coat with a matching mink fur collar that Max included to warm her bare shoulders. It also didn't hurt that the entire ensemble was undoubtedly expensive. So Mamma was able to rationalize away her values a little easier that way.

Before Sofia knew what hit her, the five of them had entered the most audacious party she had ever seen in her life. Unlike the elegant Book-Cadillac, this was Sofia's very first speakeasy.

But this wasn't a refined gathering of the old guard of Detroit. Rather, this was a racy party of have-nots finally having a little something for a change. This was new money. And it was absurdly loud, vibrantly over the top, and lewd in manner, to say the least. Sofia couldn't help but cringe at the sight of it.

Holding tightly onto Princess' hand, Salvatore led the way like Peter leading his disciples through a gluttonous display within the faux funeral home. Sofia recalled the back of Renie's heels as they clacked each step of the way. Sofia didn't understand why Renie was in such a hurry to get inside that she just had to walk two steps in front of her. She wanted the comfort of walking side-by-side with her best friend through the wild party.

Instead, she had to settle for the hypnotic rhythm her friend's heels made as Sofia's pace was weighed down by Max's arm that clutched her waist like a vice. He would squeeze her so tight at times Sofia was finding it hard to breathe. She noted to herself that he always had to feel his power over her in some way. He made sure of it.

With the image of her friend and her clacking heels still frozen in her mind, all Sofia confided to Max on the houseboat was, "Renie was so cross with me that night."

But Sofia recalled how intimidated she had felt walking

through the feral crowd while everyone else at the party seemed to be having the time of their lives. People laughed and hollered between drags of their cigarettes as they played cards and threw dice. Some people challenged their pals to drinking games, seeing who could guzzle down their cocktails laced with illegal booze the fastest. Others groped each other on the dance floor as they competed to see who could dance their hearts out the longest.

Sofia had never felt so out of place in all her life.

Meanwhile, right in the middle of the joint, a couple of flappers were enjoying their cocktails at a prime booth until Salvatore and Princess conveniently ended their strut in front of the two Janes. The odd yet very intimidating power couple didn't say a word at first. They merely stared down their noses at them as if these two unknown women should know precisely who they are and why they were there.

The flappers each glanced over at the other with a valid concern for their mutual welfare when Princess made one solitary command, "Scram." Knowing better than to fight this battle, they didn't say a word as they obediently slid out of the booth.

It seemed to Sofia like they tried their very best to get out of there as fast as humanly possible. They clearly didn't want any trouble from the likes of Sally Bottoms and his notoriously famous mistress.

Sofia also noticed Princess wore a triumphant smirk on her face. The singer didn't hide how she distinctly enjoyed the rush that came with being Sally's side dish. Between that and her celebrity, Princess was literally the most powerful woman in town.

Irene was high off of the famous couple's fumes as well when she waved a sarcastic goodbye to the two departing flappers as she added a saucy, "Better luck next time." Sofia noted that Renie would have never treated anyone like that before she started singing backup with Princess.

Seemingly like a gentleman, Max took a step to the side and cleared the way so Sofia could remove her coat and slide into the booth before him. At the exact moment he sat down, a waiter approached their table. Sofia remembered how, by this time in her relationship with Max, she noticed how all waiters had impeccable timing around him.

In fact, everybody was always on their toes when Max was around. She had never once heard one person ever tell him the word *no*.

Barely acknowledging the waiter as if the black man was nothing more than a scrap piece of paper to place his order on, Max demanded, "A round of the usual and keep 'em comin'."

Although she didn't disclose this tidbit to Max during her current rendition on the houseboat, Sofia recalled hiding her cringe of embarrassment for his rude behavior as she, in turn, kindly requested, "A Coca-Cola for me, please." The bubbles in the pop helped appease the constant nausea she had been feeling for the last week.

Irene had instantly rolled her eyes with cutting sarcasm as she asserted, "Sofia, we're not in a soda parlor. You're such a schoolgirl."

Putting Irene's smart mouth in place, Max gave her a threatening side-eye glare as he firmly reinforced Sofia's wishes to the waiter, "Ya heard her. Add a Coke to it."

Sofia, however, did choose to convey to her husband that she recalled being happily surprised by Max's support at that moment. Especially since he had such a bad habit of pressuring her to do things she wasn't comfortable with all the time. When she added that last anecdote, so as not to offend him, Sofia made sure to imply that she had since grown to love all the naughty things she now did with Max.

When the waiter had nodded affirmatively and scurried away to get their order, Sofia then recalled how Max had stopped paying attention to anybody else around. His eyes were fixed solely on her own appreciative smile.

It was then Sofia was also beginning to realize that oddly enough, Max did want her love...

And possibly even my approval?

Of course, this realization was also something Sofia carefully chose not to share with him, neither now nor then. It was best Max knew as little as possible about what she knew about him. It was easier if he never even suspected she had a brain to do such things like gather and analyze information.

Instead, she told him the story she had rehearsed for weeks in front of the mirror. She explained to Max how, at that time, she had not yet understood why Irene was being so exceptionally rude to her that evening. Despite being offended initially, Sofia now clarified to him that she still didn't want to be the only fire extinguisher in the joint that night. So she defended her nonalcoholic drink order to her friend as simply, "I don't feel well. That's all."

But Sofia did privately know at the time that she had just told Renie about her pregnancy and the ensuing nonstop nausea that started about a week or so earlier. Renie knew that even the thought of alcohol could make Sofia vomit. So Irene's response, challenging her to drink, came as a surprise to Sofia.

"Aw, really? I wonder why you don't feel well?" Irene rhetorically asked, acting all sweet but slathered in sarcasm. Still clearly miffed at Sofia, she had grabbed off of a passing waiter's tray, two shots filled with golden brown liquor, and downed the first of them in one fell swoop.

Sofia could suddenly feel her heartbeat in her ears. She feared that Irene was going to spill the beans about the baby to Max, knowing he would stop her from getting rid of it.

But knowing all too well the mess that would ensue if Irene got as drunk as she seemed determined to do, Max warned, "Slow down. Detroit of all places won't be dealin' with any shortages of hooch. That I can promise."

Feigning obedience but really pushing the situation even further, Irene then placed the remaining shot in front of Sofia. She said, as blatantly sarcastic as possible, "Well, then, Sofia can finish this one off for me. One little shot won't kill ya, right?"

Keeping her nose as far from the liquid as possible, Sofia had shaken her head. She replied, stiffly to Irene in response, "No, thank you. I'd rather not."

She felt another jab of fear within her nauseated gut. Sofia didn't even want to risk smelling the liquor's offensive scent with the heightened super sense of smell she now possessed as a consequence of her pregnancy. If she ended up vomiting profusely in response, Max could suspect something, and that would be dire.

It was then Sofia started to realize that her friend would stop at nothing to get her to have this baby, even if it meant a guaranteed life of abuse for her.

Why was my life not equally important to Renie? Why do I matter so little to her?

Sofia, once again, didn't mention that last realization about Irene to Max. Instead, still able to see the giggle juice sitting before her in that shot glass in her mind's eye, Sofia revealed a side note to him. An explanation as to why she had *erroneously* concluded at the time that Renie's cross behavior toward her was about her upcoming abortion. She confided, "Renie always wanted to be a mother."

Because of this, Sofia had felt that was the *real* reason behind Irene egging her on with her flippant retort back, "Papa still has ya on a short leash, huh?"

Being the dutiful, good girl as always, Sofia firmly replied with a deep sense of moral principle, "Ladies shouldn't drink spirits."

Irene challenged her friend's inherited, old-world outlook with a dig back at her, "What difference does it make to you? Molls aren't ladies anyway."

Sofia distinctly remembered feeling like she had been punched in the gut. Knowing what Renie had known about her situation, she didn't understand why her friend would take such a low blow. After all, she knew that Sofia didn't volunteer to be a *moll*, a gangster's girl.

Yet again, Sofia knew better than to share her hurt feelings about that word during the carefully revised rendition of events she had previously prepared to tell Max about that evening on the boat. She knew it would only offend him. Max, of course, had no problem making her a moll. So much so, he didn't even give her a choice in the matter.

She also had learned by now that for a tough guy, Max could be extremely sensitive. She didn't want to risk angering him by the fact she was embarrassed by the label.

Still sitting in her mink coat on the houseboat bed, Sofia instead decided to carry on to her next crucial point as originally intended. "So I figured Renie was mean, trying to push me to drink because she disapproved of my decision to meet with Mrs. Stoner, but..."

Sofia paused a moment as if a new awareness was dawning on her for the first time. She acted like she was finally able to see the entire big picture, seeing things in such a different way that it was mind-boggling.

She then attempted to explain the backstory that led to her newly changed mindset due to this spontaneous insight. That same night, Sofia noticed Irene caressing Max's hand with her index finger, softly back and forth along his own, while flirtatiously asking, "Max, teach me to play Craps?"

She remembered how he quickly pulled his hand away from Irene as he told her, "Figure it out on your own."

Then, Irene had dramatically exited the booth offended, finally giving up.

Feigning a hefty realization, Sofia solemnly looked up at Max from the houseboat bed, stared him straight in the eye, and declared, "But it really was about *you* the whole time."

EIGHTEEN

Sofia admitted to Max that at that time she wasn't exactly sure what was going on between Irene and him, but knowing what she now knows, the whole scene between them that night played out quite differently to her this time around.

Max seemed pleased with himself that Sofia had finally seen the light regarding her treacherous friend. He didn't want to deal with a lifetime of her throwing Irene in his face whenever she became moody with him. Despite Sofia's spotty behavior throughout this particular evening, he truly wanted to live harmoniously with his wife. So it would be best if they could get past this little problem now. After all, he reasoned to himself, they were about to have a child together.

Sofia sensed that her plan was working. Her story had put Max at ease as he leaned back in his chair, now taking his sweet time drinking the last of the wine as he swooshed it within his glass.

She took the opportunity to try again. "So where did that traitor end up anyway?

Max casually waved off her question; implying it's better for her not to know.

"Ah, come on, Max, I want to know," Sofia responded, coaxing him to change his mind. But as she spoke, she instantly realized that she slipped up. She had said she *wanted* the information. That was the wrong word to use. Knowing she may have just sabotaged her chances with that inadvertent admission, she admonished herself.

And true to her fear, her coaxing did little other than get Max to take another slow sip. As he did so, she could tell that his manner stiffened ever so slightly. The change in his demeanor was barely noticeable to the eye. Yet she could feel it; he was warning her not to ruin their night by pushing her luck any further.

Although she felt that familiar anxious jab in her belly, Sofia wasn't about to give up. Instead, much to her husband's surprise, she continued on with her story. She brought up how Princess then rubbed her satin-coated hand onto Salvatore's chest and asked with a playful smile, "Sally, baby, let's dance. Just one."

Salvatore hesitated initially. With his declining health, it seemed anyone with a set of working eyes could tell that a dance floor was no place for him, and that included Salvatore, himself. But he didn't want to disappoint his much younger mistress, and he quickly gave in to Princess' girlish pout. He had replied firmly, "Just one." Sofia couldn't help but notice how easily he was won over by her.

Salvatore then reached out for Princess by the hand as she helped lift him from his seat. He held his breath until he managed to get on his feet, at which time, he let out an exasperated huff. It was clear to everyone watching that what was a naturally easy act for them took a lot of effort for him. But he proceeded on like nothing was amiss and began to lead the way while still holding onto Princess' hand.

Sofia remembered thinking that the odd pair looked more like an old man leading his daughter than a couple in love. Her father wasn't even as old as Mr. Scalici, Sofia noted. She watched as he guided Princess protectively with each rickety step he took toward the dance floor.

As always, the surrounding partiers knew to clear a path for the powerful mob boss so he could easily get by. Even in his present condition, Sally Bottoms still garnered the utmost respect since he wasn't the actual goon who would ultimately end up giving you a good beating. He had a whole gang to do his bidding for him, so his own advancing age and declining health meant little.

Max, of course, didn't disagree with Sofia's assessment of the two. Although he would never acknowledge this to anyone, let alone his wife, he wasn't thrilled that Sally Bottoms was running around with Princess O'Sullivan either. He didn't care so much about their vast age difference but rather that his sister, Teresa, would ever find out about it. She would be devastated to know that her husband's *cummari* was a woman from Black Bottom of all places.

If any other man had done this to her, Max would have done

that guy in. But this wasn't just any man. This was his brother-in-law, his only father figure, and the boss. So Max had to sit by silently condoning the whole thing without a peep. It took every ounce of self-control he had in him.

After her commentary on Salvatore and Princess, Max noticed that Sofia had stopped midway through her story and withdrew into her thoughts. Her face seemed to go white as if she had seen a ghost.

Sofia couldn't help but recall how the nerves in her belly began to tighten more and more as each member of their gang left the booth on Valentine's Day. Ultimately left alone with Max, Sofia felt a siren go off in her body, warning her that danger was near.

She began to feel that same alarm bell resonating within her again now. She took a breath to calm down as she sat back on the houseboat bed, deep in thought.

For a moment, Sofia feared she would lose her nerve to continue with the evening. She reminded herself that she had come this far, and she would never have another opportunity like this ever again. She needed him to know how she felt. It was important to her.

Meanwhile, Max, relieved that Sofia finally stopped jabbering away, didn't bother to ask what was going on in her head but instead, decided to enjoy the silence for as long as this unexpected story break lasted.

So Sofia continued to sit there quietly as she silently recalled how on that night on Valentine's, it didn't take but a moment for Max's hot breath to land on her ear while he asked her, "Why don't we go back to my penthouse?"

Under the table, Max had placed his hand firmly on Sofia's knee. A jolt of fear had traveled up her spine.

Sofia had done everything she could to stop the frown that was fighting to naturally appear on her face as a visceral response to his suggestion. She didn't dare look at him in case she failed at that attempt. Instead, Sofia did her best to focus her attention on the loud ruckus swirling around them at the party.

She recalled that this was the first evening they had been alone together since that dreadful night in Penthouse #13, and just like that night, she didn't want Max's hands anywhere on her. But all she could do about it was reply politely, "You promised Papa, remember? I was able to come out tonight unchaperoned."

She was alluding to the conversation that Giacomo had with Max when he arrived to pick her up. Her father had made it very clear that his daughter had never been allowed to go out with a bachelor unchaperoned and wanted assurances from Max that he would be a gentleman. This was her father's way of bending to Max's will but keeping his pride somewhat intact in the process.

In true form, Max eagerly agreed to respect her with several guarantees that Sofia would be in the safest of hands. He even softly kissed her hand like a charming prince when he said it.

It didn't surprise Sofia in the least that Max had no intention of keeping his word to her father. She had caught on by now that this was how Max operated. He said whatever he needed to say, to get whatever it was that he wanted at the time, with little regard for future follow-through. She didn't expect that particular night to be any different. Max clearly said whatever he needed to say to get her papa off his back.

But even though she wasn't surprised that Max's word meant nothing, Sofia still wasn't prepared for his bad behavior occurring brazenly right out in public. As Max slid his hand up her dress, Sofia's throat tightened, and she held her breath in apprehension. It's all she could do not to move.

Sofia felt like it was fruitless to attempt to stop him. She had already learned that hard lesson the night of the Book-Cadillac Hotel's Grand Opening Gala. So she just sat there as still as a mouse, hoping he wouldn't have the audacity to continue climbing up her dress. But her silent prayers for this nightmare to end quickly went unanswered as she felt him make his way up her thigh.

Then Max's hot breath sent a second dose of chills up Sofia's spine as he whined in her ear, "I can't wait anymore."

By now, her body felt frozen stiff as she gazed blankly across the rambunctious crowd in the room. She remembered wishing she could be at home with her parents, listening to her Victrola instead of stuck in that booth.

Sofia desperately wanted to be anywhere in the world but where she was at that moment.

Then she caught sight of Irene at the Craps table clear across the other side of the dance floor. Despite Renie's recent demeanor toward her, Sofia still found the sight of her oldest friend comforting. She focused on her, in hopes that watching Renie enthusiastically throw dice across the green-felt tabletop would distract her from Max's fingers attempting to get around her underwear.

And for a moment, it did.

Sofia even had time to make a brief observation about how

Renie seemed to know how to play Craps pretty well for a gal who had just asked for a tutorial from Max. Sofia then rationalized that Renie was probably only trying to ham up their plan when she flirted with Max right in front of her, while asking for instruction that was clearly unneeded.

But as soon as Max managed to circumvent the thin piece of cloth between her legs, Sofia instinctively clasped her thighs together, stopping his fingers from entering inside her. She didn't mean to do it. Her mouth dropped open in surprise at her reaction. She remembered feeling fearful that he would be angry because of it.

Max was unhappy about her rejection. He swiftly removed his crushed hand from beneath her dress while he justified his actions, "Besides, Giacomo doesn't know you don't have anything to lose anymore."

Both Sofia and Max knew that wasn't true. She wouldn't be there with him at all if it were.

But, oh, how I wished it were true!

Sofia would have done anything to turn back time and save her father from all the embarrassment she had put him through. She wished she would have stayed home that evening Irene came banging on her bedroom window. Had she, her reputation and life would still be intact.

Not being one to take no for an answer, Max leaned in and pulled Sofia closer to him, almost ripping the delicate silk neckline of her new dress. Pinning her between him and the booth, he informed her, "I'd make you the happiest woman if you'd let me."

But his forcefulness felt more like a threat to her than a romantic gesture. He was clearly warning her to just let him do as he pleased.

If that wasn't bad enough, his hot breath smelled like burnt garlic to her sensitive nose. Again, she found herself holding her breath to keep from getting sick as he invaded her personal space.

Sofia started to feel like the walls of the funeral home were closing in on her.

Her heart began to race as she attempted to squirm away from his tight grasp.

Sofia had felt Max's .38-caliber digging into her ribs, terrifying her all the more. She pleaded, "Max, stop. I can't breathe."

Nobody, however, tells Max what to do, so he held her even tighter in response.

Then, he stuck his tongue in her mouth, making it impossible for her to continue taking the short gasps of fresh air that were keeping her from throwing up. She tried to kiss him back to appease him, in order to break the seal of his kiss faster so she could breathe freely once again.

But Sofia's skin became damp with perspiration while her body fluctuated abruptly between spells of fever and chills. She tried to resist the dizziness that was overpowering her with a deep breath. But it felt like a mere second had passed before everything in the background began to blur and swirl until Sofia ultimately saw nothing but complete and utter darkness.

The next thing Sofia remembered was lying on the cold, hard, wood floor. As she started to come to, Sofia felt sensations of all the dancing and jazz pulsating through her body. She struggled to open her eyes as she heard Max's baritone voice demand, "Brandy and keep it coming."

After her eyelids made a few fluttering attempts, Sofia finally managed to slowly open them only to discover Max, Irene, and Princess hovering over her wilted body. She recalled Renie lightly slapping her cheeks while Princess waved her peacock feather fan over her face as she assured her, "You're gonna be alright, Sofia."

As she sat up, Sofia caught a glance of Salvatore, who appeared happy to be sitting back in the booth instead of dancing nearby. His gravelly cough was coming and going as he also struggled to catch his breath with his weak lungs. He brushed Sofia's current condition off as unimportant, while he simultaneously clenched a white handkerchief to his own mouth as he croaked, "She's gonna be fine."

Compared to his own health, someone would understand why he thought that was the case; however, Sofia didn't feel like she was going to be fine. She hadn't felt fine since the night she met Max Denaro.

Sofia's surroundings perplexed her as she held her throbbing head. She recalled asking herself aloud, "How did I get onto the floor?"

Before she had time to deliberate her question, the attentive waiter carrying a full tray approached. He interjected with his message, "Here's your brandy, boss." He handed Max the glass filled midway with the sweet, brown liquid. Then, as quickly as he came, the waiter scurried off, as if fearful of becoming involved in Sofia's plight if he stayed any longer.

Max had handed the glass of brandy to Sofia and commanded, "Drink this."

Weak and nauseated, Sofia groaned, "I don't want it."

As usual, giving her no choice in the matter, Max snapped back, "I said drink it."

Sofia knew she was taking a risk drinking the hooch. The taste could very well make her upchuck, but she couldn't risk upsetting Max either. So she reluctantly opted to obey Max's command and drank the brandy down fast.

As Irene watched Sofia dip the bill, she congratulated her on her impressive performance, "Not bad for a beginner."

But Irene had spoken a moment too soon because the liquor made Sofia cough profusely. It was a miracle that the burning sensation she felt down her throat didn't make her vomit all over her dress.

With an accusatory tone, Princess questioned Max, "What happened to her?"

Princess was probably the only woman who could get away with talking to Max in such a tone. Not even Teresa had the guts to demand answers from him. But as he was well aware, nobody could touch Princess, including Max, because of Sally's personal protection. So Max just shrugged his broad shoulders as if completely stumped by what had just occurred and responded in his defense, "She just fainted."

As Sofia's coughing finally subsided, she looked up to find Max was watching Irene and Princess exchange concerned glances, which, in turn, worried Sofia.

Princess had chided, "You need to be more careful with her, Max."

Irene then heedlessly added, "Yeah, a girl in her fragile state..."

Sofia's heart dropped. For the first time in her life, she wanted to actually box Renie's ears for being such a big mouth.

Why was what I did with my own body any of my friend's god-damn business?

Even though Princess tried to shut Renie up by pinching her arm so as not to spill the beans, it did nothing but make it obvious something was going on between the women. For the first time, Sofia regretted confiding in her best friend.

Max clutched Sofia's shoulder in an attempt to steady her wavering stance, as he asked, "How ya feelin'?"

Sofia solemnly yearned to be in the comfort of her mother's arms. She quickly fought back the tears that were beginning to brim her eyes at the thought of being home. With Sofia's head still woozy and her body wobbly like Jell-O, she muttered in response, "I don't feel well. I want to go home."

Max grabbed Sofia's coat from their booth and draped the mink trimmed wool over her shoulders. He then wrapped his arm around Sofia's waist and walked side-by-side with her through the rowdy crowd toward the exit.

Sofia did her best to walk in a straight line despite her queasy head and the brand new leather pumps she wore that Max had also gifted her with that evening. Sofia noted how Max seemed to have a new pep in his step as he steadied her awkward stride through the dimly-lit exit.

Sofia also remembered feeling a sense of relief that he wasn't upset at her for having to cut the fun short. The bit of fresh air seemed to help her stomach as well. She even smiled as they passed patches of people strewn throughout the speakeasy's alley, laughing, kissing, and smoking ciggies while she and Max headed toward his car. Knowing that she would soon be home, Sofia eagerly looked forward to leaving the wild party and crawling into the quiet solitude of her twin bed.

When Max spotted the Lincoln L parked nearby, he beamed, "Right where we left her." Max whistled as he smoothly swung the steel door open, then grasped Sofia's hand, and aided her into the back seat.

As Sofia stepped inside of the luxury vehicle, she remembered how appreciative she was of Max's current good behavior. However, the thought came too soon as he pushed her further inside the back seat and sat next to her on the cold, black leather.

In shock, Sofia asked, "Max, what are you doing?"

Unbuttoning his coat, Max replied, matter-of-factly, "Baby, they don't call it a struggle buggy for nothin'."

Sofia's already sick stomach dropped even further, and she felt her heart begin to race. She felt the same panic set in like she did in Penthouse #13 as she reminded him, "You said you would take me home."

Max turned his palms toward the sky with a shrug and casually asked, "What's the hurry?"

Sofia's throat tightened as she desperately added, "But Papa is waiting up for me."

Without a care in the world, Max flirtatiously replied, "Then I'll make it quick."

The pounding in Sofia's head deepened with every button Max set free from his trousers. She tried to remain calm as anxiety swelled inside of her body. Desperately searching for a way to get out of her crisis, Sofia exclaimed, "But someone could walk by!"

Only thinking of himself, Max removed his jacket, exposing the black leather gun holster wrapped around his shoulders as he replied, "Any owl around at this hour is gonna be ossified anyway."

Sofia looked deep into Max's face. She felt that even though Max was looking back at her, he wasn't truly seeing her. She felt as if she were nothing more than a mirror reflecting his wants and desires with no consideration of her.

So, of course, he didn't pay any mind to the fact she had practically buried herself into the corner of the backseat to be as far from him as possible. All he did was slide closer to her, pinning her between him and the door. He then kissed Sofia in his usual, forceful manner.

She felt his hand squeeze her breast, rubbing her aggressively. Her body seemed to betray her dismay as she felt him stimulate her physically. The strange sensations pulsing throughout her body only confused her until she realized for the first time that her mind didn't have to be on board for her body to perform for him.

Before she knew it, his hand was making his way back up her dress. He used his shoulder to pin Sofia, keeping her in place as he quickly made his way around her panties this time.

Max's .38-caliber dug into her side so hard that she felt her ribs bruising.

She felt two of his abrasive fingers enter her in a brisk, jabbing motion. It didn't feel good to her but instead, it really hurt. Her body unwillingly responded, lubricating the situation as a defense mechanism.

Sofia struggled to resist Max and managed to break his kiss.

While pushing his hand away, she pleaded, "Max, please take me home. You promised my father."

Sofia noticed Max's irritation instantly rise as he retorted sharply, "There's a ring on that finger."

Attempting to remain the good Catholic girl she was raised to be, Sofia said, "But we're not married yet."

Max cracked back, "But we will be soon. Now lay back and pull up your dress." He had slid over to give her space as he returned his attention to freeing himself from his trousers.

Disturbed by the situation at hand and not knowing what else to do to stop it, Sofia quipped sarcastically, "I see romance isn't your thing."

Max's temper simmered as he looked Sofia directly in the eye and warned, "In a minute, you'll see how romantic I can be to a big mouth dame that doesn't do what she's told. You won't be able to sit for a week. Romantic enough for you?"

Sofia could tell Max meant business. He had never hit her before, but she knew he was the type of guy that wasn't above giving her a beating to keep her in line.

She also knew that Max would get away with it if he ever did because he was her fiancé. Had he been a total stranger, he may have gone to jail. According to the social constructs she was trapped in, Max was completely entitled to do what was necessary to keep her under his control. No cop in town would book him no matter what the law said.

So once again, she wisely concluded she had no choice in the matter. Filled with fright and nausea, Sofia reluctantly chose the path of least resistance and dutifully laid back.

Max appeared inconvenienced by Sofia until she ultimately surrendered. He crooned, "Attagirl," as he pulled up Sofia's velvet dress and effortlessly tugged down her silk underwear.

Unlike their first time together in his penthouse hotel room, Max now noticed Sofia's frozen expression and wanted her to enjoy what he was about to do to her. "Come on, Sofia. Relax."

So she smiled at him to make him believe she had suddenly changed her mind about the whole thing. She opened her legs a little wider, suggesting she was inviting him in.

But when he crawled on top of her, a grimace quickly spread across her face the moment it was out of Max's field of vision.

She could hear the squeaking of the Lincoln as it rocked back and forth to the rhythm of Max's thrusts.

She could feel her motionless body awkwardly pinned against the hard, black leather.

She felt his revolver jabbing her side, bruising her with every thrust he made.

All she could do was stare at the automobile's ceiling until Max had his fill.

It felt like an eternity to Sofia, but in actuality, it was only a few minutes until Max finished inside of her. He caught his breath as he flopped over onto the seat next to her.

Sofia felt as if she was in a trance as she pulled her silk panties back over her hips and guided the fluffy mink hem of her soft velvet dress over her knees. She cocooned herself in her fur-trimmed coat as Max fastened the buttons of his fly and said, "See, now that wasn't so bad."

Abruptly, the back door of the Lincoln opened by a puzzled

and buzzed Irene, who asked, "What are you two still doing here?"

Relieved to see her dear friend and desperate to no longer be alone with Max, Sofia hastily replied, "We were just leaving. Need a ride?"

Irene gazed at Max as she responded, "I do. Do you mind, Max?"

Having given the final adjustment to his pants, Max smoothed his jacket as he casually replied, "Not at all." Max stepped out of the car and made way for Irene, who briskly took his place.

As Sofia thought back on the final image of her dear Renie, she remembered how her friend barely looked at her for the duration of the ride back home. She had wanted to hug her even though Irene seemed as cold as the winter snow.

It was only then that Sofia realized that Irene's anger with her that evening caused her to blurt out the remark about Sofia being a double-crosser. This led to telling Max about the secret pregnancy and ended with Renie's own ultimate demise over doing so. This realization brought a tear to Sofia's eye as she finally broke her silence on the houseboat and uttered something aloud, "Not at all, you said."

NINETEEN

Trying to fight back the oncoming tears, Sofia didn't want Max to know how deeply he hurt her. She blinked a couple of times and took a deep breath to center herself.

But it didn't work. The tears came anyway.

Overwhelmed, Sofia had no choice but to let it out.

Max sat there, staring at his wife as she quietly sobbed. He had no idea what caused this rapid turn of events. He wondered if it was her pregnancy that was making her act all over the map like this.

Finally pushing down the sadness somewhere deep inside her, to gather the surrounding situation, Sofia looked up from the bed where she was seated.

She took note that his wine glass on the small dining table was finally empty.

It was also pitch black outside, and the dimly-lit candles strewn throughout the houseboat were half the size since when they started their evening together. The slow-moving boat had stopped altogether.

All these were the signs that told her it was time. Time for her to make her stand.

Sofia stood up with her head held high and her chest puffed out in confrontation as she broke her silence and accused Max, "Of course, you didn't mind giving Renie a ride home that night."

As his usual method of operation, Max acted like he had no choice in the matter. He rebutted loudly, "What else was I supposed to do? You invited her along."

In her mink coat, Sofia boldly placed her hands squarely on her hips as she shouted at him, "I didn't invite you to murder her right after you defiled me in that automobile. Where is Renie's body? What did you do with her?"

Max's jaw dropped. He couldn't believe his ears. Sofia had the guts to raise her voice at him, yet again? He had no idea what got into her that night, but he knew he didn't like it. He also knew he wasn't going to stand for her impertinence. Deflecting Sofia's question with no intention of answering, Max erupted arrogantly in response, "What do you care?"

He once again banged his fist on the table, making both it and Sofia jump a little. He could tell she was scared of him, as she should be. He intended to make this the last night she ever treated him this way.

But despite the fear coursing through her body, Sofia was determined not to let Max weasel his way out of her question.

Done with the charade, she pressed on, "I want to know whether her poor family can have a proper burial?"

Equally confused as he was irritated, Max questioned, "What happened to bein' happy that I did her in?"

As gutsy as she's ever been in her life, Sofia pushed Max's buttons firmly as she glared into his dumbfounded eyes and said bluntly, "I lied."

This time, dashing salt onto Max's wound, Sofia nonchalantly added with thick sarcasm, "I've learned from the best."

After the courageous words flowed from her mouth as freely as the Detroit River flowed downstream, Sofia felt another tinge of fear rise up her spine as she witnessed Max's eyes widen in anger.

Having no tolerance left for Sofia's dumb trap and her sour attitude, Max clenched his jaw and closed his fists as he lunged toward her. He fumbled a couple of steps, drunker than expected, missing her by a hair and tumbling to the floor.

Sofia feigned concern, "Max, baby, you need to lay off the wine."

Confused, Max stabilized himself as he looked up at his petite wife and asked, "How much did I drink?"

Sofia walked over to the candlelit table. Taking the empty bottle in her hand, she held it up in the dim light and casually replied, "A whole bottle."

This seemed strange to Max since he usually could drink a whole bottle of wine and only feel as buzzed as a solitary bee. But then he recalled that this was her father's wine, and he knew it to be particularly strong. So he brushed off his tipsiness and assured

Sofia, "I feel fine."

Max's eyes focused on Sofia's image as he regained his balance, and then like a bull, he charged at her. Despite her attempt to dodge her loaded husband, Max took her down with him onto the bed, and demanded, "Enough with this talk about Irene. She's outta the picture for good."

Before Sofia had a chance to escape, Max pulled himself on top of her and pinned her down with his sheer mass as he effortlessly opened her mink coat. Sofia pushed her palms against his chest while she said as assertively as she could, "Get off of me."

The weight of Max's body felt like being pinned under a steel car to Sofia. Max easily absorbed her struggles as he taunted her sarcastically with her own words, "I can *defile* you as much as I want. You are my wife, and you do as I say. Shut up and act like a woman should act when her husband touches her."

Disgusted by Max's demands, Sofia fired back, "That's what you think? My whole existence is here to please you?"

Offended that she would think otherwise, he wanted to show her that was, indeed, the case. So, wearing an evil grin, Max swatted her hard across the face. In case Sofia wasn't yet convinced by his superior physical strength alone, Max taunted, "You better believe it."

Sofia felt her cheek sear with pain from his strike as her face whipped to the side. Taking a hit was not what she was aiming for tonight, and she hoped with all her heart that she wasn't going to have a bruise because of it.

Usually, Sofia would have quickly submitted to his dominance to keep the situation from escalating and getting worse. But

Sofia wasn't going to let Max win so easily. Not this time.

So with all her might, Sofia kneed Max in the balls.

He instantly cringed over and toppled off her. The moment she was set free from him, Sofia jumped onto her feet and away from Max's grasp. She kept her eyes fixed onto his broad shoulders, curled over in agony as he gasped in pain.

She quickly wrapped herself protectively in her mink coat and maintained a safe distance from him. She often felt she was trapped in close quarters with an unruly, dangerous animal when she was alone with Max, and this moment was no different.

While catching her breath after enduring his crushing weight, Sofia boldly informed Max, "*Amore mio*, you see, there is something I can do about it. Although I admit, there was a time when you had me right where you wanted me…"

TWENTY

Sofia explained what she meant by her seething retort to Max with a new story. A story about the night she sat across the desk of Detective Jack Morgan at the Detroit City Police Station.

Morgan looked exactly like what one would think of when one thought of a detective. She recalled in vivid detail how he wore a three-piece charcoal gray wool suit with a matching fedora hat as he jotted down notes onto a pad of paper in front of him. His jacket was open and exposed the fitted vest that his ox-blood tie was tucked behind.

The detective was serious in nature as one would expect, too. She couldn't help but stare at the thick crease between his eyebrows as he scowled down at his paper.

When he had escorted her into his office, Sofia noticed how he quickly shot a glance here and there around the bustling police station to check if anybody was paying attention to them. As usual, going unnoticed was an impossible task for Sofia and pretty much every man in the station turned his head to watch her go by. They couldn't help but stare as if they were witnessing the Egyptian Queen Cleopatra, herself, entering the premises. Detective Morgan shot a final glare across the room warning his coworkers to get back to work as he shut the door behind him for privacy.

But then the detective had skeptically eyed Sofia through his round spectacles as he stated to her, "You have no witnesses."

Feeling embarrassed at the mere thought of an audience watching as Max did what he did to her in Penthouse #13, Sofia had responded shyly, "Of course not. We were alone."

As he reached into the side pocket of his pants, the detective exposed his worn leather gun holster before pulling a white handkerchief back up to his nose. He rubbed his large sniffer with the wrinkled square of white linen as he continued, "No bruises?"

Shaking her head, Sofia sighed and tried to explain as best she could, "He's so much stronger than me. He pinned me down easily."

"No torn clothing?"

"He did tear my dress around the neckline. But I repaired it already."

"Oh. But that still doesn't prove anything. Could have been torn in a number of ways. Even willingly."

Detective Morgan placed the handkerchief back into his pocket. He didn't know what to think of this story. Not wholly understanding Sofia's position, he asked, "Aren't you engaged to him? I thought I read in the Free Press--"

"He's making me marry him," Sofia interrupted.

She could see the instant confusion come across his face. She understood why the detective reacted as he did. He obviously knew she wasn't speaking of an arranged marriage, although those were fairly common. If that were the case, then she would have said her father was making her marry him.

But she had distinctly suggested that Max was making her marry him.

Sofia knew how strange that statement may seem in this day and age. It had just turned 1925, after all. Women had earned the right to vote six years earlier. But just because it's strange doesn't make it false, she reassured herself as she waited politely for the detective's next question.

But then Detective Morgan eyed the giant pear-shaped solitaire on Sofia's finger being the type of ring nobody could possibly ignore. A look of disbelief spread across his face as he continued his line of questioning, "Making you marry him? Huh... Did you catch him with another woman or something?"

Sofia promptly felt her temper rise within her. It was insulting that he would think this was solely about revenge, as if she couldn't simply have been abused by this notorious gangster. But she did her best to keep her frustration in check. She knew if she became flustered, this man would easily get distracted by her temperament and would lose focus on her point at hand.

"No. I know it sounds crazy, but Max is crazy. He's never cared about what I want. I'm nothing more than a prize to him. He forced himself on me that night, and now he's forcing me to marry him."

Sofia watched as the serious detective scribbled something down onto the pad of paper as she asked, "When you arrest him, my father will be safe, right?"

The detective halted his scribbling and looked up at Sofia from his notepad. He smiled sympathetically as he took in her beautiful, naive, young face. He asked, "You know Salvatore Scalici's nickname?"

Sofia pondered for a moment about where this line of questioning could be going before she responded, "Sally Bottoms?"

Detective Morgan affirmed Sofia's answer with a nod and explained, "Yeah, Sally Bottoms. Because anybody that messes with him ends up at the bottom of the Detroit River… Or at least that's the rumor, because we rarely find the bodies."

Sofia winced as she soaked in the scary reality that she was dealing with actual monsters. There were severe life-altering consequences for anybody being mixed up with this crowd. Sofia knew this to be true first-hand.

Detective Morgan continued with his explanation, "Max has been running rum in this town under his brother-in-law's protection for years. Not only can I not nail him for it, I can't even try with Sally around. Half the guys in this station are on his payroll."

Sofia stared blankly back at the detective in disbelief. Her worldview had just been flipped upside down.

There were policemen working for the Mafia?

Sofia had always been taught that policemen were there to serve and protect. This was the first time she learned about the fine line that existed in reality between good and evil.

But she didn't want to believe it to be true. With her eyes

wide in shock, Sofia asked, hoping she didn't hear him correctly, "You're serious?"

Detective Morgan nodded as he released a frustrated sigh before he replied, "So serious that I'd recommend you sign this. It says you were here to report a missing purse."

He turned the scribbled piece of paper toward her and pushed it across the desk, placing it directly in front of Sofia.

Sofia attempted to read the contents of the paper, but she was too overwhelmed with confusion to focus on it. It seemed to be about some jibber-jabber regarding her purse getting stolen by a Negro.

She looked back up at the detective and asked in a final act of desperation, "There's really nothing you can do?"

"He's your fiancé. There's really nothing I could do," Detective Morgan replied somberly as he shook his head. He genuinely wished he could make a difference in Sofia's life, but he knew all too well what would really end up happening.

He wouldn't even get the chance to arrest Max. Some undercover informant in the station would somehow tip him off beforehand, and this innocent young lady would end up getting a good beating or perhaps disappear entirely without a trace. Her family would be in danger if they dared complain about it, so nothing about it would ever be reported.

No report, no victim, no crime, no case. It would be over before it even began.

For her own good, he warned Sofia sternly, "All I can do is promise never to breathe a word of this to the snoops around here. Your fiancé would be very unhappy."

Sofia sat in anguish for a moment. She couldn't believe how the best night of her life had been turned into her ultimate nightmare through no fault of her own, unless you count being dumb enough to trust a handsome man's polite gesture as her crime.

She not only had her virginity stolen from her, but she also had her dignity stolen. And now it was becoming clear that there would be no protection, nor any justice, for her.

Sofia despairingly acknowledged that this was her only choice by signing the paper. As she got up to leave, Morgan wisely advised her to keep this quiet and between them for her safety.

Tears began to swell in her brown, doe-eyes as she said, "Thank you for your time, Detective Morgan."

The detective took the paper from her and removed his fedora from his head in an act of respect before he sincerely replied, "I wish there was more I could do."

Sofia exited abruptly without another word. She knew that if she had stayed a moment longer, she would end up sobbing uncontrollably in Detective Morgan's office. The realization that there was not one man in Detroit that could protect her from Max was more than her heart could bear, and she didn't want it to break in front of this useless stranger.

Back on the houseboat, doing her best to keep fresh tears from forming, Sofia then paused in her story to watch Max, who was beginning to recover from her kick to the groin. He had risen onto his hands and knees as she ironically informed him, "You were the most powerful person I'd ever met. You can't imagine the fear I felt when the very next day…"

Sofia returned to her story. She had been helping her mother make gnocchi at their kitchen table when she heard the front doorbell ring. It didn't take long before it began to ring impatiently. She barely had time to dust the excess semolina flour from her hands onto her apron as she scurried over to open the door to stop the incessant ringing.

However, gone were the days when she would merely swing the door open, always assuming a visitor was benign. Having learned from her past mistakes, Sofia never opened the door until she knew who was on the other side, although she did know that endless ringing to belong to only one person. She peered through the lace curtains to confirm the identity of the Spera's unexpected visitor.

Through the window, Sofia found it was Frankie Z on her front porch, wearing a dark brown plaid, three-piece suit, and holding a brown paper package. With his chiseled bone structure and full lips pursed, he looked determined, like a man on a mission as he once again rang the bell.

Sofia was used to receiving gifts from Max at this point. And by this time, she had gotten to know her delivery man. For some strange reason, the Scalici Squad's *consigliere* was the goon that ensured the safe delivery of all the packages. It seemed weird to her because he was too far up the food chain to be doing such a menial job. But when she suggested as much to him during one of his many past deliveries, Frankie responded that he's the only one Max trusts, and he was happy to do it. Then, with a friendly wink goodbye, he had tipped his flat cap and left as quickly as he came.

Knowing Frankie was probably in a rush as always, Sofia promptly opened the door with a wide smile. She always smiled big for him, so he would never suspect how much she wished Max would lose interest and these gifts would stop.

His face lit up as well at the sight of her. Playfully acting like a proper delivery man, Frankie said, "Package for a Miss Sofia Spera."

Sofia noted that he was stiffly manicured in the finest clothing just like the rest of the squad leadership, but unlike them, he had soft, kind eyes that smiled as he spoke. He seemed like a contradiction to her. Someone who was far too jovial for his line of work, which made her curious about him.

How did Frankie Z get swept up in the Scalici Squad?

But she knew better than to ask any questions. If she mentioned another man to Max, any man, even his friend, he may get angry with jealousy. It was always best for Sofia to just pretend other men didn't exist. So Sofia responded with a pleasant smile, the kind usually reserved for small children and the elderly, playing along, "That's me, Mr. Delivery Man."

Frankie placed the box into Sofia's dusty palms before he politely tipped his flat cap. He promptly headed back to his black Packard Twin Six that was parked in the driveway.

Sofia inspected the large package as she walked it back over to the kitchen. It was packed so well that whatever was inside didn't make much of a noise as it barely shifted around when she shook it.

But then, not caring one way or another, she nonchalantly set it on the counter without thinking twice about opening it.

Silvia peered over her shoulder as she kneaded a large ball of potato dough and asked, "It's another one from-a Max?"

Sofia merely shrugged in acknowledgment and returned to her task of rolling the smaller balls her mother had prepared for her into long rope-like pieces before using a knife to divide it into bite-size gnocchi.

Silvia responded, scolding her, "You need to be-a nice."

"I didn't ask for him to send me anything."

"Oh, you poor-a girl, getting beautiful presents!"

Sofia didn't understand why her mother felt she should be happy with the gifts, especially knowing the circumstances surrounding her engagement.

However, it seemed to Silvia that women rarely got much of a choice when it came to suitable husbands under the best of circumstances. Although it was unfortunate that Max of all men had set his sights on her, Sofia should just make the best of her situation like every other married woman. At least, this man was wealthy and could provide a comfortable lifestyle along with fancy clothes.

To get her mother off her back, Sofia tugged at the box's brown string bow to unwrap it. Feeling inconvenienced by this gift's arrival, she muttered aloud, "How many dresses does one woman need?"

Curious as a cat, Silvia watched over Sofia's shoulder to get a view of what was inside the box. Before Sofia even had the chance to fully remove the brown wrapping paper, Silvia, filled with anticipation, asked, "What is it?"

Feigning curiosity for her mother's sake, Sofia replied, "I don't know, Mamma."

Sofia folded back the crisp brown paper that exposed a hunter green box with the word "Hudson's" written in silver block letters centered on the stiff cardboard lid. Hudson's was a local favorite department store where Max purchased most of his gifts for her.

Sofia flipped over the lid to reveal a card lying on top of the carefully folded, white tissue paper. Sofia opened a neatly, hand-written message that bore Max's usual direct manner as she read aloud, "Next time you lose something, you come to me."

Ha! Romantic as ever!

She didn't say that out loud purposely to avoid a lecture from her overbearing mamma about how romance doesn't put food on the table. Evidently, neither does good looks or a head full of hair, although Max did, indeed, possess both.

Hands newly washed, Silvia impatiently scooted the tissue aside and pulled out a beautiful brown, hand-tooled, genuine leather purse from its box. There were swirls of flowers that were tastefully carved into the velvety leather with a geometric gold clasp closure.

Sofia recognized it immediately. Mr. Scalici had bought Princess a similar purse, and Sofia had admired it the first time she saw her with it. At the time, Princess informed her that this style of bag was inspired by western wear but modernized to fit the current art deco fashion craze. It was all the rage.

Puzzled, Silvia asked, "Why he think-a you lost a purse?"

Her mamma's question caused Sofia to freeze in fear. She just stared at the purse while Silvia merely continued examining its excellent craftsmanship. She had no idea the significance behind this gift since Silvia also had no idea that Sofia had unintentionally reported a missing purse the previous day.

One thing was for sure, Sofia was getting better at keeping secrets from her parents these days, although she clearly was not as good keeping them from Max.

Sofia hesitated for a moment wishing she could come up with something better to tell her mother before she simply replied, "I don't know."

Although it wasn't the best lie, Sofia remembered noting how lies were also coming more naturally and frequently for her as well. Another consequence of getting mixed up with Max.

Impressed by Max's kind gesture, Silvia had marveled, "It's nice! And it's expensive, too. Feel-a this leather." Silvia offered it up for Sofia to touch but expensive or not, Sofia felt extremely uneasy about the bag. She couldn't even bring herself to touch it.

If Max knew Sofia went to the police, then he might know the real reason she went there, too. Her speeding thoughts raced on as she felt the stress of the situation pump through her veins.

Maybe Detective Morgan wasn't one of the good guys like he acted?

Maybe he had told Max everything I said to him?

This purse isn't a gift. It's a warning.

Although Sofia didn't know precisely what Max knew about her visit over at the police precinct, she did have another solid realization. She realized that Max would ultimately find out anything Sofia chose to do around town when acting out of her own free will. She now truly understood the full extent of her fiancé's network of informants throughout the entire city of Detroit.

Sofia looked down at the pricey purse and felt like the ornately carved leather had eyes of its own and was watching her every move. Her stomach suddenly felt queasy before she told her mother, "It's yours. You can have it."

She took a step back away from the bag, as if it were made of dynamite that could blow at any second.

Confused by Sofia's reaction, Silvia admonished her daughter, "Sofia, what have I told you? You thank-a Max right now. I'm-a sure he's waiting for your call."

Sofia's saliva suddenly felt warm, and her body swiftly became damp with perspiration as she moaned, "I'm not feeling so well."

She abruptly exited the kitchen as fast as her feet would carry her and headed straight toward their family's only water closet. As soon as Sofia reached the porcelain floor, she fell to her knees and vomited in the toilet. She remembered how the floral patterns made with white and black hexagon tiles began to swirl before she had no choice but to lie down on the cold floor to rest.

Sofia couldn't help but pause, once again, to observe how Max currently appeared equally as unwell as she had felt at that time in her story.

He was sitting on the floor as he rested against the foot of the houseboat bed. Sofia watched Max rub his sweaty head with his thick fingers, as she told him, "I wanted to believe that I was sick to my stomach because I was frightened."

TWENTY-ONE

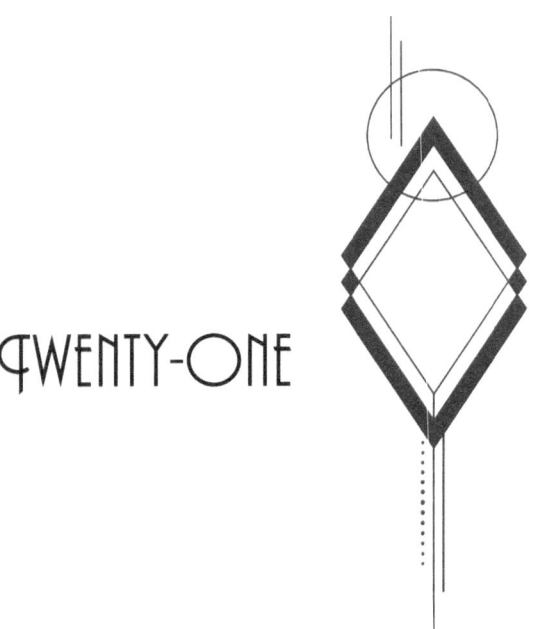

"I prayed for the worst of my problems to be that I went to the police to report what you did to me. But I knew better," Sofia explained to Max, who had progressed to dabbing his sweaty forehead with a handkerchief as he rested on the houseboat floor. "I wanted to believe that I was frightened because if you did know the truth..." Sofia shrugged, not knowing what her fate could be but knowing full well it could really be anything.

It wasn't long after the frightening gift's arrival, Sofia attended mass with Max at Holy Family Parish. Her parents had gone to an earlier mass that day because of Giacomo's work schedule; however, Sofia knew they were only trying to avoid contact with Max. Her father was having a hard time with the entire situation. She could tell because he hadn't looked her in the eye since the day Max arrived asking for her hand in marriage.

Parishioners had started to file out toward the entrance. Sofia remembered how glum she felt as the two of them both rose from their pew to follow them. As Max and Sofia approached the large carved wood doors, she surprisingly halted her mournful stride. With sudden conviction, she avowed, "I need to go to confession."

Upon hearing this, Max was annoyed since he had no interest in staying in a church, of all places, any longer than he needed. So he questioned, "You do nothing but cook and clean. What do ya have to confess?"

Sofia shot Max a sweet smile as she replied back with an innocent tone that made a veiled attempt to camouflage her sarcasm, "Then why don't you go instead?"

Max scowled at Sofia as he filled his lungs with air in an attempt to dilute his frustration with his bride-to-be. He wasn't stupid. He knew what Sofia was suggesting, and he didn't like it. She had been making little snide comments disguised as virginal remarks like this one since the day of their engagement. His patience with her was wearing thin.

But deeming it unwise to make a scene in front of the congregation, he instead retorted, "On second thought, see what that priest says about that bitter tongue of yours. I'll be out front waiting in the Lincoln."

Max continued his powerful gait out of the heavy doors as Sofia made a B-line for the confessional boxes. The parishioners who were already waiting in line invited her to go ahead of them all. It was a strange feeling for her to just cut in line but every single one of them insisted. So she thanked them for their courtesy, knowing full well it was fear of Max that prompted them, and pushed aside the red velvet curtain of the confessional box to take a seat inside.

Having already done this countless times throughout her youth, Sofia continued with the tradition seamlessly. While she did the sign of the cross across her chest, she recited, "Forgive me, Father, for I have sinned. It's been ten weeks since my last confession."

Father Pasquale was seated on the other side of the screen in the confessional box beside her. "What brings you here, my child?"

Although she knew the priest meant she was God's child, Sofia remembered how the word hit her straight in the heart. It was now clear that up to that point in her life, she had been nothing more than a child. A sheltered, innocent, stupid child.

But it was also clear that she was no longer that same child. So it felt odd to hear her referred to as such, especially since she felt abandoned by her deity when He allowed Max to take over her life.

Her sinful thoughts made her swallow thickly with guilt as she continued with her purpose. "Father, forgive me, for I have prayed for the death of my fiancé at least thirty-three…"

She took a moment to ponder the exact number. She had been keeping count every time the thought popped into her mind. She knew it was wrong to think such thoughts, even against Max, but she couldn't help but notice how relieved they made her feel when they occurred. All Sofia wanted was for Max to just go away.

She then corrected herself to the priest, "No, thirty-five times."

Knowing his congregation well, Father Pasquale knew precisely whom he was talking to, despite the presence of the elaborately carved mahogany screen between them. "Is your fiancé the same man you last confessed about?"

"Yes, and I know what you're thinking, but..." Sofia hesitated.

She had been up late in her bed, night after night, contemplating this question as she reviewed everything that occurred the night of the grand opening over and over again in her head. She knew she had sinned that night, having lied to be there in the first place. That much was clear from her last confession.

But she was unsure about how much of the blame for the rest of the stuff that night should be on her shoulders. Sofia felt she didn't adequately explain to Father Pasquale how things had occurred last time. So she drew a deep breath and the courage to blankly ask, "Is it still a sin if I was... Didn't give myself freely...to him that night?"

Father Pasquale knew his congregation well, but he knew Max Denaro, too. Everybody in town knew of him, and it was far from the first time that he had one of his parishioners in the box next to him confiding about their injuries from this man. So he was happy to reassure the beautiful young woman he had known since she was a sweet little girl, "No, you have made no sin."

Upon hearing the priest's verdict, Sofia's heart instantly felt lighter. At that moment, Sofia realized how heavy the burden of blame had weighed on her as she unexpectedly became emotional. She exhaled a sigh of relief and did her best to even her shaky voice, as she said, "That's good news, Father. My heart has been so heavy since that night."

Father Pasquale continued to soothe Sofia's grief as he explained, "If you didn't give yourself to this man, you never intended to sin. In fact, Max…" Quickly recovering from his fumble, he corrected himself, "*Your fiancé* sinned against you."

Confused by the priest's conclusion, Sofia spontaneously asked, "Then why am I being punished for his sin?"

Now confused as well by her visceral response, Father Pasquale inquired, "How so?"

Having second thoughts, she hesitated in fear, unsure of whom to trust, especially since learning that Max had eyes and ears all over Detroit from Detective Morgan. Sofia hadn't told anybody that she was pregnant other than Princess and Renie. Princess was beyond understanding about her sticky situation; whereas, Renie spent the entire time trying to save her from eternal damnation.

Sofia believed her friend was so mad over her decision to have an abortion that she was now avoiding her and thus, disappeared since the night at the speakeasy in Black Bottom on Valentine's Day. It was the longest she had ever gone without seeing Renie, so she knew something was wrong. But their recent fight was the only possible reason for Renie's disappearance that had occurred to Sofia at the time of her confession.

As she contemplated her response to Father Pasquale's question, Sofia came to her own quick conclusion that her family's priest had always been an honorable man. She had known him practically her entire life. She rationalized that inevitably some people who said they were good had to actually be good. Sofia wouldn't allow herself to completely give up on the world around her. So, feeling confident in her decision to trust the religious leader, Sofia softly admitted, "I'm with child."

Filled with relief and effused with hope, Father Pasquale instantly replied, "A child is a blessing, never a punishment. The Virgin Mary wasn't given a choice. She was chosen. She was happy to bear the son of God, regardless of the sacrifice to her own person."

Sofia contemplated Father Pasquale's words. She knew, of course, the miraculous story of the mother of Christ. Still, Sofia didn't feel like she was experiencing a miracle in the same way. She also didn't understand how he didn't see the difference between the two situations.

But Sofia was desperate to get whatever paternal guidance she could, despite the logical irregularities the priest had already offered her thus far. She didn't have the heart to tell her actual father the truth, and Father Pasquale was now the only man who knew her entire predicament.

Sofia asked him earnestly, "But what if you're carrying the Devil's child instead?"

Father Pasquale didn't judge her for thinking as such. Everyone knew Max to be a particularly cruel person that you didn't want to cross. Truth be told, the priest was well aware at that moment that he didn't want to cross the ruthless gangster, either.

Sofia also wasn't the first woman who confessed to him that she didn't want to bear a certain man's child. This issue came up more than he cared to admit. So the priest knew from previous experience how to answer this daunting question. Plus he didn't want to deviate from his usual canned response, in fear that Max may find out.

So Father Pasquale advised her with as much confidence as he could, "You must not judge the child. That would be a sin. There is a reason God sent this baby to you. Maybe this happened to make a terrible thing turn into something beautiful?"

Sofia immediately felt guilty for having judged her innocent child. She knew it didn't choose to be, any more than she chose to partake in its creation. She made an honest attempt to change what she viewed as nothing more than a terrible predicament to a Godly blessing, but the endeavor proved to be too great. She couldn't even pretend for a mere moment before she sullenly asked, "Then why would I rather die than have it?"

Father Pasquale was again not surprised by her response. Throughout the years, many women had sat in the seat next to him, confessing they would rather die than have the baby that was coming, no matter how they felt about it.

Sometimes they actually did kill themselves. As unfortunate as that was, he attributed their abnormal response as the Devil taking hold of them. He didn't know what else it could be since women were clearly made to bear children. Otherwise, it seemed unnatural to him that they wouldn't want to do the very thing they were meant to do in this world.

Trying his best to make her feel better, the priest explained, "You feel upset because you haven't forgiven him. You must forgive your fiancé, for he is only a man, full of flaws and weaknesses."

Sofia couldn't believe her own ears when she instinctively responded in surprise, "Forgive? That's what I should do?"

Sofia couldn't help but note that this was advice that seemed to work rather conveniently for men, completely at a woman's expense, on top of it. But then she reminded herself of the cold, hard reality that the whole world was built around man's convenience and on the backs of women's free labor, too.

Knowing there was a long line outside waiting to be the next to confess, Father Pasquale didn't have the time to dive deeper than this cursory advice. Besides, now knowing that Sofia was having Max's baby only sealed her fate to him. In the priest's opinion, no other decent man would come near an unwed mother. Sofia had no choice but to go through with the marriage to Max. Plus, the child needs his father, too. So Father Pasquale merely replied, "Yes, and ten Hail Mary's."

Sofia remembered feeling stunned by his seemingly simple advice as she exited the confessional box. She had no idea how she was going to achieve this act of forgiveness. It felt as if Father Pasquale had just tasked her with swimming the entire stretch of the Detroit River without getting wet. This mobster had literally torn her life apart through no choice of her own, and her only solution was to forgive Max?

How was that even possible?

Sofia also questioned whether she should change her mind and bear the unwanted child quickly growing within her. Sofia wondered whether she could be wrong that having this baby would do nothing more than cement her existence to Max. Although they were engaged, she still hoped there was a chance that Max may lose interest in her and the wedding would get canceled. That would never happen with this baby in the equation.

She had hoped going to confession would give her clarity about it, but in the end, Sofia just felt more confused than ever. Regardless, she quickly replaced her concerned expression with a forced smile on her face. She didn't want any of her fellow parishioners waiting in line to suspect from her dire look that her life was unraveling like it, in fact, was.

Sofia had to play the role of the happy bride-to-be. It was bad enough that she was marrying Max against her will. She didn't want the whole neighborhood to know about it. It seemed like she could retain more of her dignity if this insane decision were at least perceived to be her own.

Sofia had hoped for a brief moment that Max had become impatient and left without her. However, when she saw him still parked out front on Chrysler Drive waiting in his new Lincoln, she knew it best to let go of her disappointment. Taking a deep breath of courage, she scurried down the church steps and dutifully entered his car.

Sofia remembered sitting there, pensive and staring straight ahead. She had nothing to say to Max, so she always opted for the safest choice, to remain quiet.

As Max drove, he couldn't help but notice her mood had not improved from getting whatever it was she had so desperately needed to get off her chest. He became curious because of it. "Ya didn't mention anything about me to that priest?"

"No." Sofia had also learned that short answers were safer, as well. No need to go into details that could lead to potential problems.

Easily satisfied with her acceptable response, Max warned her as he switched the conversation into his Sicilian dialect, "Good. You never say anything about me or what I do to nobody, including that busy-body priest."

Hearing his warning laced with a threat, Sofia quickly pushed away any doubts she was just having at the church about keeping this baby. Instead, she reconfirmed to herself that she should stay fast to the original plan and remained as quiet as a mouse. Barely acknowledging the conversation, Sofia didn't stop staring straight out the windshield. Instead, she could only think about how Father Pasquale knew more about Max's personal life at the moment than even Max was aware of himself.

"Ya follow me?" Max demanded.

Knowing she had no choice but to agree, Sofia answered mechanically, "Whatever you say, Max."

That line had become her go-to reply whenever she needed to satisfy his overbearing need to control her. Her absolute submissiveness seemed to be the only way to appease him. She honestly didn't know how she was going to manage to do that successfully for their entire lives together. Another personal dilemma she wisely kept from Max.

Instead, they drove in silence for a few minutes, which felt like an eternity for Sofia. She just wanted to get home and away from him.

Then out of the blue, Max broke their silence and asked, "Any plans later?"

Sofia was caught off guard by the question. Max never asked about her life, so alarms went off within her because he was suddenly interested in what was going on this particular evening of all evenings.

She wished she could ignore his seemingly innocuous question. Still, she also knew that her fiancé was not the type of man you get away with ignoring, so Sofia simply responded, "Going over to see Irene."

Max quickly scolded, "I don't like ya hangin' around the likes of her. She's low-class."

You're one to talk!

But Sofia wisely bit her tongue and defended Renie instead, "She's my friend."

Max chuckled at Sofia's naivete before he asserted, "You don't know how to judge people, that's your problem."

Sofia didn't appreciate being told what her problem was by the man whom she considered her greatest problem. She found it so annoying, she couldn't control herself when her next thought unintentionally slipped from her lips, "Boy, did you nail that one on the head."

Max flared his nostrils and gave Sofia the side-eye as he sarcastically asked, "Did ya remember to include that bitter tongue in your confession?"

Without thinking twice, Sofia promptly answered in that same fake tone of innocence as earlier in church, "It slipped my mind."

Officially sick of her mouth, Max grabbed Sofia by her tiny shoulder and snarled, "Who do ya think you're talkin' to? You show me respect!"

Sofia winced from Max's tight grasp. She felt like Max was going to dislocate her shoulder if he continued to shake her for much longer. Brimming with pain and her eyes wide in fear, Sofia carefully retreated, as she assured him, "It'll never happen again, Max."

Sensing her sincerity, Max gave Sofia's shoulder one more

good push before he let her go. He then pointed his index finger an inch away from her temple as he punished her. "You're staying home tonight."

Sofia leaned her body as far away from him as possible. She remembered how she had felt like a child being reprimanded by her father as she disputed, "But I have plans."

Max retorted, "Cancel them."

The wheels of Max's Lincoln sharply stopped in front of Sofia's house. She remembered thinking how thankful she was to finally be home right before Max threatened, "And don't get any bright ideas. Bambi will be here to make sure you're going nowhere tonight. Ya follow me?"

Sofia mechanically responded, as usual, "Whatever you say, Max."

Then Sofia obediently pecked him on the cheek and exited as fast as she could without appearing too obvious that she was desperate to escape the car.

Just then, in the houseboat, Max attempted to stand, breaking Sofia's concentration on her story. But after a few stumbling tries, he couldn't bring himself to depart from the comfort of the cold wood floor.

Sofia didn't appear concerned about Max's ailing state as she peered down at him with her fuming eyes. Determined to tell her full story, once and for all, Sofia eyed him as if daring him to stop what she was about to say.

For once, it was Max who couldn't look away from the floor.

So Sofia carried on, "But that was the Sunday night I was meeting Mary Stoner, and nothing was going to keep me home."

TWENTY-TWO

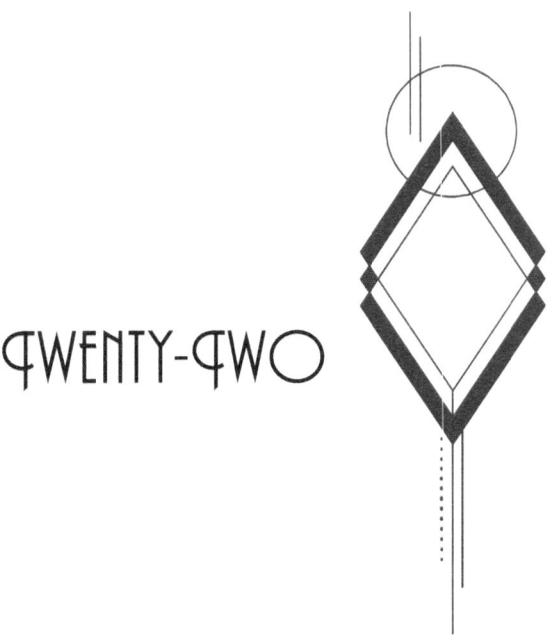

Still sitting on the floor, Max finally looked up at Sofia, who glared back down into his glassy eyes as she sneered, "Nobody was going to stop me that night. Not Father Pasquale, not Bambi, and especially not you."

Sofia recalled how she used a hand mirror to peer through her bedroom window, seeing a sliver of Bambino puffing his long cigar on her family's front porch.

He was wearing a heavy, black coat with a matching fedora hat. Most men wore fedoras, but Bambino's had a taller crown that made his already intimidating height much more daunting. Bambino's face was blocked from view by the hat's three-inch wide brim, so Sofia could only see the wide Petersham band bearing a flat bow and a small red feather on the left side of it.

Sofia recounted how she had pulled the rawhide laces of

Enrico's hunting boots, completing a bow at each of her shins. Despite their large size, his boots would still prove to be much more useful for climbing down from her bedroom window than her usual t-strap leather pumps. And she knew that even though Enrico's boots were too big for her petite feet, using her own feminine hunting boots would be a giveaway as well.

To join Papa on hunting trips, Sofia had taken her late brothers' clothing and tailored it to fit her, because hunting in a dress was as impractical as jumping out of a window in one. So she was also wearing Enrico's moss green tweed hunting breeks for that exact reason. There was no way she could ensure landing both quietly and safely on the ground without injury if she wore a housedress. So the short knickers, being the only pair of pants she owned, were her best option.

She had also bound down her breasts to help with her boyish disguise. Then she tucked in Alessandro's white hunting shirt into the pants. She felt grateful that she had this one ensemble ready to go in preparation for this evening.

Mimicking a man's hairstyle, she had also slicked back and pinned up her hair with a newsboy cap as the final touch. Hopefully, she thought to herself, the functional disguise would both allow her to escape undetected and help her make it to her destination unnoticed.

She remembered feeling her heart thump in her chest as she kept her eyes solidly on Bambino through the mirror's reflection. She cautiously watched his back as he guarded the house entrance, trying to determine the best time to make her move. She had never crawled out her bedroom window before, so Sofia hoped with all her might she could do it without him detecting her.

It also didn't help her nerves that she was worried that Max was on to her. It seemed odd that he suddenly wanted to keep her confined to her home that evening of all evenings, considering what she had planned to do that very night.

Nothing was ever a coincidence with Max.

But she couldn't figure out how Max would have found out about it. The only people that knew were Princess, Renie, and Father Pasquale. Considering that Max's demand that she stay home occurred on the way back from church, she knew that the priest was innocent. He had no opportunity to rat her out.

So that left either Princess or Renie as the culprit.

But Sofia had rationalized that there might be a chance she was wrong about one of her friends telling Max her secret. After all, he didn't mention the baby. Surely, if he had known she was pregnant, he would have acknowledged that fact, she reasoned to herself.

Then unexpectedly, Sofia heard her mother on the front porch. Her voice was muffled to her, but it seemed Silvia was asking if she could get anything for Bambino like a cup of coffee. Sofia saw the large man turn away to respond to her mamma as he politely removed his hat from his head.

Sofia's heart instantly began thumping in her throat.

She knew that now was her best chance to get away without detection from the massive goon. As quietly as humanly possible, she slowly pulled up her bedroom window. She felt the cold Michigan air whip her cheeks as she checked on Bambino to see if he had heard her. To her good fortune, he was still conversing with

Silvia, but now they were commenting about the weather.

Not wasting a moment, she dropped her coat to the ground and then swung one leg after the other outside. As she hung onto the windowsill, Sofia pressed herself against the side of the house, intending to use the small indentations of mortar between the bricks with her feet to slow her climb down to the cold, frozen ground below her. However, the borrowed boots were much bigger than what she was used to and she quickly discovered she couldn't hold her grip against the wall because of it.

When she fell, her feet landed with a crack in the air.

Sofia froze as she knew that was much too loud. She didn't dare move as she listened to whether Bambi had heard her clumsy descent.

Now her heart felt like it was thumping in her ears.

As she held her breath, the fear that she would be caught frozen like a statue outside her open bedroom window started to rise rapidly within her.

But Sofia didn't hear anything from the porch. Bambino seemed to have stepped inside the house. Knowing her mother, Silvia had probably convinced him to take a coffee break in the warm kitchen instead of drinking it out in the cold winter night.

I'm sure he assumed I wouldn't have the guts to disobey Max.

Sofia then pressed herself against the wall as she hung onto her coat, her knuckles already red from holding it so tight in the cold. She didn't want anybody to see her from the kitchen window. She shuffled alongside the house as swiftly as her brother's boots could take her toward the back.

The small backyard surrounded by a gray chain link fence was mostly frozen grass with a large patch of tilled earth where their summer garden was planted each year. She quickly headed to the fence behind it.

With considerable ease, she jumped the fence to make her getaway. It wasn't a total surprise to Sofia that she could jump that fence. Although it had been a while, she had done it several times as a young girl.

For a brief moment, melancholy thoughts of her carefree days as a child had come rushing back to her. But she couldn't afford to be slowed down with sadness regarding how much she missed her lighthearted youth. So Sofia pressed the fond memories to the back of her mind as she focused on her current predicament and moved on, stealthy as a cat, into the dark Detroit night.

She had kept her eyes to the ground most of the way to travel unnoticed. When she did look up on occasion to ensure her path, she noticed how men that passed by didn't ogle her at all. It was the first time she felt safe to walk alone in the streets since her bubs grew in.

Her disguise had clearly worked, but this time, she was surprised by the unforeseen way she felt liberated by it. It was like she was able for a brief moment to walk in a man's shoes and feel what it's like to be seen as a person. And not merely an object to satisfy someone else's desires or needs.

It wasn't long before Sofia had arrived in Princess' dressing room at the Book-Cadillac Hotel. As discussed initially between them, Princess had just returned from her nightly act in the lobby lounge. This was apparent from the beautiful beaded cocktail dress that was still on her body. Layers of long pearl necklaces dangled from Princess' neck, resting on layers of shiny, scalloped satin trimmed with silver beads that made her sparkle like a star.

Princess sat in front of her vanity as she opened a jar of cold cream, about to remove the makeup from her flawless face, when she caught the sight of Sofia at her door. Princess couldn't help but exhale in relief, "Thank God you made it."

Sofia was behind schedule due to the holdup with Bambino back at home. But she intuitively knew that Princess wasn't referring to that fact in her exclamation. It seemed to her that Princess was happy to merely see her alive.

Princess patted the chair beside her and said. "Sofia, doll, have a seat."

Sofia could tell something was amiss when the relieved smile instantly left the singer's face and was replaced with a solemn expression instead. Sofia cautiously sat down. She was out of breath from hastily trekking through side streets and back alleys to get there as fast as she could without being seen by any of Max's informants.

Worry clearly on her face, Sofia asked, "Mrs. Stoner isn't coming?"

Princess hesitated. She had practiced this speech several times in the mirror, but now, saying the words aloud was harder than she ever imagined. But she managed to respond, "No, she'll be here any minute. It's about Irene."

Sofia hadn't seen or heard from her best friend for days. Up to that point, she had thought Renie must have been mad at her over the current procedure she was about to have in that very dressing room, but something about Princess' mournful tone told her there was more to it. "What's going on? Is she okay?" Sofia asked earnestly.

"I don't know how else to tell you this, so I'm going to spit it out." Princess, again, hesitated in apprehension before quickly adding, "Renie and Max had a thing going."

"What do you mean *had a thing*?"

Sofia knew precisely what Princess meant, but she had to stick to the plan and act like she had no idea. Sofia remembered taking note to herself that acting was also getting more natural for her, just like lying and keeping secrets.

"She was Max's girl until you showed up the night of the gala."

Sofia feigned surprise and exclaimed, "But Renie never said anything?"

Princess gently smiled at Sofia, remembering sadly how she once was as young and innocent as her new friend. She then proceeded to explain the situation as quickly as possible because, despite the delicacy of the subject matter, they didn't have much time. "Max put a gun to her head. Told her to keep her mouth shut because he was going to marry an Italian. He'd never marry a Polack, so Renie was nothing more than a side dish, and there wasn't a thing she could say or do about it."

Again, Sofia pretended to be surprised as she added, "But Renie could tell me anything!"

"Sofia, Max put a gun to her head."

Princess reiterated that point, once again, to emphasize that she didn't mean this metaphorically but rather quite literally. She then added to soften the blow, "She felt awfully bad getting you in this mix. She did everything she could to get Max away from you."

What Princess didn't know is that none of this was real news to Sofia. Within a couple of weeks of the terrible night in Penthouse #13, Sofia couldn't keep the pain confined within her any longer. She had confided in her best friend about what had happened to her.

To Sofia's dismay, Renie had her own story about Max.

Although Renie had told Sofia that she had lost her virginity to a neighborhood boy, that had been a lie. Renie was equally embarrassed and afraid to tell Sofia the truth. With tears flowing from her eyes, she now recounted how Max had also forced himself on her one night after a rehearsal. Max had then taken a liking to her, so Bambi would often show up to escort her to his boss' bedroom, where she had no choice but to sleep with him.

As she sobbed, Renie had also shared her immense guilt in putting Sofia in harm's way. Holding her friend in a tight embrace, Renie admitted that she was doing everything she could to get Max's interest back on her instead of on Sofia.

Sofia tried to convince her to stop doing that for her own safety. She didn't want Renie to get hurt. She did not blame her for what occurred the night of the grand opening. Max was a grown man responsible for his own actions.

How could Renie know that Max would set his sights on her?

But her dear friend refused to give up. So together, that night, they vowed to figure out a way to get Max out of both of their lives.

They had also promised one another not to say anything to Princess about their intentions. They thought it best not to risk her telling her sugar daddy anything, as Mr. Scalici would definitely alert Max. They reasoned that the only way they were going to survive this was by outsmarting Max, and it was imperative that he didn't find out they were working together on this common goal.

"But where is she? Renie's supposed to be here." This time, Sofia asked the question about her childhood friend, not knowing the answer.

Princess paused for a moment before she solemnly replied, "She's been missing since the night we all went out in Black Bottom."

Sofia had known this to be accurate, but by Princess' serious tone, it finally dawned on her that her assumptions about Renie's recent disappearance were wrong.

Deadly wrong.

As painful as it was, Sofia began to retrace her steps from their night out in Black Bottom. Sofia attempted to only focus only on the moments that pertained to her missing friend. But flashes of her own traumatic events with Max persistently pierced into her mind like the stabbings of a razor-sharp knife.

The last moment Sofia could remember was exiting Max's Lincoln, where Renie was still seated inside. Deep in thought, Sofia responded, "But after he dropped me off, Max took her home that night... Oh, no!"

Sofia gasped in fear as her heart fell to the bottom of her stomach. She felt the sudden realization with every fiber of her being, now screaming within her, that Renie was forever gone.

Princess had attempted to stay positive about Irene's whereabouts for the past week. However, seeing Sofia's face turn white before her eyes, Princess concluded what she had feared was true. She responded glumly, "Sally says I'm crazy, but now that I know Irene was last seen with Max..."

With tears brimming in her eyes, Sofia asked with a sense of urgency, "But why? What could Renie have done?"

She knew that Princess couldn't possibly know the answer, but something inside her desperately had to ask anyway. She had to know what happened to her friend. Sofia vowed to herself that even if it was the last thing she ever did in her life, she was going to find out the answer. Nothing would stop her.

Even if it meant she would have to confront Max.

"Who knows? Renie could be a bit of a Dumb Dora. She probably threatened to tell you about the affair they were having or something like that, so he got rid of her."

"Max would really have murdered her?" Sofia asked this hoping they could be wrong in their conclusion. But once Sofia said the words out loud, she felt foolish.

Of course, Max could have murdered her. After all, he was a ruthless mobster.

In shock, they sat in silence together. Sofia's tears streamed down her face as she realized that not only was her friend not going to be by her side during the scary procedure she was about to have, but Renie was never going to be by her side - ever again.

Suddenly, there was an abrupt, loud knock at the door, startling both of them.

Touching her own heart to calm herself, Princess said, "That's just Mary Stoner." But before she rose to let her in, she added, "If anybody understands the fix you're in, I do. But let me be clear, if

Max ever finds out, I'd nothing to do with this. Got it?"

Considering Sofia just learned of Renie's dreadful fate, she understood Princess' concern completely, so she gave her word promptly with a nod. "Yes, of course."

Satisfied, Princess then allowed their expected visitor inside as she motioned for her to enter quickly before anybody saw her. "Mrs. Stoner, there isn't much time."

A white-haired woman with a grave, wrinkled face wearing a long, black coat entered with a leather medicine bag held within her mittened hands. As her eyes instantly met Sofia, she smiled warmly. "Miss Spera?" Mrs. Stoner was thrown off by Sofia's disguise. She did really look like a 12-year-old boy, so the elderly woman questioned her just to be sure.

Sofia had brushed the tears away as she rose from her chair to meet Mrs. Stoner. She faked a little smile to welcome her, trying to switch her focus back to the reason she was there in the first place. If anything, her friend's death just solidified her decision to get rid of this baby before Sofia ended up like Renie, too.

Not knowing otherwise, Mrs. Stoner concluded that Sofia was upset about the procedure she was about to endure, so she had done her best to comfort the young woman through the difficult decision. "You poor, sweet girl. Mary's here. Don't you worry about a thing."

Like a grandmother, Mary approached Sofia and embraced her in a warm hug. "Miss O'Sullivan told me all about the pickle you're in. But don't worry. It's nothing old Mrs. Stoner hasn't dealt with many times."

Hand in hand, Mrs. Stoner then guided Sofia to sit back

down. Sofia remembered how warm her hand felt holding her own and how comforting it was for that brief moment, as the older woman took a seat next to her.

As she raised Sofia's chin to look in her teary eyes, Mrs. Stoner asked, "When was your last cycle, dear?"

Sofia didn't even have to contemplate the question having prepared for this evening for a couple of weeks now. "It was mid-November. I believe I've been with child for over two months now."

"And when were ya gonna tell me the good news, *amore mio*?"

Max's baritone voice echoed within the small dressing room as he stood squarely by the door he had silently entered.

Caught off guard, Sofia looked at her fiancé, frozen in shock. She could tell he was angry by the dark scowl across his face. His cheeks were red, and his hands were balled up in tight fists as he eyed her like a punching bag.

Sofia knew she needed to defuse the situation. But there was a problem. Although she had known there was always a possibility that Max may find out about her plan, she focused her entire attention on making sure that didn't happen in the first place. So she never planned what she would do if Max did end up standing there like he was at that moment.

So not having anything better to say, Sofia played dumb as if nothing was amiss, "Max, darling, what are you doing here?"

Max challenged Sofia back. He spoke to her like she was absolutely disgusting. "Better question. What are you doing here?"

Before Sofia could answer him, Max immediately turned his attention to Princess and raised his voice while he threatened,

"That better not be Mary Stoner."

Princess stammered in fear. It was clear that their plan had somehow been foiled, and they were caught behind the eight ball because of it.

It was the first time Sofia had ever seen Princess speechless, which made Sofia feel even more afraid. If Princess was worried, she knew they were in big trouble.

Mrs. Stoner quietly interjected, "I think it best I leave you all to discuss this in private." Mrs. Stoner humbly crouched her stance as she grabbed her leather medicine bag and headed for the door. Sofia remembered how Mrs. Stoner looked as if she wished she could have disappeared through the dressing room walls like a ghost.

Max had blocked Mary's exit with his broad frame as he looked deep into the kind, old woman's fearful eyes. He said, "Yeah, I think that's best, too, and be sure, Mrs. Stoner, that ya never come near my fiancée again."

Knowing she had no say in the matter, Mrs. Stoner respectfully replied, "As you wish. I'm on my way."

Max turned his body to the side and allowed the old woman to scurry past him out the exit. His menacing stare burned through Mrs. Stoner as she dutifully departed in haste.

Then he turned his attention back at Sofia and demanded, "What are ya doing here?"

Trying to help, Princess immediately interjected with the best excuse she could come up with, "Sofia was just visiting--"

Max quickly cut off Princess' blatant lie with a sarcastic retort, "Really? She sure dressed for the occasion, too." With a threatening glare, he added a warning, "It'll be the last time that Sofia ever visits ya. And if it's not the last time, Sally will be on the market for a new whore. Ya follow me?"

Using the power that comes with being the boss' squeeze, Princess warned right back, "Sally wouldn't like you talking to me like this."

"Yeah, and my sister wouldn't like knowing about ya, would she?" Max gave Princess a hard look from top to bottom. Referring to her darker skin, he added venomously, "Especially considering what you are. She'd find it sickening."

Princess knew that Sally's wife being comfortably in denial about her relationship with her husband was crucial to its success. With all the great gigs Princess was able to get because of Sally's connections, she couldn't afford to have Teresa causing major problems for her. So, not wanting to rock the boat, Princess nodded in agreement. "You don't have to worry about me."

Puffs of air passed through Max's flared nostrils as he continued to fix his ominous gaze at Princess for a beat. He silently vowed to one day kick her ass for this little stunt.

Sofia remembered how the only noise she could hear was the sound of their breathing that varied in cadence. She remembered how much she hated Max's silence because she knew that it almost always preceded a much greater threat.

As the tension only grew, Max turned that same ominous gaze over to Sofia, and admonished, "I told ya to stay home."

Sofia feigned her innocence as she squeaked, "I needed to know if I was having a baby like I thought I was."

Swatting Sofia's fib like a housefly, Max retorted, "So ya had to dress like a boy to do it? Mrs. Stoner isn't a doctor. She gets dames outta trouble. Do ya think I'm a fool?"

Hopeless from just having been caught in her bad lie, Sofia began to cry. She didn't know what else to do.

Max's voice echoed within the walls of the small dressing room, as he snarled at Sofia's whimpering face, "Nothin' better happen to my baby. Ya hear me?"

Max grabbed Sofia's arm and gave her a good shake to make sure she knew he meant business. His grasp pinched her arm, causing her to cry out in pain. Annoyed that she dared to complain about his touch, he then swatted her across the face.

Sofia felt his hard hand slap her cheek, causing her face to whip to the side. It was the first time he had physically struck her, but she already knew to take it silently, or worse would come to her.

Max then grabbed her by the chin and turned her face back to his own. As he looked her dead in the eye, Max ordered, "Time to tell ya dear old papa that our wedding is this Saturday. And you better show up wearing a dress."

Tears streamed down Sofia's face as she whimpered, "But Max…"

Disinterested in hearing her protest, Max continued, "I said this Saturday. Unless you'd rather tell him you're pregnant out of wedlock? The choice is yours."

TWENTY-THREE

A bawling Sofia burst through the front door of the Spera home. She pushed the door shut behind her, wishing she could lock out her doomed future as she sobbed like a child.

Giacomo rushed into the foyer from the kitchen to see what all the ruckus was about. He was alarmed by the sight of his tearful daughter, whom he thought a second ago had been sound asleep in the safety of her bedroom. He was also puzzled by the fact that she was dressed in her hunting gear to boot.

Filled with anxious concern, Giacomo asked, "Whatta happened? Sofia?" With Max now in their lives, he knew absolutely anything could be the answer. So he nervously stroked his salt-and-pepper beard as he braced himself for the worst.

Sofia was crying so hard she could barely speak. She leaned against the front door as if her legs were unable to hold her up without its support. Between sharp gasps of air, she finally managed to whimper, "The wedding... is this... Saturday."

As soon as she uttered those fateful words, she immediately started to wail uncontrollably. Sofia couldn't stop herself. She had never felt more helpless in all her life, and there was nothing she could do about it but bend to Max's will.

Her puffy, red eyes looked over at her father. All she could see was a look of defeat across his face. She tried her best not to grimace. She felt like she had been lied to her entire life. Told about a life, a moral society that didn't really exist. Because *this* was their reality.

And Sofia knew from the depth of her soul that there was nothing Papa could do about it, either. The man who had sworn he would always protect his little girl from harm was as helpless as she was.

With that bleak realization, Sofia felt a sudden urge to be alone and away from the world that seemed to do nothing but disappoint and deceive her. She immediately rushed off to her bedroom without another word.

Just as Sofia was scurrying away, Silvia entered wiping her wet hands from washing dishes onto her apron, bewildered by the commotion.

As Sofia entered her room, she overheard Silvia asking Giacomo, "Whatta happened? Whatsa matter with her? What did he do?"

Giacomo shrugged his shoulders feeling as defeated as the expression showing on his worried face as he solemnly replied, "Max-a wants the wedding *this* Saturday."

Quickly grasping the reason her daughter was hysterical, Silvia replied gravely at once, "I should go to her." She knew to Sofia this news must feel like a prison sentence.

Silvia had entered Sofia's bedroom to find her on the bed with her head buried in a pillow, muffling her moans of agony and screams of frustration. It was not the image she had envisioned for her daughter on the night she had set her wedding date. In her mind, Silvia always thought it would be a joyous occasion. She imagined them sharing a glass of their best wine together around the dining room table to celebrate the upcoming nuptials.

Besides the fact Max was Max, Silvia always knew there was more to the story, but she never dared to ask Sofia about it. Silvia understood that once she knew the truth, there would be no going back for her, and she desperately wanted to keep her view of Sofia the same.

Silvia didn't want to change her opinion of her sweet, innocent daughter. She didn't want to blame her for what occurred in her life. She didn't want to face the harsh reality her daughter was going to face being married to one of Detroit's biggest mobsters. So, instead of seeking the truth, Silvia tried to stay positive about the situation for both of them and embraced denial with a smile as best she could.

But seeing her daughter this upset, Silvia could no longer ignore the evidence in front of her eyes. She could no longer pretend not to see her child's pain anymore. She, too, had to finally face reality as it now was for the Spera family.

Silvia reminded herself she had been through times like these before. After all, she had lost her two boys to war and survived.

This thought helped to finally drive up the courage within her to ask, "Whatta happened? Sofia, please tell-a me. Sofia, please."

Sofia didn't want to talk to anyone, especially her mother. She felt the last thing she needed was a lecture at the moment. Silvia would probably do nothing more than remind her about the trials of womanhood and how she should just get used to being nothing more than an afterthought in her own life from now on. So Sofia ignored her mamma's questions and did nothing more than continue to cry in her pillow.

Leaving Silvia no other choice, all she could do was rub her daughter's back softly, trying to calm her. But as if on cue, she also started her usual routine, "It won't be as bad as-a you think. Look at how good Max has-a been to you so far."

Usually, Sofia just let her mamma go on about how great her life would be when she finally accepted her fate. She knew her next line would be about how most women didn't get to marry a man they loved, so what she was experiencing wasn't unusual. Then Silvia would continue to remind her that with time, Sofia would grow to love Max. And even if she didn't, her future children will keep her mind off of him, anyway. And on and on and on she would go.

But today of all days, Sofia couldn't bear to hear this deluded fairytale once again, so she erupted at her mother in a burst of anger, "Good? He's been anything but good!"

Sofia returned to her pillow to cry at what an idiot her mamma was, on top of everything else. No wonder she was stupid enough to have believed Max's line regarding his keys being up in his hotel room when she had this blind woman guiding her through life.

Wouldn't it have been better to be impolite to Max that night in the hotel lobby?

Silvia feared that Max was pure evil. But she honestly didn't want to know what Sofia meant, because she could tell from her volatile response that it was going to be bad. Really bad. Sofia wouldn't be this upset if it weren't horrible, Silvia reasoned.

Although Silvia would have much preferred to be in the dark about the details, she also knew that her daughter needed her desperately. With another deep breath of courage, Silvia finally put her own needs and desires regarding this unsavory situation to the side to be there for her daughter.

To somehow make it easier for her, Silvia switched to her native tongue to coax her daughter's story out of her. This way, she could express herself freely without having to deal with the differences in semantics within the English language. So, in her Sicilian dialect, Silvia said, "I don't understand. What did Max do? Tell me, Sofia!"

Again, Sofia only replied with new cries into her pillow. She really didn't think it would do much good telling Mamma anything. After all, what was an uneducated immigrant woman who barely speaks the language going to do about it? If anything, she would probably just take the whole story personally as if it was her own failure. Then Sofia would have to deal with her mother's brooding as she blamed herself, in addition to dealing with Max.

But Silvia continued to cajole her, "Talk to me, Sofia."

Then it occurred to Sofia, that maybe Silvia should take it personally. That perhaps if her mamma had been able to talk to her about life without embarrassment or guilt, had Mamma been a stronger, wiser woman, Sofia would have known how to deal with men like Max that fateful night at the Book-Cadillac. Instead, all she knew how to be was perfectly polite, allowing Max to con her into his room and bully his way into her body. With a fresh bout of blame, Sofia asked, "You want to know? You really want to know?"

Silvia nodded her head despite not really wanting to know everything.

"Max forced himself on me. The night I sang at the Book-Cadillac."

Sofia remembered how Silvia gasped in pain as her immediate response. Her jaw dropped in mortification as she plopped herself on the end of the bed. Her hands had fallen helplessly in her lap. It was as if the wind was knocked out of her.

Silvia always wondered what had occurred that night. Still, she held firmly onto the hope that Max and Sofia had simply been seen together unchaperoned at this fancy party. This act alone was enough to have to promise her daughter to him. No reputable Italian man would want Sofia now that she had been alone in public with any other man. Especially a man like Max.

But what had actually occurred was far worse, and Silvia didn't even want to imagine what Sofia went through that night. The thought was truly breaking her heart. So much so, she didn't want to think about it at all.

To distract herself, Silvia instead started to worry about who already knew about this, and, of course, she worried about more people in the neighborhood finding out as well. She feared everyone would judge her a bad mother for not being able to protect her daughter, despite her best efforts to shelter her from this outcome.

"And if that's not bad enough, I'm having his baby now," Sofia added, as if she couldn't believe how rotten her luck could actually be in this godforsaken world.

She finally told her mamma because there really wasn't any reason to lie about it any longer. Everyone, including her parents, will know once this baby arrives six months after her wedding day, Sofia rationalized.

She also thought about how taking that extra time to arrange her meeting with Mrs. Stoner will end up being the reason everyone will know that she wasn't a virgin at her wedding. She had taken a risk and ended up making it worse, Sofia concluded.

For a brief second in time, Silvia thought things couldn't have been any worse. After all, she had just been told her daughter was forced to marry her rapist. But now, Sofia was pregnant because of that night. This poor baby would be a daily reminder of that terrible nightmare for her.

Witnessing how hard Silvia took the news, Sofia felt an instant pang of guilt for having told her the truth. She now regretted sharing the heavy burden of her pain. Sofia realized she didn't truly want to hurt Mamma and felt embarrassed for blaming her for what happened. Sofia knew deep down that nothing her mother could have done would have prepared her for Max.

Sofia looked into her mother's desperate eyes while she consoled, "I'm sorry, Mamma. I didn't mean to hurt you and Papa."

Gripping onto her last ounce of hopeful denial, Silvia asked, "You are sure? You are absolutely sure that you're having his baby?"

Heavy with sorrow, Sofia nodded as she undoubtedly sighed,

"I can feel it with every fiber of my being."

Silvia slammed her fist on the bed in frustration as she screamed and yelled in her Sicilian dialect, "That bastard! He's done everything he could to make sure he got you. He left us with no choice."

Sofia knew her parents would react this way once they knew a baby was involved, which is why she tried to get rid of it before either of them found out. But getting rid of it, to her dismay, was now out of the question.

However, Sofia couldn't just give up, either. "You think I should still marry him?" She earnestly inquired.

Silvia, with a similar expression of defeat that Giacomo had on his face earlier in the foyer, replied matter-of-factly in English, "It's-a that or a lifetime of shame."

Then, to her surprise, Sofia arose from her bed with a sense of urgency. She had a new, exciting idea for her mamma. It wasn't necessarily a new idea for her, though. Instead, it was one that had popped into her mind on more than one sleepless night as she would lie awake wondering how she could get out of marrying Max.

But it was the first time Sofia was bold enough to consider this option out loud with all seriousness. So she pitched it to her mamma, "Why can't I just leave? We can all leave together. He won't find us."

Silvia couldn't believe her ears. She felt this suggestion was absolute ridiculousness. "You can't run away from a baby, Sofia. This child needs a father. The father has-a rights, more than you do on that baby. Does Max-a know about it?"

"Why else would the wedding be set for this Saturday?"

That was all Silvia had to hear about the situation. It was the final nail in the coffin.

As much as she knew Sofia was hoping beyond hope that Max would lose interest in her and not end up marrying her…

As much as Sofia was prepared to live a life alone because no other man would touch her soiled reputation after Max left…

As much as she personally wished that there was another way, Silvia couldn't see one. Instead, she explained to her disappointed daughter the reality of her situation. "Max is not gonna let you disappear with his child. I wish it were different, Sofia, but a woman's burden can-a be a heavy load."

There Mamma goes with the trials of womanhood!

Sofia, out of options, had thrown herself on her bed again and had buried her head back in her pillow with fresh, heaving sobs.

Silvia felt equally as helpless as Sofia when she added, "I'll go to Holy Family and make-a the necessary arrangements for this-a Saturday. It's the only way."

But before Silvia could exit, Sofia raised her head from her pillow to request, "Mamma. Please don't tell Papa. About the baby."

Without a moment's hesitation, Silvia agreed, "I think thatsa best."

As Sofia returned to her sobbing, Silvia exited her bedroom with a heavy heart knowing if Giacomo knew what had actually happened to his daughter, he would be destroyed forever.

"Come to think of it. That was the moment when I knew I was going to marry you," Sofia interrupted her side of the story to add that sarcastic afterthought for Max, who was now crouched on the houseboat floor trying to get back on his feet.

TWENTY-FOUR

As Sofia explained her account of events, she had walked through the small room within the houseboat, lighting more candles throughout. She had purchased every candle she could get her hands on in the last month, making the houseboat look lit up like a Christmas tree.

But all Max could say in return was, "Ya lyin' little whore! Pretending you knew nothin' about Irene."

He hated it when he caught anybody trying to pull a fast one on him. But his own wife acting like she didn't know anything about Irene to pump him for information on her whereabouts...

That he couldn't stand for.

Max felt that Sofia's behavior tonight was out of control. It was time to give her a lesson she would never forget - ever. He then lunged for Sofia's neck, but she easily dodged him because he was sloppy drunk and unable to keep his balance.

He didn't expect to miss her, but he immediately used the table as support to get back on his feet. Max growled, "What else are ya lying about? If this baby comes out lookin' like him, I'll kill ya!"

Max attempted to take Sofia down once more, but she again evaded him easily, like a bullfighter who sidesteps at just the right moment to avoid the rushing bull.

As he stumbled to the floor right past her, Max felt dizzy and nauseated from the wine. He couldn't help but hold his head to steady himself.

After watching Max falter before her, Sofia made a cutting remark, "Looks like you don't have your sea legs yet, Mr. Denaro."

Sofia's sarcasm caused Max to fume with rage. His spit flew into the air as he barked, "You were lucky to marry me! Every dame in this town wanted me."

Sofia kept her distance, taking a few steps back to ensure her safety, as she barked, "But not me!"

Max wiped the drool from his lip as he slurred, "Whattaya *dooo* to me?"

Sofia ignored Max's question and continued to the subject she had been waiting all night to broach. "And you knew it too. But that didn't stop you."

"Knew what?" Max replied, challenging her as he stared with menacing black eyes straight into her own.

Standing tall and straight with her hands on her hips, Sofia confidently stared back down into Max's dilated pupils, as she clarified, "You knew I was in love with someone else…"

TWENTY-FIVE

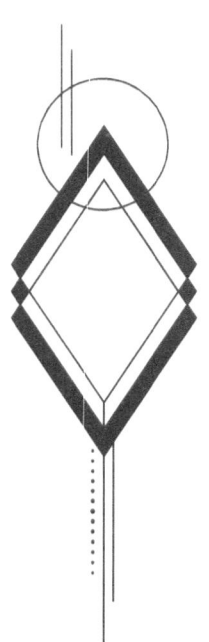

Sofia now described a very different part of that fateful night at the Book-Cadillac Hotel. The part that made her heart sink into the pit of her stomach with instant melancholy at the mere thought of it. So, she usually did her best not to think about...him.

But she felt strongly that after all that Max had done to her, he must know the truth. Not his story. Her truth.

She remembered how her black dress shimmered under the endless array of chandeliers as she hustled throughout the bustling hotel. Baring her beautified face fresh from a Princess makeover, Sofia had never worn anything that garnered so much sparkle and, consequently, so much attention. She had done her best to be as inconspicuous as possible, with her eyes focused on the floor in front of her. But being inconspicuous proved to be impossible.

As she made her way to the exit, Sofia noticed how one man

after another turned their attention toward her as she walked by. There were even women who couldn't help but turn their heads, and some looked as if they wanted to spit in her eye. Sofia didn't know what she had done to those women, but it was a look she was getting used to seeing more and more often. Tonight, she achieved a world record of spiteful stares. Still, she tried her best to ignore them.

Sofia wanted some fresh air to calm the butterflies that fluttered in her stomach. Renie advised against standing at the front entrance since it would spoil their big reveal at their performance. Instead, she gave Sofia directions to a rear service door that led to the back alley of the hotel.

As Sofia finally opened that door, she saw a man gazing up in the moonlight. His back was toward her, and even in the dim lighting, she could tell from only his stance that he was gorgeous. She couldn't help but notice his powerful broad shoulders as he leaned against the brick wall of the hotel. He wore denim overalls over a denim shirt. The same work uniform of thousands of men in Detroit. But Sofia immediately hoped that this particular auto assembly line worker was her mystery man.

It took just a second for him to turn toward her, so she could see if he was, in fact, the one she was hoping for. To Sofia's pleasant surprise, it was her mystery man.

And now that she looked straight at him for the first time, she noticed that he had the most beautiful, crystal blue eyes.

It was the third time their paths had crossed that evening alone. Was it fate?

As his eyes seemed to twinkle at the sight of her, Sofia remembered her heart began to pitter-patter uncontrollably in her chest. There was an undeniable spark between them.

Her mystery man gently smiled at Sofia, as he said, "You shouldn't be out here. It's dangerous."

Already filled with nervous apprehension, Sofia instantly froze.

Does he mean he's dangerous?

Noticing Sofia's frightened expression, the mystery man clarified, "Oh, no. I just mean that a beautiful young lady like yourself… It's not safe to be out in an alley alone after dark."

Ah! He was only being protective of me.

As she recalled prior, it had been an evening of firsts for her, and now, it was the first time Sofia had ever spoken to an eligible bachelor unchaperoned before. Being alone with him definitely felt unfamiliar but interestingly, not unnatural to her.

For one thing, Sofia knew immediately that she liked being in his presence, and she didn't want to leave despite his valid point about the dark alleyway. If anything, his protectiveness made her like him even more. But she also felt it was unwise to ignore his warning, so Sofia politely replied, "Of course. I better be going then."

As soon as Sofia turned to head back into the hotel, her mystery man asked, "Why were you coming out here anyway?"

She could tell he didn't want her to leave either. So, not having to be asked twice, Sofia quickly took the bait to stay in this attractive stranger's company longer.

"I warn you I'm not proud of this," Sofia said as she lifted a cigarette in her shaky hand.

With a mix of excitement and nervousness, Sofia continued to explain her actions. "I'm singing backup in the band tonight. It's a dream come true, but I barely even rehearsed. My friend keeps telling me it'll help my nerves."

Sofia's mystery man smiled at her, and said confidently, "You don't need that. You'll do great."

Although Sofia found it difficult to keep her eyes off of his warm smile, she humbly brushed off his compliment. She had been warned by Mamma that men love to flatter women as a way to get what they want from them. She had told her to be wary of it, even if she felt the man meant it. So Sofia pointed out shyly, "You don't know that. You just met me."

Looking earnestly into her eyes as if admiring a priceless piece of art at the Louvre, he genuinely replied, "I can tell."

Sofia felt her heart racing within her chest. Her body began to tingle throughout. She couldn't help but notice that she wanted this absolute stranger to kiss her. She blushed a deep red at the naughty thought. This must be love, she reasoned.

But their intimate moment together was swiftly interrupted when the back door swung open again, abruptly ending their bashful smiles at each other.

Out of the blue, Bambino appeared with a battered Fred Moore, throwing him on his ass into the dark alley. With a quick brush of each of his sleeves, the giant goon disappeared as quickly as he had unloaded his discarded cargo.

Sofia remembered how she gasped in shock at the sight of the beaten Irishman, who moaned after having his fresh injuries slammed on the hard pavement.

However, her mystery man wasn't surprised in the least. Rather, he seemed to have been expecting him.

As he offered a hand to Fred, he remarked almost casually, "Max got you good this time, didn't he? I'm sorry for that. I should have drowned him in the tub when I had the chance."

As the mystery man helped the bruised man off the cold, blackened ground, Fred groaned as he crouched over in pain. The mystery man responded matter-of-factly, "It's a broken rib. Let's get off to the hospital, or it'll be the death of you."

"Should I call for help?" Sofia didn't know what else to say as the whole situation was unlike anything she had ever seen in her short eighteen years.

"Trust me, you don't want to get involved in this. I've got it under control. Go. Break a leg." He then provided his shoulder to the limping Fred to help him walk toward the busy main street while Sofia opened the back door to return inside.

She had stopped a moment before entering to watch them, still in shock over the severity of the injuries she had just witnessed on Fred. She recalled how nervous he had seemed when she saw him earlier that evening, being escorted by Bambino. Now, Sofia understood entirely why Fred had been shaky and skittish.

But before rounding the corner to return to the bustling Woodward Avenue, the mystery man turned around once more and called out to her, "What's your name?"

"Sofia Spera," she replied with a wide smile across her face. She couldn't even hide how happy it made her that he asked before he disappeared forever from her life.

"Giacomo's daughter?"

"Yes," she replied again as quickly as before. Sofia wasn't altogether surprised that he knew her father, judging from his attire. Then, referring to his blue jean overalls with the oval Ford Motor Company logo stitched on his chest, she added, "You work with Papa?"

"Good guess," he replied with a playful wink. "I hope to see you again, Miss Spera."

Sofia blushed at the thought as she entered back into the hotel. She added under her breath for only herself to hear, "God, I hope so."

She didn't know why.

She didn't know how.

But she did know there was just something between them from the first moment they laid eyes on each other on Michigan Avenue in Downtown Detroit.

ᑫWEПTY-SIX

But then, Sofia reminded her husband during her current rendition of that evening's events at the Book-Cadillac that Max had ended up taking whatever he wanted from her that very night.

Sofia confided that she felt like a complete wreck after what had occurred in Penthouse #13. So much so that she had gone straight to confession, first thing the very next morning, at Holy Family Parish. She barely had a chance to process what Max had done to her, causing her to struggle with her explanation as she awkwardly reiterated the gist of what happened in Max's hotel room.

But having sought solace for her pain, she instead received an uncomforting penance from Father Pasquale. She burst out of the confessional box in tears after she failed to gather any sympathy over her lost virginity. He harshly admonished her for lying to her parents, which resulted in putting herself in harm's way. According to him, Sofia wouldn't have needed a ride from Max, if she was home where she belonged.

He blamed her for what happened, causing her many subsequent sleepless nights. This holy man didn't end up easing her mind about the entire ordeal as she expected. If anything, Sofia had left that confession with more questions than answers afterward.

How was I supposed to never leave my house?

Sofia decided to leave before the mass. She didn't think she could make it through the entire hour without breaking down in front of the congregation. She just wanted to get home so she could cry in the comfort of her own bed, alone without prying eyes surrounding her. Besides, she rationalized it would be best to get back before her parents knew she was gone.

She remembered stopping dead in her tracks, though. Through her tear-brimmed eyes, Sofia saw none other than the mystery man.

He stood there alone in his best suit beside the entrance lighting candles. His slim fitted, dark blue, three-piece suit gently hugged his trim physique. He respectfully carried his brown tweed flat cap that handsomely matched his brown leather oxford dress shoes.

It was apparent that he wasn't a butter and egg man. However, it was also obvious that this mystery man was the kind that used his humble earnings from the Ford assembly line to have a freshly pressed shirt, shined shoes, and a well-kept suit. Even if it might be his only one. Although she wasn't happy to see him right then in that moment, she couldn't help but notice how good he looked in his Sunday's best attire.

Why couldn't he have been the one to take me home last night?

Thankfully, he hadn't spotted her, but Sofia had to walk right past him to leave the church. She didn't want him to see her this way. So she lowered her head with her teary eyes focused on the floor just a step in front of her and waited for him to turn his back toward the door.

As soon as he was done lighting two candles, he did end up turning away from the church entrance, and as soon as he did, Sofia swiftly picked up her pace to make a break for it. But the mystery man caught sight of her at the exact moment she tried to exit undetected and then called out in surprise, "Miss Spera, wait!"

Sofia remembered hearing him say her name as she pushed open the heavy wood door. Still, she pretended she hadn't heard a thing and continued on her way, undeterred.

As Sofia scurried down the church steps, she wiped her tears away in case he followed her. She didn't want him to know that she was upset. She didn't want to have to explain why she had been crying this early in the morning.

He must never know what happened to me.

He must never know I'm spoiled goods.

I must pretend nothing happened.

It didn't take but a few seconds before she felt him catch her by the arm while he sincerely asked, "Didn't you hear me calling you?"

"Sorry, I was a bit distracted," Sofia lied.

"Are you alright? Something wrong?"

His forehead crinkled into deep grooves with worry for her.

He could tell she wasn't happy to see him, like she was just the night before. Something had happened since he last saw her, and it didn't seem good to him.

Sofia, on the other hand, never expected to ever see this mystery man again, let alone have to face him at this unimaginable moment in time. Nobody had ever prepared her for this conversation. All she knew to do was not tell him what happened or, she was convinced, she would definitely never see him again.

So she came up with an excuse and replied as matter-of-factly as she could muster, "I'm cold. I was getting my gloves from home."

"But it's warm inside the church. Come. Attend mass with me."

There he goes again, smiling warmly at her, she thought. Even as upset as she was, she couldn't help but admire those full lips of his. His baby blues were also so inviting with that same lighthearted twinkle. Sofia winced at the thought of rejecting him now.

But having just learned her lesson to not ever trust men, Sofia responded as she was taught upon such a request. She said as sternly as possible, "Papa would disapprove. I'm not allowed out unchaperoned."

"But why are you here alone now?"

It was an honest question that had her cornered. She clearly didn't think it through before she spouted out her father's scripted response. She usually went to church with her parents during the mass held at noon, so she normally wouldn't have been unchaperoned.

However, Sofia managed to escape her family home alone to

desperately seek guidance from her priest. Father Pasquale was the only person she felt she could talk to about it. She didn't want her parents to know that she even required a confession. She didn't want them to know that their worst fears had come true when she disobeyed them by singing outside the church. So she left before they had even awakened. Sofia noted it was one of the first of many secrets that were yet to come.

She knew she couldn't just confide in this mystery man either, despite his warm, loving smile. She had learned the hard way that warmth, politeness, and kind gestures could mean ab-so-lutely nothing. But not having the time to come up with a better lie, Sofia responded simply with a vague truth, "I had to get here early for confession."

Not knowing her actual bleak reason for her attendance, the mystery man responded by teasing her. As if she must have merely had too much fun at the party, he playfully chided, "First thing in the morning? Last night must have been quite a performance."

If he only knew…

Suddenly feeling awkward, Sofia didn't know what else to say about it, so she responded shortly, "I really must be going."

But the handsome stranger reached out and grabbed Sofia's hand, not letting her continue on her way down the stone steps. His warm hand instantly shielded her tiny one from the cold. He begged, "Please. It's a crowded church. Plenty of chaperones in here. I would love it if you joined me for today's mass."

The word *love* seemed to echo in her head. He had said he would *love* it if she joined him. Sofia noticed how she *loved* to hear the word *love* out of his mouth, especially when it referred to her presence being near him.

Sofia remembered how she looked up at him with a shy smile. He made sure that his twinkling eyes met hers directly. She recalled how she melted into those magnetic eyes. Her resistance instantly evaporated. She couldn't reject him any longer and decided to accept his invitation.

It was a full church, after all. That's a lot different than an empty hotel room, right?

Sofia also recalled how natural she felt sitting next to her good-looking admirer, despite the disapproving stares she received from a smattering of surrounding parishioners. She had already surrendered to the fact that those glaring around her were the same people who would ensure her parents found out that she was seated next to this eligible bachelor, alone.

She even knew they were also going to tell on her about how he was holding her hand during the entire service. Not once did he let her go. Not even to open his book of psalms.

They would gossip about how he touched the small of her back as he guided her protectively back to their pew after taking communion together from Father Pasquale. She remembered blushing red in response to his touch.

But his hands felt so strong, yet warm and gentle, that she didn't care what anybody else thought, including her parents. For a brief moment suspended in time, she felt like this was the only man that could protect her from Max. She felt like she had nothing to lose but everything to gain by being with him.

If anything, for the first time, Sofia wanted everyone to see what was going on. So that maybe this new controversy would possibly be tantalizing enough to distract them from gossiping about whatever occurred last night with Max at the party over at the Book-Cadillac Hotel.

Once mass had finally ended, the two of them exited amongst the parishioners who piled out the massive carved wood doors. Upon the church stoop, he asked her politely, "May I walk you home?"

Sofia allowed herself to be brazen by accepting his invitation to mass. But her newfound courage was starting to wane. When just a few short moments before, she had thrown caution to the wind, she was now beginning to fear the consequences of her decision to be there alone with him. Not wanting to push her luck even further with her parents, she replied equally politely, "I live a short walk away. I'll be fine. Thank you."

"But I wanted to hear all about your performance last night. How did you do? You did amazing, I'm sure. Right?"

Sofia couldn't resist that warm smile he seemed to always have for her, and she replied back with her own. She didn't know what else to say about it, she had hardly thought about her performance with what happened afterward, so she only said, "It was a lot of fun."

He immediately teased her, "Hence, the morning confession? God forbids fun, you know."

He seemed to want to know why she had come to confession. She didn't blame him. It did sound strange. Sofia instantly regretted not coming up with a better lie when he asked earlier because she didn't want to think about last night, especially in terms of enjoyment. She hadn't yet figured out a way to cut up her evening in parts and how to focus solely on the good parts without recalling the bad.

She attempted to change the subject to divert his attention from her awkwardness. "What happened to your friend?" Sofia asked.

"Oh, yes, Fred. Two broken ribs, a concussion. He spent the night in the hospital."

"Why did Bambino do that to him?" Sofia couldn't contain her curiosity in asking. It wasn't the first time that question had occurred to her since witnessing him dump the bruised and beaten Fred into the hotel's back alley.

"You know Bambi?" He genuinely seemed surprised that she did know him by name.

Picking up on this, Sofia wanted to clarify that she wasn't one of those people that usually knew people of this unsavory sort. She explained in her defense, "I didn't at the time, but I met him later at the party. He makes me uneasy."

"Uneasy is one way of putting it. But Bambino didn't do it…"

Sofia noticed his hesitation. To her, he seemed to be debating whether he should spill the beans about a certain situation.

Then he looked up and met her earnest eyes and decided to tell this lovely woman the truth. "My brother did."

Sofia was caught entirely by surprise and repeated what he said as if she hadn't heard him correctly. "Your brother?"

He clearly wasn't proud of this fact, but he clarified it all the same, "Yeah, my brother."

And then, Sofia felt her smile disappear with a sudden realization.

Something she had never considered until this very minute in time.

Something that felt like the worst sort of luck at a time when she felt her luck couldn't get any worse.

The mystery man had noticed she was upset by his association with the man responsible for severely harming Fred, but before he could explain any further, Sofia said as cold as ice, "I just realized that I don't even know your name."

He, once again, hesitated, knowing that once this information was shared, it could never be taken back. And it could negatively affect how she felt about him. It could effectively end them before they even had a chance to begin a courtship. It wouldn't be the first time that happened to him.

But he seemed to figure that she would find out eventually, anyhow, so he couldn't hide who he was from her any longer. With that understanding, he carefully replied, "It's Luca. Luca Denaro."

"Denaro?"

That last name was all Sofia had to hear before reacting instantaneously with a curt retort, "I really must be going." She had taken off toward her house as fast as her feet could carry her down the slippery path of icy snow.

But Luca dashed after her as he called out, "Wait, Sofia! I'm not anything like him. I don't blame you!"

Sofia stopped in her tracks. Her thoughts raced in fear.

What else could he blame me for but going to his brother's hotel room like an idiot?

Did Max already spread the news about what he did to me?

Does Luca know I'm not a virgin anymore?

Sofia needed to know what he meant by it. Her reputation was on the line. So she questioned him, "Blame me for what?"

Luca stopped chasing her and threw his hands in the air, defeated by the complexity of it all. "For not wanting anything to do with me because of my family. Please let me explain."

Sofia was already relieved by Luca's limited response. But she also didn't know what he could say that would possibly make it okay that he was actually Max's brother.

"Please let me explain," he asked, once again.

"Fine, but you only have until I get home."

So Luca began to walk her down the street as he explained, "I'm much older than Max, ten years older. When my parents died, he was adopted by my sister, Teresa, and that monster."

"Salvatore Scalici?"

"I gather you have met him, too."

Sofia nodded affirmatively. So much had changed for her in only a day. Before yesterday, she never thought she would know men like Sally Bottoms or...Max Denaro. Now, she was discussing them like nothing.

Knowing they didn't have much time before she would be home and having to face her parents' disapproval for leaving the house, yet again, unchaperoned, Sofia moved the conversation along. "What happened to your parents?"

"Papa died at work, at Ford, right on the line from exhaustion. Six months later, Mamma died of a broken heart," Luca replied sadly.

Judging from his sorrow, Sofia couldn't tell that he was talking about something that happened over twenty years ago now. She felt her heart ache for him.

Luca continued, "I was fourteen. Max was just four. We were poor as dirt. So when Scalici came sniffing around Teresa, she was just seventeen. She was an easy catch. Any roof was better than no roof."

Sofia nodded. She could undoubtedly understand Teresa's decision considering the limited options she would have had to make a living as a young single woman.

Luca added, "I had wanted Max, but she needed him more than me. Unfortunately, she found living under that man's roof equally unbearable as I did."

Sofia's stride landed in front of her parent's house as she asked, "How come you didn't stay with her, too?"

With his words coated thickly in sorrow, Luca responded, "Living with that monster was Teresa's choice, not mine. To not get sucked into her mess, I kept my distance. I don't have anything to do with those people. I've been out on my own ever since."

But then a hopeful smile stretched across Luca's face like a rainbow that suddenly appears from within the dark clouds above when he added, "So I've been alone for a long time, Sofia, but I don't feel alone anymore. Not since I met you."

She couldn't help but offer a shy smile for his confirmation that he liked her as much as she liked him. Sofia blushed, completely smitten, as she looked into Luca's earnest eyes. After hearing that he didn't compromise his integrity like so many others would have done for even less money at stake, she had a newfound, deep respect for him.

But her excitement quickly faded when she eyed the picture

window of her family home, and sure enough, her mamma was seen eavesdropping behind the curtain. She caught the distinct look of disapproval upon her mother's face right before she had released the lace curtain from her hand.

Sofia dreaded the series of explanations she would be forced to give as soon as she left Luca's company and returned inside. But, despite the amount of trouble she was about to be in, Sofia knew that she wanted to see Luca again. Sofia also knew that for that to happen, he would have to meet her father first.

So Sofia dug up a bit of courage before she asked sweetly in a soft voice, "If you'd like to talk to Papa about visiting me…"

Sofia remembered how vulnerable she felt as her request dangled in the air, eagerly waiting for his response.

Luca's smile only grew bigger before he beamed out in excitement, "You want me to talk to him?"

"Yes, I do," Sofia assured.

Energized by the thought of seeing Sofia once more, Luca gushed, "Then I would love to talk to your father." He kissed Sofia's hand in a gentlemanly gesture of respect before adding protectively, "Your hands are cold. You should get inside."

Luca had then walked Sofia up to the front door of her family home, and politely asked, "May I speak to Mr. Spera now?"

"It'd be better if I speak to him first. He'll want to know my feelings about it beforehand. How about next Sunday?"

"Same mass?"

Sofia nodded in agreement. She already couldn't wait until next week. She replied with a bashful smile, "I'll be counting down the minutes."

Luca responded with his own bashful smile, "Well, I'll be counting down the seconds."

Awestruck by the opportunity to see her again, Luca continued to watch Sofia as he grinned happily in pure delight while she safely entered the front door.

TWENTY-SEVEN

"That whole week, we wrote letters to each other every day. I thought about Luca every moment, and each moment felt like it was taking forever to get to next Sunday," Sofia reminisced as she continued seamlessly with her love story.

"Seven letters in seven days. Now that is romantic," Sofia added, clearly highlighting her current husband's lack of insight regarding true romance.

She remembered how Giacomo walked into the kitchen shuffling through the morning mail in hand. At the sight of the envelopes, Sofia felt the fear stiffened within her. She hadn't had a chance to swipe her latest letter from the mailbox before her parents knew of its existence.

And just as she feared, Giacomo found the letter addressed to his daughter in a man's handwriting. He promptly opened it without hesitation. As far as he was concerned, this was utterly his business in ensuring his eighteen-year-old daughter's safety. He read it quietly as Sofia and Silvia were putting away groceries throughout the kitchen.

"Who is-a this Luca? And why is-a he sending letters to my daughter?"

Sofia knew he was reading Luca's letter. However, she still almost dropped the can of San Marzano tomatoes in her hand when she heard Papa bark out his questions so abruptly.

She had meant to talk to him about it all week, but she hadn't gathered enough courage or found the proper time, or both, until today. Now that he had read one of the letters, she had no choice but to tell him. Sofia replied as casually as she could muster, "Oh, Papa, I've been meaning to speak to you about him."

With a raised eyebrow, all he said in his Sicilian dialect was, "I'm waiting…"

By the skeptical look on his face, Giacomo already seemed to know he wasn't going to like what she was about to say next.

"His name is Luca Denaro. I met him at church last week, and he invited me to attend mass with him."

Sofia purposely failed to mention that she actually met Luca in a dark alleyway behind the Book-Cadillac Hotel. At this point in time, neither of her parents were aware she had even been there that night.

Plus, it sounded much better that she had met Luca at church anyway. She hoped it would give him an automatic positive association with her parents because of it.

But Giacomo didn't like her response, regardless. In a huff, he tossed the letter down on the kitchen table. "It must have been some mass because he's quite smitten by you."

He also was confused by how Sofia had been at church without him being there with her as well. Last week, they had gone as usual as a family to mass at noon. He had no idea when she could have actually gone to church with this man without him knowing.

Silvia interjected, "Is this-a the man I saw you with at the front of the house?"

Last Sunday, after getting caught by her mother with Luca out front, Sofia thought she was in for an earache about it. She knew she wouldn't be allowed out, possibly ever again. Sofia prepared herself because she knew it was also likely she would get the belt over this.

However, to her surprise, Silvia only gave her a menacing stare when she entered the house. Sofia felt that if her mother could throw darts at her with her eyes, she would have at that moment. Instead, her mamma had sharply snapped her dishtowel just once at her side, giving Sofia a warning. She would be its next target if she did that little stunt outside ever again. Silvia then returned to the kitchen and didn't say a word to her about it since.

When her father never broached the subject, Sofia had guessed that Mamma didn't want to upset Papa after she had just been caught coming home alone from church the night before.

"You saw her with a man alone?" Giacomo raised his voice to his wife, not understanding in the least why she would keep such valuable information from him.

"What?" Silvia practically yelled back in her defense. "I'm-a telling you now!"

Silvia had purposely kept her findings from her husband. Giacomo had been so upset with her decision to allow Sofia to stay out alone with Renie that he had been complaining to her daily about it. As much as he cared for Sofia's best friend, having known Irene since she was a little girl, Giacomo felt she had gone bad under the influence of these modern times.

Silvia had known how he felt about Renie, and yet she still allowed Sofia to be with her without a chaperone. He didn't care that she only let them go to church. According to him, Silvia had no right to overrule his judgment by allowing it under any circumstances. Ever since, Giacomo had been particularly cross with his wife.

So Silvia decided to keep quiet about the handsome stranger unless absolutely necessary to avoid another onslaught of complaining and blame. She knew Giacomo would say that Sofia was now acting up because Silvia had given her a taste of freedom, and their daughter was ill-equipped to deal with it.

But since Sofia was now telling him about it, Silvia thought it best to admit she saw them, in case the truth got back to Giacomo later. She would never hear the end of it from him if that happened. It was better to fess up first.

Knowing he would deal with his wife's indiscretions later, Giacomo returned his attention to his daughter. He asked her with all seriousness, "Are you trying to-a destroy your reputation?"

He pinched the tips of his fingers together and bobbed his hand up and down in the Italian gesture meaning "What?" It's often used when someone is confused, trying to figure out what the hell you're doing. In this particular case, Giacomo wanted to know what the hell Sofia was doing with her life.

Sofia twisted her hands in worry as she tried to explain her behavior, "No. And it was broad daylight, after church, and there were people everywhere."

However, Giacomo didn't find Sofia's reasoning compelling. If anything, it only proved to him that there were witnesses to her bad behavior, which meant her reputation was, indeed, in question. After everything he had done to protect it, he wasn't happy to hear that Sofia risked it all over a man she happened to bump into alone at church when she wasn't even supposed to be there in the first place.

He grumbled, dissatisfied, as he took a seat at the kitchen table, "He shoulda have asked my permission first. It's disrespectful."

"Papa, we just happened to run into each other at church," Sofia pleaded Luca's case. "How was he supposed to ask you first? Besides, I was going to tell you that he'd like to come this Sunday to speak to you."

"When-a the hell were you in church without us anyway?" Flabbergasted, Giacomo gestured toward Silvia and then himself. He finally needed to get to the bottom of this nonsense.

Sofia obviously knew this question would come up since Papa was in the dark about how she had snuck out of the house to go to church last Sunday. Her mamma had left the door open and slightly ajar, allowing her to quietly enter the foyer upon her return. Her papa had been getting dressed at the time, so he didn't even know she had left in the first place. So she spent almost the entire week preparing her answer to it.

In the end, Sofia felt keeping it as close to the truth as possible was the best solution. After all, there were far too many witnesses to confirm her attendance at Holy Family that morning. So she explained as rehearsed, "I felt bad about my behavior the night before, so I went to confession first thing in the morning."

Dumbfounded by her logic or rather, lack thereof, Giacomo threw his hands up in the air. He couldn't believe his ears. "How does thatta make any sense?" He called out as if asking God Himself to literally answer in response.

Silvia, equally as displeased as her husband, ended up slamming shut one of the kitchen cabinet doors in her frustration. "Mrs. Rossi told me he was-a touching you in-a church."

Sofia instinctively understood that her mother was especially upset that she had to hear about Luca's behavior in church from Mrs. Rossi, of all people. Sofia knew that Mrs. Rossi's son was on Giacomo's list of suitable husbands for her, and he was a lawyer to boot. She knew her parents were aiming higher for her; hence, the scowl on her mamma's face as she fumed while now standing behind Giacomo in solidarity. Silvia believed, and rightly so, that Sofia's chances to marry the lawyer were now nonexistent because of this.

Giacomo couldn't even wait for Sofia to reply to Silvia's accusation when he added suspiciously, "You never go to church alone. Suddenly, you're going to-a church alone morning, noon, and night. Did you meet-a this man when you went out with-a that *puttann'*, Irene?"

"Renie is a flapper, and Mrs. Rossi is nothing but a gossip."

"You say-a flapper, I say *una puttann'*," Giacomo snapped back at Sofia. It was the first time he noticed something was amiss with his daughter's judgment, and he felt a stroke of fear that she was losing her moral compass like her best friend.

Sofia had a feeling this conversation with her father wasn't going to be easy. Still, she never anticipated it going as badly as this, either. She figured Papa knew this day was coming soon since she had already turned eighteen years old. He often talked about who he felt would be a suitable husband for her, but none of the men on his list had ever made her feel like Luca did. Not even a schoolgirl crush could rival how captivated she felt by the mere thought of him. So she couldn't give up on her new love without a fight.

She tried to reason with her father, "This has nothing to do with Irene. Mr. Denaro is a very nice man."

"Luca works atta Ford. I knew his-a father, too. He's-a too old for you. Is that whatta you want? A beautiful girl, like yourself. You want an old man factory worker?"

But true to her Catholic upbringing, Sofia didn't care about things like money. Sofia wanted to be with a man she loved with all her heart no matter what size house he could provide for her. So she respectfully made a valid point in Luca's defense, "You work on the line. What's wrong with you?"

Sofia remembered how Silvia looked over at Giacomo, waiting to see how he'll answer that one.

"You can do betta than me," Giacomo said without a moment's hesitation.

"Papa, don't say that." Sofia didn't like that her father believed that; whereas, she felt quite the opposite about him. Papa had always been there for his family. He provided food on the table. Her father was there every night, not out drinking with other women like many men were doing in the neighborhood. He was the most honest person she had ever known. To Sofia, if Luca were half the man her father was, she would still be in good, loving hands.

But Giacomo had truly meant what he said. He had sacrificed everything leaving Sicily, leaving the only life he knew and all the people he loved to come to America with Silvia. He did it to give his family an opportunity to do better than he did. With his sons gone, all he had left was Sofia, and Giacomo wasn't happy that Luca wasn't any further ahead in life than he had personally achieved. He knew his pretty daughter could do better.

Miffed, Giacomo grabbed the *Detroit Free Press* that arrived with the rest of the mail on the table. He flipped it open as he grumbled displeased, "I don't like it."

"Please, Papa."

Suddenly, Sofia was on her knees by his feet. She clasped her hands together, begging her father for his blessing.

Still seated, Giacomo looked down into his daughter's pleading eyes, and he knew immediately it was too late. He could see it in her big brown doe-eyes that she had already fallen in love with Luca.

Having once been a young man in love, Giacomo also knew if he kept them apart now, it would be torture for her. Any other man he found for her would now be a second choice, so her life was doomed to unhappiness either way. Faced with this grim reality, he finally acquiesced, "Luca can speak-a to me on Sunday."

"Thank you, Papa! Thank you!"

Sofia hopped back on her feet in utter joy. She lit up with that wide smile that always seemed to be on her face when she thought of Luca. It was almost as if she couldn't believe her good luck.

Sofia gave Giacomo a loving peck on the cheek in appreciation. She grabbed her letter off the table and left straight for her room before he could change his mind.

She continued to reminisce about how happy she was when Sunday finally did arrive. She met Luca at church and they attended mass together as they originally planned. He, once again, held her hand during the entire hour, but this time, he had even kissed her fingers as they were interlaced with his own.

When they exited the church, they were arm-in-arm. They couldn't keep their eyes off of each other. They were in their own world oblivious to all the other surrounding parishioners spilling out amongst them. She knew that people were staring at them, but she didn't care. Sofia was in love.

She recalled how they had walked together hand-in-hand, smiling and laughing the entire time. She remembered how she couldn't wait to get home so Luca could speak with Papa, but she also tried her best to savor the moment with her new love by keeping their pace to a leisurely stroll. She couldn't remember another time in her life when she was quite this happy. Her face almost hurt, she was smiling so much.

But as Sofia and Luca approached her family home, they found Silvia standing alone on the porch waiting for their return.

TWENTY-EIGHT

At the sight of Sofia's mother, Luca immediately removed his gray Homburg hat from his head in respect and said, "Good afternoon, Mrs. Spera."

Silvia responded politely, "*Buon giorno.*"

Luca, with a friendly smile, added, "I was hoping I could have a moment with Mr. Spera." As he spoke to her mother, Sofia could see that twinkle in his eye that she had quickly grown to love so much.

Sofia also remembered how she had smiled eagerly at her mother as she awaited her response. She was very excited that the moment she had been waiting for all week had finally arrived.

But her smile instantly disappeared when she sensed something was off about Mamma.

Still polite but slightly cold, Silvia responded, "I'm-a sorry,

Mr. Denaro, but my husband is-a busy."

Sofia's mouth dropped in confusion. She didn't expect her mother to respond as such. They had just gone over the plan of Luca returning with her after mass when her father dropped her off at the church that morning. She had managed to convince Papa that an entire congregation of people were plenty of chaperones, allowing her to attend mass with Luca alone. But when Papa didn't show up to drive her home as discussed, she assumed that he must be okay with her being walked home by Luca. So all she thought to say in response was, "Mamma? Papa said…"

Silvia wasn't in a position to explain as she feared they would be heard out front. She also needed to get rid of this man as quickly as possible so she sternly said, "I'm-a sorry, Mr. Denaro, but you will-a have to come back another time. Sofia, get in-a the house."

Confused, Sofia whispered to Luca, "Please wait here. I'll find out what's going on."

Luca, speechless in his unexpected disappointment, not knowing what to think, only nodded affirmatively in response to Sofia's request, allowing her to scurry after her mother.

Sofia then followed Silvia into the kitchen, asking nonstop questions, "Mamma, what's going on? Where's Papa? What's happening?"

She could tell her mother was very upset as Silvia nodded toward the closed dining room door and added in an agitated whisper, "Papa's in-a there with Max Denaro."

Sofia's jaw dropped. She felt a wave of fear vibrate throughout her body, and she knew Silvia could sense her dread.

"Do you know who thatta man is, Sofia?"

Sofia was pensive as she stood by the kitchen door, trying to eavesdrop on the conversation happening down the hall. She didn't want to answer her mother. She had happily placed Max Denaro within the wonderful realms of denial, hoping that he would become nothing more than a figment of her memory.

"How could you have met thatta man, of all men, and not-a mention it to us?" Silvia's whisper grew in volume and agitation, causing Sofia to look at her mamma wide-eyed in alarm. She worried that Max might overhear them talking about him.

But Silvia was distraught by her recent realization, and whatever else her daughter may not have mentioned about the night she let her roam free with her friend. It was now pretty clear that they hadn't been to church at all that evening. She also knew Giacomo was going to be furious with her because of it.

"How was I supposed to know who he was? You and Papa never tell me anything," Sofia responded in her defense. She knew that wasn't her mother's point, but she didn't want to get into it with her about it.

Sofia was equally distraught about why Max Denaro had decided to call upon her father. She figured she had been one of many dames for that man, someone he would have quickly forgotten within a week.

Suddenly, they heard the dining room pocket door slide open, and Giacomo called out from within it, "Silvia! Sofia! Come here!"

Silvia and Sofia dutifully emerged from the kitchen right when Max and Giacomo stepped out from the dining room. Sofia could see that Giacomo was in a somber mood with a swollen red cheek; whereas, Max seemed pleased and at ease with a satisfied smirk on his face.

"Hello, Miss Spera," Max said smugly.

Sofia wondered how she ever found him handsome and charming. She felt disappointed in herself for her lack of ability to see the obvious right in front of her face. This man was nothing more than a glib thug.

Then, to her dismay, Max pulled out Sofia's gloves from his coat pocket. He politely explained, "I wanted to get these back to ya. You dropped 'em when we met last weekend."

All Sofia wanted to do was crawl under a rock. These were the very gloves her parents had gifted her for her eighteenth birthday. There was no denying that they were hers, and of course, the gloves proved to her parents that she had met Max Denaro.

She didn't know what else to do but politely take the gloves from him. "Thank you, Mr. Denaro," was all she could muster softly in response. But her mind wasn't nearly as quiet. She kept searching for an answer to why he came to visit. She could clearly tell it had nothing to do with him returning her gloves. Fear was mounting within her at all the possibilities that could unfold right now.

"It was a pleasure meetin' ya at the grand opening," Max added.

Giacomo, not pleased by the contents of the conversation, cleared his throat and extended his arm, inviting them to enter the living room.

The four of them gathered right in front of the picture window. The sheer white drapes were drawn, giving Sofia a view of Luca waiting on the sidewalk looking in.

She began to panic as she started to suspect the reason for Max's visit. She desperately asked, "What's going on, Papa?"

"Mr. Denaro, please say whatta you have to say."

Whatever Max had to say, Sofia knew her father was melancholy about it from his solemn expression. But she also concluded that fresh swollen cheek was the reason why he allowed Max to stay despite his current unhappiness.

"Miss Spera, I've wanted ya since I first laid eyes on ya on that stage at the Book-Cadillac Hotel. And I was hopin'…"

Sofia's eyes darted from Giacomo's troubled face to Max as she watched him pull out a little velvet box from his pocket. Her mouth dropped open in shock. Alarmed, her eyes opened wide. She couldn't believe what was about to happen. Like being stuck in a nightmare, she wanted it to stop, but all she could do was cover her mouth to hide how she truly felt about this dangerous man.

After what felt like an eternity for her, Max finally finished his sentence, "…you'd marry me." He opened the little box and nestled within the black velvet was a gigantic pear-shaped diamond solitaire.

The biggest diamond Sofia had ever witnessed in her entire life. And likely every other life she had ever known on Earth. But all Sofia could manage to say in response to its grand reveal, "Mr. Denaro, you are certainly always full of surprises."

It was then that Max started to brag about its size, but Sofia couldn't hear a word he said. He seemed to fade to the background as her attention was immediately drawn outdoors through the window. Her forlorn eyes met Luca's eyes, and from the pain she saw blatantly within them, she knew that he had witnessed his brother's marriage proposal. It felt like pure torture for them both.

It didn't take long for Max to follow her gaze since it clearly wasn't on him. He didn't seem surprised to see his brother standing outside on the sidewalk. But he asked anyway, "Why is Luca here?" He seemed to be testing her to see if Sofia would actually tell him the truth.

But Giacomo gave Sofia a look of warning. It was a look he usually used when they would hunt together, warning her of a potential predator being nearby. Just this time, it's not a black bear, a cougar, or a gray wolf in their path. It's the most deadly man in Detroit.

Taking heed, Sofia thought it best not to tell Max the details and responded as vaguely as possible, "He walked me home from church." She then looked down at the enormous ring, trying to divert Max's attention away from Luca's presence. Still, not knowing what else to say about it, she awkwardly remarked, "Thank you."

"Thank you?" Max seemed perturbed by Sofia's lack of enthusiasm. "How 'bout yes, I'll marry you?"

Sofia was in such shock over this whole thing, she didn't have the wherewithal to even control her reaction. Of course, she didn't want to marry Max Denaro. Everything inside of her was screaming.

Say no!

But here he was, in front of her, proposing for her hand in marriage. Max had not liked her response of *thank you*. She couldn't imagine his anger if she actually said *no*. Sofia couldn't believe her rotten luck in being confronted with this conundrum.

In one last futile attempt, Sofia desperately looked over at her father. She searched his face, hoping beyond hope, somehow there was something that could be done to deny this man what he wants from her.

To her chagrin, Giacomo gave one sharp nod.

Sofia tried to hide her disappointment. So she bent her head low, keeping her eyes down on the large, sparkling ring being offered to her. She knew if she looked at Max's face, she wouldn't be able to spit out the words.

However, after she swallowed thickly, she still wasn't able to answer Max's question as it hung heavy in the air. Sofia didn't know if she would even be able to spit out the words whether she looked at him or not.

But she had to respond, so she decided to do something to make it easier for her. She pretended that Luca was the one standing in front of her proposing marriage. Only then was she able to respond softly, "Yes… I'll marry you, Mr. Denaro."

She remembered getting a glimpse of Max's victorious smile as he took the ring and slid it on Sofia's left ring finger. He then kissed her hand and informed her, "I want this wedding to happen as soon as possible, *amore*."

Sofia recalled how she couldn't help but wince at the sound of the word *amore* coming from him. It felt unnatural and wrong to her.

To buy her daughter time to get used to this new plan, Silvia responded politely, "We will need some-a time for the wedding preparations, Mr. Denaro. You understand, of course."

Making the best of the situation, Giacomo extended his hand to Max and said, "Welcome to the family."

Silvia hugged Sofia close as Giacomo shook Max's hand in congratulations. They did their best to be as joyous as such an occasion usually warranted, as they traded partners for hugs and felicitations.

Once Max departed through the front door, Sofia remembered how his ominous presence still lingered in their foyer like an evil spirit while her family stood in silence.

Sofia peeked out the small window beside the door and watched Max walk toward his Lincoln, parked in the street out front. Her forlorn eyes paced back and forth as they searched for Luca. Sofia's heart sank when she realized he was nowhere to be found.

Confused and afraid, Sofia looked at her father and asked, "Papa, what did he do to you?" She touched the raised bruise on his cheek.

In an attempt to appear strong, Giacomo gently brushed Sofia's hand away and said, "It's-a nothing."

In the kitchen, Silvia wrapped ice cubes within a thin white dish towel while Sofia guided her father into his seat at their table.

Sofia's family sat in silent shock from the tragic event that had just taken place. Giacomo looked pensive as water dripped from the melting ice that soothed his bruise. Sofia remembered how the room was so quiet she could hear the drops of water as they landed onto the surface of the wood table.

Giacomo's Sicilian dialect finally broke the silence that lingered, as he requested, "Silvia, a cup of coffee, please."

Sofia sat quietly beside her father as she mourned her shattered hopes and dreams. She remembered thinking to herself how happy she had felt during that single week.

How she had smiled as she read Luca's letters over and over again in her bedroom.

How her heart raced every time she imagined what her future with Luca might be like.

How she laid awake in her twin-size bed, filled with so much hope and excitement, she could barely sleep.

Now, in contrast, Sofia was sitting there, distraught and miserable, wondering how life could be so cruel to her.

What have I done that was so bad to deserve a man like Max?

A man who had, once again, forced himself into her life like a tornado, destroying every ounce of happiness within her.

As Silvia poured some espresso into a small floral porcelain cup, Giacomo turned to Sofia, and solemnly explained, "Nobody lives to see another day who stands between Max Denaro and whatta he wants."

Perplexed by the pear-shaped diamond that rested on her finger, Sofia earnestly asked, "But why me?"

Giacomo sipped his coffee as he searched for the right words that could possibly soothe his daughter's pain. After a deep exhale, Giacomo simply shook his head as he said, "I don't know. But he has his mind-a made up. There's nothing I can do."

Still lost in confusion, Sofia said, "But I don't even know him."

"Then how did he have your gloves? And whatsa this about you singing at the Book-a-Cadillac?" Giacomo boomed, showing a glimpse of anger.

Without thinking, Sofia defended her innocent decision to help her friend Renie by singing that night, "If I'd had told you,

you wouldn't have let me go."

"And with-a good reason," Giacomo shot back as he slammed his fist on the table.

Sofia felt the instant sting of Papa's valid point. Max had said he wanted her since the moment he laid eyes on her…on stage. She had put herself in harm's way by performing that night. It didn't seem fair, but it was what, in fact, had occurred. All she could do was put her head down in defeat.

Tears streamed down Silvia's mournful face. Sofia could tell Giacomo felt powerless as he turned to his wife and said, "Like I said, there's nothing I could-a do. He wants her. She's been seen with him at some-a gala alone without nobody. Whatta choice do I have?"

The blatant truth of Giacomo's response only made Silvia's tears cascade into her handkerchief even more. Silvia sniffled as she asked her husband, "How soon must she marry him?"

Her question made Giacomo's eyes turn glassy. He had a blank stare as a tiny tear emerged. Trying his best to be the strong patriarch, he fought the urge to cry before he solemnly responded to his wife, "As soon as possible."

Sofia briefly looked up at her parents, but her eyes immediately went back down to the floor. She remembered how guilty she felt for causing her family so much pain. She had lied to them about the night of the grand opening, and now she was in this terrible situation because of it.

Giacomo looked at Sofia's somber face. Her obvious pain shot through his heart like an arrow. He knew what he was about to say was going to hurt his little girl even more. So with his eyes focused on the small floral espresso cup in front of him, Giacomo said as matter-of-factly as he could, "I know this isn't who you wanted."

Sofia shuffled uncomfortably in her chair. That was an understatement.

But Papa continued, "Max Denaro is a wealthy man. He built a new home in Grosse-a-Pointe. A very private property right on the lake. You'll have servants. The best-a schools for your boys."

Sofia's glum expression didn't budge a bit. None of this stuff mattered to her now that she was being forced to marry Max when she really wanted to marry Luca.

Giacomo added, hoping it would somehow help, "And he promised to be-a-good to you."

At that moment, Sofia looked up into her father's eyes. They were filled with anguish. She could tell Max's assurances were the best her father could do to ensure her future happiness at this point. She could also tell he felt emasculated because of it. And it was the very first time Sofia realized her father couldn't protect her from Max.

Like Luca's poor sister, Teresa, Sofia's future was doomed. Her life was now squarely in this dangerous gangster's hands. Sofia remembered how the depressing thought made her immediately burst into tears as she ran to her bedroom.

"That's what Papa said. You promised to be good to me."

Sofia made an extra effort to point out that part of her story to Max, who remained nauseated on the houseboat floor. He had no choice but to listen to his wife's story, whether he liked it or not.

But he was still plotting how to make Sofia pay for her rubbing whatever she had going on with his older brother in his face.

Max's jaw was set squarely in anger as he looked up at her defiant face. He had never met a woman who deserved a good beating more than she. He was determined to make Sofia pay big time.

Meanwhile, Sofia didn't seem too concerned about Max's murderous glare. Instead, she looked as if she was about to spit in his eye as she added, "What a liar you are, Mr. Denaro."

TWENTY-NINE

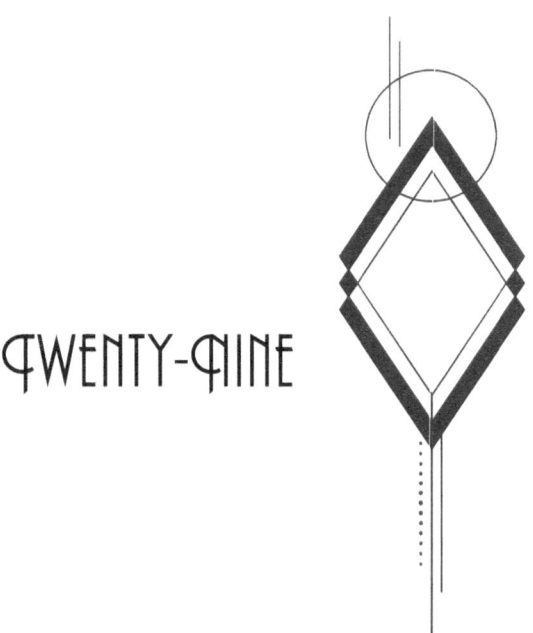

Sofia continued her recollection about what occurred during their wedding night in a very cold fashion, her usual soft warmth nowhere to be seen. She spoke with a calculated precision as she wanted to make sure Max heard every word.

With a steady, hateful glare at her despicable husband, she recalled the 500-plus headcount at their over-the-top Italian wedding reception held within the grand ballroom of Max's new gray stone manor on Lake Shore Drive -- the lake being, of course, the one they were on currently, Lake Saint Clair.

She was amazed at how many people were able to attend, considering the date had only been set less than a week prior to the wedding. But every single invitation sent received an immediate affirmative response. It was as if their guests were also afraid to say "no" like she had been when Max proposed, Sofia mused to herself.

Sofia also remembered how she and her mother planned and arranged every detail of the wedding within that short week. It was a full-time job for both of them - morning, noon, and night - although they were able to spare no expense since Max wanted it to be known as the wedding of the century, so that did make it a little easier to do.

Most brides would have been in heaven. Sofia was not most brides.

But Sofia was grateful to be distracted by the many things that needed to get done in order for the church ceremony to occur that coming Saturday morning, as Max required. Selecting the linens, cake, and menu at least helped keep the dread at bay. She noticed how that terrible feeling seemed to continually rise in her throat. Without her long list of things to do, Sofia would find herself lamenting about how she was going to survive this marriage to a man she didn't love and with his unwanted child on the way. So it was an understatement to say she was very grateful for every distraction that came along with planning an elaborate wedding.

Although Sofia wasn't happy about this marriage, she did everything she could during that week to make sure nobody else knew the truth but her. As far as the neighborhood was concerned, she was madly in love with Max, and she was going to throw the most lavish wedding to prove it.

For instance, Sofia searched every single department store in Detroit for the perfect *bomboniere* to hand out as favors to the guests. She finally had to settle on five different crystal vases with coordinating art deco floral designs; she couldn't find enough of one design in stock and there wasn't enough time for a special order to be delivered.

Sofia had also purchased the most expensive wedding dress she found. She stayed up till all hours sifting through dress catalogues to find the perfect style, and ended up choosing a handmade lace headband encrusted in swirls of tiny pearls and white glass beads. It wrapped around her long sheer veil embroidered delicately throughout with roses that landed just above the floor. She wore a white French lace gown with long, fitted sleeves and a square neckline that matched the beaded texture and opulence of her headband.

Sofia never imagined she would be wearing such an extravagant dress on her wedding day. She had always thought she would wear her mamma's simple white dress from when she married her papa.

Max, however, had forbidden Sofia from wearing what he deemed were her mother's rags to their wedding. He didn't want his beautiful bride to look like some poor old-fashioned immigrant. So Sofia followed his orders as best she could and spent every penny possible on the beautiful masterpiece she was wearing instead.

Although she purposely bought the most expensive of everything in a gleeful effort to upset him over the insane cost of this wedding, Max didn't even blink twice at any of the bills that came across his desk. Rather, he seemed pleased with her ridiculously excessive spending. Sofia determined that Max approved of all the razzle and dazzle, because it was his chance to flaunt his immense wealth and power.

So instead of becoming upset, Max loved that Sofia secured the very best in entertainment out of Black Bottom (besides Princess, of course, because she couldn't perform for the obvious reason of Teresa's attendance). He was thrilled when she booked the most widely acclaimed photographer in Detroit. And he couldn't agree more when she carefully selected to serve only the top-shelf wines smuggled in by his own network.

The dark mahogany walls of the grand ballroom dripped with gorgeous overflowing arrays of white and red gladiolus flowers with soft blush pink Tiffany roses. All were flown in from some exotic country on a rush order especially for the wedding, with such a hefty price tag that Silvia almost fainted.

Yards upon yards of white satin fabric with soft pink ribbon were draped behind the flowers along the walls and on anything else they could find.

Fine silverware and crystal rested upon round tables coated in white linens and topped with bursting white, red, and pink floral arrangements.

Servers wore crisp white jackets that matched their short white gloves as they held polished silver trays filled with wine, prosecco, and canapés. The servers swirled about the extravagantly dressed guests that treated the occasion as if it were the heiress Cornelia Vanderbilt's wedding.

Most of the men wore black silk top hats, including Sally's goons, who traded in their usual fedoras for the ultimate symbol of class and sophistication. Sofia remembered thinking the mobsters looked almost comical as if they were wearing costumes in their garish attempt to be classy.

This was especially true when she and Max made their entrance into their tastefully decorated reception under the tasteless arch of Tommy guns the goons held up for them. It was a detail Max found particularly amusing. Sofia smiled and laughed as she made her way under the terrifying arch pretending to be equally on board with the so-called fun.

Unlike the other men, Max wore a white fedora with a thick black Petersham ribbon and white spats over his shiny, black oxfords so that he could stand out amongst what he called a sea of stuffed penguins. Sofia would have found him handsome if she didn't hate him so much.

But Sofia still tried to focus on the good stuff since there was nothing she could do about the bad. She recalled how much she enjoyed holding her beautiful cascading bridal bouquet. After all, it isn't every day a woman gets to hold a handful of white orchids, roses, and calla lilies, surrounded by luscious ferns and white ostrich feathers. Sofia also loved how the long streams of ribbon in her wedding colors of white, red, and pink flowed down her bouquet. Not only did the flowers have a fragrant perfume she loved to inhale, but they kept her hands occupied, being a good excuse to not have to touch Max.

The five-tiered, white frosted wedding cake had geometric shapes on it, contrasted by the soft curves of flowers made of sugar and pink frosting. The giant cake rested near the long and seemingly never-ending dessert table covered in every Italian cookie ever invented.

The gift table overflowed with beautifully wrapped presents of all different sizes and shapes from the American friends who attended, while the Italian guests followed tradition with gifts of cash, and those were placed in a bursting white satin satchel on a table beside the presents. The satin bag contained so many envelopes stuffed with thick stacks of cash that it looked more like Santa's sack than anything she had ever seen at a wedding before. At one point of the evening, Sofia spotted her parents as they discreetly slipped their thin humble envelope into it.

Knowing her parents well, Sofia could tell that they weren't thrilled, despite the broad smiles they kept permanently on their faces that night. Like her, they didn't want anybody to know exactly how they felt about this marriage. They knew better than to risk Max hearing anything derogatory, which would cause them to lose their ability to see their daughter once he married her.

Sofia also did her best to keep a smile on her face. She knew she needed to keep her new husband happy with her performance as the blushing bride in front of the guests. But in reality, she was pregnant and nauseated and wished she was anywhere but there. Throughout the night, she often wondered if everyone was buying her act. She couldn't find any indication that they weren't.

So everything was going along smoothly until several wedding guests had circled around and started clapping for the bride and groom as Sofia and Max cut the cake hand-in-hand.

Only Luca was solemn as he sat quietly alone in the corner, watching the seemingly happy couple. Sofia always knew exactly where Luca was the entire time. But she would only give her searching gaze a second to register her real love's whereabouts before doing everything she could to return her attention to her husband. Everyone attending needed to believe she was happy to be with Max. Otherwise, it was all too embarrassing to bear for her.

It was bad enough that there were already rumblings around the neighborhood about how she had conveniently dumped the poor brother for the rich one in a week. Nobody had told her this to her face because ever since she became Max's fiancée, nobody could look her in the face. People seemed to tip-toe around her now, even cater to her whims.

It was Silvia who found out about it. From her friend, the reliable old gossip, Mrs. Rossi, who was equally miffed that things didn't work out between Sofia and her lawyer son. She had taken it as a personal insult that Sofia actually chose an uneducated assembly line worker over her learned and handsomely paid son.

Silvia noticed that Mrs. Rossi seemed to relish the thought that Sofia was, in the end, a gold digger. She was happy about it because it at least changed the narrative on how this whole situation reflected upon her Johnny. It was better to have Sofia choose a richer man than a poorer one over him. Everyone can understand that especially with the wealth Max had. Nobody could compete with that.

Knowing that her brief romance with Luca and their brazen public appearances together at church had been the talk of the town, making the rounds in every bible study and sewing circle around, Sofia had wanted to avoid the awkward situation entirely. She didn't plan on inviting Luca to the wedding because he hadn't spoken to Max in more than a decade.

However, Teresa insisted. Max's older sister reasoned that despite the distance he had kept from them since their parents died,

Luca was still their brother and should be invited to something as important as a family wedding. Being isolated in her own mansion, nobody clearly had the guts to gossip to her about the love triangle involving her two brothers. And Sofia certainly wasn't going to be the one to tell Teresa about it.

Max had agreed a little too wholeheartedly with his sister for Sofia's comfort. She could tell something was up with Max and wondered why he really wanted Luca at the wedding. It made her worry that Max somehow found out about the romance that had flared up between them.

At one time, she believed that men were above gossip. But she had since learned about the intricate network of informants Max had throughout the entire city. It now occurred to her that Silvia might not be the only one to have received reports of Luca touching Sofia in church. It also didn't seem like a coincidence that Max showed up, out of the blue, the following Sunday morning, bright and early, to beat Luca in asking for her hand in marriage.

But, whatever the reason, Max didn't seem to pay any mind to his brother being there. Instead, he seemed to be enjoying himself thoroughly from the church wedding ceremony to the ballroom reception afterward at his mansion.

And Max, as usual, was getting a real kick out of himself as the cheering guests encouraged him to act up. One even yelled out, "Give it to her good, Max!"

So he thought it would be hilarious if he crammed a piece of cake in Sofia's mouth. Of course, everyone roared in laughter as she got frosting smeared over her whole face by him.

But she wasn't amused, as she wondered whether she was

going to choke to death on the cake. Sofia didn't even know it was possible to fit that much cake in her mouth.

Rather than being amused, Sofia found it disrespectful, but she had no choice in the matter. She played along, pretending to be a good sport, flicking some of the whipped frosting from her face right at her laughing guests. They roared in response as they jumped back to avoid the splash.

But that's about the time when the fun ended.

THIRTY

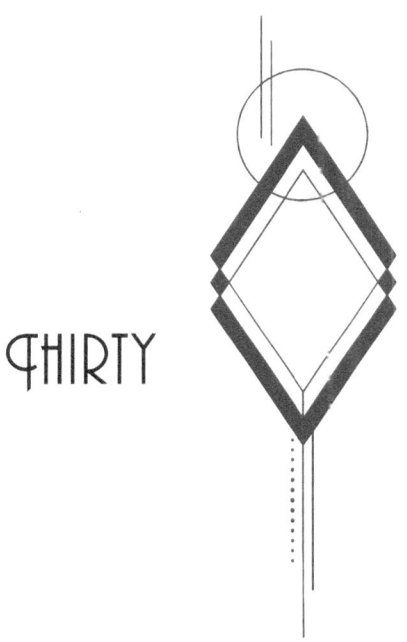

Unfortunately, the mess with the cake had caused her to go clean up. When Sofia finally removed any trace of frosting from her face, she found Luca there in the hallway, alone, right outside the water closet at the back of the house. She had gone to this one specifically to get some privacy away from her guests. There was no reason for him to be back there, so she was genuinely surprised to see him.

"Luca," Sofia said, in almost a whisper, as if she had seen a ghost. Up to this point, he had done his best to avoid her the entire evening.

"Congratulations, Mrs. Denaro."

Sofia had never heard a more melancholy congratulations in her life. But she could empathize with his depressed tone; she was starting to feel a little dead inside, too.

She also ignored how much it hurt to hear her new name out of his mouth, because they didn't have much time to talk before someone would notice they were missing from the celebration. She pounced on her only opportunity to ask, "Why didn't you answer my letters?"

She was referring to the letters she wrote Luca every single day since she last saw him through her family's picture window. She tried to communicate with him, but she couldn't go over to his house without either Giacomo or Max finding out about it. With God only knows how many goons keeping an eye on her, the letters were the best she could do to contact him.

Luca knew precisely what she was talking about, having received every single one of them, and replied to her now, down and brokenhearted, "Were you trying to get us both killed?"

"But we could have run away. I had a plan." Sofia desperately searched Luca's eyes.

Maybe it wasn't too late for the plan?

"Would it even matter?" Luca checked down the hall to make sure nobody was approaching who could overhear what he was about to say next. When he confirmed there was not a soul in sight, he added, looking her directly in the eyes, pleading with her, "Max would have hunted us down and killed us like animals. You hear me? So I burned them. Let's forget it ever happened."

Like everyone else Sofia knew who came up against Max, Luca could see how futile it was to try to fight his brother. Max was a man who would stop at nothing. How does someone win against that?

Not thinking, Sofia threw herself into Luca's arms in desperation. "But you said you loved me," she reminded him.

"You're married to my brother, Sofia."

Sofia didn't know what she was thinking. All she knew was she wanted to be married to Luca. She wanted to be *his* Mrs. Denaro.

So she kissed him. It was their first and only kiss.

She had waited so long to kiss his lips, she was almost as forceful as Max. But it didn't matter, because Luca kissed her back just as passionately.

Once she broke away from him, Sofia said, "We can still run away. We could go to Mexico."

"And do what? I love you. But there's nothing we can do."

There wasn't anything else she could say to change his mind. Luca had already given up in defeat. She knew it because she was now familiar with that look. She had seen that look on Detective Morgan's face. She had next seen that look on Giacomo's face. And now, she could see it clearly on Luca's face. Max had, once again, won victoriously.

Tears brimmed in Sofia's eyes as she embraced Luca close, knowing it would be the last time she would ever get to hold him like this.

"But I love you, too," Sofia said as if that is all that should matter in life.

"What's goin' on here?" Max barked out, demanding to know.

Caught in their close embrace, Luca immediately let go of Sofia at the sound of Max's voice. Luca looked her in the eyes one last time. They knew they were, indeed, in trouble.

Sofia remembered how Max's unexpected baritone struck

her with so much fear, she felt as if she had been electrocuted by lightning. Panicked, she spewed out the first fib that came into her mind, "I was just feeling a little faint...from all the excitement."

Max never appreciated attempts to pull the wool over his eyes. Not only would he take it as a personal stab, he simply didn't have the patience to tolerate it. Not from his squad, not from any guy, and most certainly, not from his new wife. Unfortunately for Sofia, Max was not fooled by her lie in the least.

He pulled Sofia to his side as he glared into her teary eyes and said, "Feelin' faint? I guess that's a likely story comin' from a dame in your condition."

Max then shifted his cold gaze to his older brother, "We was gonna wait until after the weddin' to spread the good news. Sofia is havin' a baby."

Sofia remembered how Luca appeared as if he had been punched in the stomach. The blood drained from his face, and he was then paper white.

Noting Luca's visible shock and disappointment, Max playfully asked, "Surprised?" He gave a maniacal laugh enjoying how much that stung his brother. Max looked down at Sofia and then back at his brother as he added, "Come, Sofia, tell Luca 'bout our first night together. At the Book-Cadillac Hotel's Grand Openin' Gala."

Sofia shifted nervously as she whispered, "Max, you're embarrassing me." She tried to step away from him, but he kept a firm grasp on her.

Taking her by the wrist, making her face Luca head-on, through his gritted teeth, he said, "Luca needs to know how I fucked you the first night I met you."

Sofia tried to hide the pain she was experiencing from Max's tight grasp. "Please, Max, stop."

Luca knew Max was hurting her more than she was letting on. He had seen him hurt many people, but never the woman he loved. He wanted to knock Max right on his ass, but he knew that about forty goons would appear out of nowhere and beat him to death if he did.

Instead, he attempted to calm his hot-headed younger brother, who seethed like a feral beast. Luca raised his hands in the air as a sign of surrender and pleaded, "Massimo, you don't need to do this. I got the message. Sofia is yours."

With his chest puffed out and his eyes as dark as the waters of Lake Saint Clair, Max scowled at Luca as he questioned him combatively, "Yes, she is mine, but now I need to know... Was she ever yours?"

Sofia's blood boiled. She quickly defended Luca and her reputation as she snapped back, "It's not like that! Dirty and wrong, like you."

Luca's eyes darted over to Sofia. It was a dire look of warning, reminding her of how dangerous a person they were actually dealing with. And it also reminded her of when her father, Giacomo, had done the same. She instantly knew to stay quiet.

Luca knew from experience the more information you gave guys like Max, the easier it would be for him to snap and become enraged. Working on the line with all sorts of guys had taught him a thing or two about defusing an escalating situation with hotheads. So he kept it simple. Luca calmly stated, "I only know

Sofia from church."

Max snapped like a vicious wolverine. He grabbed Luca by the lapel and banged him against the wall. Spit flew into Luca's face as he snarled, "Don't fuckin' lie to me! I invited you here outta brotherly love, and this is how you repay me?"

Sofia attempted to pry Max away from Luca as she pleaded, "Please, Max. Let him go!"

Max easily brushed her away with his elbow as if she were a mere housefly. Sofia crashed to the floor, hurting her forearm. He ignored her cries and focused on the words that came out of his big brother's mouth, "I didn't know there was room for love in your line of work."

Max retorted back to Luca, "What choice did I have, my dear brother? I couldn't run away like you did."

Then Max stared down at the whimpering Sofia, as she rubbed her injured arm, utterly disgusted by her behavior with his brother, and then returned his murderous glare to Luca. Warning him, Max said through gritted teeth, "But I hope my bride wasn't the only person you were hopin' to speak with tonight and that ya had the decency to say hello to our sister."

Sofia helplessly watched as the two brothers continued to fight in the middle of the hallway on what was supposed to be one of the happiest days of her life. So much for fucking fairytales, she thought.

Luca shook his head as he earnestly told his younger brother, "You are such a disappointment."

Max deflected his brother's statement, and quickly threatened, "Yeah, if this kid comes out lookin' like your scrappy ass and not mine, you're not gonna be the only one that's disappointed. But you're the only one that's gonna be dead."

Knowing that both their lives were at stake, Luca assured, "We only attended church together. I swear on our mother's grave."

Max released his grip on Luca. As he straightened out his suit sleeves, he responded in such a menacing tone it made the hair on the back of Sofia's neck rise, "Good. Now get the fuck outta here."

Luca didn't dare look at Sofia, although her eyes couldn't help but search for one last glance before he left her forever. Max noticed and pulled her behind him to block her view as he waited for Luca's departure.

To both their surprise, Luca hesitated and turned to look Max right in the eye and said, "I'm not the only one. Papa would have been disappointed, too."

Nobody had ever had the guts to say such a thing to Max, and he was caught off guard by his brother's brutal honesty. His eyes opened wide at the sting it caused. He thought about punching Luca in the face. But for some strange reason, he didn't do it. He just stood there, staring at him, frozen.

Because what Luca said was true, and Max knew it.

Luca decided it was best not to push his luck any further by sticking around. He nodded his hat respectfully toward Sofia, although he didn't dare look her in the face. Then he left swiftly for the front door before Max could call his goons on him.

Sofia remembered wiping the tears from her eyes, wishing she could leave with Luca. But she had no choice. She had to stay behind with her new husband.

As if concerned she would somehow sneak out of the place,

Max kept Sofia by his side for the rest of the evening. If she even took a step away, his arm would guide her right back next to him. But he seemed to be his usual smooth-talking self as he continued charming guests at the celebration.

Sofia also did her best to get that wide smile back on her face and to resume her performance as the happy bride. Meanwhile, she kept a careful eye on Max, wondering how much he had heard and seen in the hallway. She was scared to death that he heard her tell Luca that she loved him. But she did everything she could not to show it, just in case Max hadn't heard much at all.

It wasn't long before the guests were saying their goodbyes and heading home. Sofia could tell that they were in awe by the grandeur they had witnessed that night. Everyone treated Max with the utmost respect as if he had performed miracles before their eyes that evening, like turning water to wine. As the biggest players in town shook his hand, enthusiastically pumping it up and down, congratulating him one more time before their departures, they bowed their heads like they were nothing but his humble servants.

Sofia recalled how just after midnight, the butler held the formidable wood door for their last remaining wedding guests, Silvia and Giacomo, in the foyer of the grand stone manor.

Silvia had hugged Max goodbye, and then she hugged Sofia tightly like she was never going to let her go. She was fighting back tears. All she could say without crying, "It was a beautiful wedding."

"It was," Sofia agreed softly. She smiled at her mother, now attempting to assure her worried face that she was going to be alright living with Max.

Silvia finally acquiesced despite her concerns and even managed to smile back as she pushed up Sofia's chin. She really hoped for the best for her daughter, although Silvia knew this wasn't going to be it.

Giacomo then interjected, "Don't forget to visit us."

Sofia turned her attention toward her father. She warmly stroked Giacomo's beard as she replied, "Of course, Papa." She gave him a loving peck on the cheek like she has done since she was a little girl, and he hugged her tightly as well.

Once he was able to let her go, Giacomo turned to Max and said, "Take-a-care of my little girl."

Max quickly retorted, "She'll get everythin' she deserves."

They each took one last look at Sofia, trying now to reassure her with forced smiles despite their own brewing concerns for her safety. Finally, there wasn't anything else Giacomo and Silvia could do but accept it was time to leave and they solemnly departed out the front door.

Once the heavy door closed behind them, Max then turned his attention to his bride and gestured up to the grand staircase. "Let me show ya to our bedroom."

Sofia knew this time would come, and she swallowed thickly in apprehension, wishing she could have just left with her parents out the door. She didn't know how to act at the moment.

But just when Sofia thought things couldn't get worse, things actually did.

Max suddenly kicked her in the behind just hard enough that she knew he wasn't being playful. It caused her to stumble toward the stairs, where she barely caught her balance in her t-strap heels.

Max then grabbed her by the hair and proceeded to pull her up the staircase. Controlling her by the chunk of hair in his large hand, he pushed her head down, forcing her to bend over, and crawl up the stairs. As he dragged her, she screamed in pain and tried to claw at his hand to break his grasp.

When that didn't work, Sofia tried to punch his hand to get him to release her. If any of her blows landed on him, Max just responded by kicking her ass twice as hard. He even kicked her in the stomach once, knocking the wind out of her. It was as if he couldn't care less about the baby, or Sofia's life, for that matter.

Her efforts to get away from him were to no avail. Max easily held her head down as he took confident strides, pulling her like a wild dog as he went upstairs.

Sofia's last view before being thrown down on the floor at the top of the stairs was of the butler still standing at the door below. She saw him shudder at the sight of her abuse. But despite her cries for help, the butler didn't even attempt to get involved in a private, domestic dispute, especially concerning his boss, the ruthless Max Denaro. He merely walked away to help with the cleanup in the ballroom.

As Max shoved Sofia by her hair into the newlyweds' master bedroom, he demanded, "What happened between you two?"

As Sofia tumbled onto the pristinely polished hardwood floor, in her elegant wedding gown, she thought to herself of all the times she ever imagined being carried over the threshold, not once did it involve getting shoved into the room headfirst by her veil.

Sofia heard Max slam the giant mahogany French door behind them as she desperately struggled to regain her footing. She didn't know exactly what to do or where to go, but she felt with every fiber of her being that she needed to run away from her husband as fast as her feet could carry her. Terror pulsated through her body as she continually tripped on her wedding dress and veil that had awkwardly wrapped around her during the fall.

As soon as Sofia was able to regain her stance, she felt Max's tight grasp wrap around her tiny arm. He twirled her around and slapped her across the face, as he scolded, "Take care of my little girl. I wonder if dear old Papa knows what a whore his little girl really is."

Sofia placed her hand onto her cheek to relieve the stinging sensation left behind from Max's blow. Tears welled in her eyes as she whimpered, "It was nothing, Max. Really."

Without hesitation, Max whacked Sofia, again and again, across her face, "I want to know if I need to give ya somethin' to cry about. What's goin' on with you and my brother?"

Sofia recalled how her sight briefly went black before she saw purple and green spots swirl about in the air as Max's furious face came back into view. His cheeks were red and his eyes wide with rage as she pleaded, "Please, Max! I've only been with you. I swear the baby is yours."

Max grabbed Sofia by her arm and pulled her toward the bed. She lost her balance and fell to the ground. As he kicked her while she was down, he warned, "It better be. Because if it's not, I'm gonna fucking kill you."

She attempted to defend herself by flailing her arms and legs, but Max easily absorbed her strikes as he began to drag her across the floor. Sofia remembered how she was fearful that Max would end up pulling her shoulder from its socket.

"If anythin' happens to my baby… If you try anything, I'm gonna fucking kill you," Max threatened as he grabbed the skirt of Sofia's wedding dress with his free hand and threw her onto the bed. She remembered hearing the sound of her silk chiffon and lace dress rip.

"You are my wife," Max reminded her, but it came out as a barked order. "And it's death do us part."

All Sofia could think to do was nod apprehensively, and all that did was anger Max beyond belief. He took it as an insult that she wasn't more enthusiastic about spending the rest of her life with him. His entire face was now a bright crimson red as he pulled Sofia to him by her dress. It ripped in response to his violent tug, which gave him the idea to rip the entire thing to shreds.

Her whole body was aching from the thorough beating she just received, so Sofia could no longer fight. Instead, she whimpered in agreement, "I know, Max, I know."

"You are mine. Ya follow me? This kid…" Max punched Sofia in the stomach just in case she didn't know which kid he was referring to, causing her to gasp out in pain. "Betta be mine!"

"The baby is yours! Please, Max!" Sofia cried out, begging for mercy as soon as she could catch her breath.

Then he placed his mouth next to her ear and said in a very slow, calculated fashion so she could never ever pretend she didn't hear every single word he uttered to her. "You say so much as one word to my brother, and he's finished, ya got that? It'll be all your fault."

"Whatever you say, Max. But please, stop!" Sofia's tears were streaming down her bruised and bleeding face. Pain was emanating from her entire body like steam rising from the lake at dusk. But she still managed to flinch when his response was to pull her closer to him. Having torn her dress open, he easily ripped her lace underwear off, too.

She was naked before him. Although she desperately wanted to run away, to fight him off, or even to protest, she couldn't attempt to stop him. Sofia knew it would do no good. She was only able to wait there, defenseless, as she quietly sobbed.

But Max had no sympathy for her. "You did this. This was your fault," was what he said as he pinned her down and entered her body. This was part of her punishment.

She felt like she may throw up, but she focused on breathing as steadily as she could with his crushing weight on top of her. With every grind he made inside her, she felt a jolt of pain as if he was using a knife to do the deed instead. She grimaced as she endured the relentless violation of her body. Sofia could only pray it wouldn't last much longer.

Then to her surprise, Max whispered in her ear, "You think ya love that sap, Luca. He's nothin' but a cog for Ford like all the other cogs in Detroit. You'll see what ya got here one day, and I'll hear ya say to me the words I heard ya say to him. I love you."

Fear shot through Sofia like a lightning rod. Her face froze with her chin dropped as she realized that Max did, in fact, overhear her declaration of love for Luca.

QHIRTY-ONE

As she ended her story, she drifted off for a moment, gazing out blankly to nothing but pitch-black darkness surrounding the houseboat. Since that dark night, she had pushed the painful memory to the back of her mind, focusing instead on creating and executing the plan at hand.

But now recalling what Max had done to her on her wedding night gave her renewed strength to finally confront him, as she planned to do. So with a deep, brave breath, Sofia returned her attention to him when she remarked, "I'll get everything I deserve, huh?"

Max could tell Sofia was angry, although this was the first time he had ever seen that emotion on her. He looked over at his gun on the table in case he needed it to put her in her place.

"So...I guess I deserve you?" Sofia added sarcastically. "What did I ever do to deserve you?"

According to Max, if any woman ever deserved a good beating, it was Sofia on their wedding night. Despite her sad rendition of it, he had no regrets about what he did. If anything, everything she had just admitted to him about her romance with his brother convinced him that she should actually have gotten worse.

Max couldn't believe she dared to question his actions. "What did ya think you were gonna get? I caught ya with my brother."

With a sardonic smile, Sofia stood tall and confident as she replied, "You misunderstand, Max. I'm happy you gave me the beating I so desperately deserved!"

Her mocking had gone far enough for Max. He now felt a good pistol whipping was what this mouthy bitch needed. He lunged for his gun, but he was still dizzy when he rose. His knees felt stiff, and he fell to the floor like a tree sawed in half. His reaction time was so slow, he barely was able to catch his fall. Realizing something was really wrong with him, he demanded to know, "What did ya do to me?"

Sofia ignored his question. Tonight, she was following her own agenda. She continued where she had left off in the conversation without missing a beat. "You want to know why I'm so happy you did it?"

She looked directly into Max's eyes, who frankly didn't care an ounce. He was far more concerned about his own symptoms as he tried to rise from the floor.

But Sofia didn't care about what he wanted to hear, either. She merely continued as she originally intended and added, "Because that night, you freed me."

THIRTY-TWO

The grandfather clock in the corner had just struck two.

Even though Sofia's eyes had adjusted to the darkness, she still couldn't make out much in the unfamiliar bedroom. It was pitch black because the heavy drapes were drawn shut.

Sofia hadn't moved an inch since Max finished and rolled off of her. She feared waking him as she lay in bed, listening to his snoring for over an hour. Sofia just breathed as softly as she could, trying to avoid the sharp jab she felt with every inhale. She pondered whether there was a square inch of her body that wasn't experiencing the most pain she had ever endured.

When she felt confident that Max wouldn't wake up, Sofia slowly crawled out of bed, wearing nothing more than a bed sheet wrapped around her. Her body ached with every movement she made, and she wished she could just stay in bed and never move ever again. However, Sofia felt like she may finally throw up. She felt sick to her stomach at the very least and she needed to find the master bathroom, just in case.

Once on her feet, she felt a little dizzy, but she did her best to tip-toe slowly in the dark. One hand holding the bed sheet, the other hand out in front of her to help feel her way around.

She could make out a door across the room that she guessed was the water closet. As she took each careful, achy step, she stopped to make sure the rhythm of Max's sound snoring didn't change. Luckily for her, the path straight to it was free of any obstacles for her to bump into in the dark, although she could hear her heart pounding in her ears the entire way.

When Sofia was finally at the door, she heard Max snort loudly, and she froze, feeling the fear vibrate throughout her entire body.

Was he awake?!

She didn't know if her punishment was done, according to him. All she knew was she couldn't survive another beating like that. So she was not going to take any chances by waking him.

She couldn't believe she had been careless enough to hug Luca like that when anybody could have walked in on them. But it was like she had been possessed.

Love made her do it.

But Sofia had just paid the ultimate price for her rash judgment. Or almost the ultimate price because she was still alive, and Max could have easily killed her.

When she finally determined that Max had only turned over on his side and continued snoring away, Sofia turned the knob to open the door as slowly and quietly as possible. She stepped inside, closing the door carefully behind her. She didn't make a sound.

She flipped on the electric switch next to the door, and the bulbs buzzed to life, showing off the grandest master bathroom she had ever seen. Floor to ceiling Carrera marble with gold-gilded mirrors, faucets, and accents throughout. But she wasn't tempted by it. She couldn't enjoy its opulence for even a second.

Instead, Sofia instantly crouched over in pain. She bit down on her own hand to keep from yelling out. She managed to stumble over to the sink, barely making it.

Sofia looked at her reflection in the mirror and discovered she looked pale, sweaty, and sickly. Dried blood was peeking out from her nose and there was some along her hairline.

But before she could do anything to clean herself up, Sofia felt a jab of pain striking through her. She crouched over, hoping it would help it go away, and then fell to the floor when her legs gave out from underneath her.

As she lay on the cool marble floor, all she could remember was the whole room swirling around her until nothing but blackness engulfed her.

Then she heard the sound of the grandfather clock booming four strikes, causing her eyes to pop back open in fear.

Where was Max?!

Disoriented from fainting, Sofia had found herself on the floor with the bed sheet still loosely wrapped around her.

With the last crash of the striking clock, Sofia sat up and noticed a large bloodstain on the bed sheet. She opened it to investigate and discovered her thighs splattered with blood. She managed to lift her body from the floor to find she was lying in a red pool.

She took a deep, stabbing breath with her eyes closed. She still felt the throbbing pain throughout her body, but one thing she no longer felt was nausea. She had been perpetually sick to her stomach for more than three weeks and throughout the whole wedding reception. Now, she felt nothing but the worst abdominal cramps ever.

Sofia concluded she must have miscarried the baby. She wasn't surprised by this, considering everything that Max had just done to her.

But she was still fearful of Max's reaction. She vividly recalled how he had, in the most menacing tone, threatened her life if anything happened to the baby. It terrified Sofia.

Still wrapped in nothing but the bloody bed sheet, Sofia made her way back down the grand staircase. She tried not to whimper with every cautious step she took down the stairs. Since her body was weak and shaky, she leaned heavily on the banister for support until she finally entered the foyer.

She came upon the bureau by the front entrance and began rummaging through it. Her hands brushed past loose papers and writing utensils. Nothing useful to her.

Then Sofia came upon a letter opener. For a brief moment, she was filled with hope, but it quickly dissipated when she decided it wouldn't work and returned it to the drawer.

As Sofia searched in the darkness of her new home, she felt as if she was stuck inside a haunted house. Its high ceilings overwhelmed her, and the dark carved wood looked eerie inside the ornately decorated home filled with taxidermy and hunting rifles hanging throughout. It was the type of place where a ghost would surely live. The thought made Sofia shudder.

But then she couldn't help but smile a little at the thought of haunting Max, concluding she would surely haunt him when she ended up dying there herself. At the time, that seemed the only way she could get him back for everything he had done to her.

Sofia moved onto the nearby den. A stately wood desk faced an equally large picture window, letting in an expansive view of the moon hanging low over the dark and peaceful lake.

She headed straight toward the desk, fumbling through the drawers, one after another, until she found only a pair of scissors. She held them in her hands contemplating whether they would serve her purpose. She considered continuing to the kitchen, which made her wince, anticipating each additional agonizing step it would require. She figured they would work just as well as a knife anyway.

At that moment, all she could think about was ending her suffering. She'd rather kill herself than let him kill her.

Sofia raised the scissors ready to surge them into her heart when the blade reflected the moonlight streaming in. The flash of light caused her to gaze over at the large picture window, as she found herself compelled to walk over to it.

Instinctively, she began to softly sing that same bible hymn from her audition with Princess. It seemed to soothe her current heartache, although it made her wish she could go back to being that girl at that audition, singing her heart out.

But Sofia knew that girl no longer existed. She had seen too much since then.

As she sang, Sofia remembered how beautiful the dark water looked below, sparkling in the moonlight as if the lake were made of diamonds.

She then noticed how the moon hung low above Lake Saint Clair, much like it did the night Max raped her at the Book-Cadillac Hotel. She hated that word. Rape. She wondered if there would ever be a time when she could look at the moon and no longer think of that terrible word.

Sofia stopped her song when she sensed some movement out near the shoreline. She peered intensely out the window, wondering what it could be at this early hour. Her eyes then spotted a majestic buck suddenly appearing out of the woods. The sight of him made her lower the scissors to her side.

He was grand with his tall rack of antlers, and seemed to acknowledge her when he looked up and returned her gaze. The mighty buck was a sign.

After a silent moment observing his large, powerful body walk toward the lake's edge and peacefully take a gentle sip, Sofia decided there wasn't any time to waste.

She made her way back into the master bathroom where she turned on the hot water in the large slipper bathtub. As Sofia waited for the water level to rise, she hobbled over to look at her reflection in the mirror again.

She looked like she had been to war. And she needed to do something that would help her forget it. She desperately wanted to be a different person. A woman that wasn't the perfect victim.

She glanced down at where she had set the scissors, and an idea struck her. She didn't think twice about it and began to cut away her wavy locks. As each long strand of hair fell to the floor, Sofia stood a little taller, like a stronger woman. The type of woman that didn't allow anybody, even Max Denaro, to disrespect her.

When she was done, she admired her short bob in the mirror. She actually liked the new look on her and tried to smile, although her sore jaw wouldn't allow more than a small smirk.

Now it was time to get rid of the blood that had splattered and dried throughout her. She looked forward to the metallic smell in her nose to soon be gone. She slowly lowered her throbbing body into the bathtub filled to the brim with hot water. But she had to be fast since her continued bleeding was making the water pink.

Newly bathed, Sofia grabbed a white terry cloth robe. Having no idea where her trunk of clothes was placed once it was delivered the morning of the wedding, Sofia had no choice but to use a towel to diaper herself due to the blood that flowed between her legs.

There was also the red pool remaining on the bathroom floor. Sofia took the bed sheet that was wrapped around her earlier and wiped up the blood with it until there was no trace of her injuries on the pristine bluish-white marble.

She managed to find the laundry room, which was logically off to the side of the kitchen downstairs. Sofia pulled the string on the lone light bulb above. Once illuminated, she was able to see a big wash basin standing in the corner.

She immediately threw in the bed sheet and turned on the cold water faucet. She grabbed the large bar of laundry soap and scrubbed as best she could in her pain. She desperately needed to get rid of all the evidence, fearing what Max's reaction would be to her losing the baby.

Sofia scrubbed and scrubbed until the housemaid, Marta, entered surprised to find her there. She declared, "Mrs. Denaro, what are you doing up at this hour? It's five o'clock in the morning!"

Sofia was startled by Marta's entrance. She still had to get used to the idea of having servants in her home at all hours. Sofia answered, "I'm sorry. I just wanted…"

"Mr. Denaro will have my neck if he sees his new bride scrubbing bed sheets."

Sofia could hear the high anxiety in the housemaid's voice and knew too well that it was warranted. She wasn't about to argue with her.

She kept her head down to hide her injuries as she let Marta scoot her to the side so she could continue scrubbing the bed sheet instead.

The housemaid assumed Sofia's inability to make eye contact was due to modesty and said, "There is nothing to be embarrassed about, missus. Every woman has her wedding night."

Luckily for Sofia, she had had enough time to wash most of the blood out of the sheet before Marta took over the job. Sofia understood that to the housemaid, it looked as if she was witnessing the amount of blood that usually occurred when a woman loses her virginity.

Sofia softly asked her for reassurance, "So you won't mention any of this to Mr. Denaro?"

"I was hoping you would do the same," Marta replied earnestly as she began to rinse the bed sheet clean.

"Of course. Thank you," Sofia replied with her head still hung low.

The housemaid didn't look up from the task at hand as she responded frankly, "My wages are thank you enough. Now get to bed. I'll have the cook send up breakfast in a few hours."

Sofia didn't have to be told twice. She exited as quickly as her battered body let her. There had been so much blood to clean, she had lost track of time and wanted to get back into bed before Max woke up. She worried she may already be too late.

She staggered up the grand staircase and back into the dark master bedroom, where she was met with the sound of Max snoring. Exhausted beyond belief, Sofia crawled back into bed and finally fell asleep until there was a knock on the door.

Sofia could hear the knocking as if it were happening far, far away down a long tunnel. She was still in a deep sleep, having gone to bed only a few hours prior.

She then heard the bedroom door open. For a brief moment, she thought her mother was waking her for school like she did every morning, until Sofia had to quit school to get married and have a baby.

But when she heard the mild clanking of a breakfast tray as someone hobbled over to set it down on a table near the bedroom window, she quickly recalled with dread that she was in Max's bed. At the sound of the servant's entrance, Sofia remembered that it was the old cook bringing up her breakfast, as promised.

As Sofia began to register her surroundings, she listened intently and noticed that Max's loud rhythmic snoring had stopped.

As far as she could tell without daring to open her eyes, he was no longer next to her. Otherwise, Sofia would have kept her eyes shut to this nightmare for as long as humanly possible.

As the old cook, Catalda, arranged the utensils neatly next to her plate, Sofia felt it was safe to finally stir in bed.

Catalda politely said, "I'm-a sorry I woke you, Mrs. Denaro."

Sofia sat up on her elbows in bed and took note that the rumpled spot next to her was, in fact, empty. "Where's Mr. Denaro?"

The cook pulled back the drapes allowing in the gray Michigan daylight as she responded, "Mr. Denaro said he had-a business to do. He said not-a to wake you, because you needed your rest."

Sofia blocked her face and turned away from the light. She squinted and pretended that the soft haze drifting through the cloud covered sky was far too bright for her eyes. In reality, she just didn't want Catalda to see the bruises forming on her face. She needed to get her out of the room before she noticed her wounds. Sofia quickly agreed, "Yes, Mr. Denaro is absolutely right. I am exhausted. Barely slept a wink this past week. I'll be in bed for the rest of the day."

Catalda approached to pick up Sofia's wedding dress that lay in a heap on the floor beside the bed. Not expecting the shredded rags that remained of it, the old cook let out a, "Oh, dear."

"Mr. Denaro has no patience for buttons," Sofia explained. Not wanting the woman to get a closer look, Sofia rolled over and away from her as she added, "Please draw the drapes shut."

Following orders, Catalda immediately made the room pitch black again. As the old cook hobbled back toward the door, Sofia raised her head once more from her pillow and asked curiously,

"Did he say when he'd be back tonight?"

"Tonight? Oh, no, missus, Mr. Denaro won't be back until Friday."

"He's not coming home for a week?" Sofia didn't know whether she should be relieved or offended by the fact he had left her alone for that long.

"You know he stays in-a Detroit to work?" Catalda asked.

Sofia rolled onto her back in bed and stared blankly at the dark ceiling above. She was relieved that Max had left while she was sleeping. She also took a silent moment to rejoice that she wouldn't have to see him for a whole week. She could heal in peace.

But she knew she needed Catalda to think that she was having the opposite reaction. For all Sofia knew, the old cook was one of Max's many informants. Sofia was young, but she was smart enough to know that she could no longer trust anybody, except for her family.

So she acted like she was sad that her new husband was already back to work on a Sunday, no less, and replied with a sigh, "No, I know. At the Book-Cadillac. I thought that might change now…"

Catalda took her opportunity to share years of experience with the newlywed before she made her final exit from the room. She responded earnestly, "I've been married for over forty years, and I promise you one-a thing, missus. Men-a-never change."

Catalda's words of wisdom stung Sofia.

That meant only one thing to her. Last night would be the first of many over the lifetime of her marriage with Max. That's if she didn't end up like Renie, over this miscarriage.

But once Catalda closed the door behind her, and Sofia was finally alone, the only thing she knew to do about it now was to get out of bed to eat her breakfast. Sofia dragged the drapes open, allowing the light in as before. This time no squinting necessary.

As she sat at the table to eat, she solemnly stared out the nearby window, watching the dark storm clouds forming in the sky. Interestingly, her mind felt like it was doing the same.

Sofia thought about how she would use the upcoming week to lay low, heal her wounds, and gather the strength she needed to put her hunt together. She definitely had learned the harsh lesson that if she didn't take care of herself, nobody else would do it for her.

This is when Sofia finally decided to take matters into her own hands.

THIRTY-THREE

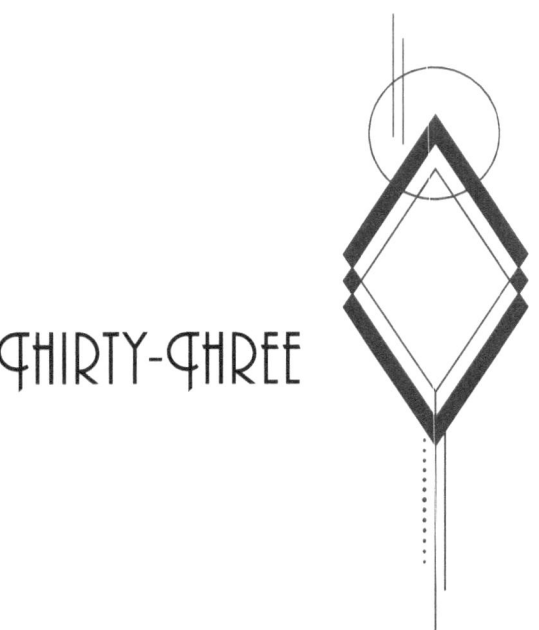

"So what business needed to be attended to the very next day? On a Sunday, no less," Sofia confronted her husband on the houseboat during their so-called romantic boat ride.

Despite his drunken stupor, Max managed to grab the gun off the dinner table, and he now aimed it at Sofia.

As if she were suicidal, she didn't seem to be concerned about it. Instead, she continued to taunt Max for an answer, "What was so urgent that you had to leave your new bashed-in-bride for?"

"You have some nerve questionin' me. I ought to pop ya one," Max threatened. He gave the gun a good shake, just in case she didn't believe him.

"You'd bump off your own wife?" Sofia feigned being surprised by his threat before she added sarcastically, "That old cook was right. Men rarely change. And if you were willing to bump off your own brother--"

Max cut her off, declaring, "Your precious Luca tripped. It was an unlucky accident at the Ford Highland Plant. They happen every day. Ask ya dear old papa, if you don't believe me. He told me he saw it happen with his own eyes."

Sofia rolled her eyes and spouted back, "What else is Papa going to tell me after what you did to him? After you threatened him..."

Max recalled how he slammed Giacomo's face down onto the formal dining table and placed his loaded gun to his temple. He was angry because the old man had the guts to say no to him when he initially asked for Sofia's hand in marriage.

He remembered making his next pitch, "Think 'bout this, Mr. Spera. Who's gonna stop me from marryin' her when you're dead?" Max then cocked back the gun just in case the old man didn't believe him.

Giacomo didn't know what to say in response to that, but Max could tell he was scared out of his wits.

Then it started to occur to Max that this really wasn't the best way to begin his relationship with his future father-in-law. He realized that he needed this guy on his side and shouldn't have let his anger get the best of him. So he decided to let up. Slowly de-cocking the gun, he put it carefully back in his pocket and then helped Giacomo sit back up in his seat.

As if to signify a fresh start between them, he offered his hand for a friendly handshake. He made his final pitch for Sofia's hand, "So whattaya say, Mr. Spera?"

Frightened, Giacomo quickly touched the smarting cheek

that had just been smashed onto the tabletop before he solemnly nodded in agreement.

"Come on. That's not the warmest welcome to the family."

Max recalled how badly Giacomo stuttered as he finally spit out, "Yes, of-a course, you have my blessing to marry Sofia."

To Giacomo's surprise, Max hugged him and replied with a satisfied grin, "Ya have no idea how much this means to me... Papa."

As Sofia now stared down the barrel of his gun, Max couldn't help but conclude he had been such a sap. He had no idea at the time of his proposal how much trouble this woman would end up causing him. For the first time ever, he wished he had never laid eyes on Sofia that night at the grand opening.

She stood in her dark mink coat, shoulders back defiantly, as she questioned Max, "You want me to believe Luca died at Highland, on the line, in some freak accident, the very next night after our wedding? The night after I declared my love for him?"

Max still flinched in response. Even after everything Sofia had just confessed since arriving on the boat, it continued to bother him that his wife had told his own brother she loved him on their wedding day. It deeply offended his manhood.

But Sofia no longer seemed to care about Max's manhood or the sense of entitlement that came along with it when she coldly added, "Fuck you, Max. I'm not as dumb as you need me to be."

Max lifted the gun higher firmly aiming for Sofia's head. "Who knows? Maybe that sap killed himself at the thought of his precious love carryin' the baby of the brother he despised?"

Sofia didn't even wince in response to his new deadly target.

Instead, she spouted back with as much vitriol as she could muster, "Despised? I think it was the word disappointment that Luca used. So did you kill him because he was *disappointed* in you?"

Sofia took a step closer to Max, making it a little easier for his aim. She added, "Or was it because you kill everyone I love?"

Max had just endured an entire evening of his wife's blubbering stories, and he now felt the need to give her a taste of her own medicine. So he cheerfully declared like a mad man, "Ya lookin' for a confession? Fine. Have it your way."

CHIRTY-COUR

As usual, the desk lamp provided dim lighting while the out-skirts of the room remained camouflaged by darkness. Max did his best to focus on the newspaper as he sat at his desk in the penthouse at the Book-Cadillac Hotel. But no matter how hard he tried, he couldn't push the image of his bride in his brother's arms out of his mind.

There was one solid knock at the hotel door alerting the anticipated arrival of his requested guest. Max could then hear Bambi's key jiggling in the lock until the door opened, causing him to look up from the one particular news article he had repeatedly tried to read in its entirety.

"Everythin' alright, Max?" Fred Moore anxiously asked upon entering the dimly-lit room.

Nothing was alright, but his life was none of this cog's concern, Max thought to himself. He remembered the apprehension in Fred's voice at not knowing why he had been summoned there early on a Sunday morning. But Max, as usual, had no desire to relieve the Irishman's tension. After all, causing that tension was his goal.

Instead, Max gazed at the assembly line worker with a pensive stare from above his *Detroit Free Press* sprawled before him. He squinted at Fred, assessing him one last time to make a final determination as to whether his last-minute plan would work with this amateur in front of him at the helm.

Feeling nervous by Max's silence, Fred carefully approached him as he jabbered on to fill the air, "Bambino says you needed to talk to me. I thought we were doin' good? There hasn't been any more problems, has there, Max? I thought everythin' was workin' like a charm, really, Max. You're a genius, really."

Max ignored Fred's flattering remarks. He certainly didn't care what this jobbie thought about him or his ideas. The only opinion that mattered to Max was his own. So, in response, he merely gestured for Fred to take a seat at one of the two gold-gilded armchairs in front of his desk.

Max knew he didn't have much time to execute the plan that he just devised on his drive over from Grosse Pointe to Detroit that very morning. So he quickly made up his mind. He concluded that his gut had been right to call in Fred on this job because he was his only choice if he wanted to get it done undetected.

Without another moment's hesitation, Max continued with the purpose at hand for this surprise visit. He replied matter-of-factly by referring to the article that sparked his current idea. "It says here…" Max began to read directly from the newspaper print. "The Ford Motor Company Highland plant recorded 192 severed fingers, 68,000 lacerations, 5,400 burns, and 2,600 puncture wounds this year alone."

Uneasy about where this conversation could possibly be going, Fred remarked as he took a seat, "It's a tough job workin' the line, it is. Pays good, but tough."

But then Max curiously asked with a raised eyebrow, "But how many die?"

Fred's back straightened up stiff; now on alert, his eyes started to dart back and forth toward each of the dark recesses of the room.

Max could see the fear that was instantly visible across this working man's worn and weathered face at the mere thought of where this question could possibly lead. He could tell Fred was trying to see if there was one of the Scalici Squad lurking somewhere in the darkness, waiting silently to snuff him out while they first nonchalantly discussed what could easily end up being the cover-up for it. Max was well aware that Fred knew he was sick enough to do such a thing…to torture a guy with planning the alibi for his own murder before he had to face his untimely death.

Max's deadly reputation amongst his fellow Detroiters was the sort of thing he was especially proud of because he had worked hard over the years to build it. Nobody dared fuck with him.

But unbeknownst to Fred, it was important to Max that there were no witnesses to this present meeting. So much so, Max lied for the first time to Bambi, the man he trusted completely to protect his life, about the reason he asked for Fred's presence there that morning. He said he needed to question Freddy again about that lost shipment back in December but in private. Bambi was to stand guard out in the hallway.

"Oh, I don't know exactly how many die, but it happens from time to time," Fred finally responded.

Max rose from his leather desk chair and then sat down on the end of his desktop closer to Fred. Despite the dark subject matter, he acted as if they were having a friendly discussion about something utterly benign like a Tiger ballgame. He answered, "From what I hear, accidents happen all the time on the line."

Max could tell that Fred was taking some time to consider whether to agree with his assessment of the Ford Motor Company's workplace dangers. But not having the guts to disagree with this temperamental man who probably murdered more than the assembly line ever did, Fred swallowed hard and then added, "Yeah, I guess ya can say that."

"I need ya to do me a favor, Freddy."

Now knowing his own skin was safe, Fred had let out a sigh of relief without thinking. For a brief moment, this novice even relaxed back in his chair.

Meanwhile, Max had pulled out his flask from his pocket and took a big swig, still bothered by what he had witnessed the night before between his slut wife and back-stabbing brother. If there was ever a time he needed to drink, it was this morning.

He also felt uneasy about this particular job. Although he never felt more convinced that someone deserved what he had coming as much as Luca did, Max knew his sister must never find out about his involvement in their brother's death.

This was really the driving force behind his oddball choice of involving Fred in this most unconventional of murder plans. Usually, cutting a guy down in the street was about as complicated as retribution would get for the squad.

But Max wanted to keep Teresa in the dark. He even went as far as asking Jesus for reassurance that Teresa would remain clueless about it for the rest of her days. Max wasn't the sort of guy who relied on prayers. He usually didn't sit around asking for favors from the unknown; he was an active problem-solver in his own right. Whether knee-jerk or premeditated, Max was, undeniably, a man of action.

But he knew that if she did find out about his current solution, Teresa would give him an earache about it for the rest of his life. And he wasn't in no mood to deal with her nagging on top of a cheating wife. So he figured it wouldn't hurt to ask for some extra backup this time to keep this particular matter quiet.

Sofia, on the other hand, would automatically suspect Max's involvement once the deed was done. But unlike his sister, Max actually wanted his wife to be suspicious; hence, his need to act swiftly the very next day. He was going to great lengths to make it appear as if it was accidental for the benefit of Teresa, and for the added benefit of keeping the coppers off his back. However, he knew the timing would always make Sofia wonder whether her husband had a hand in her lover's death.

Max specifically wanted to punish his wife by making her wonder for the rest of her days, never really knowing the truth about Luca's death. He planned to never tell her the truth, only to sock her in the kisser if she dared to question him about it. All

Sofia needed to know was what would happen to her if she didn't know her place.

"Sure, Max. Whatever ya want, ya know ya can always count on me," Fred said cautiously, as his eyes couldn't help but continue to shift nervously from shadow to shadow within the dim room. He was back to sitting straight up in his chair at attention, awaiting the details of his assignment.

Max took it as a good sign that Fred was smart enough to know what was being asked of him even if it was the first time he had ever asked for such a big favor. Usually, Fred was only his inside guy. The one who would just arrange access, ensure delivery, and provide payment of bribes to the mugs at the Highland shipping yard. This was one of the many ways the squad smuggled Canadian booze, hidden safely within legitimate automobile shipments sent throughout the entire United States.

Max also knew there was no way Fred could say no to him even if he wanted to, and he could tell by the anxious look on Fred's ruddy face that he wanted to get out of this favor with every fiber of his being. It was apparent because Fred seemed unable to control how he fidgeted in his seat. His hands were tightly interlocked with his thumbs twiddling nonstop in his lap. Beads of sweat started to appear along his hairline.

To get out of this fix, Fred made an attempt to get Max to change his mind by adding in his heavy Irish brogue, "But are ya sure I'm the right guy? This ain't me sort of thin', ya know. I'm no button man."

Max didn't respond right away but instead pulled out a cigar from his interior breast coat pocket and took a moment to light it. It was as if he was taking a little time to consider Fred's valid point as he puffed and circled the cigar around in his thick fingers. But it was for dramatic effect as Max already knew he had made his decision, and once a decision is made by Max, nothing could change his mind.

All Fred could do in the meantime is wait as patiently as possible with his knee nervously bobbing up and down while the beads of sweat slowly made their way down his forehead.

Once Max had finally lit his cigar successfully, and with a big puff of smoke, he replied with pride for being the one that came up with it, "Nope, you're the right guy, alright. He'll never suspect ya."

Fred made one last attempt to persuade the mobster as he responded, "Smugglin' I'm good at, but what I'm thinkin' you're askin', I don't think I'm that good a choice. I'd hate to be a disappointment to ya."

There was that word again. Disappointment.

Hearing that word caused Max to see red as he suddenly shouted out, "Ya owe me, Freddy. Ya fucked up that shipment. Ya didn't think you was gonna get away with not havin' to repay all that dough ya lost for me?" Max grabbed Fred by the collar and lifted him off his chair as high as his right arm could lift him as he asserted, "Ya think one ass kickin' was all ya was gonna get for an entire shipment lost? Next time, bump off the Purples stealing my booze."

The Purples was another name Detroiters used to refer to the Scalici Squad's archrival in booze funneling, the Purple Gang. Despite their reputation for being absolutely cutthroat, there had been a truce delicately in the balance for years allowing both mobs to do business peacefully.

When Fred lost an entire shipment and claimed it was the Purples who made off with the loot, that was a big problem for Max. Not only did he lose a whole boatload of dough literally, but making an accusation like that against the Purple Gang could very well start an endless mob war.

To avoid that drastic situation, Max saw to it that Fred faced the consequences by getting a good beating the night of the Book-Cadillac's Grand Opening Gala. He rationalized that Fred was the one in charge of getting the booze safely hidden onboard Ford's Model T shipment, which he clearly failed to do.

Besides, Max had no proof that the Purples were involved other than this jobbie's word. For all he knew, this could be nothing more than Freddy doing a Chinese squeeze. No point in starting a deadly street fight over that.

"I don't care what ya do. Push that boob in front of a flivver coming off the line, for all I care. But make it look like an accident, ya follow?"

As Fred hung by his collar with his feet barely on his tip-toes, he reassured Max with a gulp, "Sure thing, Max. There's so many nooks and crannies in that there factory, an accident won't be hard for me to do."

"It's gotta happen tonight. Got it? And nobody in the Scalici Squad can hear a lick 'bout it. That's why I got *you* on this. *Capisci*?"

Max couldn't risk Salvatore finding out anything about this because anything Sally knows might end up in his sister's ear. He usually wouldn't keep something like this from the squad, especially not his brother-in-law. But Max noticed lately that Salvatore's mind wasn't quite the same. He seemed to have developed loose lips with age, which was another issue Max had weighing heavy on his mind and would have to deal with soon enough. So this particular hit was a little secret between Max and Fred only.

"If ya say a fuckin' word, Freddy... One. Fuckin'. Word. I tell ya, I'll shiv ya right in front of that fat, fuckin' wife of yours and make those eight ruddy kids cry their fuckin' eyes out over their dead papa, ya follow me?"

Max released the Irishman as soon as Fred acquiesced with desperate pleas that he can be trusted to get the job done right and without yapping about it around town.

When Fred was finally back on his feet, he asked, "Who do ya want me to bump off?

"Why, my brother, Luca, of course." Max remembered how Fred's jaw instantly dropped in horror at the mention of his friend's name as he added with a sneer, "Oh, and on second thought, push him into a wood saw or something. I like that better. He'll bleed out fast."

CHIRTY-FIVE

Not having tortured Sofia enough with the details, Max then pointed the barrel of his Smith & Wesson between his wife's defiant eyes. "So there ya have it. I had your precious love cut down by his own pal, and that sap never saw that wood saw comin'," he snarled with an unusually calm and collected insolence. "Your papa said his arm came clean off. Bled out so fast, they didn't even make it to the hospital. Luca was nothing but a bucket of sand by Tuesday morning."

With that same sneer he once had for Fred, he cocked the hammer of his handgun as he threatened, "What are ya gonna do 'bout it, ya dumb dame?"

To his surprise, Sofia didn't even flinch. In fact, she still acted as if she couldn't care less that a pistol was pointed squarely in her face. That made it clear to Max that she'd rather die than continue to live on as his wife, which made him even angrier.

Sofia merely responded casually without fear, but thick with sarcasm instead, "I find it very interesting, *amore mio*, that you would pop me one, after everything we've been through together."

Max was sick of his wife's sour disposition and bitter tongue. He felt that Sofia had been a bit of a pain in his ass in the past, but tonight, she really took the cake. Now knowing she had lost his baby on their wedding night, Max had little reason to deal with her brazen disrespect. He reasoned to himself, he could always get remarried to a better dame.

He flashed that same sly grin at his wife, just as he did the night at the Book-Cadillac Hotel months ago, as he cruelly retorted, "Doesn't matter what ya think cause you're 'bout to join my brother. I guess ya were soulmates, after all."

Max then pulled the trigger.

But, to his dismay, the gun didn't fire.

His grin fell as he cocked the hammer back and pulled the trigger once more. Still nothing.

With a furrowed brow, Max checked the gun's chambers. There wasn't a bullet in sight.

Sofia remarked coolly, "I'll give ya one thing, Max. You at least look as dumb as you are."

She smoothly slid her hand inside the pocket of her mink coat and pulled the gun's remaining five bullets out of it. With a triumphant smile across her face, Sofia held them in her open palm, showing Max the evidence of what she had done while he soundly snored in bed earlier that evening. Sofia was quite pleased with herself that she managed to pull that trick off on her husband. Although she had just called him dumb, she knew he was actually quite cunning as well as devious and evil.

"But how did I know that you'd be the type to cut down your own wife?" Sofia asked rhetorically. She shrugged her shoulders for added dramatic effect and ended with a sarcastic pout like she was the dumb dame he just accused her of being. "Lucky guess, I suppose."

Max growled in anger. He couldn't believe the audacity she had touching his weapon. He was determined to make Sofia pay dearly for her disobedience. Instead of a quick, peaceful bullet to the head, Max was going to beat her to death with his pistol instead.

Sofia could tell she hit the nerve she was vying for, right on schedule, in the middle of the night. Nothing could have pleased her more than rubbing his face in her ability to outwit him. She knew how much Max prided himself on always being the smartest guy in the room. To have a woman dupe him was the utmost humiliation.

So Sofia also looked forward to his next reaction as she nonchalantly threw the lead out the houseboat's window and into the surrounding dark water. With several plop, plop, plopping sounds, the two of them quietly listened in the silent night as the bullets landed one-by-one in the peaceful lake.

Max's nostrils flared with rage as he barked, "You're done after this lil' stunt. Ya know that?" Despite his rapidly debilitated condition, Max managed to fling his handgun at Sofia with a wooden sidearm throw. He had such strength that even in his weakened state, he was able to easily send the heavy metal weapon through the air.

She attempted to dodge the hurled object, but it still managed to graze the top of her head, just above her temple. But Sofia was able to catch her fall as she tumbled backward toward the floor.

While she regained her balance, she rubbed the tips of her fingers against her hairline where Max's pistol had struck her. Sofia looked down at her damp fingers. They were coated in blood. If she had been hit a half an inch lower, it would have killed her, and she knew it. She looked at her dangerous husband and wiggled her red-stained fingers femininely at him as she replied, "I guess this means there's no backing out now."

She then rose confidently before him, with her shoulders back and head held high. She felt that her diamond-crusted hairpin had shifted during the whole ordeal. She straightened it back into its proper place, which kept her hair out of her eyes. Sofia was ready for the fight that was about to happen.

Her casual taunting made Max want to break every bone in her body. He felt the desire burn within him to smash her face in with the butt of his pistol until he could see nothing but a pulpy, bloody mess. Her boldness was beyond anything he had ever dealt with, especially from a little woman that was so small he could easily break her in two.

And he could no longer wait to do her in. Until he could grab the gun that was now out of his reach across the room, beating Sofia with his bare hands would have to do.

But when Max, once again, attempted to get on his feet to charge full speed ahead to begin his brutal beat down of his wife, he discovered he suddenly couldn't move his left arm.

Instead, he felt as if his body was rebelling against his mind just as Sofia was rebelling against him. He could barely move now with the stiffness that had slowly spread through him as the night unfolded. He had been zozzled many times before, so he knew this was different. Max finally confronted the reality that something strange was, in fact, happening to him.

Perplexed that now he was the one with sweat beading down his forehead instead of some other victim he was torturing for fun, Max managed with his equally stiff knees to hobble onto the bed as he growled at her, "Somethin' ain't right."

The quiet stillness surrounding them suddenly rung with Sofia's abrupt laughter. She laughed and laughed and laughed callously as blood dripped from the bleeding gash above her left temple. According to her carefully devised plan for the evening, she was purposely giving Max a dose of his own maniacal laugh as she admitted with glee, "I slipped you a Mickey Finn, you idiot."

Max's jaw dropped in shock.

"But it's an extra special concoction I had made for my extra special guy with a little extra special punch to make it particularly painful before it slowly sends you off to sleep." Sofia added with verve, "The big sleep."

He glared up at Sofia, not quite sure whether she was just fucking with him or not. Despite his apparent symptoms, he couldn't believe a dame like her had it in her to pull the wool over his eyes. But as his arm continued to stiffen in pain and become completely motionless, he recalled that he never saw her uncork the wine bottle before dinner. Max started to realize this wasn't a sick joke but that his supposedly submissive wife was, indeed, telling him the truth.

Sofia stared directly into Max's dilated pupils as she explained to him about what she had done. "It was easy, really. You know that old, fat pharmacist across from the Eastern Market?"

Sofia had been waiting patiently all night long to be able to tell Max this part of her story. She couldn't help but smirk down at her dying husband as she began to recount how she managed to outfox him. Now, this was *her* salt to *his* wound.

ƬHIRTY-SIX

It was right at closing time, but the pharmacy had a few remaining customers being serviced by the pharmacist behind the counter. Sofia was there, trying to evade the attention of others. She avoided eye contact, pretending to be interested in the wares stocked on the crowded shelf in the very back of the store.

Her shiny, black Ford Model T Fordor Sedan was parked at the curb right outside. Every so often, she would take a quick glance out the storefront window checking on the solitary passenger within it -- her driver, Bambino. Max assigned him as her personal chauffeur along with the automobile on their wedding day. Although her husband said it would give her the freedom to go wherever she desired, Sofia knew that the gesture was more about keeping track of her every move. So it felt more like a curse than a gift. Much like her wedding as a whole.

Luckily for her, Bambino found the assignment boring. He currently had his head laid back with his fedora hat over his face to catch a moment of rest before driving her home. She remembered how his massive body engulfed the driver's seat. It made her skin crawl to think what this giant goon could be capable of doing to her if he ever caught on to her unfolding plan.

She managed to convince Bambino not to make the run inside to pick up her medication on her behalf -- since, as she explained, it was particularly embarrassing to her. Sofia had no problem blushing shyly as she further explained in her soft, sweet-natured voice that she needed a little privacy to talk to the pharmacist about the delicate nature of her situation. It was "lady problems," as she put it.

Once that was said, Bambino, equally embarrassed, didn't need to hear another word. He was one of the few in their inner circle that had been told in confidence by her husband that Sofia was happily pregnant. So Bambino automatically believed her and quickly volunteered to wait in the car.

As Sofia pretended to pick out the perfect shade of Rigaud's rouge in their little golden pots of pink powder, the store finally emptied, leaving her alone with the pharmacist. He was a middle-aged, balding Italian man, a *Calabrese*. He was wearing a navy silk, polka dot bow tie around his thick, wrinkly neck. His dark brown vest was wrapped around his squishy torso with buttons that looked as if they were ready to burst under his white lab coat. His name, Dr. Ferraro, was stitched on his lapel.

Dr. Ferraro was her neighborhood pharmacist growing up. Sofia knew him for as long as she could remember, and he knew her entire family as well. Throughout the years, when she would go shopping at the Eastern Market with her mother, they would often head to the nearby pharmacy to grab a soda pop.

During their recent wedding planning, they had gone in there a few times, and it was then that Sofia noticed Dr. Ferraro was one of those older men who couldn't seem to keep his eyes off her. And that's why she had chosen this particular pharmacist to ask for her special favor that day.

Sofia waited to make her lingering presence known until Dr. Ferraro had locked the front door and turned over the hanging black-and-white sign letting customers know the shop was closed for the day.

As planned, she dropped her winter coat from her shoulders onto the floor in the aisle that she had made her makeshift hideout. She wore a sexy rose-colored silk dress with a layered lace skirt and matching satin trim. She wanted to look especially good for this moment, so she even had a soft pink rosette neatly tucked behind her ear. The monochromatic look made her seem as if she were a delicate pink rose.

Dr. Ferraro was startled at the sight of her. He had no idea there was somebody else left in his pharmacy. But once he saw that it was Sofia before his eyes, he didn't mind that she had given him such a shock. In fact, his face spread into the widest smile as he apologized for missing her and promptly returned behind his counter to service her needs.

She did her best to sway her hips like she had been taught by Princess as she approached him. With her big, brown, doe-eyes looking up at him, wounded and in need of his help, she apologized for taking up his time after hours. She acknowledged that he had his own wife and family to get home to, but Sofia quickly confessed that she had purposely stayed to see him…alone.

Dr. Ferraro was surprised, to say the least. It was quite apparent that young, attractive women wanting to spend time with him was something that rarely, if ever, occurred in his life, especially at his age. He was immediately interested in knowing what he could possibly do for Sofia.

It didn't take long into her story for Sofia to start sobbing in front of the pharmacist. She asked politely if she could sit down so she could have a little privacy. Although Dr. Ferraro was initially taken aback by her tears, his eyes quickly softened behind his round spectacles as he attentively guided Sofia to his lab in back.

To comfort her, the pharmacist reached into his crisp lab coat pocket and kindly offered his handkerchief to her. She made sure to brush his hand with her own as she took it from him. There was no electricity between them, but Dr. Ferraro didn't seem to notice as his eyes lit up at her sensual touch.

As she sobbed, Sofia confessed to him that she had lost her baby due to a miscarriage and that she was frightened for her life because of it. She further explained how her tyrant of a husband already ruled her life by his mighty fist and had already warned her, on multiple occasions, that if anything happened to his baby, he would kill her, too.

Normally, Dr. Ferraro would have thought she was being a hysterical woman exaggerating. But he already knew who Sofia's husband was and he was well aware that Max was capable of anything. He had his own troubles dealing with the notorious mobster.

So he felt like he could empathize with this pretty woman. Dr. Ferraro also admitted to Sofia that the Scalici Squad had been coming down on him pretty hard with threats of broken limbs and such since he'd been late on a few payments. As luck would have it for Sofia, they had even given him a black eye recently. So he completely understood her fears.

Sofia pretended to be moved by this newfound connection they shared between them, built upon their mutual life-threatening fear of Max. Flushed with tears, fears, and emotions, she rushed into Dr. Ferraro's arms. She did her best to press her breasts close as she hugged the pharmacist.

It didn't take but another ten seconds before she could feel he was aroused. At first, Dr. Ferraro tried to pull away from her, embarrassed.

But she wouldn't let him. Instead, she pressed him closer until his breathing became heavy. She looked up at him and she could see genuine shock across his face. She could tell that never in a million years had he ever thought he would be in this situation. She could also tell he wanted her badly.

But Dr. Ferraro wasn't a stupid man, and he quickly began to list the many reasons, including the obvious, why they should stop. Sofia only put her index finger to his lips, stopping him from speaking any further. Then, she pushed him down into his desk chair.

Kissing him the entire time, she unbuttoned his lab coat. Dr. Ferraro was in such shock that this opportunity had sprung upon him that he behaved like nothing more than a pile of mush.

Sofia even had to place his hands on her breasts for him and he squeezed as directed.

Then, she freed him from his pants. She hiked up her dress and was about to climb on him when Dr. Ferraro stuttered, "Mrs. Denaro, are you sure you want to do this?"

As she lowered herself onto him, letting him enter her body, she hushed him and whispered flirtatiously with a playful giggle into his ear, "I just have to tell him that I fucked you."

She made sure she did what she could to make that balding, middle-aged pharmacist feel like he was none other than Rudolph Valentino. In the lab of his pharmacy, as she rode him in his desk chair like a thoroughbred racehorse, Sofia remembered how he grinned from ear to ear, having the time of his life.

She even had to remove that polka dot bow tie around his neck to muffle his mouth for fear his loud grunts of pleasure would cause Bambino to wake from his nap outside. Sofia did such a good job, he made his final muffled groan of joy only a few minutes later.

And then Sofia promptly rose from his lap. She quickly smoothed down her hair and readjusted her dress to hide the evidence of what had just occurred between them.

There was a time that sex was regarded as a sacred act to her; now, it was a way for Sofia to get what she wanted. It seemed, she reasoned, that was the only thing men really cared about when it came to her and she figured at this point, after everything she had been through, what difference did it make anyway.

As the blood returned to the pharmacist's head, what Sofia said earlier struck him as peculiar. He assumed she must have been joking at the time, because it would be a death sentence for them both. Otherwise, Dr. Ferraro would have never let it get that far. Just to be sure, he asked, "You're not really going to say anything about this to your husband, right?"

Sofia responded bluntly, "Of course, I'm going to tell Max."

Again, he thought she was teasing him. Dr. Ferraro chuckled nervously at her response until he realized that she was serious when she clarified for him, "That was the entire point of this."

"But why?" Dr. Ferraro's face fell to the floor in fear and disappointment. He had worried that this fortunate turn of events was too good to be true. And it was now clear that his initial concerns were valid.

She then took a moment to delicately dab away her last remaining tears with his handkerchief as she finally asked for her big favor. If Dr. Ferraro agrees to make the poison for her, Sofia agrees to only tell Max about them right before he dies from it. "That way, we both get to live," Sofia added.

The pharmacist was alarmed at such a crazy idea. If he did such a thing, to actually make the poison she would use to kill Max Denaro, he would be putting his own neck on the line, not only with the Scalici Squad but also with the police.

But Sofia gave his handkerchief in her hand a closer look and commented, "Your initials are B.F., huh?" She then acted like she nonchalantly tucked it into her bra for safekeeping. However, it was clear she was going to use it somehow against him.

"Or I can go right out there and that giant goon would come right back here and kill you like that," Sofia informed him as she snapped her fingers, it would be so fast.

Being the smart guy he was, Dr. Ferraro quickly understood the only way he would get out of this sticky situation alive was by giving Sofia what she wanted. So he went straight to work.

THIRTY-SEVEN

Sofia stood there with her bow and arrow pointed at Max as she ended her story.

During her rendition about what had occurred between her and Dr. Ferraro, she had seductively sashayed toward Max. Now able to sway her hips with ease, she behaved as if she was about to give her husband one last joy ride as well.

However, with a sly smirk, Sofia stopped short of him and merely grabbed a dinner knife from the dining table instead.

Painfully stiff, Max watched his wife's every move suspiciously, wondering what she planned on doing with the weapon. At this point, he had no idea what this crazy woman was truly capable of. Max tried to massage his stiff arm with what little mobility he had left in a desperate attempt to revive it and somehow save his life.

Meanwhile, Sofia unexpectedly stopped in the middle of the

boat and had pried up a loose floorboard with the utensil. As the blood continued to drip down the side of Sofia's head, she pulled out her bow and arrow that she had planted beneath their feet, ready for this very moment.

Before she had stretched back the tight string aiming straight at his heart, she first pulled out a large, white square piece of material from her mink pocket.

It was Dr. Ferraro's handkerchief.

It was evidence that everything she just told Max was the truth. She wrapped it like a feminine scarf around her own neck to let him know she was proud she had done it, too.

Now, with her story finished and her arrow aimed squarely at Max, Sofia continued to rub her infidelity in his face, "Since we've been sharing all night, it's important for you to know that I didn't mind fucking Dr. Ferraro."

Max wasn't a fool. He knew he was utterly cornered. But being true to form, Max wouldn't give up. Even if he could do nothing more than give an ominous stare at Sofia as he scowled and sputtered out, "Ya ungrateful whore."

Sofia's eyes kept her aim carefully on Max as she calmly responded, "You took everything from me."

Max's words slurred with spit as he retorted, "I gave you everything! You are nothing but an ungrateful *whorrre*!"

She knew Max never cared a lick about her feelings, especially now more than ever. However, she needed to tell him just the same for her own sake. Sofia had never told anybody before, not even Renie. It felt as if this last painful memory would somehow disappear from her past if she were able to finally get it off her chest.

Unwavered by Max's pathetic attempt to wound her one last time with his degradation, Sofia asked, "Do you have any idea how hard it was to face them after what you did to me?"

CHIRTY-EIGHT

Sofia recalled how her worried parents had jumped to their feet at the sight of her. Their daughter had just returned home alone well after midnight. This had never occurred before, so they were convinced something terrible happened to her. They didn't know if they would ever see her again.

Silvia blurted out in her Sicilian dialect, "Thank you, God. She is safe!" She immediately wrapped her arms around Sofia. She clung to her only surviving child, giving her a big kiss on her forehead.

Sofia fought back her tears as she retreated into her mother's embrace. She was truly relieved to finally be home and in the safety of her mamma's arms. She wished she never ever had to leave again.

With his Sicilian accent unusually thick due to his fear and frustration, a distressed Giacomo also blurted out, "Where were you? You look-a mess?"

Not having the heart nor the right words to tell her parents the truth, Sofia simply replied, "It's snowing," as she brushed the wet flakes from her disheveled hair. As Max warned her earlier that awful evening, she wasn't able to catch a cab at that time of night and, instead, was forced to walk home in the dark alone.

"We came to get you at church. There was nobody there. Where were you?" Silvia questioned, still speaking in her native tongue.

Sofia replied as matter-of-factly as she could muster, "Renie wasn't feeling well, so we left early, and I walked her home."

Sofia felt guilty because of her lie. She couldn't help but think about where she had actually been this entire time. She then couldn't help but think about what had happened to her because she had lied to get there.

She could feel the heat build in her cheeks. She kept her eyes to the ground, knowing she was turning red because of her lie. But she hoped, as she solemnly put her head down in remorse, that they thought her blushing was over her bad decision to walk home unchaperoned.

Although Sofia felt she had paid the consequences for her sins, she didn't understand why those consequences were so unfairly disproportionate. What had started as an innocent attempt to help her friend and have a little fun in the meantime had turned into her greatest nightmare.

Sofia knew that her pain would be magnified if her parents ever found out what actually took place that night. She didn't want them to feel the terrible heartache and humiliation she was currently enduring herself. She couldn't hurt them like that on top of everything else she had done to them.

Despite not knowing the absolute worst of it, Giacomo still couldn't believe the words coming out of his daughter's mouth. He banged the table with his fist as he badgered her with questions regarding her irresponsible behavior, "Walking alone? At night? You lost-a your mind, young lady? What if something happened to you?"

Silvia examined Sofia's untidy appearance as if to make sure her daughter still remained in one piece. She quickly noticed Sofia's cold, shaky hands and wrapped her palms around her daughter's chilly fingers as she said, "And without your gloves. You could catch-a cold."

Sofia gently pulled her shivery hands away as she assured them both, "I'm fine, Mamma, really. Nothing happened to me, Papa."

"Did somebody see you?" Silvia questioned, still filled with worry. Being from a small, ancient town in Sicily, Silvia learned to be very concerned about other people's opinions. Nothing was worse than a tarnished reputation fueled by gossip. A young woman even suspected of having lost her virginity while unmarried was better off dead in her view, since it would mean a life sentence of shame, scorn, and ridicule from those around.

"No," Sofia replied. "Nobody saw me." This was the only thing Sofia had said that was true. She had swiftly walked the entire way with her eyes straight to the ground to avoid detection. Due to it being well past midnight, she hadn't seen anybody she recognized from her conservative neighborhood.

Giacomo wagged his calloused finger at his daughter as he admonished, "You know betta, Sofia. Think of your reputation. Mr. Manetti's daughter walked-a home alone from a shift at the soap factory. Not one respectable man will look her in the face now."

Silvia quickly layered, "Forget about getting-a married."

Sofia had never spoken to Mr. Manetti's daughter, nor had she seen her around the neighborhood for years. But she still had to endure lectures from her parents of the spinster's sad and lonely existence. Her tale of woe was always the one used as a warning to keep Sofia's behavior in line and her reputation as a good Italian girl intact.

But Sofia defended her own native country's modern times, "That was ten years ago. It's the Twenties now. Times are different." It didn't occur to her at that moment that defending Mr. Manetti's daughter was actually defending herself. But it had since.

Silvia shook her head in pity at how young and naive her daughter was, as she doubled down on her husband's original point, "But Valentina's alone till this day."

Giacomo lectured, "Valentina should have-a waited for her papa to pick her up and so should have-a you. Promise me you'll never do something so stupid like this ever again. You hear-a me?"

Sofia didn't want to endure this lecture from her parents any longer, especially after what she just survived. Sofia remembered how badly she wanted to wash that fateful night from her body, ever since she looked at her defiled image in the mirror in Max's hotel bathroom.

Craving to end the conversation, Sofia obediently retreated.

"I don't know what I was thinking."

Giacomo grumbled to himself in his Sicilian dialect, "You were thinking like a woman. If God knew I'd be left with only one child, why did he send me a daughter? Nothing but headaches!"

Covered in sadness and guilt, the corners of her mouth down, Sofia apologized, "I'm sorry. It'll never happen again."

"You betta believe it won't happen again because, the next time, you are going to get it. You hear-a me? I've never had to, Sofia, but I will make you black and blue. You hear-a me?"

Sofia obediently nodded with tears brimming in her eyes. She wished her father would beat her with his belt now. She never felt like she deserved it more.

Sofia witnessed her parents exchange a look of disappointment out of the corner of her teary eyes as she trudged to the water closet to finally rinse the evidence off her body. That look between them made her want to die. They only thought she had walked home alone unchaperoned. She couldn't imagine how they would feel about her if they actually knew she was no longer a virgin.

Later that night, as the moonlight streamed through Sofia's bedroom window, she was in bed, quietly crying herself to sleep when there was a soft knock on her door. It then jarred open, and Silvia's head had popped in as she asked, "Sofia, what's wrong?"

Sofia tried to brush the tears from her eyes to hide that she was crying and answered softly, "Nothing, Mamma."

"I know-a Papa can be hard sometimes, but if anything ever happened to you…"

"I know, Mamma. You'd never be able to live with yourselves," Sofia had finished her sentence having heard this explanation, time and time again, as the reason why they had kept such a close eye on her. It was the reason why they never let her go anywhere without them.

Silvia assured her only daughter, "When you're a mother, you'll understand." Silvia then gently kissed Sofia's forehead, once again, wishing her a good night, "*Buona notte, tesoro mio.*" Thinking she had made her daughter feel better, Silvia had quietly exited the room.

When, in reality, Sofia was left to suffer alone in silence.

ꟼHIRTY-ꟼINE

"Your dear old Papa is *rrright*. Women are nothin' but headaches," Max sputtered in response, still as unapologetic as ever, although his statement was apropos, considering his current physical state.

But Sofia made sure to give Max more than a headache this time. As she pulled back the string on her bow as tight as she could, she responded, "Because there are men like you in the world."

Max attempted to move, but he couldn't budge. Sofia only knew he tried because his head shook a little. He was now paralyzed and could do nothing more than sit there on the houseboat bed as still as a brick of straw used for target practice

Sofia let go of her arrow.

It skimmed Max's right ear.

Unable to even flinch, Max wailed, "Captain! Get here now!

Now, I said!"

Sofia just watched his pitiful pleas and taunted him, "We're miles and miles from shore. Nobody can hear you."

Max could only respond to her with a threat, "You'll never get away with this. The captain is gonna tell Bambino. Sally is gonna find out what ya did to me. Don't think your pretty little ass is too good to get pumped full of lead."

As Sofia reached for the second arrow in her quiver, she explained, "Papa always told me, once people believe in someone -- like really *believe* in someone -- once that person has a good reputation amongst the people, you see, that person can then take two slices of bread and put a piece of shit between them. And serve it up, telling them it's good for them like marmalade. The people will gobble up that shit sandwich without even blinking twice, although everything about it stinks."

As she pulled back her next arrow, Sofia added, "Now, when Papa says this, he's always talking about politicians, but it got me thinking…"

As Sofia aimed, once again, straight at Max, "Who would suspect your sweet, innocent wife is capable of murdering her strong, powerful mobster husband? Your sister, perhaps?"

FORTY

With a sweet smile, Sofia had turned to Teresa, a hardened mob boss' wife draped in way too many jewels. Sofia recalled that Max's sister looked much older than her actual age of thirty-eight, despite her stylish silk dress. She also seemed to have an expression of perpetual unhappiness on her face.

Her own mamma scowled a lot like Teresa, Sofia had thought to herself. She wondered if any wife was actually happy in the world. Or, if all of it, the happily-ever-after, was nothing more than a tall tale spun to get women to readily volunteer for a life of subjugation. All in the name of *love*. Phooey, Sofia thought to herself.

Sofia now knew that she would also end up just like Teresa, or even worse off, dead, if she wasn't able to keep it together and get out of this mess. That critical thought helped Sofia keep focused on the task at hand.

They both were standing in a spare bedroom, as Sofia had an array of coordinating fabric and wallpaper samples spread out and on display for her new sister-in-law to see. Sofia said brightly to Teresa with as much enthusiasm as she could drum up from within, "It's perfect for his nursery. Don't you think?"

"It's gonna be just beautiful," Teresa responded as she touched the wallpaper sample with a hand-drawn pattern of baseballs and bats.

Explaining her choice of motif, Sofia said, "Max is such a Tigers fan." As she gestured to the right side of the room, she seamlessly added, "I'm thinking of putting his cradle against this wall here for him."

"And you could put a dresser here. Rocking chair there," Teresa had said, as she pointed out the perfect locations for those items.

Sofia remembered how she joyfully agreed with her as she exclaimed, "I'm so excited to hold my baby boy in my arms!"

But then Teresa paused a moment to consider her next statement before she added, "But how can you be so sure it's going to be a boy?"

Sofia, of course, knew this was coming from a woman who had five daughters, much to her husband's dismay. She tried to be sensitive to that fact as she responded to Teresa. She blissfully rubbed her flat belly, which only she knew was empty at the time, as she reacted exactly like an obedient wife in love should. "Max is dead set that it's a boy. And he's never wrong about *anything*."

It was the only example Sofia could think of that would prove to Teresa that she was, in fact, happily married. It was imperative that Teresa believed that Sofia believed in Max. Sofia silently prayed to herself, hoping that Teresa would actually buy that she could love and admire a monster like Max.

But then Sofia reminded herself that this was not only his sister but more like a mother who helped make Max into the monster he was. If anyone had blinders on to his many faults, it would be the woman who helped shape him to be the man he is today.

Sofia may be young, but she had already witnessed a mother's blind love for her son too many times to count. Everywhere around her, there was nothing but examples of women silently ignoring or even sticking up for the bad behavior of their fathers, husbands, and sons. What other choice did they have?

But now Sofia also understood that many of those women were like she used to be. They may not have known it, but they had given up before they even tried. They were so immersed in a world where there wasn't any other option. Because if you tried to complain, you were ignored or ridiculed or beaten into submission. Sofia realized that those were the only three options women were actually given in life, not the ones that her father loved to bring up at the kitchen table.

No wonder women seemed to do nothing but strive to be good little girls in men's eyes.

The whole thing felt like a circus act to her, she reasoned. And women were the seals balancing red balls on their noses to avoid the ringmaster's whip.

Sofia knew she had achieved her goal when Teresa took her

hands into her own. It felt like a real moment of bonding between them as she said, "Oh, Sofia, after what our family has just been through…"

Sofia knew Teresa was referring to Luca's recent death. Still, she gulped down her own sadness, reminding herself that if she could pull this off, her current plan in motion would eventually avenge her lover as well.

Teresa continued with tears in her own eyes, "A baby in the family. It is exciting! I'm so happy Max finally found a wife like you."

With tears of supposed joy brimming in her own eyes, Sofia responded, "Teresa, that means so much to me. My only wish is to be as good to Max as he has been to me. Look at me. I'm a princess in my own castle."

Sofia then warmly hugged Max's older sister so Teresa could no longer see her face. She feared her true feelings about her abusive husband were still too hard to hide. She was afraid her expression would somehow betray her, and she needed to hide her real disgust. As she held Teresa tight and close, Sofia recalled rolling her eyes behind the unsuspecting woman's back.

To make sure Max, immobilized on the houseboat floor, knew just how miserable it had been to be with him, Sofia added, "Little did Teresa know I was talking about a fairytale in Hell…"

ϤORTY-ONE

Princess practically jumped out of her skin as if she had seen a ghost when Sofia entered her dressing room. The singer had been applying her makeup while seated at her vanity as Salvatore sat nearby, keeping her company. Princess was still the resident lounge act at the elegant Book-Cadillac Hotel, and she was in the middle of getting ready for her next performance.

The singer was expecting her usual delivery of red roses when she nonchalantly invited a knocker in. But to her dismay, the person behind the door was Sofia, looking like a much different woman since Princess had last seen her. Since her wedding day, Sofia was now always dressed fashionably from head to toe and, of course, she had her new bob hairdo.

With fear clearly splashed across her face, Princess said, "Sofia, please tell me Max knows you're here."

Sofia shyly responded, "Of course, he doesn't know a thing."

"Then, get out." Princess returned her attention toward her reflection, letting Sofia know she was done with this conversation.

"But I need your help."

"Listen, doll, I know when to heed a warning. As much as I think you're a fine gal and all…" Then Princess turned to Salvatore and added, "You're my witness, Daddy. I didn't ask her to come around here."

Sofia knew that Princess had every reason to be scared. But she pretended that the singer was being overly dramatic. "Oh, don't be silly. Nothing is going to happen to you. Max was just mad. And Renie will come back around. You will see."

By this time, Sofia had already known her best friend was as good as dead. And, after the severe beating she had endured herself, she believed Renie was murdered by Max. However, she couldn't let on that she had any motive to exact revenge on Mr. Scalici's brother-in-law. Max was too crucial to the Scalici Squad, being the very important second-in-command of their entire operation. So the more clueless Sally Bottoms thought Sofia was about Max's involvement in Renie's disappearance, the better it would be for her later on.

"Are you…?," Princess retorted, dumbfounded as if Sofia was, indeed, a daft idiot for being such a ridiculously naive woman. Especially considering they had discussed this very topic the last time they were together. "All I know is I'm left without any backup singers."

"But I helped you when you really needed someone. I came and sang at the grand opening to help you out in a pinch," Sofia gently reminded her with pleading eyes.

Princess didn't respond but looked over to her sugar daddy for his opinion on the precarious situation at hand.

"Please, Mr. Scalici, it's about Max. I need to learn how to make Max happy. Like Princess does for you," Sofia begged in the sweetest, most soft-natured way she possibly could.

Intrigued as well, Salvatore responded to Princess, "Don't worry, I'm here. Max won't do a thing to ya."

"Fine. But I'm singin' like a canary if need be," Princess warned Sofia as she straightened up in her chair and continued to apply her rouge.

"Mr. Scalici, with the deepest respect for you, would it be too much trouble if I spoke with Princess alone for a moment?" Sofia had asked innocently before she added, "It's about lady matters." She batted her eyelashes and gave him the most endearing look. She couldn't flirt with him outright in front of Princess so she went for the sweet-little-girl-asking-pretty-please angle instead.

In reality, Sofia was only pretending to ask for some privacy because she really wanted this conversation to unfold in front of him. She needed the mob boss to know in no uncertain terms what a devoted wife she was to Max. Salvatore needed to never suspect her in the slightest in Max's upcoming disappearance.

As she expected from a macho man like Salvatore Scalici, he responded bluntly, "Whatever you gotta say, it can be said in front of me."

Sofia knew that he would never do as she asked because, as she had so quickly learned, mobsters like him never allow a woman to dictate the terms. Evidently, to them, compromise with a woman somehow causes a mysterious condition that makes their dicks fall off. At least, that's the tale men seem to spin.

Twisting her hands together, Sofia blushed with embarrassment as she continued as planned, "Princess, I need help… How do I go about… You know...making Max *happy*?"

"You're askin' me for pointers in the bedroom?" Princess asked with her lipstick stopped in mid-air. It was as if she couldn't believe her own ears, knowing the uptight, conservative background that Sofia stemmed from.

"All I was ever told by Mamma was not to do it until I got married, and now that I'm married, I don't know what to do to make Max happy."

Having heard enough, Salvatore slowly rose from his seat with his usually heavy breathing and hacking cough. He then, by his *own* volition, announced, "I'll leave ya two girls alone."

Knowing exactly why the old man had abruptly changed his mind, they didn't respond but instead patiently waited for him to exit the dressing room. The only thing Princess said as he departed was, "I'll see ya later, baby."

Now that they were alone, Princess replied frankly to Sofia, "You're quite a trooper, I must say. But since when do you care about makin' Max happy?"

"Max's my husband now," Sofia responded matter-of-factly as she displayed her left hand showing off the massive diamond to the singer. She then gestured to the rest of the expensive jewelry her body was dripping with before adding, "I'm lucky to have him, and he deserves a good wife in return." Sofia tried her best to come off like all the other submissive women she knew who were groomed from girlhood to focus only on the good while ignoring the bad in their husbands.

Princess replied with a tinge of disappointment in return, "You always struck me as the dutiful wife type."

"I just want a happy marriage. Can you blame me?"

"I guess it's not a total shocker Max won ya over in the end. He can be quite a charmer when he wants, and havin' a mountain of dough never hurts, I'm sure. Anyway, what you're askin' about is easy to do."

Sofia's eyes opened wide, eager to hear the more experienced woman's pearls of sexual wisdom. She did desperately need to know this information for her plan to work successfully. So Sofia was well aware that her life depended on it.

Soaking up the flattery that comes with being asked for advice, Princess continued with her life lesson, "All men are the same. Act like his buddy during the ball game. Act like his mamma in the kitchen. And act like a whore in the bedroom. You'll have Max happy as a clam."

Horrified, Sofia asked, "How do I act like a whore?"

As Princess primped her hair, giving it her final touch, she replied without hesitation, "Just do whatever he asks of you, and no matter how disgusting, pretend you're lovin' it."

"And that's it? What if I can't pull it off?" Sofia's initial reaction was genuine and had just popped out of her mouth. She hated Max to such a degree, she didn't know if she could pretend to love doing disgusting things with him.

"I've seen you on stage. Anybody that can capture an audience like you do can capture one man. Even Max Denaro," Princess assured her with a sassy wink.

That's when it occurred to Sofia that the singer was absolutely right. She only needed to think of this as a performance, and that was something she really could do well. She had proved that on the night of the grand opening.

And if that failed, she could always just pretend she was doing it with her beloved Luca. Her vivid imagination would finally come in handy.

With a smile of gratitude for her beneficial guidance, Sofia said from the bottom of her heart, "Princess, I can't thank you enough."

₣ORTY-₸WO

"Mrs. Denaro, are ya ready to go home?" Bambino asked surprised when he answered her knock at the hotel room door of Penthouse #13. He had driven her to the Book-Cadillac so she could visit Princess in her dressing room earlier that evening. She had initially told him to meet her in the lobby in an hour, and there was still about fifteen minutes to go.

"Hello, Mr. Cercone. Is my husband here?"

Before he could answer her question, Max had yelled out from within the room, "Sofia, get in here."

Sofia could tell he was brooding from his tone, so she took a deep breath of courage before she entered the hotel room. She didn't have time to waste. God only knew how long it would be before she could catch Max in a good mood, so she decided to proceed ahead as planned.

She found Max sitting in the high-back leather chair in dim lighting, waiting for her with his hands interlaced on the desk. His lips were tightly pursed together with the corners of his mouth drawn down in a frown. He definitely wasn't happy to see her.

"I tried calling first from the lobby, but you didn't answer," Sofia explained apologetically.

"I don't talk over party lines. Everythin' goes through my guys," Max retorted as he gestured over to the giant of all the goons in the room, Bambino. "Ya follow me?"

"I'd have never come up if I knew it would disturb you. I know how important your work is. But I was hoping to talk to you about something I think you will like to hear. Alone?" Sofia asked softly as she demurely eyed the dim room, referring to the spattering of mobsters within the shadows around them.

Max didn't say a word but merely nodded to Bambino, who instinctively opened the door again, allowing the rest of the men, including himself, to depart.

Once Max and Sofia were alone, he said dryly, "Spit it out."

Sofia, twisting her fingertips together nervously, said as soft-natured and sweetly as possible, "I feel horrible…"

She shook her head as if the pain was too much for her to bear any longer. "I can't believe how I behaved… How I treated you… On our wedding night… And I was hoping you could find it in your heart, *amore mio…* "

Sofia noticed how Max had perked up in surprise when she referred to him as her lover, but he didn't say a word, with his grimace still in place. So she continued on sounding as apologetic as she could possibly muster, "I'm hoping you will find a way…to forgive me."

Max quickly replied, "What 'bout Luca?" Being a master con artist himself, he naturally didn't believe her.

Sofia took a step closer to him as she carefully continued her explanation. "I've been doing a lot of thinking since…"

She wished she could say since he had beaten her so severely that she had to lay in bed for a week healing, but she knew better. Instead, Sofia said, "Luca is gone. And the truth is I barely knew him. I don't want to ruin what we have together… Our marriage, our baby's family, over a childish fantasy."

Sofia was now standing right next to Max, finally sharing a little of that dim lighting from his desk lamp. "So, I was hoping you'd forgive me for being such a stupid, silly woman…."

She began to unzip her dress as she added, "I want more than anything for us to finally be…*happy* as man and wife."

Although Max's mood seemed to soften as he unlaced his hands and laid back in his chair, he still replied coldly, "I've important business that needs my attention, Sofia. Whatever this is, can wait."

Sofia pouted like a little girl as she let her dress fall to the floor showing off her new sexy lingerie. She was thankful for the dim lighting. It helped camouflage the yellowish marks that were the last remaining evidence of the bruises around her body.

"What's got into ya?" Max had asked suspiciously. Despite his unease, his eyes couldn't help but stare at the black lace bra and tiny short silk slip she had on.

"I am up to something," Sofia admitted. She then got on her knees before him. She couldn't think of a better way to show him she had officially submitted to his will as his obedient wife. Acting like she wanted him, she added, "I think you're going to like it."

This was the first time Sofia had ever initiated a sexual encounter with Max. And she knew he wouldn't be able to help but be intrigued by her change of heart. It didn't take but another moment for him to willingly turn his chair around to allow her unfettered access to his lap. Max leaned back with his hands, cradling his head, ready to relax and enjoy her offer as she unbuttoned his pants.

Although nothing within her wanted to remotely touch his body, let alone put him in her mouth, Sofia knew he would never believe her unless she did it.

She recalled Princess' sage advice...

Sofia knew for this plan of hers to work, if she were going to be successful in making him believe she was in love with him, she had no choice but to give the best performance of her life.

Which is exactly what she did.

The next morning, Max was still soundly asleep alone in bed. Sofia had taken note that nothing seemed to wake him, especially after he had sex. He didn't stir at all as she ordered room service, then drew back the drapes letting some light in and quietly picked up their clothes that were scattered throughout.

She had come across Max's Smith & Wesson, still sitting in his holster, in a pile with his shirt and jacket next to the desk. For a brief second, she thought about pulling that gun out and shooting Max right there while he slept. But guns scared her. That's why she always preferred hunting with a bow.

But even if she could shoot straight with the force of the gun pushing her tiny body backward, the loud popping noise would alert everyone in the hotel that someone had been murdered. The cops would immediately be called. Sofia knew she would end up getting caught fleeing the scene, considered a hysterical woman, and sent to prison for life. After all, when what he did to her was completely protected under the law, how could she convince a court that she was justified in killing Max?

So, instead of shooting him, she folded his clothes neatly and set them on his desk. She did inspect his weapon. Felt its weight. Checked out its chambers. It held six bullets. And then set it carefully down next to the clothing.

She tried her best to enjoy her breakfast while he merely continued to snore through it all. As she was trying to push the images from her mind of all the disgusting things she had done and had let be done to her last night, she heard Max finally stir in bed.

"It's Saturday, Sofia," He grumbled at the sight of her.

She knew that was his way of reminding her that she needed to leave because he had to get back to work. But Sofia pretended she didn't understand his implication when she responded cheerfully, "It's not raining. What do you want to do today?"

As Max finished rubbing his eyes, he was met with Sofia's bright smile. "I have a big shipment comin' in," he responded dryly.

"You act like spending the day with me is some form of punishment."

"Funny, cause that's what I thought ya felt about me."

Max had a valid point because that is precisely how Sofia felt every time she was with him. But she needed to change his belief as quickly as possible. She only had so much time.

"You still haven't forgiven me?" Sofia asked with that same girlish pout that helped her persuade him last night. "Are you going to make me beg again?" She added flirtatiously.

"I knew ya would come around in time. But this is fast... too fast." As Max sat up in bed, he eyed her. Sofia could tell his gut seemed to be telling him something was suspicious about her current behavior. Up to this moment, his new wife had always acted like she was his prisoner, who would rather be killed with lethal gas than spend a lifetime with him.

When she arrived at his hotel door last night, Sofia was sure he assumed she had finally gathered enough courage to make her anticipated accusations against him related to Luca's recent untimely death. She was convinced he thought he would be giving her another one of his lessons with his fists and definitely didn't think he was about to get lucky with her like he did last night.

"You'd rather have my bitter tongue around longer? Is that what you prefer? I'll do whatever you want, Max." Sofia responded playfully flashing a sarcastic wink but still making a valid point.

"So that bitter tongue of yours is gone forever?" Max responded, needing some further reassurance, although his tone suggested he was considering the possibility that his last lesson was quickly learned by his wife.

He did give me a good beating!

"What will I have to do to prove it to you?" Sofia opened her terry cloth robe revealing her nude body.

A wide smile spread across Max's face. She knew that he had

thoroughly enjoyed the new Sofia last night. He looked over at the clock and then back to her. "I have a few ideas about what ya can do with that new *better* tongue," Max replied as he gestured toward his lap.

"Then let's spend the entire day together making love."

"But I've got business to take care of, Mrs. Denaro."

As she let the robe drop to the floor, she decided not to push the issue but instead took the opportunity to flatter him. She bit her lip sensually as she began to rub her body, enticing him, and said, "I guess I need to get used to how important you are. It's going to be *hard* being married to the Big Cheese."

"Sally is really--" Max began to correct her, but Sofia boldly interrupted him, "Sally is an old man who can barely walk without a cane. We both know you're the one really calling the shots."

Not being one to argue against his own greatness, Max quickly acquiesced, "Okay then, the Big Cheese wants ya to get over here and *pronto*."

Sofia gleefully giggled as she scampered over to his bedside and Max immediately pulled her back in for a morning frolic.

ᖴORTY-ᖴHREE

"So, you see there, Max, if the Big Cheese was dumb enough to be duped, who else is going to suspect your loving and doting wife?"

Sofia then pulled back the string on her bow extra tight. She carefully aimed the arrow at Max as she caustically added, "If anything, they'll think what everybody thinks happens to a dirty gangster like yourself."

Sofia smirked at the wisdom of her own statement as she let go of the second arrow, which skimmed Max's other ear.

On either side of his head, he had two arrows stuck in the wall behind him. They looked as if they were holding him in place, but in reality, he was paralyzed unable to move regardless. "You shoot like a woman," Max croaked. He had nothing left in his arsenal except to disparage her.

"Ha! Papa used to say the same thing," Sofia scoffed, letting his remark bounce right off of her. She then began her last story of the evening as she explained, "Since I was a young girl, I would go hunting with Papa."

She recalled being in the forest with her father, thrilled to be able to spend time with him. Hunting excursions were the only time she ever truly had Papa to herself.

She further described a young Sofia taking each step slowly and carefully like she had been taught by her father so as not to scare away the majestic young buck just ahead of them.

"But the thought of killing that magnificent animal…" Sofia explained as her younger self carefully aimed her bow and arrow. "It always made me shiver."

She recalled how she had let go of her arrow. And, once again, how it grazed above the buck's head. This wasn't the first time she had missed. She had missed many times before. Sofia remembered how she had looked over at Giacomo, who stroked his beard and shook his head in disappointment.

But now as Sofia, the young woman, pulled out her third arrow from her quiver, she said, "Little did Papa know…"

Pulling back the string tightly, Sofia aimed her arrow, smooth and steady, at Max's heart.

With his dilated pupils, Max stared defiantly at her. "Ya don't have it in you. I dare ya."

With a sly smirk, Sofia continued unphased by his jeering, "Little did Papa know that his daughter wasn't only the best-looking dame in Detroit… She's the best shot, too."

Sofia shot her arrow.

With a swift whoosh...

It sped speedily through the air...

It pierced Max right in the heart, just as she intended.

The only movement his face would allow was for Max's eyes to open widely, in shock that Sofia actually had both the audacity and ability to do it.

"Whatever you say, Max," Sofia said triumphantly, thick with sarcasm.

Max's eyes remained frozen in shock forever as he died.

She dropped the bow and quiver, letting it clang onto the floor with a sigh of relief.

But she didn't have much time to let it sink in. She quickly approached Max's body, taking a closer look, checking to be sure he was really, truly dead. Max was such a monster that she felt superstitious about him. She reasoned, if anybody could survive what she had just done to him, it would be Max.

"But you are certainly no magnificent animal," Sofia commented as she watched the blood gurgling at his lips, telling her Max was a goner.

Her nightmare was finally over.

Without another moment to waste, Sofia opened the nearest window and yelled out, "It's done!"

Within seconds, at the houseboat's door, the clean-shaven boat captain appeared holding a canister of gasoline.

It was Giacomo.

ǶORTY-ǶOUR

"Is he really dead?" Sofia's father asked, feeling the same apprehension that she did as if Max was supernatural and could never be stopped.

"Yes, and good riddance. What time is it?"

"After two o'clock. Not a soul has been up-a for hours."

"Good. Now get into the lifeboat," Sofia instructed Giacomo as she gestured for him to give her the canister in his hand. This was the first time she told her father what to do. It had not taken long for murder to change her.

"No, I want to finish him."

"I said get into the lifeboat," Sofia responded sternly.

Giacomo referred to the gasoline as he replied equally as sternly, "This is-a dangerous."

"What? You don't think I can do it?" Sofia said as she motioned toward her dead husband's body as proof she could accomplish anything.

Giacomo's face softened as he replied sadly, "Sofia, I spent-a the last hours listening to your story... What this man did to you... What I let this-a man do to you. Let me do this now. For you."

Sofia looked into her father's sad eyes. The disappointment she had seen as a young girl was nowhere to be found on his face now. Instead, she saw a man before her who wanted to make amends for anything and everything he may have done throughout her life to have unwittingly put her in this current situation.

But knowing, of course, she couldn't have defeated Max without his help, Sofia rushed over to him. She hugged her papa tightly as she offered a compromise, "But I get to light it."

"Of course," Giacomo quickly agreed, letting her go so they could continue with the plan.

Sofia grabbed her bow and quiver of remaining arrows from the wood floor as Giacomo began to pour gasoline all over Max. "Be careful, Papa."

As Sofia entered the deck, she could see Giacomo's handiwork. There were several canisters of gasoline strewn throughout having been emptied on every square inch of the boat along with a small pile of firewood right in the middle of the deck. Sofia walked past it over to a lifeboat strung up and waiting to be lowered alongside.

Sofia entered it and pulled the lifeboat down to the water. She then used the paddle to get a bit of distance from the houseboat to give her some safety in case something went wrong. She then quickly changed into the clothes placed there for her for this exact moment. Finally fully clothed, Sofia sat there quietly alone under the dark, solemn sky praying for her father's safe return as he splashed gasoline in a room filled with burning candles.

With the thick cloud cover above, she could see a gentle fog rolling in as she suspected it would earlier in the evening. It would help camouflage the flames from shore, so Sofia welcomed it as good fortune. She had already spotted the one bright light in the far distance to guide her home but in case the mist became too thick, her mother would play her Victrola next to one of the church choir microphones, loudly from the open office window above, like a jazz blaring lighthouse. But despite the backup plan, the sooner they left, the better, Sofia reasoned.

She suddenly heard a loud splash. It didn't take much longer for Giacomo to pull himself into the lifeboat from the water.

"He's ready," Papa announced.

Sofia handed him a towel along with her mink coat to shield him from the crisp night air. She then grabbed a rag-tipped arrow from her quiver and a box of nearby matches.

She struck a match and lit the tip of her arrow as Giacomo jerked on the rope to the small motor latched onto the back, causing it to roar alive. They needed to get out of harm's way as quickly as possible. He did his best to keep the motorboat steady while he warned his daughter, "Be careful."

As she aimed her flaming arrow at the houseboat, she replied, "You don't have to worry about me…"

Sofia let it go.

The arrow swiftly glided through the houseboat window, piercing Max. His body burst into flames.

"...anymore." Sofia ended her previous sentence satisfied by how quickly her husband's dead body was engulfed by the fire. She watched as the fire spread throughout the room that she had just shared her last hours with Max. It spread quickly, helped out by the many candles Sofia had purposely lit in preparation.

She promptly lit another rag-tipped arrow, aimed, and let it go.

Suddenly, the prepared pile of gasoline-soaked wood on the deck burst into flames. It spread instantly. The boat was so thoroughly saturated in gasoline, it didn't stand a chance.

They had carefully planned every detail for a quick, quiet burn that hopefully, nobody noticed in the dead of night. As Giacomo guided the lifeboat away to safety, they both solemnly watched in silence as the houseboat rapidly disappeared under the calm, dark water.

Reminding her father, Sofia finally broke the silence, "Mamma lit the lantern. It's right there." Sofia pointed in case he didn't see it as well as she did.

Giacomo continued steering them toward the distant lonely light in the darkness as Sofia kept her eyes straight ahead on their destination. They were several miles from shore, and it would take some time for them to return to the grand stone manor. They needed to get back and have the lifeboat hidden in the woods before the staff arrived for work. She needed to be in bed as usual when Catalda came to serve her breakfast.

"Sofia..."

"Yes, Papa."

"That night Luca died, at the factory."

Sofia turned to her father, wondering what he may want to add about Luca's last moments on Earth.

Maybe the love of her life had given her father a departing message for her?

Giacomo's breathing was heavy, thick with guilt, as he found the courage to tell his daughter the truth. "There wasn't an accident."

"What are you saying?" Sofia asked, confused. She didn't understand what her father was trying to communicate to her. After all, they both knew for sure that Luca's death wasn't an accident. She had managed to at least get a confession out of Max about his plot to kill his brother.

Giacomo explained, "Fred could not-a do what Max wanted him to do. Not to Luca, of all people. Luca was his friend. So they faked an accident. Fred told everyone Luca died on the way to the hospital."

"How do you know this?" Sofia asked, completely shocked by this revelation. She had cried so many tears for her lost love, she could barely register this new reality with him back in it again.

"Fred asked for my help, and I drove Luca as far as Chicago. Last I heard, he went on to Los Angeles."

"So, Luca is alive?" Sofia asked with a joyful smile.

"He gave me the boat as a gift. Figured he wasn't going to be able to use it anymore. Felt I deserved it for putting my neck out, driving him-a like I did."

"So, that's where you got it?" Sofia felt there was something deeply romantic that it ended up being Luca's boat that helped set her free. But her smile quickly faded from her face when she made the next realization. "And he left Detroit without me?"

"I wanted to tell you, but I needed to protect you in case of Max ever..."

"When are fathers going to learn their job isn't only to protect their daughters from the world but to prepare them for it? Even make it better for them?" Sofia asked, with all seriousness.

By now, Sofia firmly believed that adhering to society's rules had done nothing but groom her to be the perfect target for a monster like Max. She had many sleepless nights to contemplate how she was forced into her dire situation because of them.

And then, on top of it, with every heartbreaking turn she experienced since the grand opening of the Book-Cadillac Hotel, the world did nothing but turn its back on her.

Suddenly, the rules no longer mattered.

She felt like a second-class citizen, as if someone would have literally swept her under the rug if they could. She was tired of the injustice.

But it finally made her realize that if she was going to survive in this life, she would have to turn her back on the world, too. Sofia was finally okay that she was never going to be a good little girl - ever again.

"Sofia, I am very proud that you are my daughter."

She smiled warmly at her father, Giacomo. Sofia had never heard those words from her father before, and she was happy to finally hear them now.

But she noticed that she didn't need them as much as she once did. So Sofia just turned back around and stared straight ahead toward the bright light in the distance, never looking back.

ꞆORTY-ꞆIVE

A telephone loudly rang and rang and rang--

Putting a stop to the shrill bell, Sofia finally answered it, "Hello?"

As she discovered who was on the other end of the line, she thought about how Papa always told her women had it easy because they only had three big choices to make in their entire life.

"No, Mr. Scalici, I still haven't heard from Max," she politely replied.

Sofia continued to listen to the mob boss as she also recalled her father's words of wisdom. Women could choose to become a nun, a wife, or a prostitute.

Sofia again responded as respectfully as possible, "Max told me to mind my own business, and that was the last of it. He's always gone from here for a week or so at a time. You're not worried, are you?"

She listened to Salvatore Scalici's response for a moment longer before replying back into the telephone, "What do you mean you found his automobile abandoned near the Purple Gang's hangout? You don't think…?"

She paused for dramatic effect as if she couldn't even bear to think such a terrible thought. "Of course, I'm worried! I figured he was in Detroit working this entire time. But if the Purples did something to my…to my…"

She pretended as if she couldn't finish her sentence, the thought was so utterly painful. Her breath started to get heavy as if she were about to burst into tears. Sofia finally spit out, "Please, please call me when you hear from him. Promise me. Promise me!"

Once the mob boss made his promise to her, Sofia hung up the telephone, causing her distress to evaporate immediately.

Sofia was in her grand stone manor's kitchen, which was empty at the moment. She eyed the window and walked over to it.

As she pulled out a cigarette, Sofia noted to herself that she had successfully referred to Max as if he was still alive on that call. She was constantly going through every detail of her plan to make sure nobody ever suspected her. Especially Sally Bottoms.

As she lit the cigarette, she gazed out back. Sofia remembered how her father had once stood there, looking like a stranger, freshly shaven in disguise, waving to her, letting her know their plan was ready to go.

But this time, Giacomo wasn't there, and there was no houseboat docked beside the long, narrow pier.

After she took a long, deep drag of her ciggy, Sofia murmured to herself, recalling her girlhood memories, "But Papa forgot about one option for a woman."

Outdoors, the gray clouds above finally parted ways, allowing sunlight through the window for the first time in months. Springtime was officially here.

The warm sunshine felt like a sign. Her destiny would be bright.

A sly smile appeared across Sofia's face as she recounted her father's mistaken omission, "A woman can always become a widow."

END OF BOOK ONE

ACKNOWLEDGMENTS

It has taken many years to get this story into your hands. So there are many people to thank over that time. From the ex-fiancé who encouraged pursuing the kernels of that dream that happened one night in Italy to all the beta readers throughout the years whose feedback helped shape Sofia's story.

And, of course, family. Our family has been supportive along this entire journey being everything from those beta readers mentioned above to our biggest cheerleaders. Mom and Dad - you are our #1 Fans, and we are grateful for everything you've done to help us. Mike, John, Adrienne, and Elena - thank you for everything, especially the emotional and even financial support at times and for being our first patrons on Patreon.

The rest of our family and friends who have donated to our creative projects in the past in both time and money -- a group that is, gratefully, too many to list here, we thank you for your support as well. Without it, we wouldn't be where we are today.

We want to thank all our current patrons on Patreon. Your assistance helped us pay for our monthly subscription for Adobe Creative Cloud, which allowed us to save thousands by designing this book ourselves.

A big thank you to Susan Moss and Ed Davids for being such detailed and thoughtful editors.

We would also like to thank Howard Kaufman, Mike Simpson, Arnold Rifkin, and Pilar Savone for being the original Hollywood players to believe in *Giacomo's Daughter*. Again, without your encouragement, this story may have never made it this far.

THE SAVONE SISTERS

Rosanna Savone and Diana Savone are the authors of their debut novel, *Giacomo's Daughter*, the first of a trilogy, about a young 1920's Detroit Mafia wife. Michigan-born by Italian immigrants, currently California-living unapologetic feminists, and entertaining yet thought-provoking storytellers, one of their passions is sharing the Italian-American female perspective.

You can follow Rosanna online at rosannasavone.com.